UNDEAD

GODS

CAITLYN BATTELLE

Paperback ISBN 979-8-9911125-0-5
Hardback ISBN 979-8-9911125-2-9
Ebook ISBN 979-8-9911125-1-2

Book Cover by Story Wrappers
Developmental Editor: Elora Ramirez
Line and Copy Editor: Dragon Smith Publishing LLC
Proofreader: Brittany Gossin

For all the girls who hear music inside of books, see magic instead of dust, and stay up till dawn enchanted by other worlds.

PROLOGUE

FOURTEEN YEARS AGO

SHINY BLACK CROWS pecked dull dead eyes in the Kavian main square, and young Elysia Parker couldn't tear hers away from the sight.

It was a hanging today. Yesterday a beheading. The bodies accumulating like some bizarre, macabre décor that everyone wished would just be put away already.

Elysia watched the woman's body sway gently, the tips of her bare feet brushing against the welcome sign that sat beneath the gallows.

Welcome to Kava, where the undead gods neither hear nor care, but you'd best pray to them anyway lest they curse you with their gifts.

Magic in Kava was dead. There would be no resurrections here. It was for fools and thieves—a crutch that would not be tolerated. Kavians could stand on their own two feet without false aids from the undead gods who clearly did not hear nor care.

She'd heard in stories whispered after dark that Kava was once lush with magic and wonder. Such ease for all its people. And then one day, from one breath to another, it was gone. In a world of magic, they were left barren. Even the soil responded in kind.

Magic lived on in other lands, but much like the flowers and plants that did not bloom in Kavian soil, all it took was one foot into the sunless country and even outsiders would lose their magic until they left again. It was as if the magic had been ripped from the sprawling, thread-thin roots of Kava, leaving them a land without a heartbeat or pulse. Other lands came and slaughtered and stole until King Garrison brokered a deal, the Treaty of the Fall, preserving what was left of their kingdom.

Elysia traced her boot in the dirt.

Mandelyn.

That was the name of the woman whose dull eyes would soon be pecked by crows. Elysia stared on as stoically as any child could. Her father demanded she attend because after all, it was her fault the woman swung, just like it was her fault that a neck had snapped or a head had rolled every day this week.

"Are you watching, Elysia?"

Her back straightened at the reprimand, her foot erasing the name she had written in the dirt. "Yes, Father." Her eyes latched onto the blue of the woman's dress, knowing what would happen if she didn't.

There was still flour dusting the woman's sleeve, a powdery cloud against the sky blue. As if she'd been in the middle of baking her famous tarts for Fillie's Café when the guards stormed in and dragged her here.

Relaclave, the capital city of Kava, would never taste a tart quite like hers again. Elysia swore she could smell the sweet scent of lemon custard even now. But that wasn't possible. Mandelyn's specific combination of magic and love had been extinguished today.

"And why are we here?" Jack Parker kept his voice down, making it rumble even more inside the barrel of his chest. He tapped his hands against the charcoal formal jacket he wore bearing Kava's insignia, waiting for her to answer.

"I must bear witness to the cost of my curse." Anyone else listening might have thought her strange. But Elysia's dark eyes were like the grave as she spoke. Her small mouth was serious and the lift of her chin already hinted at the severity she would hold herself to in all things as she grew.

Her father's trim beard dipped closer to his chest as he nodded. "And how must you atone for your evil?"

The blue of Mandelyn's dress rippled in the breeze. Her legs no longer moved easily, already becoming stiff with death. Elysia watched and recited her atonement.

"I must see the cost of my curse. I must understand the death that will befall our family if I cannot be better. And I must pay the Crown with secrets, as is only fitting." She looked up at her father, hoping to see the intoxicating flare of pride in Jack Parker's eyes. But her father was rarely impressed with her. His disappointment was a much more familiar drug, and so was the feeling of drowning which accompanied it.

Her father crouched, careful not to kneel in the blood and vomit covering the cobblestones of the square. Humming his agreement, he hooked his thumbs into his jacket pockets. "You endanger your family with every breath you take. You will never be able to pay this debt, child. Always remember that."

He straightened and looked beyond her to the gallows.

Elysia flinched. How could she ever forget? Yet her steady gaze did not drop even as a familiar sense of terror threatened to become a tempest within her. She smothered the inner turmoil before it could so much as peek out of her eyes. Insides tight, she clenched her fists within the folds of her matching gray dress. She welcomed how her nails cut into her palms, chasing the ache from her voice. Bitterness was all that remained.

"There is no repayment for a crime such as mine."

"That's right." His hand settled heavily on her shoulder and the weight was a boulder.

She was vile. A disease they would be better off cutting away entirely.

She would be why her family died. She just knew it. Mandelyn stared back at her lifelessly in agreement.

Elysia's nose wrinkled. The damp smell of decay made her

want to retch. You would think she would be used to it by now. The ever present pile of bodies waiting for pick up created an odor that would likely stay burned inside her brain for the rest of her days.

"King Garrison!" her father's voice boomed, causing her to startle and focus on her surroundings once more. She forced herself to be attentive, ready to play her part—Elysia Parker, daughter of the Crown.

The king slapped a hand against her father's shoulder with a squeeze. "Good of you to come, Jack. I think we've culled the last of them for the time being. Your tips were most appreciated, as always."

The men continued to speak, but Elysia's eyes drifted to the lanky boy with electric green eyes standing off to the side of the king. Her breath caught. She hadn't seen the prince in over a year. He traveled kingdom to kingdom with his tutors, preparing for his role. A wide jaw and lifted cheekbones brought an untamed feeling to the boy in spite of the fact that he was dressed head to toe in formal finery. She almost laughed at the look of pure boredom upon his face. He stuck his fingers through the tufts of his hair and a loud sigh hung heavy on his lips as his eyes wandered.

The king turned in irritation.

"Is there somewhere else you'd rather be?" A warning. Elysia was familiar with the sound.

The boy transformed. Intelligence shot through his green eyes and he suddenly somehow looked perfectly kempt, even though not one hair on his head had been subdued.

Topp Blatz, Crown Prince of Kava, let his face twist. "Nothing is more important than this work. Our kingdom is better off now."

His look of disgust narrowed on the bodies, and Elysia's stomach sank. The bodies that were cursed just like hers.

Her vision faltered, the terror rising back up with a vengeance. Black spots danced within her line of sight and heat rushed her body. Suddenly, it was *her* up there. She could see it. Her face shoved down against a blood-soaked stump and a sword plummeting down to excise her from this land.

She wondered how long she could possibly last—how long she could possibly hide her secret. She wondered if her mother would cry—if her sister would scream. She swallowed. She didn't have time for such thoughts.

Elysia smiled prettily at the prince, imagining she had razors for teeth. The look in his eyes said he knew all about smiles hiding weapons like a sheath.

Resting a hand on her father's forearm, she thanked the gods who did not hear that this boy was almost never in Relaclave. The cunning in him would have her strung up by next week. His smile widened, as if he could hear her thoughts.

This is what it was to be cursed by the undead gods—to always think twice and to never trust. Yes, this is what it was to be cursed, she thought.

Her curse led her to traipse far and wide through Relaclave, as if she were walking a tight line between her and the other cursed souls of her city.

She found them. Her father dropped a tip on them. And the king killed them.

But really, she could find anything. The truth tucked in your pocket. The lie beneath your tongue. The room long bricked shut within home or soul.

Her father wanted her to know just how precarious, how fragile her life really was as a cursed daughter of the Crown. He wanted her to wield this curse and control it.

If not? There were always the gallows.

CHAPTER 1

PRESENT DAY

ELYSIA WAS FALLING. Her arms shot out to brace herself, and her knees cracked against the floor like dusty bricks. Pitch black and hours before dawn, she couldn't see shit. She swore silently at the oversized muddy leather boot lying on the floor that had done its best to take her out. Never mind the pain flashing through her kneecaps, the damn thing was trying to get her caught.

Ever so quietly, she stood and carefully picked her way to the curved wooden door. Heart racing, she ignored the little thrill soaring through her. One hand on the iron handle, the other holding her shoes, she glanced over her shoulder at the prince.

A novice mistake, really, but she couldn't help but steal one last look before she went. Blanket loose around his bare chest and one muscled arm pulled in close to his body, every single cell of her being wanted to crawl right back to his bed where it was warm and smelled like a woodland storm.

It really was too bad she had to run out like this all the time now.

She pressed down on the door handle.

The ear-splitting shriek of iron grinding against iron shattered the middle of the night silence like a bucket of water to the head.

The prince shot up, his hand immediately grasping for the blade on the table beside him.

Elysia closed her eyes, head falling back in irritation. Spinning around, she kept her voice soft. "Go back to sleep. It's just me."

His chest deflated, one large hand rubbing his face while the other tossed the knife aside.

"By the gods, Elysia, you scared the shit out of me. What are you doing out of bed?" Topp's eyes tracked her hand on the door, his brow pinching. His low voice caught on a rasp as he called her out. "Is this how early you've been leaving? All those mornings I wake up and you're gone, and you make some excuse about meetings or work with your father?"

The sound of his sleep-laden voice did something to her that was entirely unhelpful right now. Ignoring the flush of heat begging her to forget her senses, she coughed lightly. "If you really want to know, you snore terribly and I've been leaving so that I can actually get some decent sleep."

She crossed her arms and leaned against the door. The lies fell from her mouth with practiced ease even as the acrid taste of guilt was familiar on her tongue.

Topp tucked one hand behind his head, the movement defining the strong curve of his arm. A lazy grin slid across his face. "Come back to bed, Parker."

Elysia acted as though she hadn't heard him, sticking her feet into her boots.

"Seriously? Lys, you can't go walking around Relaclave right now. The only people awake are the kind who would wear your skin as a coat."

She stopped in the doorway, twisting so she could see him. "You're a sick man, Topp Blatz."

She heard the soft thud of his bare feet on the floor. A breath later, warm hands captured her face and green eyes drilled down into hers.

"I don't like it."

"Then quit snoring like a cressin."

"A cressin?"

She tipped her head at the stack of books behind him. "I was reading your book on the creatures that used to live here. Before the Fall."

His cheeks lifted and he shook his head, burying his lips into her hair. "That book was supposed to be burned with all the rest."

She pulled away, moving out into the hall. "I can keep a secret."

Topp followed her into the open doorway and caught her wrist, stopping her. His face indicated just how much he didn't care for her gallivanting through the streets during the darkest hours of the night.

"Send word when you get home." He dropped her wrist gently. "Please."

Fond exasperation colored her response. "None of the messenger kids are going to be out at this hour."

He gestured at his bed. "One of two options, Parker. Take your pick."

Rolling her eyes, she wiggled her fingers in a wave and disappeared.

Hours later, Elysia was safe in her flat and the dawn still had not crested. The sky remained dark with only the shadows of clouds breaking up the blackened expanse of night. Her oil lamp was near its end, the light flickering instead of steady. She sat at her desk, thumping her forehead against the pages of a book. A singular page stuck to her face and she groaned.

The stubborn desire to stay alive and out of the gallows kept her searching through the forbidden text in front of her for answers to questions she couldn't speak aloud. Her eyes itched and blinked with red, and despite the hours searching through the book, she had come no closer to discovering the truth behind the nightly invasion of her psyche.

She wished she could leave her questions behind. Pretend her curse wasn't changing and that her life was exactly how it had been six months ago. Her life hadn't been perfect—not with a curse from the undead gods and a blackmailing, manipulative father, but she'd been managing. She had a plan, and it'd been working just fine. But now, everything she'd ever hoped for was about to slip through her fingers. All because her curse seemed to be growing, and she had no idea how to stop it.

Every night now, she fell into some otherworld. The dark beauty of this realm haunted her past sleep and well into the waking hours. Much like the ivy in the Lovestone Woods, the essence of the dream wound itself around her mind. It clung ferociously to her thoughts, leaving a beautiful, ominous trail that left her no choice but to follow.

And so she did. Because she couldn't seem to not.

Elysia rubbed her eyes and stared at the ceiling. A headache was on the horizon. The muscles at the base of her skull throbbed, tired and angry. Stress and no sleep tended to have that effect. She pushed away from her desk, stepping over a pile of clothes with her thoughts still spiraling.

She had business to attend to—both Crown and personal. A miscreant of a sister who she couldn't quite tolerate lately. And a family that expected things.

But never more than she did of herself.

Then again, maybe that wasn't true. Her expectations sliced through her mind like a blade while theirs silently pinned her down, stealing all her breath. She rubbed her chest. At least a blade could keep you alive. You were just dead without your breath.

She was Elysia Parker, and like the long line of Parkers before her, she could shove this unnatural dream with all its dangerous questions down so far within her it might just turn into a diamond. She could, she really could... So why wasn't she?

Because she was curious. She had always been curious.

Her virtue and her vice.

Beyond curiosity, the threat of death loomed, refusing to be ignored.

Elysia walked into the kitchen and looked inside her metal tea tin, setting it down a little too hard on the counter when she found it empty. She only had tea when she stole it from the castle, and she'd been avoiding her family like a plague. *Great, no tea.* Her fingers smeared her face, stretching her skin taut.

It was no surprise she hadn't made any progress delving into the arcane matter of her dreams. All those long nights she'd spent wearing down candle after candle reading had been fruitless. If she was honest, she knew the answers she sought would not be found within the old, crumbling pages of a book.

Because the answer was simple. There was no cure for the cursed. Even children knew that.

But she still had to look—she would drop to her knees and beg the undead gods who did not hear for an answer if it would stop the dreams. She could handle the secrets. Finding hidden truths was an invisible magic. Hard to prove. But what was happening while she slept? *Next to the prince.* That was going to get her killed.

Cursed to know what she should not, to find what she should not. And yet, the answers she needed eluded her. It was maddening. It was enough to make her question whether she knew anything at all. Of course, that wasn't true. She knew plenty. The things she did know just seemed to be useless in this endeavor.

Here is what Elysia did know:

The hidden streets and tunnels of Relaclave as well as the freckle below her lip.

That she liked flowers better than most people.

Enough gossip to make you blush.

And how to slip through a crowded room without a soul noticing her steps.

She would have once told you that the last thing she knew in her carefully curated life was that sooner rather than later, she would find herself engaged to Topp Blatz, Crown Prince of Kava.

It was simple, really.

And it had all been going to plan. Her father's plans. Her mother's plans. *Her underminings.*

Her entire life she had known there were only two options for a woman like her. A woman who should have already been dead. The first was to hide away in obscurity and live a life so bland that no one ever noticed there was something different about her. A safe, boring life somewhere far from the whispers of Relaclave. Unfortunately, this had never been an option for the daughter of Jack and Georgia Parker. Born into the politics of the Crown, everyone knew her face and everyone knew her name. Running away was impossible. Her father would rather have her executed than let his prize bloodhound escape. This left her with only one path forward.

She pictured the king, Garrison Blatz, with his fawning crowds and golden crown atop his head.

She had realized one all-important truth as a child growing up in this magicless kingdom. The one who wears the crown can do no wrong. They become *untouchable.* She didn't have any romantic notions of saving the land—saving the ones cursed like her. Her greatest and only ambition was to save herself. And if that meant marrying Topp Blatz and wearing the crown that would see her destroyed, then so be it. She had given up any naive ideas of morality long ago.

Until the dreams swept in like a tidal wave, destroying all she had once been so certain of in this life. All the work she had put in to ensure that her curse was undetectable. That she would survive this world where any false step could be her demise. That one day she would wear the Kavian crown and be safe at last.

Uncertainty and vexation were her constant companions now. She'd been navigating her curse just fine these last twenty-four years. Years of jobs for her father and no one was the wiser about her little *predicament.* A prickle of guilt gave her pause at the thought of all those jobs, but she stomped it dead. A hoarse growl echoed in her throat as she paced the length of her flat.

She knew better than to dwell on the work she did for her father.

She stopped, bare feet cold against the wood floor, staring out the window at the wisps of smoke rising off of chimneys. Underneath her strivings, true fear pushed her, never allowing her to rest.

It was like someone had taken a seam ripper to the fabric of her life. Thread by thread, they plucked, snapping her fate in two. And no matter how she grabbed or clutched at the tapestry, she would not be able to stop it from unraveling in her hands.

Elysia threw herself onto a chair littered with clothes, still ruminating on her father and his demands. It was easier to focus on his smaller requests. The bullshit political maneuvering. The leverage that moved the scales. Because otherwise, she had to remember that her hands were covered in blood. That she'd traded innocent lives to protect her own.

When she was younger, she had liked to imagine that if she was careful, then perhaps one day she could find freedom and use her talents for something better.

Now, she harbored no such delusions or musings about if she'd use her curse for good.

All she wondered now was if the part of her that was a quiet, long beaten-down scream for vengeance would cry true. Truth be told, she knew it was equally likely the more pathetic side of her that still vied for her parents' approval would win out in the end.

The metal plate of the mail slot clanked against itself, drawing her eyes and attention. A cream envelope poked through the slot, and she could already guess it was from her mother, given no one else was insane enough to be up in the middle of the night issuing a summons.

Leaving her morbid reverie behind, she stood, tossing the pillow she'd been holding aside to where her cat would once again claim it for its own. Hunched down in a squat, she attempted to pull out the envelope. Cursing, she yanked even harder, but the courier had somehow jammed the thick paper into the crevices of the mail slot and it wasn't budging. Thinking it would be easier to pull it out from the opposite side, she opened the door.

Elysia stopped dead in her tracks. There was a package. Beneath the dim amber light of the poorly tended hall lamps was a small brown box with burgundy liquid seeping out onto the black-and-white tiled hallway floor. It was tied with a perfectly happy twine bow. Frozen, she stared down at the box, knowing she wouldn't like whatever was inside.

A heavy breath filled her chest, sounding like the sea, and then practical resolve squared her shoulders. This mess wasn't going to clean itself. She snatched the envelope out of the mail slot, damn near ripping it in half, and grabbed the bloodied box off the ground. Marching back inside, she dumped the box with a loud thump into the sink and hurried back to the front door to wipe down the floor with an old rag. The last thing she needed was the landlord on her ass about *blood* staining the tiles.

She opted for the easier of the two deliveries first. It's not like the bloody box in her sink was going anywhere. Tearing open the cream envelope, she found a note from her mother, as expected.

Did other people's mothers send calls to action at four in the unblessed morning? Elysia squinted at the honeyed demand for both her and Beatriz's presence. The *please* and *thank you* were perfunctory. Georgia Parker did not ask her daughters, she told them, and she was telling them to be prompt and present for a strategy session regarding the upcoming Raven Ball.

She cringed at the idea of debating food choices and centerpieces, but when she thought about the possibilities of the Raven Ball, a flicker of excitement raced through her.

Yes, the Raven Ball was a feast for a girl like her. Every single important person in the kingdom and from lands beyond gallivanting in a bubbly, liquor-fueled daze. The work practically did itself on a night like that. If she was lucky, she'd be able to scrounge up enough dirt to hold her father off for months. She practically salivated at the thought.

The rancid smell of decay brought her back to reality in a hurry.

Elysia looked down into the sink, grimacing at the box. Knife in hand, her stomach rolled as she put off what she needed to do.

"Come on, Parker," she chastised herself. "You're made of stronger stuff than this."

Wariness twisting her face, her knife slashed through the bow of twine before she could overthink it. Box flung open wide, a fresh bloodied tongue stared back at her, pink and red, with a film of white on the top. Elysia swallowed down the instant surge of bile in the back of her throat and grabbed the blood splattered note pinned to the top flap of the box.

Too bad you didn't hold yours.

Elysia didn't blink until the words on the note began to blur. She had zero questions about who this little love note was from— the disgusting creatures who had been stealing women and draining them of their blood. Ever since the Fall, a new illness had cropped up, and eventually your blood ran black with it. These con men were selling *fresh blood* to the desperate folks infected, but instead of finding willing donors for their harebrained scheme, they were murdering women.

The women were typically a specific demographic. Single, childless, and addicted to whatever street drug was the current trend. In other words, women who wouldn't be held as credible or missed.

But they were missed.

These women moved in packs, taking care of each other the best they could, and the more of them who disappeared, the louder they grew. Brushed aside by the Crown, Elysia let her magic and curiosity carry her away.

She hadn't expected to discover a bloodletting healing sham. Collecting enough information had only taken a few evenings, and then she'd anonymously dropped off a file of facts to the

Crown's investigators. They might not care about the women, but they did care about infected citizens guzzling blood like it was some sort of magic cure-all. There was obviously no logic in this action. Healers had tried transfusions years ago to no avail and putting blood in your stomach wasn't the same as replacing what was in your veins. Elysia could only imagine the hopelessness that led to being willing to swallow down gulps of blood.

While there wasn't technically anything magical or forbidden occurring, the unnaturalness of the situation was disturbing to the Crown. If people were willing to drink blood, then the next thing they knew they would be seeking magic. Better to snub it out immediately.

Given that she had basically handed the Crown a map to the bloodletters, she'd assumed they would take care of the guilty parties. Clearly, she had been mistaken. Someone had gotten away, and they seemed to be well aware of who had gotten all their scammy friends strung up in the square.

Elysia slowly lowered the note to the counter, feeling tired down to her soul. She should've known better than to get involved in this mess. As if her father hadn't already punished her enough, now there was a tongue in her sink and death threats to contend with, and her day hadn't even begun. Her mouth tightened. There was only one place for her to go now.

It wasn't to the castle or her parents, and it definitely wasn't to the bumbling Crown idiots who had let this person get away.

No, she knew a man who could fix this before the sun could so much as rise.

CHAPTER 2

Elysia clambered up onto a turret. Inside the turret was the bedroom of the man known as Kava's Shadow. There was no doubt in her mind that he'd heard her not-so-subtle scraping and cursing as she climbed up the side of his damn house. Ass firmly planted on the roof, she kicked her legs and looked out at the horizon. Still two hours from sunrise, there was barely any light to be seen. Only a dim sheen filtered through the heavy sky. But that was normal here at any time of day.

The roof's layered clay tiles were slick, slippery from the constant soft but steady rain. Soot was a dark, mournful veil upon Relaclave. Mixed with the rain, it became an oily substance that had sent many victims tumbling from roofs, balconies, and even on the solid cobblestone roads.

Watercolor streaks of charcoal ran down the sides of the cream-toned homes surrounding her. If she had been feeling poetic, she would have said they looked like tears. A torrent of wind whipped her dark hair back, and she was grateful for the stimulus. Every inch of her body cried from the lack of sleep. It was a miracle she was even still awake. The venture over here had left her with burning muscles and her breath coming short and fast, when it should have been slow and controlled.

But the icy wind and water stung her wide awake, forcing her to be alert. Rain continued to splatter against her skin. She picked at the wet fabric clinging to her body. *Disgusting.* And there was her heart thumping erratically, unable to withstand her usual physical torture. Frustration cracked through her cool focus. *Get it together, Parker.* The question of how long she could keep this up was becoming pressing.

The lack of sleep. The rabid, but necessary obsession.

All the while pushing herself through her normal routines and duties.

The sounds of Gage shuffling around inside his room carried up to her. She knew he was just making her wait. The man had likely known she was on her way, long before she stuck her butt on his roof and settled in. She dragged her finger across a tile and inspected the nasty film now infesting the underside of her nail. Relaclave was undoubtedly a city of gray. The sky. The speckled buildings. The people and secrets that it held close.

Elysia's secret was that she traded in those secrets.

She'd been born into the court and its politics.

Her father, Jack, controlled the region's trades and imports. A highly necessary and important business in a land where the sun hid and barely anything grew. Her father, like many of the current regime, had come from nothing. Instead of gold and silver running in his veins, it was a brutal, undying need to prove himself. To maintain security at all costs. This was buried deep, of course. She doubted he had any idea what was beneath his own skin. He didn't worry about those sorts of things. He was too busy being vigilant about how to continue scraping his way to the top. If he could do it, then anyone could. And if they couldn't? That was their own damn problem.

There are some things people never want to experience again. Hunger that bends you in half. The loss of a place to rest your head. Your body being used in ways that are not your own. Rage that blinds you senseless. The whispers told her that Jack Parker once knew something about those kinds of things. He was ruthless now. No one would ever imagine he'd once been scared or helpless.

He'd taught her to never apologize.

That her only responsibility was to herself.

And her only loyalty was to her family and the Crown.

The sun would shine in Kava before her father felt so much as a shred of remorse for all he had demanded of her. All those bodies. She wondered what the total was now. The rain drip, drip, dripped down her nose. She'd stopped counting near her sixteenth birthday. There wasn't any point. Because it was never going to end.

Thankfully, it was rare she had to find a tip now. The king believed the worst of the curse to be decimated. But it was a constant threat in her father's hand. That she'd have to go find someone to be put down like an animal. That he'd hand *her* over to the king instead if she didn't obey.

And then there was her mother, Georgia. She carved out the social face of the Crown with expert strokes. Parties, cocktails, and gold flatware were her weapons.

Born into the Crown's circle, she had used poise and grace like an ax to hack her position into existence. And now she wielded her power with the best of them. Who to invite. Who to ostracize. The art of putting someone in their place by seating them at the children's table. By accident, naturally.

She made careers. And she broke them. People sweat in her presence as if she were the queen herself. If her mother had ever learned how to get her hands dirty, she would have made a terrifying general.

Elysia brushed the water off her face. She had always been a quiet child, unlike her sister, Beatriz, who screamed and raged like a soul caught between the dead and the living. While Beatriz was politely dragged out of sitting rooms that rolled with smoke and banter, Elysia had been allowed to stay, often tucked away in a corner long forgotten by the people who made the wheels of Kava turn.

And so Elysia began her training in the ornate halls and parlors of their kingdom's finest. She collected secret after secret with no one the wiser. Because no one pays attention to sweet, soft girls in the corner.

And she liked it that way.

Rough fingers captured her ankle and yanked, startling her out of her thoughts. An embarrassing squeak escaped her mouth, but Gage's strong hands had already grabbed her waist and pulled in her through the open window. Set on her feet, she teetered like a baby deer with her heart pounding loud enough she was sure he could hear it.

"You didn't even notice me opening the window." His deep voice normally settled around her like a warm blanket, but today the subtle reprimand sank beneath her skin, grating against her already raw nerves.

"*Maybe* I have a good reason for being so distracted, did you ever think of that?"

His dark eyes twinkled, amused at her rancor. "Please, do share."

A small laugh rumbled in his chest, and with her temper filed to a point, Elysia glared but didn't say a word, knowing she'd regret whatever came out of her mouth.

Making his way to her, he pried her arms apart from where they'd been folded across her chest and looked down at her with genuine affection. Her frown softened, the tight ball of anxiety and anger melting a fraction under the warmth of his friendship. Moments like this made it easy to forget the man was a trained assassin who'd been born to continue his family's empire.

Gage rarely talked about his family, but from what she'd gathered, they were indigenous to Bellia, the next closest country to Kava, and it remained the seat of their power. No matter where they called home, you could find a Reyez in every important kingdom and city, keeping a finger on the pulse of things. The family business extended far past the unseemly matter of relieving people of their lives, but as Gage said, it was important to stick to your talents, and there was no use crying about what they were.

Kingdoms were intricate and complicated pieces of embroidery, stitched together with lies and truth and dead-end dreams. People like the Reyez family were the back of the needlework. They were the knotted and tangled mess everyone was happy to pretend didn't exist.

But they did.

The false beauty of the many kingdoms in their world lazed on. And the Reyez empire counted their coins, knowing their business would never cease. Because people were knotted and tangled on the inside, too.

Gage rested easily in front of her, and even after so many years of training beside him, Elysia still noticed how his body was an instrument that sang with even the most simple of movements. He waited patiently for her to tell him what was going on, his stare quickly becoming an uncomfortable weight against her.

"Let me guess, you went after a tip without an exit plan, got lost in the thrill of it, and now you're in trouble? Or is this about what's actually been going on with you?" His voice was torn between brotherly amusement and parental concern.

Elysia remembered the feeling of adrenaline as she attempted to escape Topp's rooms only hours ago, and her mouth pinched at the both accurate and inaccurate observation. She *did* enjoy the thrill of chasing secrets, but she also had no choice about working for her father. And more importantly, that wasn't why she was here at all.

Gage noticed her reaction and clamped his mouth shut. She could tell he was itching to pry. Her behavior over the last few months had likely been driving him up a wall. He wasn't a man who did well with information being withheld, but he also knew she was about as skittish as an alley cat and would bolt if he tried too hard to get her to open up.

His current silence was probably for the best, considering she didn't want to hear anymore of his *concerned* questions. Not today and probably not tomorrow, either. She could practically hear the questions stuck behind his lips and even the thought of them left her feeling exposed. *"What's wrong? I've noticed how you've changed. Please tell me, so we can fix it."*

She wasn't ready for that conversation, and for once, she had an easy card to play to get him off her back. Elysia pulled the note out of her pocket, handing it over to him. He looked curious until she tacked on what felt like pertinent details.

"Came with a box and a bloody tongue."

Elysia stepped back, wrapping her arms around her middle as she watched his face work through flashes of emotion. Surprise. Anger. Resigned violence. Yes, this is what she had expected.

It was a strange miracle that she had ever met Gage. Even now, it was a puzzle to her why he had made himself such a permanent fixture in her life.

In some circles, Gage was a legend.

The one you brought your plea to and prayed to the undead gods that his price was not too steep. Because for his kind of work, there was always a price unseen. It was never going to be just coins. In other circles though, Gage was no one. He simply did not exist because how does one even trace a shadow in a city without the sun?

Expression hard, he handed her back the note. "What did I tell you about working alone?"

Elysia swallowed the vile barbs building behind her lips. She was here to beg his help, and she wouldn't come out on top of a verbal pissing match, anyway. Not today, when she barely had her wits about her. The venom slipped back down inside her for another day, another fight, but fatigue slapped her in its place.

It was exhausting to always pretend.

She hedged, picking at her gross wet clothes. "Will you help me?"

His hand clasped against the back of her head, his grasp firm and steady. "Always. That doesn't mean we're not going to have a conversation about this at some point."

Relief swept through her, her head tipping forward and tears stinging her eyes. She blinked, wiping at her face with the back of her hand. Stepping away from his touch, she tried to hide her discomfort, but even his palm against her hair felt too intimate at this moment. Her instinct was to hide, and it was proving difficult to override it.

Gage studied her. "You've never crossed this line before. There's a difference between an informant and an executioner. Do you want to keep your hands clean, or do you want to come?"

Palms open in front of her, she thought of the long tally of lost lives behind her name. Was she really so different from an executioner? She wasn't sure all the people who'd died because of her tips would think so.

All the emotion left her body as she answered. "It'd be smarter if I stayed out of it."

"But you need to know it's been handled."

"Something like that." She looked up from the floor, their eyes meeting in understanding.

Gage flicked off the lights as they walked through his home. One by one the lights went out, and with each switch he flicked, his movements grew smoother and somehow deadlier as he slipped into a dangerously focused state. Elysia trailed behind him. The man had more money than was healthy and a love for the boom of technology slowly crawling through Kava now that magic was gone. The end result was a home fitted with electricity and running water and the kind of tub she dreamt about. Her own flat only boasted a washstand and a communal toilet.

Her eyes went back to Gage as he strode in the direction of the docks. They both knew something about terrible choices made out of necessity and survival, but there was no joy or even vengefulness pumping through her now that the task was before her. As was often true, she was simply left with a grim resolve to make it through the day, and today that meant shadowing an assassin through dark alleys and strange buildings until the problem was solved.

The sun had risen when Elysia finally collapsed onto her bed.

She'd wondered if what she had seen would keep her awake with her brain spinning. Violence was nothing new in her world, though. Not with a hanging or beheading happening at least weekly since she'd been a child. In some respects, this had felt cleaner. Gage knew exactly who to go after, given that he had tracked every guilty individual since she had involved herself by tipping off the Crown. Usually she scoffed at his over-the-top protectiveness, but today she was glad for it. He knew where to go and who to seek.

Their mission had been simple, efficient even. Find the guilty parties. Remove them from the picture. Regardless of his feelings for her, Gage's kills had been fast and neat, his crew always only a few steps behind to perform cleanup. If anything, the most shocking part was how organized and rote the entire operation appeared to be.

Sprawled out and finally safe, exhaustion overcame her. Her last waking thought was that there was still a tongue in her sink.

Chapter 3

GAGE'S COMMENT about working alone and chasing secrets rattled around in Elysia's mind. He was right. Inevitably, sticking your nose where it didn't belong would bite you in the ass. The tongue she had just disposed of was a clear example. Given her nature, she wasn't sure she knew *how* to stay out of the fray.

She did know secrets, though. The shape and sound of them. How they fizzled with excitement or fear and arched up to their breaking point. Because almost every secret had a breaking point. The key was to capitalize just before the threads snapped loose and the secret was gone.

Her midnight-black cat wound around her legs, and Elysia smiled faintly. Yes, secrets were just like cats. They could smell desperation and longing. One must remain neutral. Keenly present while also thinly disinterested, and they would slink right to you.

Elysia scooped up Sir Larkspur, and he circled thrice before settling haughtily into the warmth of her lap. She rubbed his velvet ears and pretended she could just stay right there in her favorite plush chair with him. She was beginning to dread seeing anyone and everyone. After months of her increasingly odd behavior, it seemed everyone who cared for her was set on demanding answers. She couldn't blame them, but she didn't have to like it.

Remy and Daphne were not neutral nor remotely disinterested.

They were going to swarm her like vultures in search of their last bone-picked meal.

Elysia stood, brushing Sir Larkspur to the floor, where he glared at her with purple eyes.

"I'm sorry, Sir. I'm afraid I must beg your leave." Elysia sketched a bow in his direction. Sir Larkspur merely showed her his ample behind in response.

He sashayed into her bedroom, hips curving in a feline figure eight. The urge to slip in behind him and swiftly lock the door grew with each passing second. Tea date be damned.

She knew what this tea date really was.

There were tea dates, and then there were *tea dates*. The former was when you got together with your girlfriends and laughed openly over drizzled scones about the latest harebrained antics of your lovers. The latter were penciled into your schedule, when these very same friends became *concerned*.

We're just worried, that's all. We care about you.

A poorly disguised intervention, that's what this was.

Elysia grumbled to herself. She'd been avoiding this little meeting as long as she possibly could. And how terrible was that? To avoid your oldest friends. *Never said I was a good person*. Elysia walked over to her vanity, dropping onto the stool. Gods forbid if she showed up looking tired.

The most laughable part was that she had kept her biggest secrets from them since they were children. They had no idea that she sparred with Kava's Shadow. That she cursed him when he struck too hard and brought him sweets on his birthday. They would die if they knew that her elusive skill for aiding in court matters was often the result of her climbing in and out of windows and blending into busy rooms to listen in on delicate conversations.

She looked at her hands, a familiar bitterness falling over her. They would turn her in faster than a wolf in the woods if they knew the truth of her. The curse. All she'd done to hide it.

Elysia leaned in toward her mirror to dab a bit more concealer upon the dark clouds resting beneath her eyes. *This,* of all things, was what they had noticed. That she was tired. And a bit short-tempered. Forgetting their usual weekly tea and gin dates.

She dropped the makeup with a clatter. What's the worst they could say? She pursed her lips at the thought. Knowing Daphne, they could say an awful lot.

Slipping into her favorite emerald cloak, she gave a little twirl. An effervescent laugh tinkled out, the sound so contrary to the dread she felt inside. The cloak's smooth lining hugged her close while black ribbons at her neck swept into an elegant bow. She tugged at the ribbons until they nestled perfectly at the hollow of her throat and watched as Elysia Parker, daughter of the Kavian court and the Crown, so easily fell into place. She lifted the hood gently over her loose dark hair before stepping out into the faded gray of a Relaclave morning.

The entire kingdom decayed beneath a film of soot, but here in Relaclave, the filth was made into art as it settled layer by layer over the beautiful cream buildings their city was known for. It wasn't actually soot, not in the truest sense, but that was what it looked like, and that was what everyone called it.

The heels of Elysia's buttoned boots thudded rhythmically against the worn cobblestone streets. There wasn't a street or building in Relaclave that had not been tinged with the gray veil that had begun with magic's end. Some of the cleverer architects and planners had even begun to account for the hazy filter that would layer over their meticulous designs.

The older half of the city, the north side near the sea, boasted of curving cream buildings made soft with soot and contrasted with stark, sharp dark lines.

The city of charcoal came to life on the north side.

Indeed, at night one could see its famous doors of every color holding fast against the dinge. Swashes of blood red and the coldest of blues held the locks and keys to this part of Kava's world.

Elysia had wondered for years what the colors meant, and how they came to be in a city such as this, but whenever she asked someone old enough to know, they looked away, reminding her not to ask such questions about the time before the Fall. They were fascinating, though, colorful and untouched by the grime layering over everything else.

The doors were a beacon of sorts, always guiding people to where they needed to be.

Elysia trained her eyes ahead, searching for the yellow door that would bring her to this trial. She wove in and out through the crowds with practiced ease and paid no attention to the scurrying droves of people that foretold a wretched storm arriving.

Her gloved fingers pressed down upon a black iron handle. She shoved firmly until the sunshine-painted doorway budged, its heavy frame cracking open just enough for her to slip through. She paused, inhaling the mouthwatering scents of almond and hazelnut wafting through the air. The flames within the wall-mounted oil lamps danced, their soft light warming the hallway. Between the cozy lights and sweet smells, a sense of comfort enveloped her, easing her tension.

More than that, this was their spot. Somewhere to meet and laugh and just be. At least it used to be—she hadn't come in quite some time.

Elysia walked with measured steps down the narrow and deceptively dilapidated hall until it melted into the snug, candlelit haven that was Fillie's Café. As much a spot for lovers as it was for friends, Fillie's rarely had an empty seat.

Despite their lack of reservation, Remy lounged in a high-back velvet chair. Then again, most businesses in these parts could find a spare chair for Remelda Wincraft. Better known as Remy to those she called friends, but to the many she was Ms. Wincraft. And Ms. Wincraft was good at what she did.

Elysia couldn't help but feel another fissure of warmth crack through the wall she had been steadily building while schlepping across the city as she let the sight of her oldest friend wash over her. She was a shark with the curves of a panther, and Elysia loved her for it.

Her cherry-red dress drew out the warmth of her deep brown skin, and tiny cap sleeves armored her shoulders. She set a trap in the sweeping low-cut of her dress and executed it well with a waistline that nipped in, the fabric smoothing over her hips down to midcalf. A sharp jacket with a high buttoned collar rested on the arm of her chair.

Elysia felt her lips tip up as she drew closer to the table, her hands tucked within the folds of her emerald cloak. Remy was making the poor waiter sweat as she trailed a finger down the menu that she already knew by heart.

Remy's daddy ran the treasury for the Crown and had passed on his gift for numbers and figures. By the time she was sixteen, Remy knew the Kavian tax code better than most of the decrepit, cheating accountants who swindled folks left and right. All it took was the girl's favorite local café bankrupting for her business to be born.

Elysia slid silently into an open chair and smiled appreciatively as she always did that Remy had saved Fillie's. It turned out that Fillie's wasn't really bankrupt; they were just getting really, royally screwed. The Crown taxes were like that sometimes, when you offended the wrong person—like the treasurer.

Remy's daddy still wasn't sure if his wife had given birth to a terror or a prodigy, but it seemed he held out hope that one day she would come to her senses and leave that nonsense behind. Good girls didn't fight back against corrupt tax practices. They especially didn't do it when their father was the face of said corruption.

Elysia thought he was better off taking a swim in the venomous-fish-infested waters of the Valvere Sea.

She tugged off her leather gloves. "Where's Daphne?"

Remy gave a dip of her chin, and Elysia glanced in that direction. She let out a huff, and Remy nodded dryly in commiseration.

From her baby blue sheath to her icy-blonde locks, Daphne fluttered in like a winter breeze. She made warm hellos to the hostess and offered a knowing wiggle of her fingers to at least three separate groups of people before finally gliding to their table.

She plopped several small brown shop bags to the floor and sat back with a satisfied sigh, crossing one leg over the other. Her bright eyes scanned Remy and Elysia. "Finally, we're *all* here."

Daphne picked up the teapot that had been delivered in her absence and poured out a small cup. Elysia pretended to not hear the words beneath her remark. Pretended that irritation did not flare within her, threatening to tense her posture and heat her gaze. Instead, she settled back in her chair. She let her eyes drink in the delicate gold filigree swirls and dots that danced across the ceramic pot. And let out a soft murmur of agreement.

She ran one finger along the rim of her teacup. "I've missed you both."

The words felt forced. Chalky and dry in her throat. But it was the best peace offering she could scrounge up at the moment. She was too tired for pretty words or sparkling apologies she wasn't sure she even meant.

She looked between Remy's shimmering hazel eyes and the light aqua, startlingly pale tones of Daphne's. The former looked on with neutral curiosity and the latter ready to brandish a Fillie's jam knife in friendship and propriety's defense.

Remy paused, considering her words, long fingernails tapping against her arm. She then spoke gently before the jam could fly, cutting a firm glare at Daphne. "We aren't mad at you, Elysia, but we would like to know what's going on. There have always been parts of you and your life that are only yours, but now it's as though all of you has gone away somewhere. I wouldn't even know where to look to find you."

Elysia burned with shame as the love in Remy's words flowed over her. She ignored Daphne's not-so-subtle mumbles. "What she means is, you're a sneak."

She'd been such a terrible friend these past months. But even as the shame pricked her eyes, she could find no words to tell her friends what was wrong. She had known this conversation was coming, but if she couldn't tell Gage, the most trusted person in her life, then she surely could not tell Remy or Daphne.

Anxiety closed its fist on her lungs as the wordless realization hit her that if this many people had noticed something was off, then it was extremely likely others had noticed as well. Her time was running out before the wrong person noticed and cried magic.

She looked at her friends waiting for her explanation and prepared herself to throw them off her scent for good because she knew exactly what would happen if she didn't.

Once when she was a small child, Elysia had escaped the castle gates, waiting until the guards laughed and joked as they always did at shift change, and skipped right out the doors.

Because rumor had it that it was Day of the Moths.

It was a time to celebrate the death of autumn, and Elysia longed to see the street filled with vendors and celebration and plumes of scented smoke.

She had heard whispers of this rebel celebration. Curled like a kitten within a library shelf, barely visible to the adults who loomed above her, she listened to them speak of what must be done to these wandering charlatans and thieves.

But she had been transfixed with what she found on Relaclave's cobbled streets.

Women floated through the city in faded shrouds, their faces painted in shades of bone white and wretched black, all to carve them into ethereal creatures of death. They moved like shadowed wraiths, slithering and writhing like the smoke that coiled up and off of the streetlamps.

Elysia listened in rapt attention to their strange mix of accents and lamenting songs. They were priestesses from the temples in the city of Ryspur in Bellia, celebrating the Day of the Moths. A day to honor all the souls who had returned to the light from whence they had come. A practice Kava no longer knew or acknowledged. Yet old Kavian men who dared to remember Kava's past offered them coin and food for their travels. Old men who knew they were in their own autumn and wished to pay their tokens to the priestesses as they had been taught.

There was such a mournful joy that evening. The women whirled and danced, their limbs and song pulling everyone back into a world where magic might exist. But it was fraught with fear. The invisible fear that whispers *this cannot last, cannot last, cannot last.*

They should have listened to that whisper.

One of the priestesses had spotted Elysia, so out of place with her wide eyes in her black woolen dress with its red sash marking her as Crown. The woman threw her head back and laughed to the smoke-laden sky at the sight of her.

Elysia trembled even as curiosity sparked within her.

The woman walked closer with wanton steps meant to ensnare and delight. Ducking down low, she stared baldly into Elysia's eyes. She clutched her small, soft child arms. "Did you feel it, child? Did you feel the call from behind the towers and gates?"

Curiosity curdled back into fear.

The priestess grinned wildly and rubbed a finger upon her painted face before pressing it to Elysia's brow. She smiled more gently now because death could be kind, too. And then death blessed Elysia with its mark and peered deep into her eyes. "You will know when you hear your call."

Death's servant left as swiftly as she came.

Elysia's heart pounded and shook within her chest.

Tower bells were ringing now. Feet and armor clashing closer.

Yet small Elysia stood frozen with fright. Her body was heavy with the weight of questions her child's mind did not know how to form nor answer. So, she stood there clutching an uneaten sweet and sticky treat until a rush of guards flooded past her into the streets.

Because the Crown did not celebrate such things, nor would it tolerate these travelers with their strange, unwieldy customs.

The undead gods of Kava were gone.

The undead gods had no ears here and no one would dare act as their hands.

There was no magic here. There were no gods.

Shocked into numb motion, Elysia had crept inside a wooden vendor cart and listened in bleating panic to the sounds of knives and swords meeting flesh. Through the slats of wood, she watched fresh blood spray onto the streets only to run dark as it mingled with Kava's soot. A murky lake pooled beneath the vendor's cart and stung her nose with its copper scent.

Elysia stayed tucked tight into that small cart long after the sounds had stopped clanging and squelching. She stayed until the cart was pried open and curious eyes swept over her sash up to her new mark.

Her heart was too tired to beat in fear. It whimpered on in a slow rhythm.

The stranger held out a hand, a sure kindness in his face. "Hello, little one."

And with her hand in his, the stranger guided her past the woman with wanton steps with her throat slit so wide, out into the dark beyond that would become hers.

No, the Crown did not tolerate any sign or inkling of strange behavior that did not belong in this land, so Elysia looked up at Remy, and she lied to someone she loved for not the first time that day.

You have to make it real—you have to keep them safe, she coached herself.

She summoned real tears to coat her eyes and gripped her teacup a little tighter. "Work has just been so challenging lately. You know how he is..."

She glanced between them and bit down on her lip, registering their lack of conviction. The heat of the café and its coal powered ovens seemed to envelop her, but she remained cool, processing their reactions and adjusting her response. Her father was not an easy man to work for, but as far as they knew, she had by no means ever become the walking dead in her attempt to please him.

Well then, she'd come prepared for a moment like this.

She clinked the teacup down, lifted her chin, and dropped her voice down low. Tears still glittered in her eyes, adding a thickness to her voice. "Okay, the truth then. You know I wanted to tell you, but I couldn't. This stays between us. Understood?" She paused, looking between them seriously.

Both women nodded. Remy's the barest movement, her eyes focused. Daphne's chin going up and down so fast she might hurt herself.

Elysia refrained from rolling her eyes. Daphne had never kept a secret in her damn life.

"I happened to do a little side work these past few months. While assisting my father, I kept overhearing all these strange accounts about women disappearing. They made it sound like the women reporting were just hysterical addicts. But something felt off to me. I couldn't get myself to ignore it, and I ended up making a few folks... angry."

A truth to set the foundation.

The slight catch in her voice was real as she admitted tensely. "The people involved threatened me. They—they sent me a bloody, chopped-off tongue."

One more truth to hold the walls.

She knew they would know what she was talking about. Everyone in Relaclave did by now.

She looked her best friends in the eyes and spat out the rest. "I've been terrified. Can't eat, can't sleep. I'm not supposed to tell anyone while they try to find out who's threatening me."

And a lie to cover them all.

Daphne's already alabaster skin became gray. She latched onto

Elysia's arm, the stone of one of her rings digging in. "Have they hurt you? Have you been given a guard? Are there any leads? It's their job to protect the court of the Crown!" Her fingers dug in deeper with each frantic question and her eerie eyes grew round.

Elysia kept her own features dismayed and gently pried Daphne from her arm. "No, Daph, they haven't found anything yet. That's why I haven't been around." Never mind that the threat had only occurred a few hours ago.

She looked back up, her eyes blazing with one last truth. "I would never want either of you to be harmed because of me. I had to turn in what I found, but you don't deserve to stand in the wake of my decisions." There was a razor-edged fierceness beneath her words. Their friendships were complicated, but so was every relationship in Elysia's life—it didn't mean she didn't care.

Remy, calculating as ever, tipped her head and tugged on a tight curl. The curl sprung back, but she didn't say a word, and Elysia internally heaved a sigh of relief.

Daphne remained confused. "Why haven't you moved back into the castle then? A death threat is the perfect opportunity to end your little *I'm so independent* streak. No one could possibly blame you for such a poor decision like moving out when they're busy feeling bad for you. Besides, then you can stay with Topp *all the time*. I know I would." She unleashed a dazzling smile, laughing at her own joke while nodding encouragingly, as if she hadn't just insulted Elysia ten different ways in one breath.

Elysia shook her head and sorted through the plate of tiny cookies, searching for a chocolate one. "Daph, I can't bring that danger into the castle, and my father wants me to act as if everything is as normal."

Remy flashed a ruby-red smile. "Then we can expect you to start showing your face again? To stop holing up in your flat all the time?"

Elysia forced herself to sit still even though the question made her squirm. "Only if you promise to tell me all about your latest string of suitors."

Daphne snorted. "You should ask her about the fisherman."

Elysia grinned, but let a hint of vulnerability shine through as her smile faded. "I'm really sorry I worried you both. I just really haven't been doing well. I'm barely sleeping, and I'm shit at pretending everything is fine around people who know me as well as you two."

Truth and lies. Truth and lies.

It was the only manner of existence that she knew.

Remy nodded in understanding, forcing Elysia to meet her eyes. "But now we know, and if they haven't caught the bastards yet, then who knows how long it will take. Until then, you can't let this run your life. This won't be the last time someone gets pissed off if you insist on cleaning up the trash of Relaclave. Trust me, I would know." She made a face, likely thinking about all the threats she'd received over the years.

Remy, who fearlessly took on corrupt financiers and lawyers, even when she knew they were backed by men and women who would not so much as blink at removing her from the equation entirely. No, Remy, the shark that she was, would not allow her to wallow or hide.

A wave of anxiety rippled through Elysia. *This conversation needs to end now.* Before clever, clever Remy spoke all that she might actually be seeing.

"You're right. As usual," she acquiesced.

Remy smiled broadly, leaning back in her chair while holding her teacup out in the air. "Why yes, I am always right, aren't I?"

Elysia's voice became dry. "I have a meeting with the Golden Seal herself soon. I'm sure I can snag us an invitation to some gala or another."

Her mother was diabolical and likely to give her an aneurism one day. She also threw a damn good party.

The Golden Seal. *Such a ridiculous title.* Her mother's porcelain smile was never brighter than when she bestowed her seal. Like she was doing the person some benevolent service. Parties, funerals, weddings, they were all nothing without the Golden

Seal. If the Golden Seal was etched like a tiny medallion onto the calling card, then you had at least for the moment made into that elusive tier of people who steered the tides of Kava.

Daphne's face lit up. "Yes! That is *exactly* what we need. Less tongues, more parties." She nibbled on a shortbread cookie before poking it at Elysia's face. "Nothing stuffy. I want *scandals*, dammit. And imported alcohol, I'm sick of gin."

Remy rolled her eyes, but her smile was genuine as she squeezed Elysia's hand. "A scandalous evening for all of us then, but no more secrets, okay? I would never tell you to not chase your crazy dreams, but I *am* glad you're alright."

Elysia's heart squeezed as tightly as her hand. "No dreams here. We all know Jack Parker would never let me go far. Just a one-off, I promise."

Oh, she was scum. The dirty scum that grouted the cobblestones. Lying like the Crown fools who had raised them.

And even though the rest of tea went smoothly and all had been forgiven, Elysia could not shake the feeling that the lifeline of her secrets was dwindling to its end.

Chapter 4

The sun was past noon when Elysia left Fillie's and struck back out into the heavy rain. Her beautiful velvet cloak did nothing to stop the pelting rain drops from soaking to her skin. She didn't mind, though. You'd never go outside in Kava if you were afraid of a little rain. Besides, it wasn't a long walk to the castle, and in spite of getting her own place years ago, her mother liked to pretend she hadn't moved out at all and kept a room for her filled with fresh clothes and necessities.

She replayed the web she had spun at morning tea as she walked. She'd done what needed to be done, and they hadn't *all* been lies. Her self-consolation was half-hearted at best. Even she was tired of her own excuses, but unless the king suffered a stroke and declared magic legal again, this was her life, and lying was nothing new.

Dropping the tip on the blood drainers had been the first and last time she'd done something good with her curse. Something in all of those women's accounts had struck a chord within her. *The desperation.* The fact that they knew no one would believe them.

It had been a mistake. Likely driven from her own guilt buried in some unreachable corner of her soul so it didn't leave her frozen and useless when she needed to be vigilant.

The mud slid from her boot as she stepped out of a puddle. She wondered what it would take to wipe away the filth of the work she did for the Crown.

Whatever the answer was—it didn't matter. She never should have indulged herself. The scars that wound around her feet prickled, and she forced herself to breathe, to smile at the people she passed. Her feet were healed. The skin now dead and weird, yet new. A healer whose curse she had managed to keep a secret from her father for years had seen to healing her up the best she could—she owed that woman more than she could say. It was likely she wouldn't have been able to walk properly again without her.

Two months ago, her father had lost it when he found out that she had turned in the names of people involved in the murders and assaults of those women. Said she was out of control —out of her mind. That she must be raving mad if she thought that behavior was acceptable. That she must want her whole family to be killed.

Elysia waved to a courtier hurrying down the street, and turned a corner, dodging a woman dragging a toddler. When she was younger, she struggled to ignore her curse. How it demanded she follow its call. Her father thought this incident might have been the same. His solution had been to carve her feet with a small, sharp collapsible knife. It was the same knife he'd kept in his pocket since she was a child. The one he peeled fruit with and sliced open letters with when the seal stuck.

Now, the next time she thought about prancing off to help women *dumb enough to be in a position like that,* her feet would be a reminder. The pain would help her remember what would happen should she slip again.

Elysia plodded on through the rain. She was going to be a damn prune by the time she arrived at the castle. Her eyes snagged on what once had been a brewery run by a woman with the ability to work with yeast magically. The golden sign with wheat and hops painted onto it was faded now, and even though she hadn't experienced Kava when it had magic, the sight still made a pang shoot through her chest.

It sometimes felt as though the older generations had made a silent pact not to speak of how they once had magic in their fingertips and a sun that shone over a sootless land. Instead of the sun, Kava now boasted an almost constant haunting, ethereal mist. It rolled through the streets now, quieting the ache and replacing it with awe. Elysia ran her fingers through it, marveling at the dewy chill.

Kavians had lost their magic overnight. Soon they lost their businesses and homes. Their lives had been structured around magic—it was an integral and expected part of who they were and what they did. Until it wasn't. No one had ever so much as thought to be prepared for a moment like that. The entire economy collapsed in the aftermath, and the plundering by other kingdoms had not helped.

King Garrison was the hero in this story. The man's wife had just died in a tragic horse riding incident, only for magic to disappear while he was still clothed in his grief. Soon after, their home was under attack. His people were dying and their kingdom was failing.

The king brokered a deal. *The Treaty of the Fall.*

The treaty became a safeguard. The pillaging, the ravaging—it was over as suddenly as it had begun. Relief had come just in time. Another few weeks of upheaval and Kava would have likely been absorbed by another kingdom, their people and culture washed away like it had never been there at all.

A political miracle was what the people whispered. The love for Garrison Blatz was almost akin to worship amongst the older generations. In the darkest night, he had preserved their home even if it was no longer what it once was, and for that they loved him.

But ever since that fateful day when magic died, every last thing within their kingdom had become kissed with soot. Elysia had once seen a tear rolling down a child's face leave dark speckles in its wake. The sight had nearly broken her, given that it meant the child would soon die. Once the soot was inside you, there was no stopping it. Eventually, your blood ran black with it and your lips turned gray. People called anyone who contracted it the Fallen.

The charcoal laced mist suddenly looked far more haunting than ethereal. If the gray tinged skies in their infinite freedom could not escape this destiny, then neither could the ants of civilization below.

Elysia sped up her steps as the castle came into sight. Wet and bedraggled, she was more than ready to be dry. She approached the servants' entrance, eyeing the singular man in uniform. He stood there, resting against the wall, cap tipped down over his eyes. *Nothing like getting paid for an afternoon snooze.* Not that she was complaining. This was exactly why she preferred the servants' entrances.

The front gates tended to be overstaffed. A pompous show of strength that was ridiculous, considering the guards were more gossipy than a bunch of women in a sewing circle. Eager to earn a coin or favor, they'd happily narc on her in an instant for parading around muddy and unkempt. No reason to piss off her mother before the meeting even started.

The sleeping guard didn't so much as stir as she strode past. She smiled and lit a single candle before descending beneath the castle. Lower and lower she went, the air quickly turning stale and old. She ducked into the old concrete corridors that wound below the enormous castle like a labyrinth. The halls crumbled with dust and it was only the candle in her hand that pushed back the dark even in midafternoon.

She'd always felt at home in these twisting, winding halls, though. There were no marks, no signs. She wondered if one could even learn their way if they had not crept through the tunnels since birth. Remy knew a few shortcuts throughout the castle, but Daphne had always declared them to be *quite creepy* and never set foot within them.

She turned one more corner and paused, feeling for the rounded entrance that would open into stairs and then a closet near her room. A few moments later, the fresh smell of linens hit her nose. Her shoulders relaxed, enjoying the pleasant familiar scent. And then the door swung open. Flame beneath her face, looking like a long-lost ghost, Elysia nearly startled a maid half to death.

Her lips turned up laughingly, a shine gleaming in her eye. "Oh, I scared you! I'm sorry—I didn't want to drip down the main halls." She held her drenched cloak out in explanation.

The maid couldn't have been much older than sixteen years, with curly auburn hair and fair pink skin. She darted back, apologizing profusely. "So sorry, so sorry."

Elysia started at the sight of the woman's abject terror, but before she could offer another word of comfort, the young woman fled the closet with two towels tucked under her arms.

She frowned. A maid who she didn't recognize that almost peed herself at the sight of a Parker? Her mother must be on the warpath again. *Typical.*

Her mother was not what she needed today.

She needed a damn nap and to be left alone.

Elysia trudged the last few waterlogged steps to her old rooms and dug out her castle keys. She'd always enjoyed studying any of the castle keys she could get her hands on. They were so unlike the keys anywhere else. Perhaps, in the older northern half of Relaclave, one might find something similar on occasion, but not in the south side.

For all its modern buildings, the south side always felt lacking to Elysia. She could never quite put her finger on it, but there was something missing with all the standardized and oh so practically designed floor plans. There were no sweeping arches with curves like a woman's back. No ornately carved buildings that had all been touched by an artist's hands, or brilliant domes stretching their finger to the sky. She missed the sharp dark lines outlining the cream shapes.

She illogically loved the charcoal city, no matter how it wronged her over and over again.

Elysia held her old room key to the light to inspect the scrolling marks and symbols etched into its body. Despite the key's age, the markings held true. Her eyes drank in the clear craftsmanship and skill that had turned a mere key into art.

The locks tumbled like any other door, though, and she brushed aside her fanciful questions. She was to meet Georgia Parker in less than an hour and she looked like a cat thrown into a muddy puddle. Flicking a switch, she listened to the hum of the light bulbs as they began to glow. Amber tinted light streamed across the room and she smiled. She still wasn't convinced electricity wasn't magic. Unlike the average home in Kava that still used oil lamps and chandeliers, the castle was slowly being renovated to include electric lighting. They lived in a strange world of innovation now, with new inventions from Relaclave's iconic gas lamps to coal kitchen ranges and steam-powered ships constantly springing up. She'd even heard the engineers who'd designed the steamships were tinkering with steam-powered carriages.

Wet clothes fell with loud slaps to the floor as she tossed them overhead. Thank the undead gods for whoever kept up her room —her own flat was a hopeless mess that she had given up ever keeping completely clean. She shivered, dancing her bare feet on what felt like ice beneath her toes and berated herself for not first lighting a fire.

The fireplace's sea-foam white bricks swept up in a low, deep arch and a flame-darkened grate rested in the space below. Carefully positioning a few logs, she sprinkled a pinch of dried juniper and rosemary.

Damn near nothing grew in Kavian soil, and it killed her botany loving soul. Herbs, spices, vegetables. *Flowers.* The majority of these prizes were imported from other lands. There were forests and mosses that managed to survive the loss of magic, but that was about it. As much as she'd like to blame it on the shit weather and lack of sun, that wasn't the whole problem. Things like potatoes and carrots should have still done alright then. The soot, the inability to grow food, and the blackened sky were all consequences of the Fall.

Given how expensive food had become after the Fall, the average Kavian diet relied heavily on what could be mined from the sea. Growing up within the castle, she'd been spoiled with all types of meats and vegetables and spices imported from around the world. Now living on her own, she sometimes ate chowder three times a day, just like anybody else. She knew how lucky she was to have been fed a varied and nutritious diet throughout her formative years, to be able to swing the occasional treat at a place like Fillie's.

She struck a match, pausing to watch the small, smoldering flames. She stayed there an extra moment, mesmerized by the sight. *There's just something about a fire, isn't there?* Elysia took a deep inhale, the sweet smoke curling into her nose. It brought a fleeting peace that was gone too soon, leaving a bittersweet weight in its place. Brushing ash from her fingers, she stood, knowing she was running out of time.

A quick bath and she was wrapped in a towel, rifling through her closet, hunting for clothes that would appease her mother. Clean and simple would be best. A woolen burgundy skirt that swirled around her thighs and a silky long-sleeve top tucked in neatly. Fumbling to wrench on her stockings, she cursed and almost toppled to the ground. Tugging everything into place, she fanned her face. Why did getting dressed feel like exercise sometimes? Hands on her hips, she glanced at the timepiece on the mantel, thinking she should be on her way.

A heavy knock rapped on the door. Elysia opened it and was handed a small envelope. The envelope bore the seal of her family, and Elysia let out a groan of annoyance, already knowing what its contents would bear.

Must reschedule. Meet me in two days. Same time. GP

Elysia crumpled the note into a ball and chucked it straight into the fire. This was just like her mother. Demanding she come today, and then rescheduling no more than ten minutes before the meeting as if she wasn't an adult with her own life and schedule to navigate.

Unbearable. She was honestly unbearable sometimes.

Elysia stalked over to the great wooden chest and flung it open, rummaging for shoes. She wasn't sure anyone could get on someone's nerves quite like their own mother. Or perhaps it was just her mother. She snatched out a pair of soft, supple black boots that ran the lengths of her calves with tiny buttons up the side and yanked them on before stomping back out the door.

If dear Mrs. Parker could not be disturbed, then Elysia had her own mysteries to solve.

It was time to visit an old friend.

She'd been putting off this visit even though she'd felt a whisper of knowing that he'd be able to help. Not that anyone could blame her for avoiding Rollie.

Last time she'd seen him, he'd chucked a lit candle at her head from a foot away. Hair singed and wax blobs dripping down her face, she'd bolted from his home as he screamed at her.

Elysia's hand drifted to her hair in apprehension.

Yes, she was going to need reinforcements. If she wanted to keep her hair, anyway.

CHAPTER 5

Elysia walked with her chin held high and a cordial expression pasted onto her face, making sure to greet any servant or fellow Crown member as she passed.

Hello.

So good to see you.

No, no, I haven't seen Beatriz lately.

She was no longer sure how much of it was an act. Maybe it had once been real as she streaked through these halls with Remy and Daphne, laughing as they hid behind heavy embroidered curtains and chased the castle hounds and cats. But now, she smiled to keep her parents' questions away and to ensure that they would not rip away her life outside these walls. She smiled because she was in the business of procuring truth and lies, and should she fail, her father would not hesitate to ruin her.

She peeked her face around the archway into the kitchens and found them bustling, as expected. The smell of fresh bread had her mouth watering before she even took another step. Elysia liked living on her own. Really, she did. But soot and storms, did she miss the food here! The scent of roasting meat hit her nose and her stomach grumbled on cue, as if she hadn't just eaten her weight in cookies at Fillie's.

She stayed tucked out of sight for a moment longer, enjoying the familiar sight of the organized chaos that was Lynd's kitchen. Pans clanging and shouts of *behind you* rang out. Never a dull or leisurely moment, that was for sure. The head chef was a culinary genius with mouths to feed and young women to train. The culinary arts were one of the few paths where a woman of any socioeconomic status could find herself elevated to a position of security if they were willing to leave Kava, and Lynd felt it her duty to equip as many women as she could with the skills to provide a life for themselves.

It wasn't uncommon for the girls or women to arrive at her kitchens withdrawn or even bruised and broken. A few months or even years under her firm but caring guidance and you wouldn't recognize them. They became precise and assertive miniatures of the woman who'd given them a chance.

Yes, Lynd would very well tear apart anyone who threatened her kitchens, or the young girls and women whom she trained. Elysia thought you'd have to be an idiot to threaten anyone who could handle a knife that well, but some people were just plain stupid, she supposed.

Lynd's proteges went on to the finest kitchens and bakeries around the world. She sent them out to different countries, knowing they'd be better off there than scraping to get by here. It was almost impossible to secure a culinary position within Kava given how few restaurants still existed after the Fall. Importing the necessary ingredients was expensive and too few people could afford the experience.

Fish stew stands were the main market in Relaclave these days. All the more reason somewhere like Fillie's was so special. It was the only café in the entire capital city.

"Whoever's dawdling in my doorway, either get your ass in here and work, or get out."

A smirk crossed Elysia's face, but she listened, dropping down the steps into the kitchens. *One of those days for everybody, I guess.* Based on Lynd's tone, she knew damn well not to interrupt. She stepped out of the way, waiting patiently, and watched Lynd carefully inspect a child's pastry.

"More butter next time," she critiqued, and then turned with floured hands already reaching for the next pastry to review.

Her sharp eyes caught on the dark-haired woman hiding quietly, almost invisible in the corner, and gave a shake of her head.

"Come to steal some cakes, have you?" She directed one of the girls to grab a basket and tea towel as she spoke.

Elysia walked up to Lynd with a little shrug, enjoying how the heat sucked her into the heart of the kitchen. In the dead of winter, she used to sneak in here not only for the snacks that filled her pockets when she left but also simply to bask in the warmth and camaraderie found within the kitchen's walls. She'd found it odd at the time how they all interacted so honestly and with such good humor.

"Would you believe me if I said they aren't really for me?" Elysia leaned against a counter, careful to not place her elbows on anything sticky or covered in flour.

Lynd grumbled goodheartedly. "We all know these cakes won't escape without at least a few sliding into your belly."

She glanced up and frowned as she took in Elysia's slighter than usual frame. Too many angles. Too little curves. The thoughts were clear as day on Lynd's face.

"A few more pastries as well," she ordered the girls scurrying around like mice. "The meat ones too—yes, those." She nodded approvingly before turning back to Elysia. "Not feeding yourself in that dingy wreck you call a flat?"

Elysia snorted a laugh and swiped a small chocolate hazelnut confection from a tray, popping it into her mouth. "It's just a bit old is all. You know how the north side is—it has its charms and its faults."

Lynd shook her head in the disgruntled way that only those who love you can. "You have proper rooms, my good food, and everything else you could possibly want here."

Elysia bit down a smile at her fussing.

Lynd wiped her hands on her apron and leaned forward to pick out a bit of ashy soot from Elysia's hair. "What difference does a couple of blocks make? She rang your bell and you're still here, aren't you? Just had to walk farther in the cursed rain."

Elysia felt her weariness lock down around her, heavy and unforgiving. Lynd was not wrong. In spite of being grown and moved out, when her mother or father called, she answered. But she was not without her reasons.

Lynd sighed, taking in her stillness and smudgy, tired eyes. She tucked the beautiful pastry basket into her hands and pressed a rough kiss to her head. She then looked at Elysia with all the seriousness of a man standing trial. "I'm going to start sending you dinner once a week, and you will eat it, do you understand? And don't you dare leave this castle without saying goodbye."

Dampness lined Elysia's eyes, and she choked back the discomfort that grew in her throat. She managed one sharp nod before turning heel with the basket clutched tight in bone-white fingers.

She walked away from the sweet kitchen heat and the keen eyes of Lynd before hurriedly slipping into a curtain-covered alcove. She breathed steadily in and out, one hand rubbing against her breastbone until the brisk air emanating from the glass window beside her soothed the lingering ache in her chest. Between the lack of sleep, a tongue in a box, and meeting with the girls, her feelings were brimming to the top instead of staying down where they belonged.

She could never quite say why Lynd's brusque love hurt so much. But it did, and for that she was glad.

Elysia closed her eyes and buried that love away. Caring for someone was a dangerous thing. Someone was always watching here in the castle walls. Always reporting back to her parents. That was why she limited her visits to the kitchens. Her mother had commented about how often the servants found her perched on the kitchen counters. Eating, enjoying. She'd stopped visiting after that. Lynd didn't deserve to be collateral.

She'd found that love inspired a fear deeper than any other. A fear that caused an instinctive, irrational desire to protect. She sometimes wondered if that was the force behind her parents' actions. Love soured by the need to protect. *You're too old for such thinking,* she chastised herself. Whether they experienced love's poison or not, the people in her life were experts at wielding it against others. That much she knew for sure.

Love is a liability and an affliction. A crushing insight from one Parker sister to another. She'd carried Beatriz's words with her ever since.

Elysia strained her ears. When she didn't hear any footsteps or other sounds, she slid back into the hallway, setting off to see her old friend.

The Relaclave library was not *technically* part of the castle, but it was connected if you knew where to go. Basket in one hand and an oil lantern in the other, Elysia walked leisurely through the corridors beneath the castle.

She could have marched through the front doors of the great Relaclave library as she did any other day of the week. It was not unusual for her to while away her hours amongst the dusty tomes, but the friend she was to meet was peculiar, to say the least. He would not be found *in* the warm, cushy reading nooks above her, but rather *below.*

Long forgotten by the librarians and even the Crown itself were the levels of tunnels and rooms that ran far below the servants' corridors. The tunnels had called to her when she was a child, much like all the hidden things did, and soon she knew their secrets just the same.

Elysia stared at the small hole in the middle of the servants' path and regretted her choice of stockings and skirt. Lantern tucked into the basket, she stuck her lower half through the clay covered hole and balanced precariously upon its timeworn edge.

And then she slipped like liquid silk down into the lower tunnels that she hoped held answers to her questions.

She landed softly on the balls of her feet and brought the lantern back out before her. The light barely made a dent against the dark. She prayed Rollie was in his usual haunt. She had no desire to disturb anything or anyone else that may live down here. *Why does it always smell like someone shit in these tunnels?* She grimaced. She had a love-hate relationship with the tunnels.

She crept along the dirt-crusted paths, ducking to keep her head clean. No matter what, she'd need a solid scouring after this. The sound of shoes scuffling in the distance had her pausing.

Elysia smiled. *Some things never change.*

She called out into the darkness before he could scuttle off into the shadows where she'd never find him. "Rollie, I brought you food from Lynd."

The shuffling paused. And then a head with erratic white-blonde hair popped out of the dark. "Maple cakes?"

Elysia held the basket out like she was luring a feral creature. "And her meat pies. A whole meal, right fresh from her kitchen."

His eyes squinted in a glare from behind his thick glasses. "Fine."

He disappeared into whatever room he had been squatting in, and Elysia hurried along in his trail.

The room was awash with soft candles lighting its edges. The glow of the candles let her see just how much of the walls and ceilings had crumbled, and not for the first time, Elysia felt uneasy creeping this deep beneath the city. She never did quite trust all of this old dirt. *Maybe it's because you're not a rodent.*

But this was where Rollie could be found, so this is where she went on the rare occasion that she demanded his services.

Rollie had already begun carefully inspecting the cakes within the basket. He finally selected what must have been deemed a worthy maple cake and took an untrusting sniff before taking an equally cautious bite.

Rollie, also known as Rollickus Timmons, was not the social

sort. He was possibly the only Crown kid who had truly made his own life away from the court. He spent his time like a mole beneath the city, and Elysia sometimes wondered if he might be the only person in Kava who knew more secrets than her.

Then again, most folks found him a bit mad, which was exactly why they never would believe a word he said, anyway.

He was undeniably one of the most intelligent people she had ever met, though. She chased the secrets of Kava. Rollie chased the secrets of the universe itself.

It did help, of course, that she could tell him anything and no matter who he told, they would not believe him. A secret's best friend was an unreliable source.

Elysia carefully weaved through the room and perched on the edge of an ancient table. She crossed her ankles and watched Rollie heartily tuck into the maple cake. He ignored her until he ate the last morsel of the cake.

Elysia cleared her throat to talk, and he held out a finger.

She huffed at the silencing gesture, but Rollie continued as though he had not even heard her, and pulled out a cloth napkin, dipped it into the water glass beside him, and proceeded to clean his fingers slowly and thoroughly of any sticky maple residue.

He finally set the napkin down and looked at her with a tilted head. "Well?"

Elysia folded her fingers. "There is a mystery that I seek your help in solving."

She had to be careful, so very careful, even with Rollickus. Every fiber of her being was screaming to keep her secrets and to find another way, but she'd made her decision. Rollie was her best shot at finding an actual solution and fixing her life. Whatever magic drove her into the arms of Kava's secrets had steered her down to him, and she was banking on him being able to help.

She continued, her eyes drifting to the ceiling as she spoke. "What would you make of someone who, instead of falling into slumber, perhaps they fell into another world? Another place?"

Rollie sat up straighter, his fingers pausing right above the pile of pastries. "A dream you mean?"

She gripped the table's edge. "No, not a dream. This person leaves their body, but also takes it with them to this new place."

The fizzing eccentricity that kept others at an arm's length from Mr. Timmons seemed to die in that moment, and only the cold, stark clarity of his brilliance shone through his deep blue eyes.

He leaned back against the table and mulled over her words, mulled over what knowledge he felt safe enough to share.

He stared at her unflinchingly and finally spoke. "Elysia Parker, swear upon the undead gods that Kava denies. Swear upon the lives of everyone you hold close to your wretched, beating heart that this conversation does not leave this room."

Elysia had heard conversations that could ruin a kingdom flung into the world with drunken frivolity. She'd heard them delivered with vengeance. But never had she heard such a demand for protecting hidden words.

The death moths with their pretty red-lined throats danced behind her eyes as she returned Rollie's fierce gaze. "I swear it."

He clipped his chin in a nod and tugged on his already disheveled hair, beginning to pace.

He stopped abruptly and faced her. "There are people who may be able to answer your questions. It's better that you bring your claims to them. It's not my knowledge to share." His face turned shrewd, but his voice was free from condemnation. "This is about you, isn't it? You wouldn't be here for anyone but yourself. Maybe Beatriz, but we both know this isn't about her."

Unease and dread filled her gut. People were nothing more than behavioral patterns to some extent, and unfortunately, Rollie was extremely good with patterns. He called it like he saw it, knowing that Elysia needed him and wouldn't do anything to harm him in spite of him now knowing her secret.

"Rollie, I don't want to meet with other people." *He has no idea what he's asking.*

She remembered all the people she had accidentally brought to death's gate without meaning to as a child, and her stomach clenched. People she'd been drawn to because their secrets flared brighter than all the rest. It'd taken her years to control her curse well enough that heads stopped rolling in her wake, years before her father quit tailing her every move, knowing that she would somehow inevitably end up on the doorstep of someone who'd managed to cling to some wisp of magic.

And then there were all the lives she had taken later. When Jack Parker said it was time for another sweep. That he needed another feather in his hat. She lost sight of Rollie and the tunnels, feeling only the hollowness inside her. It could be worse, she reminded herself. She could be working for the king. Searching every day through the whole kingdom. She could just be dead.

You would think any magic in their land would be a blessing, but the people had been spurned once by the fickleness of fate, and what was once a gift was now a curse. Illegal and to be rooted out at all costs lest they find themselves reliant on a force outside themselves once more.

She stared pointedly at Rollie, her eyes imploring him. "Isn't this, just between us, unsafe enough? You *know* how dangerous this is. Or you would not have asked for such an oath."

The pacing resumed, but he shook his head, looking pained. "Elysia, you don't understand. What affects one could affect all. It is not my place to answer your questions."

He paused. "Does anyone know? Has that over-pressed royal Crown squinch noticed yet?"

Elysia blinked, her voice going flat. "Royal Crown squinch. *Really*, Rollie?"

He shrugged. "You knew who I was talking about, didn't you?"

She scowled. "No, Topp hasn't noticed. I think I threw Remy and Daphne off for now, but if I don't start controlling it, then I'm going to have a problem. I already have a problem." Gods knew how long she could hold Gage off, she thought to herself. *It's a miracle I've lasted this long.*

"What kind of boyfriend doesn't realize their girlfriend has become an insomniac who is projecting out of her body every night?" His brow creased in disbelief.

This was the Rollie she knew from childhood. Smart-mouthed and unfailingly without a filter. A bit odd, but never mad. Sure, he didn't see the point of social niceties and was far more at home with his books than stuck chattering with court members, but he had always been perfectly sane. More than competent. It was as if she'd woken up one day and her uncouth but gifted friend had become a paranoid hermit that she had to bribe in order to see. But standing here now, she took in how unfazed he was by her story and wondered if there was one more person in her life hiding in plain sight. She wondered if perhaps he was not unhinged at all, but merely protecting himself the best way he knew how—by keeping everyone and everything he loved far, far away.

The thought pressed down on her, but she brushed it aside, knowing he would not want her sympathies. "Mind your business, Rollickus."

He blew out half a laugh, but his gaze went dark. "You're out of your mind if you're still sleeping with him. Never mind that he's an old squinch." His eyes demanded her to see reason. "He would have you killed without even blinking, Elysia. He will always choose the Crown because *he is the Crown.*"

His words cut to the quick, severing the tenuous leash she held on her fear. The same fear that coated her insides each and every night as she snuck away from the prince's bed.

Her response was immediate and sharp. "You don't even know him."

Internally, she cringed. *Gods, did she hear herself?* If another woman spoke like that, she'd be rolling her eyes so hard it'd hurt.

But the prickle of fear that zipped up her spine and had her fisting her hands told the truth. She slept beside the Crown Prince of Kava, and she played a most dangerous game.

It was a game she had been born into, and there never had been any chance of winning.

Survival had always been her aim.

She let the air slowly hiss out of her nose and tried to calm her stuttering heart.

When she spoke, her teeth barely came apart. "I am handling it. Now either tell me what you know, or connect me with those who can."

She could've sworn a flash of pity crossed his pale features, but then it was gone, and he was digging in his pockets. He held up an old, worn out coin and flipped it a few times before extending it to Elysia.

She gingerly plucked the coin from between his two index fingers and examined the etchings still present beneath the heavy layer of grime. Families, businesses—they often had coins which matched their seals. The one in her hand boasted a spray of sparks with a small key set in the center. She ran her thumb over the marks and looked back up at Rollie.

"And what do I do with it?"

He shoved a hand into his pocket and pushed up his glasses. "Nothing for now."

Her head snapped up. "What?"

"I'll talk to who I can and see if they're willing to meet you. If they are, and it is an *if*, Elysia"—he stared at her unblinkingly—"then you'll need the coin."

Rollie grabbed a few more pastries and began walking back into the dark halls of the underground. He called out, knowing she could still hear, "Don't follow me, Elysia Parker, we'll know."

Elysia stood in the dark clutching the coin, praying to the undead gods that no one prayed to any longer, that Rollickus Timmons could help her.

CHAPTER 6

Two DAYS LATER, Elysia's back slammed up against the sharp edge of a wooden bookshelf, but a breathless laugh fell out of her mouth. Her laugh was immediately swallowed by firm, familiar kisses. The taste of him sent her spinning into a high that she never wanted to come down from. This week had been so awful. She needed this, needed *him*.

Strong, warm hands roved beneath her sweater, pulling her hips against his, only to let go as he planted his forearms above her and tore his lips from hers. Green eyes bright with lust stole over her, the prince's full lips giving way into a grin. And then he hoisted her up, back pinching against the shelves once more, as her legs wrapped around his waist and her arms looped behind his neck.

The person most likely to realize she was cursed and turn her in for treason was currently sucking on the spot below her ear. She wasn't thinking about treason, though. She was thinking about how she couldn't make a sound because they were in the library and they'd already been caught once in the last six months alone. Topp's thumb smoothed over her breast, making her forget her ambition to be silent as her eyes rolled back and her head smacked against the shelves. Books rattled, a few falling down to the floor. Elysia blinked, pulling away and panting as she looked down at the minor destruction.

Lightly dropping her onto her feet, Topp lowered his face and ran his lips up her neck, causing a shiver to ripple through her.

"You keep disappearing on me." With his mouth against her ear, a blush bloomed instantly on her face, giving away her sense of guilt. He drew back and fixed her with a look.

Elysia grabbed a fistful of shirt, yanking him down to her level, and fastened her mouth to his. The prince responded immediately, clearly not too set on finding out what had been driving her bizarre behavior. Fingers stuck through his hair, she kissed him until she was winded and wished she could rip off his clothes.

Breaking the kiss, Topp brought one finger to his lips and cocked an ear. Heeled footsteps clacked closer. *Fucking librarians.* The prince stepped back, his lips swollen and set in a grin that promised trouble as he straightened his shirt and trousers.

He ducked down so his face was barely a breath from hers, his broad face lit with determination. "You think I'm that easy to distract, Parker? I'm insulted. We're going to talk. Soon."

The prince strode away, leaving her to drop to her knees to collect the scattered books. He turned the corner just as the librarians came upon her, clucking at the sight of all the books strewn about. Cheeks warm, she muttered an apology, and the women carried on with their noses in the air. Elysia scoffed quietly as they walked away. It wasn't like they could actually punish her given who her partner in crime was, so instead, they would happily feed the gossip mill. Elysia was fine with that. The more everyone thought she and the prince were *in love,* the safer she was.

Legs out wide as she sat on the cold marbled floor, Elysia reached for the last book from their little avalanche. This book had fallen on its binding, gilded pages crashed open. Just out of reach, she crawled over to slide it closer. Skulls littered the background of the page and a man stood amongst them with a hood pulled over his shadowed face. A dark, winding river ran beside the lone figure. The sketched drawing made her skin prickle with vague recognition. Eyes moving fast, she scanned the words on the opposite page.

Shock had a small gasp tumbling from her lips and her wrists folding like paper. The book crashed back down to the floor as she continued to gape. Hastily, she grabbed it, shutting the book with a loud clap, and shoved it back onto the closest shelf. She sprang to her feet, wishing she had never looked inside that dark book.

Elysia stared at the gorgeous iron-paned windows nestled into the stone walls of her mother's sitting room. The rain beat a steady tempo against the glass.

The song might be a dirge.

She glanced at the clock and stopped herself. Beatriz would not be attending, regardless of the time. She knew this down to her frozen toes. But it didn't matter. *She wouldn't have been any help, anyway.* The rain dirged on, agreeing with her thoughts. Elysia knew better than to expect anything from her sister.

A person didn't have to be a keeper of secrets to hear what was whispered about Beatriz Parker. Sharp as glass. She left impossible slivers in your skin. A woman who hid herself in debauchery instead of perfection. She slid in and out of carriages, and waltzed like smoke through dark, liquor-filled parlors. Boys, girls, dresses, or suits. It did not matter to Beatriz as long as she had a good time.

Elysia still wouldn't have minded her company. Their relationship had always been strained, but now that they both lived beyond the castle walls their main contact was limited to the occasions on which her sister slyly asked for information about certain Kavians, and then she disappeared again until she needed to be fed another secret.

She always did seem to need another secret.

But Elysia worried, so she doled out the secrets like money that might keep her big sister safe one more night.

Elysia's thoughts were broken as Georgia Parker walked briskly into the room. She adjusted the position of three priceless works of art by just a hair and fluffed all four pillows in the room before Elysia could even blink. A breath later she was on to refolding the rich maroon blanket that lounged upon the overstuffed loveseat.

Elysia straightened in her chair before she could become the next possession to be adjusted.

Her mother finally settled onto the intricately stitched armchair resting across from her. She crossed her ankles. "Did you call for drinks yet? No? Good, they'll be hot then." Georgia stood and lightly tugged the golden cord that would alert her staff to haul ass like the Kavian winds.

Elysia was caught between a laugh and a cringe at the thought of how fast her mother's servants must dart through the castle halls. The same servant Elysia had nearly collided with days before, curly haired and with cinnamon freckles dusting her face, appeared in the doorway. The girl was breathless and color spotted her cheeks.

"Yes, Mrs. Parker?"

Georgia looked the girl in the eyes. "Two steaming bumblebees, please."

She was gone without a word.

Georgia smiled with closed lips and leaned back in her chair.

"Skittish that one. Still haven't caught her name."

She shrugged as if it didn't matter, but Elysia knew she would find out. Georgia Parker was both the best and worst person to work for in this castle. She would run you ragged and demand perfection where there was none to be found, but she would also discreetly slip Crown catering leftovers into your hands and ensure your family was fed and housed within the castle walls.

She used to think it was out of some motherly kindness, but Elysia had come to realize that it was simply an extension of her pragmatism. Servants with round, full bellies who slept soundly in their quarters worked harder and were far more likely to keep their lips shut than ones you kicked outside to find housing and food with their meager coin. So, her mother knew their names and treated them like their positions really meant something.

Elysia smiled at her mother. She knew the positions meant nothing. At least to her mother.

A heartbeat later, the girl silently placed the tray of drinks and scones on the table between them. Georgia caught her hand before she could get away. "Dear, remind me of your name?" Her patented smile felt so warm that Elysia almost believed it herself.

The girl's eyes shot between Elysia and her mother.

Her voice was a squeak. "Hannah, ma'am, Hannah."

Georgia kept smiling and snuck a scone into the girl's apron. "Thank you, Hannah. Have a good afternoon."

She turned back to Elysia, taking hold of a mug. Bumblebees were a common enough winter drink in Kava if you could afford tea. The simple mix of gin and tea smelled divine and was strong enough to warm your bones after being in the rain.

She sipped her drink. "I imagine your sister is not attending? Have you spoken to her lately?"

Elysia resisted the urge to crack her neck. It was the same questions all the time. *And the answers did not change.* Smiling pleasantly, she shook her head. "No, I haven't heard from her recently."

A look that said Beatriz would be getting a *nonnegotiable* type of summons crossed her mother's face. "Hm. We'll have to see about that."

She handed a mug to Elysia. "On to business. I'll be hosting a cocktail party for all the diplomats coming into Kava next week, and I'll need you in attendance."

She waved a hand. "Nothing exceptional. But I'd like you there nonetheless—the old bats always like to see the younger generation." Razor eyes slid over Elysia. "Wear something flattering."

Elysia stiffened, but merely took a small pull of her drink. "I imagine that Remy and Daphne will be welcome, then?"

Her mother snapped her fingers. "Good thinking. The three of you are such a striking set all together."

Georgia's eyes were focused, scheming even as she rested back like she hadn't a care in the world. The sight put Elysia on edge. Her mother was always making moves, forever thinking of politics, and Elysia was under the growing impression that she herself was on the docket today.

"Have you given any thought to the Raven Ball?"

Her discomfort increased. Her father didn't like to involve her mother in her *errands* for him, but perhaps he had looped her in for an event as important as the Raven Ball. She tiptoed around the question. "What do you mean? Food, décor, guest list?"

Georgia smiled like a cat with a mouse, and it was all Elysia could do to keep her eyes from narrowing suspiciously. She had not heard any rumblings about the Raven Ball yet. It was nearly three months away. But her mother was looking far too satisfied. Georgia lifted a strong shoulder, leaning in conspiratorially.

"Some might say it would be the most perfect evening for a royal proposal."

Elysia froze. Fire and alcohol raced through her veins and yet she froze down to her very bones.

Georgia's smile was not fake as she laughed deeply at her daughter's shock and dropped a sly wink. "Oh, you had no idea! But us girls must keep on top of these things. It will be the best Raven Ball Relaclave has ever seen."

The gleam in her mother's eye did not lie. It would be an extravagant and audacious affair. But it was not shock plastered upon Elysia's face.

It was terror.

Rollie's words resounded in the confines of her skull.

He would have you killed.

He will always choose the Crown.

Because he is the Crown.

Elysia swallowed her panic and painted herself elated. The prince was to propose in two months' time.

Two months, she had two months.

It had already been so tricky. Always disappearing for hours at a time to train with Gage. Scavenging secrets from both the fair and deprived of her city for her father. And then pulling back from the prince ever so slightly once this nightmare began.

She thought of his parting shot in the library. That he wanted to *talk* soon. She chewed on her lip. Topp was smart, but usually he was so preoccupied with his own business that any strange behaviors on her part went unnoticed. But that had been before her curse had changed. Maybe he *had* noticed something after all.

No, she decided, Topp would not pry or ask questions. They laughed, they played, and the sex was phenomenal, but it was a rare moment they delved into the sorts of things that made them tick. What went on below the surface stayed where it belonged. If she was honest, it was one of the many reasons she loved him.

It would be fine, she had to be fine.

ELYSIA STRODE out of the castle that evening with another of Lynd's baskets secure beneath her cloak. The woman would not be deterred, and Elysia really didn't have the heart nor belly to stop her.

She made it all of two blocks when a floppy-haired young boy sped around the corner, collided against her legs, and fell back with a humph. Elysia paused, her irritation quickly melting into amusement at the sight of him shocked and sprawled on the ground.

She held out a gloved hand, and the boy took it with a grin. "Sorry, miss. I've got a letter for ya."

Elysia scanned him and did not find a sash or any other insignia to mark the boy as Crown. She took the letter curiously and went to grab a coin in payment, but he had already charged away, reckless in his pursuit of his next delivery victim.

Stepping out of the crowds, Elysia leaned against an old closed-down eatery's walls and tore the note open.

See you tonight, dollface. BP

She had not seen Beatriz in nearly four months. Elysia pressed her lips together. No doubt, Beatriz needed dirt on some pretty rich boy that she'd pissed off or stolen drugs from.

Her heels struck the streets angrily. Frankly, it was shocking that her sister even bothered with a note. Last time she'd just snuck through a window at three in the morning, and Elysia had stuck a knife to her throat before her feet had even hit the floor.

Then again, maybe it wasn't such a surprise she sent a note this time after all.

Gage had laughed himself hoarse when Elysia had told him about it the next morning. Elysia's lips almost gave into a smile at the thought. The man didn't laugh enough. Not that she could blame him.

She twisted the locks into her dingy flat, as Lynd had so lovingly called it, and heaved a sigh of relief. Behind this door, these walls—there was no one to hide from but herself.

She set her goods on the table and dropped her cloak onto a chair. Within minutes, the fire was blazing and every stitch of uncomfortable clothing was tossed to the winds.

Better, much better already.

Between her buttery soft deep blue pajamas and the woolen socks covering her feet, Elysia soon felt the damp Kavian chill dissipate. Walking around, she lit enough lamps to brighten the small living room.

Her flat was a luxurious, eclectic mix of old steals from within the castle walls. It had been no small feat to lug the plush, velveteen poufs and worn, stuffed leather couch to her flat in the dead of night, but Elysia had paid off Gage's men handsomely to carry her forbidden cargo.

Gage called it an abuse of power and threatened to smoke out her new furnishings.

She called it absolutely necessary and had handed him an ancient Kavian blade she'd found beneath the castle that swiftly melded his lips into a shit-eating grin.

The thick rug she sat upon had been tossed from the royal sitting room ages ago only to collect dust in a closet. Elysia had been more than happy to rescue it from decay. She ran her fingers over the smooth cream fibers, feeling herself relax even further as she settled in for the night. In truth, her flat was not dingy at all. It was filled with the treasures of a queen.

She laid out a small sheet and held the edges down with two old books. She'd really hate to accidentally grind dirt into the rug. Then she placed a few pots and various dead flowers out in front of her.

The live ones, they were her secret joy. Few knew how much she enjoyed her time spent knuckle deep in the soil trying to cajole seedlings to life and whispering encouragement to the rare bloom.

Kava had no sun. It had no flowers.

But she had seen a picture book of them as a child and became obsessed with finding a way to harvest them even here in Rela-clave. They had moss and mold aplenty, but not the blooms she dreamed of holding.

Rollie, tiny scientist that he was, had pushed his glasses up, and set to work at crafting her the sun. No small feat for a boy of eight years. She imagined that was why he had succeeded, though. No adult would be brave enough to think they could capture the sun.

Rollie had.

He'd dug through books on other lands that still met the sun without Kava's constant filter of soot and haze, and created what he called a flower house. It was child sized and easily carried, only able to grow a few plants at a time. Elysia still did not understand the mechanics of the reflective devices Rollie had installed on the top panes of the little house, but light was collected and magnified, and it created the perfect womb from which her seedlings could grow.

She sat contently in front of the fire with dirt under her nails and a jug of stolen wine off to her side. Wine was an expensive indulgence. Gin remained the drink of choice for most Kavians given the abundance of their forests. And yet a good deep red was still her favorite. She'd swiped this latest bottle on her way out of the castle. Brain still buzzing with thoughts of Topp, proposals, and her looming execution, it'd seemed necessary. Bringing the bottle to her lips, she took a swig. A dark drop clung to her mouth. She absently wiped it away, debating internally which flowers to plant next.

Carefully pressing dirt on top of the new seeds until each little pot felt just right, she then placed them in the flower house. After a quick mumbled prayer to the gods-knew-who, she returned the flower house to its home on the windowsill.

Elysia scrubbed her fingers clean of dirt the best she could and then sat back down in front of the fire. *Time to earn this month's rent.* She took another swig of wine and rubbed her hands together, the image already filling her mind's eye. Delicate glass in different shapes and sizes lay before her, waiting for her to begin.

She held a single bloom out, inspecting it as if it was a gem. It was one of the few flowers that had held on for her this month. Knees folded beneath her, she lowered her arm to rest against her thighs with her eyes still hooked on the flower as if mesmerized. Her gaze softened, the beauty of the flower working its own subtle magic. Tension drained down and out of her. Her whole body relaxed in an airless exhale. Small white diamond specks that looked like stars against the velvet blue-black of the petals coaxed out a hidden sense of wonder within her. The flower's delicate, faded scent lulled her even further.

It was with regret that she placed the pressed flower upon a thin sheet of glass.

She glanced out the window, a sense of forlornness rooting in her chest. She would never know what Kava had once been. She would never know wildflowers instead of decay. Her blooms all had an expiration. At their peak, they were snipped. A life cut short. Stuck flat between the pages of a book. Flattened, but still vibrant, she crafted them into art. At least this way, more people had a chance to experience their beauty, she supposed. Everything died eventually, after all.

She studied her small collection, picking out accents. *Yes, those.* Her hands moved almost of their own accord. Peppering sprigs of greenery around the bloom. Adjusting the design until her heart quietly glowed at the sight. She gave a satisfied hum and decided it would do.

She had just unstoppered a small pot of paste when a series of loud knocks with no rhythm shook the door on its hinges. One would think a drunk ex-lover had come to visit rather than a young woman.

Elysia frowned at her unfinished work, but got to her feet, and peered out the looking hole. There was Beatriz, alright. As tall as most men with a silver mane that hung like a sheet of deathly sharp metal.

Her foot tapped against the black-and-white tiled floor. "I know you're standing there," she drawled, arms crossed.

Elysia didn't respond, just picked at her fingernails. *Damn dirt. Impossible to get out.* Provoking her sister was one of her greatest joys in life. Unfortunately, Beatriz felt the same. Her drawl became an annoyed growl and her fist slammed against the door.

"*Elysia.*"

Elysia grinned and slowly started to count to ten. She only made it to five before her sister was banging against the door like she could break through it with her fists alone.

"You're such a brat—"

Beatriz swung a swift foot at the door right as Elysia ripped it open. Beatriz toppled into the room, legs buckling and arms flailing.

Elysia smiled sweetly. "You need to be careful! Could break an ankle like that."

Beatriz glowered, shooting her a look as she straightened out her lanky frame. "Don't use that gross Crown voice with me. Gives me the creeps."

Walking back over to her project, Elysia settled down onto the floor once more as if she hadn't just antagonized a viper.

"Shut the door, will you? And lock it. Who knows who followed you here with the company you keep."

Elysia smirked as Triz's dark plum lips grumbled. The old nickname still fell out sometimes. Familiar and foreign, just like them. Her sister twisted all the locks and strutted into the living space with her hands upon her hips like she owned it.

Ignoring her, Elysia proceeded to paint a thin layer of translucent paste on the matching sheet of glass. After corking the paste, she finally turned her attention to Beatriz.

"So, what do you want? What do you need this time?" Her tone remained matter-of-fact. They both knew there was only one reason Beatriz ever visited.

She lined up the edges of the glass and pressed the sheets together.

Perfect. It would be ready to sell once framed.

Her sister stared over her shoulder. "You... You're the one who sells these?"

Elysia glanced up. "Keeps this roof over my head. Not all of us can swindle our endless lovers into paying our bills."

"You're *literally* dating a prince." Her face tilted with a knowing sort of pity. "You're that bad at sex, huh?"

But then her demeanor shifted from mocking to a narrow, scheming type of focus as she stared at the flower art. "How much?"

"Hm?" Elysia stood, not answering Triz's question. *Why do you suddenly care?* was the real question. She'd been living on her own for a few years now, selling her pieces the whole time. It wasn't a hidden operation. Every week, she was at the market.

Even her parents knew about it. They hated it, of course. Said it was wrong to remind people of what Kava used to be. *Wrong to wish for anything different.*

Beatriz's long fingers motioned impatiently at the framed flower pressings that were ready to be sold. "How. Much."

Elysia shook her head at Beatriz's agitation with a little grin. *Too easy.* Carrying her latest piece to a safe spot where it could rest and dry, she answered. "Depends on the piece. About ten coins, though."

Triz's eyebrows shot up. "Ten coins? Ten measly fucking coins? Most folks have never even seen a damn flower in Kava! You could make a killing if you wanted."

Elysia bristled, muttering under her breath as she put away her supplies. "I make enough, okay? You drugged-up cow's ass."

Grinning, Beatriz tossed the small pot of paste up and down. Elysia snatched it out of the air. "Give me that. And stop *touching* things."

Beatriz waved away her insults and orders as if they were a fly, already examining a knickknack that Topp had given her. "At least us *drugged-up cows* don't have assholes so tight that we walk funny." She gave Elysia a look while miming a ridiculous walk, her legs stiff and butt puckered.

"I do *not* walk like that."

"Sure, you don't." She grabbed a framed flower pressing, making Elysia's blood pressure jump.

"If you could do more of this"—she gestured around at the dirt and plants—"would you? You could have a serious business. There's no one else in the land with flowers, dead or alive. They're not worth importing, either."

Elysia's head slanted, gauging her sister's sharp observations as she sank onto the arm of the leather couch. "Can't. Rollie made the flower house, and I don't think he's too keen on doing me any favors right now. Besides, since when does Relaclave's favorite party girl care about anything serious?"

Her words were curious but still caustic. Once again, Beatriz didn't even bat an eye. Elysia hadn't really expected her to—her sister was well aware of what people said about her. Star of Relaclave's most salacious tales, her sister never missed an opportunity to reprimand her for caring what others thought.

"You'll never win them all, Elysia. Those sniveling old bags of bones wouldn't know a good time if it smacked them in their fake teeth."

Elysia's lips twitched at the memory. Her sister, drunk and hanging out of a carriage, giving life advice.

She left her memory and found Beatriz looking at her in annoyance, an expression that was usually followed by snide comments about Elysia being such a *precious little doll*. Beatriz kept her mouth shut for once, though. Instead, she filled it with wine. Tipping the jug back with expert ease, she smacked her lips once finished and looked around expectantly.

"Don't you eat around here?"

Elysia huffed at the unspoken demand. Wordlessly, she grabbed two tea plates and plopped down Lynd's meat pies . Handing one off to Beatriz, she curled up on the couch to wait. She allowed her sister all of two bites before placing her own pie back down.

Any day now.

Triz licked her fingers and leaned back against the wall. "Scarzan. What do you know?"

There it is.

She frowned. Beatriz didn't usually get caught up in political affairs. Scarzan was a disgusting specimen. He also happened to be one of the Bellian representatives visiting soon. "What is it you want with him?"

The diplomats had not even arrived yet. How could she possibly have found herself ass up in their matters already?

Beatriz shrugged. "We have a common interest, that's all. Never hurts to have a little leverage in your pocket. And you, sister dear, seem to have large pockets these days."

Taking a bite of pie, her sister spoke through her mouthful of food. "I heard about those con artist bloodletters. The undead gods know who you paid off to get those tips, but you did it somehow."

Irritation boiled within Elysia, building like a geyser of steam, but her sister continued, oblivious as ever.

"And you still spend half your time up the Crown's skirt. Doing all of Father's dirty work." She swallowed and grinned wickedly. "Or perhaps I should say, down the Crown's pants."

The geyser almost blew, heat rising rapidly from her chest to her face. She didn't care about the sexual innuendo, but the jab at being their father's pet was a poke against a bruise that would likely never heal.

Jaw tight, she spat out an ineloquent rebuttal. "As if you know *anything* about my life. All you ever do is show up when you need something like some kind of leech. I'm not helping you this time. *Get out.*" She gestured pointedly at the door, her eyes cold and voice harsh.

Unfazed, Beatriz chewed slowly, staring her dead in the eyes and waiting. Her comments had hit their mark and she knew it, thanks to Elysia's oversized reaction. This wasn't the first time they'd played this game. Beatriz would say something terrible, setting off Elysia's temper, so she could pretend she wasn't going to help and feel like she had a spine for all of two seconds before inevitably caving. But they both knew she'd cave.

She always did.

Beatriz might not know what exactly Elysia did for their father, but she was smart enough to capitalize on the oily self-loathing her sister tried so hard to hide.

Elysia felt the muscles in her neck grow taut as her frustration mounted. Every last drop of cool, collected logic seemed to abandon ship when it came to Beatriz. She imagined throttling her sister. Beatriz didn't know shit about *why* she worked for their father. She just liked to judge her and throw it in her face whenever she got the chance. *Selfish, ignorant bitch.*

"I need to know before that damn party Mother is hosting."

Beatriz tossed her plate aside carelessly, scattering crumbs everywhere.

Elysia glared at her sister, her temper falling and annoyed embarrassment rising in its place thanks to her own inability to maintain her composure. She sifted through what she knew about the incoming diplomat and tried to find a single trail that could possibly connect back to her sister. On paper, diplomat Scarzan of Bellia ran their neighbor's treasury, much like Remy's father did for Kava. Off paper, he was a connoisseur of a Bellian card game called fitz. He spent much of his unreasonable salary playing both fitz and any other game that could swallow money.

She ignored her sister's impatient foot tapping, taking her time to weigh out the value of her secrets.

Rumor had it that Scarzan had bet off one of his daughters to a Bellian crime lord. No one had seen or heard from the girl in months. But it was merely a rumor. A rumor that Elysia would need to confirm before it was of any use to her sister.

Her fingers combed through her hair as she thought.

Bellians valued their daughters deeply. Unlike most lands that Elysia knew of, the Bellians considered their daughters to be gifts. Gifts that grew into oracles, warriors, and the mothers of every single future Bellian. If the public learned what he had done, it would leave the diplomat not only shamed but likely dead. They were as ruthless as they were wise in that land.

It was a secret that could break this man. And that was fine if the information was true. She could appreciate a culture that meted out swift justice for a crime such as that.

Still nestled in the safety of her couch, she mused that this wasn't the type of secret to be gifted lightly. It wasn't the type to be gifted at all. *Because she wanted this one for herself.*

She toyed with keeping it. She'd had plans for this little tidbit. Been holding onto it for the right moment. The only reason she hadn't dropped it in her father's lap already was because international accusations were tricky. She needed something truly solid, *irrefutable* even, before she made her move. Her father hated Scarzan. She could've milked it for time off. Time off that she desperately needed.

Beatriz's unblinking eyes beat down on her, and she sighed. *There goes those plans.* Looks like she'd be going out into the night and listening to Relaclave whisper. All so that Beatriz could wield the truth like a scythe.

Elysia studied her sister. She was expectant and waiting. As if there wasn't a chance Elysia would leave her hanging. *She's always so sure I'll bail her out.* A staggering wave of resentment crashed over Elysia. Bitterness filled her mouth even as she agreed. "Fine."

Her resentment turned to ash, though, as the one thought that never failed to sway her hand returned. *Please don't wind up dead.* The plaintive words were quiet in her mind. It wasn't a new thought. She wasn't even sure it was from the good of her heart. There was just something unbearably lonely about imagining a world without her sister.

Her wild, infuriating sister.

She envied Beatriz. The pure freedom she'd clawed out and clung to. It was a life that had never been in the cards for Elysia. *Uncontrollable.* That's what Beatriz was. Their parents despised it. Had long ago given up on reforming her into someone they could use. If drugs and alcohol were the cost, then Beatriz was more than willing to pay it.

Elysia straightened and crossed her legs. "I may have something that could help you."

Beatriz smiled smugly. "I knew it." Her words cut short as she devolved into a coughing fit. Shaking her head, she wiped her mouth with the back of her hand and gave a half grin. "Smoking too much."

Elysia ignored her and held out a hand in pause. "It's too big to offer for nothing. Family or not, I will need something in return."

A frown creased Triz's smooth face. "You want to bargain?"

Elysia let a little bit of the woman she had become shine through her eyes and watched for the moment it registered on

Beatriz's face. *There.* Uncertainty hidden behind a patronizing smirk. Good. Her sister could bother with a little respect.

"The information you request is worth far more than whatever juvenile tangle you find yourself in. I will tell you now with your assurance that you will not act until I can verify its truth next week with the diplomat's arrival. It comes with a cost." Even Elysia could hear the snootiness rolling off her words, but she couldn't help it—Beatriz brought out the worst in her sometimes.

She watched her sister closely. She could have sworn the glint in her sister's eye was one of thrill and excitement.

"Name your price."

"I shall hold you in my debt and you must fulfill whatever it is I desire when the time comes. Do you agree?"

There was a formality to her words that had Beatriz recoiling, considering carefully. It was like Elysia could see every thought race through her hard gray eyes. She pitied the fools that thought a vapid, long-legged waif had climbed into their bed.

Beatriz nodded once sharply and stuck out a hand. "You have a deal."

The situation must be worse than she had thought for Beatriz to agree so easily to such a terrible bargain. She had expected at least a small amount of negotiation. Perhaps her sister still thought that she was not capable of her own machinations.

Elysia was not sure if she was wrong or not.

Time would tell.

But like Beatriz said, it was always good to have a bit of leverage in your pocket.

Elysia stood and slapped her palm into her sister's outstretched hand, giving it a firm shake.

"Good." She made quick work of explaining the Bellian diplomat's vices and blunders, not bothering to mince any words.

Beatriz's eyebrows lifted and she shook her head. "Bastard. Send word when you've done what you need to do." She stretched and made to stand.

She was almost to the door when her eyes snagged on something resting on the table. Elysia watched as the angles of Beatriz's body became harsh, the blood rushing to the edges of her cheek-bones in a bright pink flush.

Beatriz snatched the grimy coin off the table and held it out like it was treason itself.

Her mouth became a harsh slash. "*Where did you get this coin, you pilfering, glorified busybody?*"

Chapter 7

____

ELYSIA LUNGED FOR THE COIN. *That's my lifeline, you harlot.* But Beatriz flung an elbow into Elysia's gut, attempting to manhandle her like a sack of potatoes back onto the couch. She held the coin far out of reach, and Elysia's anger soared to where she could barely think.

Through sheer mental grit, she willed herself to remain in control. *I must not react. I must not react.*

"So easy to"—Beatriz flicked her on the forehead with her free hand—"*rile.* Doing you a favor, trust me."

Elysia's temper snapped the moment her sister's fingers reverberated off her forehead. Years of training aided her. Her leg swept out, collapsing Beatriz from the knees. One more breath and her sister was flat on her back. She dug her knee into Beatriz's chest and wrapped her fingers around her throat.

Her sister's pulse was warm and erratic under her fingers. She plucked the coin from Beatriz's now rigid grasp.

It was then she saw her sister's wide, fearful eyes. How they tracked her like she was a rabid animal.

Her rage drained in an instant. She sprung back with her palms facing her sister.

"I'm sorry," she breathed. "I'm so sorry, did I hurt you?"

What was I thinking—I should have just let her. Elysia's thoughts became a torrent.

Beatriz just blinked and gingerly propped herself up to a seated position. "How in the name of the undead gods did you learn to do that? *Why* did you learn to do that?"

It was Elysia's turn to feel her face turn fiery and warm. She ignored the pointed questions. "What does that coin mean to you?"

Beatriz held her stare in a way that clearly noted Elysia's evasion, but answered her anyway. Her voice was low, serious. "Stay away from them, Lys. This isn't some silly castle intrigue or case for you to break open."

"I can't."

"What do you mean, you can't? Just mind your own damn business for once, Elysia, and stay away from them."

Elysia shook her head and tears pricked her eyes as she slumped down to the floor. "There is no story." She looked up to meet Beatriz's eyes. The last week had broken her. She'd like to blame it on her bellyful of wine, but the truth was her life was crashing down around her ears and she desperately wanted to shove all the fear and anxiety into someone else's hands. She hadn't expected those hands to be her sister's, but here she was, saying what she shouldn't. "I want to meet with them because I need their help."

Elysia ground her palms into her eyes, not wanting to see her sister's face after how Beatriz had reacted to the coin in the first place. Fear clenched her throat. How terrible it would be to be turned in by her own damn sister. No one would be surprised—a Parker eliminating another Parker. They would call it poetic. The Crown's children had turned out to be the beastliest of them all.

Her sister did not snarl or shout now. Her face lost its color entirely. If Elysia didn't know any better, she would have said she just broke her sister's nonexistent heart.

But Beatriz did not have a heart, unpolished angry child that she had been, and Elysia did know better, which was why it could not possibly be a tear, silent and gleaming, in her eye.

Beatriz shook her head, her normal sharp light dimming, and grabbed the wine jug one more time. The arrogance in her posture fell away as she held the bottle back with just the sound of the wine glugging down her throat. She paused and held the bottle out to Elysia wordlessly.

Elysia grabbed it only to find the dregs. She stood to dig out another bottle from the cupboards, glad that she'd been hoarding a few for times like these. She plunked back down on the floor, bottle in tow.

Beatriz sat with her legs bent and forearms resting loosely on her knees. "Tell me where this story starts. Because I can promise there is no happy ending involving that coin and those fools."

Elysia pulled out the dagger that had been tucked into the pocket of her pajamas. Gage's lessons to always be prepared were hard to forget. She began mindlessly spinning it between her fingers, letting the rhythm soothe her jagged thoughts. Biting her lip, she weighed how deeply she could trust the woman sitting in her living room who shared her last name.

Maybe it made her naive, but she wanted to, she really did. *Desperation will get you killed.* She ignored the thought. Even if it was the truth. She had told Rollie the facts, but tonight, she wanted to tell the story and pretend her big sister would actually show up for *her* for once. Against her better judgment, her mouth opened.

"It started months ago," she began. "But today, I was at the library and something happened."

She lost track of herself for a moment as she flashed back to how Topp had pushed her flush to the shelves, not caring that books had rattled and fallen like gilded, crashing bricks to the floor. Her back pinching against the wooden edges of the shelves. His fingertips pressing into the hot skin beneath the edge of her shirt.

Elysia blinked and found her sister grinning like a cat with a bird. She tried to fix her face, but it was too late. Beatriz might not live and breathe secrets, but she had their father's gift for being an uncanny reader of most situations. If she could use those skills to torture her little sister, then all the better.

Beatriz pounced, knowing exactly what she was doing. "By yourself in the library, were you? Didn't think so. But do go on. I love a steamy bedtime story."

"Oh, shut up." Clearing her throat, she kept her face perfectly even. "As I was saying, I was in the library when a book fell and caught my eye."

Beatriz's grin widened as she let out a lustful sigh. "I bet it did. I could use a little book shaking, if you know what I mean."

Elysia's fingers flexed on the hilt of her dagger in exasperation. *So annoying.*

Mostly because she wasn't wrong.

Elysia recalled what had happened next. How she had dragged one particular old volume closer across the cold stone floor. Trailed a finger down its golden edges, feeling the slip of the gilded pages. She'd whispered the title aloud and shivered. *Travels of the Undead.* It was a book on the many gods that had been revered before the Fall. It was a book that should have been burned with the rest of the religious and magical works. Cracking it open, she had found a purple flower pressed between the pages.

It wasn't one of her own flowers, though. It had been left between the pages like some dark beacon pulling in stray maidens who made the mistake of kissing amongst dusty tomes.

Elysia released the memory, crawling over to her flower house where she had stuck the bloom earlier. She gently brushed her fingers over its still soft edges. Velvety and pliant, she had a sinking feeling the petals were not going to dry out. "This flower was in the book. I think it's in some kind of magical stasis."

Beatriz dropped her head to her knees. "Of course it is."

"It held the book open to a story. A story of a girl who went to a dark, dark land and retrieved the light for all her people." Saying the words aloud gave her chills.

It was just a story. Just a silly book that had been knocked from its home. *That drawing, though...* Elysia shut down the thought. The drawing was a coincidence. Nothing more.

But beneath the chills and her fright, it was as though the smallest tendril of warmth sprawled within her chest, telling her this was just the beginning, and for some reason, that scared her more than anything else.

"Is that all?"

"No, no it's not."

She stood and began pacing the room, feeling the need to check all the doors and windows. She of all people knew that someone could always be listening. There was no silent listener at her door or window though—just the irregular rhythm of her heart and breath reminding her of the thin line she now walked.

Beatriz slapped a hand to the floor, impatient as ever. "Just tell me already!"

Elysia halted. "I've been having dreams. But they're not dreams."

She leaned against the windowsill, staring out at nothing. Her body warred between frustration and an all-encompassing numbness. The cool glass touched her forehead and she closed her eyes. Beatriz still waited behind her. She could hear her shifting on the floor. Impatient, but waiting.

Her eyes grew distant. "It's like I leave my body, and at first, I can see my body still lying there. But then I go somewhere else, and wherever I am, my body is just as real as the one that's back on my bed. I tested it once, took all my strength to stay there long enough, but I brought my knife to slice my hand... When I came back, it bled." She looked down at her palm. The scar stared back, taunting her.

Her sister, who had seen every vulgar and delicious happening in all of Kava, had eyes the size of saucers.

"No one knows?"

Elysia glanced back. "No, no one knows. Well, Rollie some-what knows. He gave me the coin. I haven't stayed a full night with Topp since it started, but he caught me leaving in the middle of the night this week. I think I've thrown Remy and Daphne off for now." She trailed off, her anxiety reaching new heights as she worried over what people may have noticed and what they would do if they realized she was cursed.

Beatriz nodded darkly. "Good, you'll keep your distance if you're smart. Tell me what happens in these dreams."

This was the part Elysia really did not wish to remember. Because remembering made it real. And she still desperately wished to pretend it wasn't. She had searched and studied to no avail, and yet, there was still a tiny voice that begged her to ignore it all, as if it would go away. *It wasn't going away.*

She grabbed her house robe from where she'd last thrown it and tugged it on, pulling the edges close. The thick fabric warmed her but did nothing to soothe the turmoil within.

"I don't know where I go. But it is not here or of this land, I can tell you that."

Some of the fear in Beatriz's eyes lightened into curiosity. "What do you mean?"

Elysia shook her head. "Honestly, I believe it's a place of death."

The curiosity vanished and Beatriz blanched. "Death?"

"Yes, it's dark, desolate." It was also beautiful, but she kept that hidden thought to herself. Instead, she told her sister of the deep, rich soil that was foamy and cool between her bare toes. How the river sang her the most haunting and eerie song, raising a tear to her eye every single night.

"Does anything happen?"

"I'm barely there for more than a moment. But I swear... there's someone else. And they've called to me. Before I can do anything, I'm gone. Slamming back into my body."

They were both quiet a moment.

Beatriz came close and clasped Elysia's hands. "Don't go to that meeting. Please, I swear I will find a way to help you with this. Just don't go."

"You fear them this much?"

She snorted and dropped her hands. "I don't fear them. I fear what those idiots may do and who may find out. The fact that their little ragtag group has lasted this long without the Crown discovering them is nothing short of a miracle."

Elysia hesitated. "Rollie thinks they could help."

"They will get you killed. Is that what you want? To join the others at the gallows?" Beatriz breathed heavily. "No, you keep this to your damn self, and we—we will find a way to stop this."

Elysia wanted to believe her sister. Her sister, who never showed up when she was supposed to and only called for black-mail. She believed that Beatriz did not want her to die. That some shred of protective sisterly instinct remained beneath the clothes and reckless behavior. But what could Beatriz, who couldn't stay out of trouble herself, possibly offer?

She deflected. "Mother says Topp is proposing."

Beatriz's mouth dropped. Whatever she saw on Elysia's face must not have been reassuring. "You know you can't, right? You're supposed to be the sensible one!" Disbelief softened the cut of her words.

"You want me to turn down the Crown Prince in front of the entire court at the Raven Ball? I'm not sure if Mother or Father would kill me first. Mother *is* oddly light on her feet," Elysia noted dryly.

Beatriz glared in response. "Then stop the proposal alto-gether. Break his heart. Smash it all to smithereens and come up with some story. Get pregnant by some commoner for all I care. You've grown up in this jungle, now fucking act like it, or you'll be the king's most favorite example. His own son's true love beheaded for the sake of the Crown." Her words were mocking, but the bite of her fear was true.

Elysia said nothing, made no false promises that she had no idea how to keep.

Beatriz looked at her with pity. "What has woken will not die. But maybe we can stop it." Her gray eyes doubted even as she spoke. They both knew magic was not so easily killed or hidden. The headless and broken bodies decorating the main square proved it.

"I'm going to that meeting," Elysia said softly.

Beatriz nodded shortly and stood up to leave. Tight anger cut into her words. "Fine. It'll be your own fault when they take your head for treason. Imagine that, the crown prince's betrothed left for the birds in the square."

And with that, she stalked out the door, slamming it behind her.

Elysia thought she heard her loose a fist into the wall as she stomped down the stairs.

Chapter 8

For the next week, Elysia stayed hidden in her flat, regretting her recent choices and not wanting to face anyone in her life besides Sir Larkspur, who asked for nothing more than his daily meals. But as dawn broke, Elysia knew that her time of wallowing had come to a close.

Bleary eyed, she stumbled out of bed to find several letters shoved through the mail slot. It seemed the rest of the world was done with her hiding as well. There were three messages in total.

One from her mother with detailed instructions regarding the upcoming cocktail party from time of arrival to the exact style of hair and dress required. Because gods forbid that someone in their midtwenties chose their own *hairstyle*.

The second letter was from Rollie.

Your presence will be accepted but a favor is needed. Details to come. Good luck.

Both relief and frustration ran through her. Relief that they were even willing to speak with her given who she was and frustration because nothing ever came free, did it?

And finally, a short yet very colorful note from Gage

describing exactly what he would do to her if she did not drag her sorry carcass from her home and meet with him to train.

Shit, shit, *shit*. She'd missed at least three of their usual training sessions.

Elysia tossed off her robe and pajamas in a frenzy and almost died tripping over Sir Larkspur, who darted in and around her feet. Snatching up a pair of soft leather leggings, she shoved her legs through and danced to wrench them up over her hips. She barely spared a glance to see which top she had grabbed before yanking on her boots and practically throwing herself out the door.

The muted sun had already started its grim ascent, which meant she was late and being late never boded well when meeting Gage. Her mind raced, wondering exactly how much time it would take her to streak across the city to where they always met. Her mind raced so fast, in fact, that for once in her life she did not check her surroundings.

Which was how she found herself dropping to the ground like a brick as a dagger whizzed past, grazing her cheek. Twisting, she turned and fired back a blade of her own.

A bare hand caught the handle with practiced ease.

The smug bastard sat with legs sprawled on her roof and was calmly eating a sandwich. She'd nearly pissed herself collapsing on the street and he sat there eating a fucking sandwich.

Gage took another bite and sunk her knife into his own sheath. "Sounded like a bit of chaos down there. Weren't in a hurry, were you?"

She scowled. "You're a bastard, you know that."

His lips twitched, but he didn't answer. He just dropped to the street and held out another sandwich. "Here."

She waved him away, chest still heaving. Lifting her fingertips to her face, they came back bloody. "Do you want me to get caught? All these cuts and bruises and someone is bound to notice one day."

He just grunted and held out the sandwich again. "You don't eat enough when you're stressed. Take it."

She sighed and snatched it from his fingers before plopping down on a nearby bench. Taking a small bite, she spoke absently. "My mother is going to be so pissed about this cut. There's a stupid party with the Bellian diplomats this week. I doubt Topp will go, but she wants to show me and the girls off, as usual."

His grin held for a moment, but then his eyes turned dark with condescending ire at the mention of the prince. "Forget your mother noticing. What kind of man doesn't notice that their woman is nearly always bruised? Or that you are not soft like any other woman he would touch?" His voice lowered. "What kind of man doesn't notice there is nearly always a knife between your legs?"

Elysia choked on her sandwich. "We are *not* having this conversation." She shoved more food into her mouth and gave him a grossed out look. Their relationship was far too familial to be discussing... *that.*

"Why, because you know I'm right?" he continued before she could respond. "I've been thinking you should stay at my place for a while."

Barely done choking, Elysia proceeded to inhale a breadcrumb and start hacking all over again. Had he just asked her to stay at his home? Gage smacked her back as if that would help, while she glared and tears streamed out of her eyes.

"Clearly, you need to be monitored," he muttered.

Wiping her face, she stared at him in disbelief. "You cannot be serious."

He stood and stretched, his muscles straining with the movement. Like most warriors, he had no qualms or false modesty. Bodies were bodies. They were what you needed them to be in that moment, and that was all there was to it. Instead of beauty, there was a brutalness to Gage's form. It wouldn't have mattered if you dressed him up in the prettiest of trappings. There was always going to be something about his body and the way it moved that stirred an unconscious fear in those around him.

"I wouldn't have said it if I wasn't serious." He shifted his weight back and stared at her.

"You don't need to lock me in your tower. Is this about the other day? Because I thought we were done with that." She tensed, unsure if it was worse to have to discuss the aftermath of the tongue, or that he might have picked up on something else.

His hands clasped onto the bench. He sighed then, as if she were being particularly annoying. "As if you wouldn't climb out the window. Elysia, you're not well. There's more going on that you're not telling me, and I don't understand why. Have I, of all people, not earned your trust since the day I met you?"

Her heart caught on his words. The similarity between his words and Remy's. The frustration and hurt they betrayed.

Her own words were a whisper. "It's my job to keep you safe, too."

The lines in his face deepened. "Elysia—"

She drew in a deep breath of morning air and waved her hand, cutting him off. "I'll come by late tonight. Don't wait up." That would buy her time. To consider her words. Her story.

His lips pressed thinly, like he could see right through her. "Fine. Let's train."

She recognized the conversation was far from over. Everyone only wanted to help. She knew that. But what they didn't understand was that with each person she told, the rope that kissed the blade frayed a little more. How many people could she tell before it broke?

Elysia tracked him through city streets and alleys to the edge of Relaclave, where the Lovestone Woods began. She entered the forest behind him and stilled.

Fog and mist swirled around her feet, her eyes. It reminded her of that place of nightmares in her dreams. She half expected the eerie song to fill her ears. *Focus, he's here somewhere.* Cool forest air filled her lungs, calming her as she scanned her surroundings.

She shifted her weight, a rush of fear and excitement coursing through her veins. He was in a mood, no doubt. And that meant nothing good for her.

A crack sounded to her left and she spun. She squinted, but there was nothing there. *Shit*. That meant—she tried to turn back, but he'd already dropped beside her and snapped out a punch that rocked her head back.

She danced away, blinking back the tears that instantly blinded her eyes. "What was that for?" she gritted out, rubbing her jaw.

He said nothing, just waited.

Fine. No words were really needed, anyway. She darted back into his space and struck, knowing he would easily deflect her first blow. But then they were dancing, a wild yet strategic frenzy of limbs bringing them together and then apart over and over again.

Tired with muscles shaking, she slowed for just a moment, and that was all he needed.

She was flat on her back, staring up at misted trees with a dagger to her nose.

With an arrogant smile stretching across his face, he tapped the blade to the tip of her nose just because he could. "You're out of shape."

She smacked the blade away from her face and huffed, shoving herself back up. "I've been busy. Can't always be rolling around in the dirt with you."

Something closer to anger than disappointment touched his eyes, but his words were even. "Then we better use the time we have."

He lunged, driving harder and faster than before. The man was a whirl that she could barely track. She had already been winded and now all she could do was deflect hit after hit, never once getting close enough to strike back. He was showing her just how far she'd fallen in these last few months. She knew it and hated every breathless second of his punishment.

An angry snarl rose in her throat and she lashed out with her dagger instead of her fist.

But he caught her wrist and backed her easily into a tree. The rough bark and tiny broken branches stabbed into her uncomfortably. She snapped her teeth at him. "Enough, Gage."

A wide smile spread across his face, showing all of his beautiful teeth right back. "Is it? I don't think it is, Elysia. I don't think we're done until you're ready to tell me the truth."

He laughed from his chest, and it bounced through the trees. "Reminds me of when you were a little feral thing in your stupid Crown dresses and kicked and screamed because I wouldn't let you practice with a real sword."

He stepped back, leaving her heaving against the tree. He shook his head with a grin she knew well. "They all thought you were so perfect in your curls and little sashes and never even noticed what has always been right in front of their eyes. Do you remember what it took for me to allow that little feral kitten to finally have a real sword?"

She threw her head back against the tree, not caring that it hurt or she would have bark in her hair, and bit out her answer. "Years, that's what it took, years before you'd let me touch a real blade."

Gage sighed, and the sound reminded her that even though she was now grown, he was still older than her and was no stranger to her behavior.

"Elysia, you were this small, quiet child who crept through tunnels and stole secrets without even trying. You heard and saw things that no child ever should have, and by the time I found you in that cart surrounded by blood and death, any sense of trusting others had been shredded. I didn't give you a blade until you trusted me. Until you knew I would not hurt you, and I knew you wouldn't stab me in the eyeball in a moment of panic."

He stalked in closer to her again, leaving just enough space while staring her right in the eyes. "Let me help you. Just like I always have."

Her forehead dipped, resting against his shoulder, and she allowed herself to feel that comfort, to wonder for a whole breath what it would be like to not hold all her weight herself. His chin came down atop her head.

"I thought you would stop being such a pain in my ass when you got older."

She snorted and slapped a hand against him half-heartedly, pushing away to look up at his sharp eyes.

"I'm cursed, Gage, always have been." The treasonous words slid too easily off her tongue.

"Elysia, I've known that. It's why I'm—" He cut himself off, running a hand through his dark, cropped hair.

She laughed hollowly. He knew. Of course, he knew. "There's nothing to talk about, then."

"Something has changed, and you need to *tell me* so I can help you. That is how this works."

"There's nothing anyone can do about it. You can huff and puff at me all you want, but it won't change anything. If you want to be helpful, then I could use some backup later," she smiled. "I'm going after a diplomat."

Gage's nostrils flared, and he pinned her back against the tree with one hand.

She sighed. "Really? How mature."

"Is that how you think this works? That you can just brush me off, and I'll go so easily? Have I taught you nothing about family?" he growled.

But he wasn't done, his chest working up and down as he finally unleashed his worry-coated anger. "You think you can just demand my services as if I am some common servant? I am well aware you're one of the few who managed to cling to a drop of magic in this horrible kingdom, but something else has changed and you need to tell me what it is. Is it your magic? Because pretending nothing is happening won't fix your problem. You're smarter than this, godsdammit."

Elysia's temper ratcheted up a notch from where it had momentarily slumbered. She pressed off the tree and shoved right back into his space.

"You want trust, Gage? Then trust that I am doing everything I can to solve this, and solving this is going to require a few of my *little schemes,* as you like to call them. I need *information*, not a lecture."

His tone went flat, his hand lifting in exasperation. "You ask for trust and lie to me in the same breath? Gods, you don't make this easy." With that, he turned, stalking away from her and out of the woods.

He called back over his shoulder as he went. "You can handle Beatriz's dirty work on your own. Bother me when you have a real job. And I *will* see you at my house tonight."

Elysia bit back a scream. He was such a dick sometimes. She planted a hand on her hip, patting her sheath as he disappeared from sight.

"Motherf—" she cursed. *He took my fucking blade.*

Her blood pressure shot up, her irritation immediate and consuming. Oh, he thought he was *real* funny. Having the last word wasn't good enough, he had to nick her blade as well. A little guarantee that she would show up tonight if only to ream him out properly.

"You arrogant, thieving ASSHOLE!" Her rage sounded all the way to the forest's edge.

The woods were kind enough to carry his low chuckle back to her.

CHAPTER 9

Once she had looked forward to nights with Topp. She'd thrown dresses and skirts and tops in a ridiculous pile, trying to decide what she wished to wear. Her worries had been limited to him asking too many questions about what it was *exactly* that she did for her father. That he might wonder where her clever instincts and tips really came from after all.

Now she worried that falling asleep in his arms would be signing her own death warrant.

All relationships have problems. Elysia cracked a grin and held up a black dress with silver stitching.

An envelope popped through the mail slot, whizzing forcefully through the air and smacking against the ground. Elysia dropped the dress she had been considering and picked up the envelope.

She peered curiously at the seal.

It was an exact replica of the coin that hid in her flat. She immediately lurched forward, ripping open the door to the castle halls, looking back and forth for whoever had delivered the envelope. The halls were empty, though. Not a servant or stranger in sight.

Padding over to her vanity, she pulled out a fresh blade from the bottom drawer. Her small stockpile gleamed back at her and she smiled, a little rush flitting through her at the sight.

Lipstick and daggers. Every lady's favorite.

Elysia cracked the knife through the wax and tossed the weapon aside.

Her eyebrows rose higher and higher the further she read.

We would like to welcome you, Ms. Parker.
But first, we will need something in return.
Three evenings from now you will deliver:
A distraction of grand proportions.
A guarantee your royal attachments will be occupied.
A promise you are not compromised by false love.
Give us this and you will be welcomed kindly.
Your response shall be collected soon.

She shredded the letter and all its stupid demands without a thought. Bit by bit, she fed the pieces to the fire, watching them turn to ash. *A distraction?* What did they expect her to do, set the godsdamn castle on fire?

Fuck.

She collapsed onto her dressing chair in front of the fireplace. In the next three days, she must confirm diplomat Scarzan's actions against his daughter, find a suitable distraction for Rollie's rebel network, and attend her mother's party.

Good thing she hadn't been sleeping anyway.

Her thoughts stopped. *The party.* The party was in three days' time.

What a blessed coincidence from the undead gods.

The wheels of her mind began to spin. Perhaps, this would not be so difficult after all.

ELYSIA WALKED at a brisk pace through the castle halls. The heightened tension of the servants as they all but bolted from errand to errand was an echo of her own. Normally, she would have been plotting for weeks how to make the most of the diplomats' brief time in Kava. She'd have scouted their schedules and made herself invisible amongst their vices with no agenda really, other than to collect information for whenever a deal was truly needed.

But now, her priorities had narrowed. Pin down Scarzan. Create a distraction of royal measure. And figure out how to save her own life. *Easy.*

She turned the corner, mind focused on the first steps of her insane plan. *There are so many ways for this all to go wrong.* Elysia arrived at her destination, and after knocking soundly upon the closed door, she stepped back to wait.

The young maid, Hannah, opened the door just a crack, peering through with her watery blue eyes.

She whispered, "Yes, Ms. Parker?"

Elysia smiled and looked on curiously, dropping her voice low in good humor. "Why are we whispering, Hannah?"

The girl's cheeks tinged with pink. "Mrs. Parker is hosting our foreign guests. She does not wish to be disturbed."

Elysia raised her voice loudly, "Oh, of course, Hannah, I wouldn't dream of being a bother! I will have to come see my mother later then."

The girl's eyes widened, and Elysia gave a wink.

Heels pounded the floor, and the door flung open, poor Hannah barely escaping its path. Not that Georgia Parker noticed.

Her mother was wrapped in a tulle and silk concoction of black with a waist sash of red. The black and red reminded their guests she was the Crown's woman through and through. Elysia admired the dark creation and wondered at how what would be both garish and far too girlish on most women was a refined statement upon her mother.

Georgia pulled Elysia into the room and lightly kissed each of her cheeks. Guiding her over to the crowded sitting room, she demurely announced, "Elysia Parker, everyone, my daughter and a most valued member of the Crown."

Elysia kept her face fixed. Her mother loathed her recent *dabbling* outside of her father's assignments. Even though it'd been just the once, and ultimately, still for the Crown, she'd much prefer Elysia use her considerable skills to build upon her and her father's legacy rather than sift through the mud she found within the city.

Today was not for standoffs between mothers and daughters, though.

Today was a day for gaining secrets and bringing grown men to their knees.

Elysia smiled softly at their guests. "An honor to have you in our beloved home. Have you seen much of Relaclave?"

There were four in total.

Four overstuffed men in boring clothes with golden rings and dirty cigars stinking up her mother's beautiful sitting room. Diplomat Scarzan had the teeth and eyes of a rat. She continued to smile gently even as his eyes raked over her.

So, it was tables *and* women for him then, she noted sourly.

The man to his right sat with a stiff back and his black hair coiled to perfection. She could almost admire his beauty if not for the words that came out of his mouth. He ignored her polite question altogether, turning to her mother instead.

"I had always thought you Kavians had gotten it right with your women, unlike the Bellians." He eyed Scarzan derisively, who grunted and muttered his agreement in spite of the criticism against his people. The Peretian diplomat continued, chuckling as if what he was about to say was absurd. "I've heard your daughter often sits in on Jack's business dealings. That she goes so far as to whisper counsel in his ear. Verging on inappropriate for your customs, isn't it?"

What. A. Dick. She was surprised his ego could handle the

affront it must be to have to review his schedule with her mother right now.

But the gentleman with the perfect hair and deep complexion from the land across the great waters, Peretia, did no more than speak the opinion of the masses in Kava. And it seemed the women in Peretia did not fare much better if his comments were any indication.

Elysia blinked her eyes a little slower, letting out a throaty laugh.

"You're so kind to worry, Diplomat Batar." She gave a teasing smile. "But I promise you, my position is secure." *Barf.* Her mother was clearly made of steel because five minutes in and she wanted to smash their heads against the castle walls.

And yet, if her smile was that of a mouse, then her mother's was that of a barracuda.

She ran her fingers over Elysia's dark, loose waves. The gentle touch of a doting mother.

Georgia's voice flowed like cool water. "Elysia, the prince mentioned he was unavailable for cards this evening. I imagine you are the one who is stealing him away from our fine guests?"

She forced a blush, letting her eyes shoot to and away from the diplomats. "My apologies—I hadn't realized. His days are always so full. I can't bear to say no when he finds a little time. I *actually* was wondering if I could borrow some jewelry? We're going out this evening."

The twinkle in her eyes was real this time as she looked on imploringly—her mother's jewels were legendary. Sapphires. Diamonds. Golden cuffs. Silver rings. If it gleamed when the light hit it, then Georgia wanted it in her trove. Jack Parker was a merchant, after all.

Elysia could hear the men twitter, laughing at her wide eyes and innocent air. She was just a girl. A girl who wanted silly things like jewels. Her father must indulge her because there isn't a thought inside her pretty head.

Vapid faces hide brilliant minds. She should make that the

Parker women motto. Men like these were no bother. They saw what they wanted and acted accordingly. Frankly, that was the truth of most people. It was rare that anyone truly paid attention. And she thanked the undead gods for it. Made her job that much easier.

Georgia pulled a small key from within the folds of her dress and waved Hannah back over. "Please escort Elysia to my rooms." She pressed the key into Elysia's hand and gave her a knowing smile. "Enjoy your evening with the prince, darling."

Elysia turned to follow Hannah, but was stopped by the sound of Scarzan's voice.

"Ms. Parker, will you be joining us for our farewell party?"

She turned on her heel. "Of course, Diplomat Scarzan. My mother has worked very hard to create a lovely occasion for you all."

His returning smile made her insides slick with dread. "Then you will save me a dance. I've heard such interesting things about you."

Incredible how so few words and a single look could make her feel the need to bathe until her skin turned red and wilted.

She barely managed a polite nod before grabbing Hannah by the hand and forcing herself to walk at a measured pace to the door. It was impossible that Scarzan knew anything—there wasn't anything to know. She stopped herself from looking back over her shoulder, where she could still feel him staring. She had mentioned her plans to no one. And yet the sick feeling persisted. *I'm being ridiculous.*

The servant clicked the door shut, and Elysia gave herself one long exhale to allow the awful sensation to slide away. Truth or not, she could easily see how the rumors of Scarzan dumping his daughter to crime lords like trash had come about.

Honestly, she imagined it would be a waste of her time even bothering to confirm his disgusting actions. But she would. Because she was better than that.

Negligence bred negligence, after all.

"Are you alright, Ms. Parker?" Hannah looked on in concern.

She held out an arm to the girl. "Let's move along, shall we?" She tapped her ear, making her message clear.

Hannah's eyes grew, but she stepped closer to Elysia, taking her offered elbow. They walked in silence away from the politics behind them, and both women breathed a little easier with each step. She pressed her lips, thinking as they strolled. "Hannah, Diplomat Scarzan has many, many needs. So many important needs that all the ladies waiting on him would do well to work in pairs. Tell him it is due to his stature that he receives such care. Do you understand?"

Elysia continued to smile blandly as she spoke her words of caution, and she knew her meaning was received when the young maid's grip tightened on her arm. Oh, she knew alright. Elysia was sure they all did.

"I'll make sure my mother knows you are to work in pairs. It will not be a problem."

They stopped in front of the wide double doors leading to her parents' rooms. The wood was heavy and dark with smoothed etchings of ships, coins, and treasures splayed across a map of their land, a subtle indication of her father's role within the Crown. Elysia had always thought it rather brainless to declare who slept where in a castle, but maybe she had just spent too much time with an assassin.

Hannah opened the main room with her service key, and once the doors thudded shut, she finally spoke.

Her voice was lower than Elysia would have expected, low, but sweet. "Thank you, Ms. Parker. Working in pairs would make our jobs much easier while the diplomats are here." She shifted from foot to foot.

Elysia's smile faded, her brow wrinkling in knowing expectation. "He's already attacked someone, hasn't he?"

The girl looked up with a bit of fire in her eyes. "The maids have done a fair job of avoiding his *needs*, but I am not sure the same can be said for those who work elsewhere in the city. I... I heard things."

Elysia gave a slow nod, thinking through the gift she was just given. "Of course..." She sighed, shaking her head. It was too bad Gage didn't want to help with this one. She wouldn't mind his assistance one bit with someone as slippery as Scarzan.

She brought her attention back to the task at hand, glancing around her parents' suite. She had to get through dinner with the prince before she could worry about Scarzan.

"I should grab those jewels then."

Hannah recognized her dismissal and left quietly.

Guilt flooded in as the door shut behind the young girl. Elysia stared at the door blankly, lost in thoughts of how the maids stood no chance against Scarzan if he truly attacked any of them. If he ordered one to leave and kept another behind. How no one would believe them or care. Even when it was someone as obvious as Scarzan. He was not golden. He had no charm or false veneer. But he was powerful.

Maybe if he went after the wrong woman, there would be fallout—but the maids? Her stomach felt sick and anger writhed somewhere deep inside her. You didn't work within the Crown's court without realizing there were only two necessary ingredients if you wanted to get away with wrecking someone's life. The first was power, and the second was a fragile appendage swinging between your legs. That was it. If the man was sweet and easy on the eyes, then their path to destruction was even simpler, but it was far from a requirement.

Elysia turned back to face her parents' rooms and inhaled deeply. Tobacco smoke clung like a second skin to every inch of the room. The smooth warmth of her father's cologne layered over the smoke, leaving his fingerprint on every surface. Larger than life, he'd become the very air. The rich scent settled her bones, leaving a pang behind in its wake. Comfort, pain. He was both. And all these years later, she still didn't know what to do with that.

Some might expect the Golden Seal to have rooms filled with excess and decadence, but then they didn't really know Georgia Parker at all.

Soft grays nuzzled against deeper shades of charcoal. Cool, sea-glass-blue blankets draped over muted brown furniture. It had almost a foggy effect, reminiscent of a Relaclave morning by the docks. That was where her mother had met Jack Parker. It was where she had spent many a morning, waiting, watching—hoping he would be back from his travels. Now, he almost never left. Well into his fifties, he had young ambitious men to do that hard work for him.

Elysia snagged her father's pipe and sniffed it before setting it back down. She supposed she would have to see him as well this week. She wondered what he made of the possible proposal.

He was hard to pin sometimes, unlike her mother, with whom she always knew where she would stand. Her father swung between his heart and the politics that ruled them all. Sometimes she thought that it was almost worse. The not knowing if it was *her* that mattered, or just how she impacted the bottom line. It was a strange sensation, being equally convinced of someone's love and disgust for your presence. At least her mother was consistent.

She left the sitting room, drifting past her thoughts over to her mother's vanity. A carved chest made from driftwood stood tall, each thin drawer set with a tiny golden key hole. Elysia freed the drawer she needed with the key her mother had loaned her and stood on tiptoes to see inside.

Two small sapphire drops for her ears. A stack of silver bands for her wrist. Both gorgeous yet understated. They were perfect for dinner. And they were also not why she had come here.

Elysia squatted down, unlocking the bottom drawer of the chest. Sliding her knife out from her ankle, she used it to gently pry the drawer's false velvet bottom free. Her breath sped a little at the sight of the jeweled hairpin her mother had squirreled away from even her father's eyes.

Thin, burnished silver branches with edges so sharp they'd slit your skin. The branches intertwined, curving to rest on one side of the owner's head. A spray of dark rubies and milky opals dripped down the branches.

Elysia dropped the hairpin into a drawstring pouch, careful not to cut herself, and knotted it tightly. There were some doors in Kava that not even Elysia had dared sneak, buy, or trade her way into, and the House Gardenia was one of them.

The House Gardenia had a very particular guest list. Curious and frustrated that she had not received an invitation, Elysia had studied who came and went from the House for years. Followed people in. Followed them back home. She had found that the Doorman curated the guest list based on vice and value.

What was it you really wanted? And what were you willing to give up?

A guest's first evening—the night their invitation indicated they should arrive—tended to be a wicked, unforgettable thing. An evening personalized to your own shadowed tastes. Cost determined upon departure. That was the gamble of the House.

Some people couldn't stay away after that. Others never stepped foot in twice.

On any regular evening, every manner of delight or horror could be found within its walls. One need only whisper their longings to the Doorman and for the right price they would deliver. Secret loves, secret pains. They were the same, really.

The most important rule of the House was silence. Without it, there would be no House. People of every class and order visited the House, all with the expectation of a secret night that no one would ever be the wiser to. The person next to you might work beside the king, or just as easily be the woman who scrubbed his floors. Either way, to divulge identity or happenings was strictly forbidden.

This was the part that Elysia still did not understand. *No one ever told.* Something happened between entrance and exit that it was truly rare anyone ever broke this rule.

The ones who did? They were found with their eyes blank and bodies bloated by the sea. Dead and branded with the House's crest.

It was brutal. Enough to scare the soot off of you. But she didn't buy it. People weren't made for secrets. It went against their nature. Always wanting to drop a little gossip, chat over a morning brew. The average person was far too stupid and arrogant to keep their mouth shut even when faced with the threat of death. Especially if they had just seen their neighbor fuck a stranger in a bird mask.

Now, the Doorman of the House Gardenia was something of a legend.

For each hand selected guest, the House gifted a precious bauble. A token of entry, if you will. It was the Doorman's privilege and requirement to know the exact design, color, and shape of them all. Years of little treasures stored in finite memory.

People worried the House would fall if the Doorman ever did. Someone like that was bound to have enemies. It seemed a reckless, foolish system. But Elysia doubted this would happen.

For when did the House ever truly lose?

CHAPTER 10

NIGHT STRETCHED ITS FINGERS, slowly pushing back the day's burnt umber skies. Without pause, the ashes fell like rain, misting over the smoldering remains of the sun and disappearing into the swaths of night. At this hour, the world was a smog-ridden dream. In a strange way, it felt as though she could slip into its folds and disappear.

That was just wishful thinking, though. Elysia hadn't even seen Topp yet, and her heart was threatening to explode. She rubbed her neck, her throat tight and hot with anxiety. She'd been dodging him more and more over the last few months. Easy enough when he'd been gone, working in other parts of Kava. But lately, he'd been home.

She'd done her best to see him during the day. Tried to keep her midnight escapes to a minimum. She blamed the unavoidable departures from his bed on early mornings with her father. But he wasn't buying it anymore. His cunning green eyes had finally latched onto her bizarre behavior and he wanted answers. Elysia felt a chill run over her arms—she would just have to stay. Pick a day next week and stay. Stare at the ceiling all night and refuse to sleep. *How in the world do you plan to marry him?*

Fear gripped her chest. She was getting ahead of herself. All she had to do was get through tonight. She was an expert at hiding right in front of people, she reminded herself. The problem was, none of the people she hid from were *him*.

She swallowed and stepped in front of her mirror. Iron vines crawled and bloomed into the flowers that Kava could not have along the floor-length mirror's edge. She stood, twisting this way and that to see her work. Wide straps met a sweetheart neck, the dark green silk flowing down and pooling around her feet. And the woman in the reflection stared back, eyes dark enough to hide the turmoil within.

Elysia let the door of her building fall heavy behind her, tugging on the bronze handle until the stubborn wood finally wedged itself all the way closed. Pulling her black cloak a little tighter, she stuck her face into the swell of frosted air and set off. *Showtime.*

Topp had offered to send a carriage, but she'd declined. She wanted as many people to see her as possible tonight. Hood down and ears stinging with cold, she lingered as she walked, making sure to stop for quick hellos and dropping empty promises for drinks.

By the time she arrived at the Boar's Bones and slunk her way to the table, her nose and ears had been bitten a rosy pink. While the blush staining her cheeks originated from the ever present chill, the ruddy tinge high on Topp's wide cheekbones was undoubtedly thanks to the dwindling gin in his glass.

The Boar's Bones held the faintest reverberation of long lost magic. There was the magic that people once carried and then there was the magic that lived and breathed in all things. And in this instance, the culprit was both. Hanging from the ceiling were aged leather pouches filled with bones. Bones of the men, women, and children who had died when magic disappeared and Kava was almost overtaken. It was a Kavian tradition to keep a few bones of anyone who passed. Their people once believed that the spirit remained in the bones. Now, the bones hung as a reminder of all who died because of the fickle nature of magic. A visceral reminder not to trust magic or spirit in any form.

Elysia untied her cloak and handed it to the hostess, feeling the weight of Topp's gaze as it followed her every movement. His head tilted. Green eyes glimmering as they traveled from the crown of her head to the silk that dusted the floor.

His eyes roved freely, studying—always studying—even if it never was the right thing. Her body, her breath. Oh, he loved to study those. And who was she to stop him? Especially if it kept him from turning those shrewd eyes where she did not wish for them to stray. By now, he was just as aware as her of the power of the lust between them and had no scruples about using it to his advantage.

But *that* wasn't what made him dangerous.

What made him dangerous was that every single bright moment in her life had been a moment stolen with him. It was his loud ridiculous whispers that got them caught and her chaotic laughter as they broke every rule. It was squealing leaps from trees and forest chases that had grown from innocent to heart racing. It was his lips soft against her neck. And infinite locked, knowing gazes in rooms filled with people who were all pretending. It was the illusion that it would always just be them.

Standing here now, the sight of him made her ache—the fantasy of their love fading to nothing but a cold, hard crown.

Get your head in the game, Parker. She came here to find out what he knew. And that was exactly what she was going to do. She was on a schedule, for the gods' sake.

Elysia let her eyes go heavy and a touch of a smile played at her lips, fingers dragging over the gentle line of her throat. "Hi, Topp." His name was a barely there sound and yet his focus on her turned brilliant, as if she had spoken some truth he longed to hear.

And just like that, she was irrationally angry. So godsforsakenly angry. That he could *look at her that way* and still miss so much: the lost hours she couldn't explain, the lies that fell like a veil over what had once been vibrant between them, the irrecoverable distance between who he was and the magic that would get her killed. She needed him to not notice, and yet, it killed her that he didn't.

Topp lifted his chin, giving her a tempting sort of smirk. "You look good, Parker."

Much to her fury, he was an expert at evading her frustration. Always defusing her anger in just the nick of time before she blew. It didn't help that when he was in a good mood, he walked around with tricks playing in his gorgeous eyes. One look at them and a laugh wanted to bubble up like spring no matter how mad he made her.

If she was meticulous in her beauty, then he was unkempt perfection. Tousled and defiant, he always looked like he'd just been outside. She wanted to run her hands through his hair until it was mussed beyond all possible redemption. *That* was how she liked him.

He was magnetizing. An ax-wielding, forest-raised bear of a man with the brains of a fox who had been given a crown. And she was the fool who had fallen into his path, thinking she could outwit him.

He swiveled, his feet spreading wide and palms coming to rest on the smooth curves of her hips. His fingers pressed until she stumbled forward, her thighs now brushing his. He held her there, hands running up and down from thigh to hip as he stared into her wind-flushed face.

"You are such a curious thing," he murmured, his eyes a vivid green spark in the low light.

The warmth of his breath ghosted over her, and she inhaled instinctively, pulling in the scent of him. Violent flutters rose within her chest and she cursed herself. Silent and ensnared, her attention was fully diverted.

"Tell me, why did you subject yourself to a thirty-minute walk in this unbearable weather?" His fingers trailed over the goosebumps covering her skin. Her responding shiver had absolutely nothing to do with the cold, and the wicked shine in his eyes said he knew it.

She pulled back against the loop of his arms, answering honestly. "Can't stand being inside all day."

He laughed, a short sound that broke the building tension. It was a sentiment he knew all too well. Always trying to hide such untamed blood behind a prince's face.

"Ah, but you hate ruining pretty things even more." He lifted the skirt of her dress to reveal her soft, practical leather boots. The silk fell back down, hiding all evidence of the sensible shoes.

She scowled, swatting his hands away and settling into her own chair. The server wisely chose this moment to step out of the shadows. Setting down a steaming bumblebee next to her, he departed without a word.

Elysia toyed with the cinnamon stick garnish, swirling it until the lemon twist swam through the drink's amber waters. Taking the mug by its handle, she gingerly blew on its surface before taking a scalding sip. Eyes closed, a small sound of contentment slipped out of her. The spiced tea and gin was the perfect winter tonic, warming and loosening her frozen muscles.

She opened her eyes to see Topp's face soften, his own eyes drinking in the sight of her melting—the day's stress turning her languid instead of harsh. But then his eyes focused, narrowing the slightest bit as his mouth formed an unspoken question.

Her attention flared, seeing him lean back and kick his long legs out, crossing one ankle over another. She knew that face. It was the face of a man who was about to be a serious thorn in her side. *Tap, tap.* His fingers moved restlessly against his glass.

Oh, he was paying far too much attention this evening. She really had been hoping things wouldn't have to go this way. She loved the food here, and now she wouldn't get to eat it barely at all.

"You know," he drawled slowly, "I seem to have been remiss in my duties to you, sweet Elysia, and I want you to know that the Crown takes this matter very, very seriously."

She kept her face in her mug, hiding the stupid smile doing its best to take shape at his words.

"Is that so, Prince?"

He sat up straighter now, his elbows resting on his knees as he leaned forward. "The servants whisper that the reason the Crown Prince's woman looks so tired all the time is because the cold bastard never lets her stay. They say her heart beats anxiously with unrequited love."

There was something in the shape, the glint of his eyes that had never seemed quite natural to Elysia, like there was a part of him that belonged to the woods and the trees and the hidden wild things that had no right or wrong, and she saw it there now, gleaming in the shadowed light of the flickering oil lamps.

It frightened her almost as much as it called to her.

Months of sliding out of his bed like a wraith in the night, and now he pinned her here without ever asking a single question.

One finger continued tapping the edge of his glass as he waited. Waited for the lies to spill off her sugared tongue.

But he knew lies as well as she knew secrets, and Elysia knew better than most when to hold her cards.

His hand stilled, the only hint of his frustration in the subtle work of his jaw when she didn't respond to his subtle opening. "I knew I should have saved this conversation for after dinner."

"And why didn't you?" She kept her voice light, as if his insinuations meant nothing.

He held her eyes, his voice taking a heated edge. "Because I didn't think it would be fair to ask you with my head between your thighs."

He tossed back the rest of his glass, setting it down with a crack that made her jump. "If I was as cold or as ruthless as they say I am, then that's what I would have done. What a smarter man would have done, since it's the only time you seem to show yourself these days." A short laugh rolled through his chest as his grin took a sharp twist. "But look at me. Being generous. Playing fair and giving you a chance before I lick the truth from your pretty cunt."

Her eyes went wide and every last word choked in her throat.

Heat roared through her. Blood pounding and throbbing in inconvenient places. She should have known he would act out like this. Even on a good day, he loved torturing her in public. Seeing how flustered he could make her before he took her home and worked her over. His grin widened. He knew exactly what he was doing. And he clearly thought it would work.

Smug. Cocky. *Bastard.*

The waiter bravely cleared his throat and spoke dryly into the mounting tension. The tension Topp had so purposefully crafted. Elysia watched it all evaporate with four simple words.

"Your dinner, Your Highness."

The server looked down his thin nose at the prince. His lips pressed into a smirk as he waited to be dismissed. *Oh, he had definitely been listening.* Elysia really couldn't fault the man. Snooping *was* how she made a living, after all.

Topp stared as if he could light the man on fire with looks alone. Elysia raised a brow, watching him struggle to contain his blatant irritation. A feeling of airiness swooped through her as she bit back a grin. It was never fun having your plans foiled. But personally, she could have kissed the brash server for his interruption. His polished disregard for the crown prince was a delight that brought Elysia back into the room and out of the clutches of Topp's filthy words.

"Thank you." She gestured for the waitstaff to begin serving, shooting Topp a look that had him rolling his eyes and flopping back into his chair, his easy grin returning as quickly as it left.

She slowed now, basking in the ambiance of the candle-soaked room. Somewhere in a hidden corner, a woman poured herself into the keys of a piano. The rich timbre of her voice lamented that she was already one foot out the door while a man begged her to stay with the croon of his reply. Elysia sighed, sipping her drink and letting the music wash over her. There might not be a lot of restaurants to choose from within Relaclave—but the places that had survived the Fall sure did deliver.

She tore off a piece of bread, chewing and thinking carefully. Yes, she'd been worried. Worried that Topp might have noticed something was amiss. But the question was, what *exactly* had drawn Topp's eye back to her? She needed to know just how fucked she really was before making any drastic decisions. He'd been distracted, content to let her come and go as she pleased. Months without comment and yet he struck now.

Somewhere there was sand running through a glass, and like animals closing in, those nearest and dearest to her were letting her know they were on her trail.

Elysia rolled a few pinches of herbs between her fingers, releasing the aromatics before dropping them into her soup.

"It's funny," she began. "I've been sneaking in and out of your rooms since you first came back to Relaclave after all those years away. And you know, I don't think a servant ever once saw me."

She stirred her soup leisurely and took a small mouthful of soup, musing on her own words. "It's almost as if they were always sent away when I came over. Threatened, I would even dare to guess."

She rolled her eyes at the unabashed expression on Topp's face. Of course, he'd been threatening them within an inch of their lives all this time. Honor and propriety and all that nonsense. *So ridiculous.*

"Strange that they would now suddenly know my comings and goings, even though I have not seen a single face in these long months." She kept eating as if this were their normal talk.

"Servants, guards, people in the street. They all watch you, Elysia, they watch you because who would not?" He crooked a grin, but then became deadly serious. "And they also watch you because you are with me."

He raked a hand through his hair, the motion only serving to emphasize the thick muscle of his arm and make his hair even more unkempt than before. Elysia ripped her eyes back to his face.

He was honestly trying to kill her. With looks and muscles. It was downright foul play.

Frustration bracketed his mouth. "Forget the servants. *I* don't like you leaving in the middle of the night. *I* want to know why you've been slipping out like some one-night stand instead of the woman who's been by my side for years. I've been busy, Elysia, but I have never been close to a fool. I don't have to tell *you* that. You know exactly who I am. You know that I am many things, but blind and stupid are not on that list." He breathed the last words, leaning closer over the table.

She choked, her spoon hovering in midair. "Topp... I just—" She should have planned better for this. She should have come up with something to say. Anything to say—

The electric current that always seemed to spark like lightning on his skin, in his space, now viciously thrashed through his contained words.

"Didn't want to tell me that someone threatened your life?"

Her spoon dropped, clinking and splattering soup on the table. The thunder that was his energy rolled over her, lifting all the tiny hairs on her skin. She lived for when he was like this—a raw, inhuman storm of emotion. She dreamed of being in the eye of that storm. Getting to see him unleashed and true. Maybe it was because no one here ever was and she was desperate for even a taste.

Elysia caught herself—her stomach bottoming out as reality crashed back in. It was too easy to see things where they were not when the heart was involved. It was too easy for her to want to believe the broken little girl's dream that he would save her, protect her. That the man who had been her friend and lover would choose her in spite of her curse. She knew better than that. *He will be your death.*

She held still, her lips pressed. "Daphne. Daphne told you, didn't she?"

Damn Daphne and her giant pastel mouth.

He took several breaths with his eyes clenched closed. "The

problem, Elysia, is *not* that Daphne told me. The problem is that *you* didn't."

And then her gut rumbled on cue. A loud, painful cry from the pit of her stomach that made it clear what was to come. Sweat beaded on her brow and a fevered coloring blotched across her cheeks.

Call it a hunch. Woman's intuition. The secrets that sung to her ears.

Or maybe it had been because he said *they needed to talk*, but she had come to this dinner prepared to make her exit from Topp Blatz. And because people did not often survive lying to their Crown Prince, Elysia had thought to make it real.

Just a pinch of zorela in her soup was all it took.

The person she got it from just called it pukeweed.

She doubled over in her chair with a gasp, her insides writhing. *Gods, I hope I measured right.* She had plans for tonight and really couldn't afford to die. Oh, gods, she was going to puke all over at her favorite restaurant. Why couldn't they have gone somewhere she hated?

Topp moved in a blink and was crouched at her feet, running a hand over her face.

"You're burning. Are you going to be sick on me, Parker?" His voice, furious moments before, was now the voice that she knew few ever heard.

She nodded miserably.

He stood, sweeping her up onto her feet, and demanding her cloak. Top hat clutched in one hand and Elysia swaddled like a sweaty babe, he guided her, dazed and stumbling, outside.

Legs weak, and experiencing an altogether new kind of regret, Elysia held back a belch and swayed on her feet. *This. Was such a mistake.* She closed one eye, trying to steady herself and failing. Topp stopped in the alley of the Boar's Bones, still holding her close and looking down with such concern that guilt rose up alongside her bile. The winds blew around them, tussling their hair, and a look crossed Topp's face that she couldn't distinguish.

He buried his nose close to her as he held her and sighed, cursing more to himself than anything.

He didn't say a word, though, just held her hair and stroked her back as she retched and heaved until she was limp in his arms, her eyes barely staying open.

She wasn't sure how he knew she'd rather go to her flat than her rooms at the castle, but he got her home in a hurry, and rested beside her on the bed.

Her head pounded and her mouth was dry. He needed to leave, godsdamn it all, he needed to leave, or there was no point in her vomiting like she'd been exorcized of some putrid ailment.

"Topp."

"Hmm?"

"Go home, will you?" Her voice cracked, and she tried to roll away from him. She must have puked more than just in the alley and simply couldn't remember. It seemed like she could cross off healing and herbalism from the list of viable career options. There wasn't a chance in the realms she'd dosed the zorela right.

Topp tugged on the blanket, rolling her back into his side. "And why would I do that?"

"Let me die in peace, for the gods' sake," she muttered into her pillow.

He paused. "If you hadn't just lost your weight in fluids, I would properly let you know how I feel about you saying such things, sweet poison."

Her eyes darted toward him nervously. *Sweet poison?* That was new. And a little too on the mark.

She'd willingly barfed her brains out in front of the crown prince. If the undead gods had an ounce of mercy in their bones, then he did not know what she had done.

But he stood from the bed, filling up the room with the crackling energy that was him, and made her flat suddenly seem a hair too small for them both, only to do something totally normal— he grabbed a cup and set about making her tea.

He opened her tea tin only to find it empty and sighed. "Seriously, Lys? You steal it from the castle, anyway."

"Apologies, I'll be sure to amp up my thieving as soon as I'm right again." She shifted to sit up a little taller amongst the pile of pillows.

Elysia rested her eyes. "Thank you for getting me home." She opened her eyes to find him looking at her intently, but she couldn't quite hold his gaze. Not tonight.

He sat down beside her, the bed dipping with his weight, and brought his lips to her head, speaking against her hair. "You owe me a date. And about six months' worth of sleepovers. I don't care if I snore, or you have to work at the crack of dawn. I hate waking up and worrying about you."

He kissed her hair and then he was gone. The door shut. And with its closure, all of their unasked questions slid back down to the unlit place between them—the place where all of their secrets lie with tangled limbs and eyes shut tight—never knowing the other.

CHAPTER 11

Elysia gave herself two whole minutes after Topp left to pull herself together, and then she dragged her sorry self to the washstand where she scrubbed her teeth and body as if she could wash the feeling of sick down the drain. Toweled off, she worked scented oils into her skin, wishing to bring some life back into her worn out body.

Pukeweed.

Understatement of the century.

Her guts still twisted unpleasantly and her bones felt thin, but she had this night and this night only to seduce secrets from the House of Gardenia, and she had no intention of letting it go to waste. It wasn't just that she had promised Beatriz to look into Scarzan. It was that she could still feel the scum he had left behind on her skin. The way his eyes had trailed over her like a slug—as if he was weighing the cost of her, considering if she was worth the risk. The knowledge that he was harassing the women at the castle and out within Relaclave as well.

It felt personal now.

She hoped that whatever Beatriz needed this tip for, it would cut the man down like a blade of grass.

Over the years, Elysia had repeatedly made her peace only to lose it again when it came to what Gage did for a living. There were nights like the one where he eliminated the threat against her and what he did made sense in a brutal, practical kind of way. Then there were other days she couldn't reconcile the man who had helped raise her with the one she knew went out and did terrible, violent things. She'd never asked how Gage decided which marks to take. But it was hard to imagine a world in which anyone was better off with someone like Scarzan still in it.

Elysia lurched out of the bathroom, still wobbly on her feet, and heaved herself into the chair in front of her vanity. Tying her robe a little tighter, she glanced at the old timepiece resting to her right and winced. She had far less time than she had been hoping for, but that simply meant she had no time to waste.

She pulled her hair back and got to work.

In spite of the explicit code of silence the House Gardenia demanded, many patrons opted for masks or a face covering to blur their features. Of course, there were just as many who wore their faces proudly into the den. They wanted the whispers of those who lurked outside the entrance. Wanted the rumors to carry out past the night.

Elysia would be donning a mask. It was the only way she would be getting in, after all. Scooping out a small blob of skin tint, she adjusted the shade until it was pale with a touch of pink, unlike her own cool neutral tones. She warmed the cream between her fingers, smoothing it over her face and down her neck.

So much of the Crown's politics came down to the personal whims of people like Elysia's mother. It was a flawed system propped up on a rotten foundation that had been painted fresh. But sometimes, someone like her mother actually did something good, even if it was just a selfish whim.

Georgia Parker *loved* the arts. Theater, dance, music. Beneath her rigid exterior, she wanted to be swept away. So every year she laughed and smiled and plied Remy's daddy with drinks and favors until he ended up giving more to the arts budget than was remotely reasonable.

During show season as a child, Elysia would crawl from her seat until she found all the dancers hustling and laughing in the back. They pinched and pinned and painted themselves until they shone like evening stars, and Elysia, delicate child that she was, fell in love.

And with her red sash and dark curls, they never dared escort her out. So, she sat quietly, watching as they set themselves up in front of the lights, enamored with how they carved new bones and noses on their faces with nothing more than pots and paints. A soft, plain woman could transform into one with edges and hollows and lips that could swallow a man whole. A sharp, stunning creature could become sweet and barely noticeable. With the right clothes and the right paint—you could be anyone.

Elysia thought it was magic. And she was right. It was a magic that anyone could claim, and not even the Crown could take it away.

With fingers that cradled plants and delivered daggers, Elysia fashioned herself into someone new. Someone with vigilant eyes and a strong, classic face. She pulled shadows out of powder and cut her jaw until it was wider than hers had ever been.

Elysia did not consider her eyes to be unique or beyond the ordinary. Alluring perhaps, with their velvety darkness, but nothing that would stand out in a crowd. And yet she would know her father's or her sister's eyes anywhere simply because they were theirs. Which meant hers had to change. Holding a small brown vial up to the light, she grimaced. *It couldn't be any worse than the pukeweed, right?* Head back and eyes wide, two small drops hit her eyes.

Fuck.

Her fist slammed down on the vanity, shaking all the little vials and pots. The burn in her eyes had her cursing and sweating in an instant. Gritting down, she counted. *One. Two. Three. Four... Five.* Blinking, she used a small cloth under each eye to catch any escaping liquid that would dare disturb her face. She kept blinking until the urge to rub her eyes finally quit, and then she looked up to see a disturbingly familiar face with light sea-blue eyes staring back at her.

The final step to her creation had been stolen from the arts closet. A long summery blonde wig, brushed to perfection. She secured it as tightly as possible, testing it before deeming her face and hair a success.

No longer herself, Elysia knew it made no sense to dress in her normal habits of deceptive velvets and ribbons and wide-eyed confusion. Tonight's attire was an all too recognizable look. A black dress flaring into a full satin skirt paired with staggering heels. She threw on a red scarf, tying it around her wrist, and shook her head at her reflection. *Terrifying.* Elysia let out a disbelieving laugh and grabbed her already packed oversized purse. Dagger in her boot, she was as ready as she would ever be for an evening in the House.

The House was built on the undeniable truth that no matter how society disparages the spirit of pleasure—it cannot die. They can spit upon it. Place false shame on its name. But the spirit of pleasure in both its enticing and distasteful forms will never die. It will only grow stronger. Coming up through the cracks, taking solace in hidden rooms. Rearing up in even more twisted and delightful and curious ways.

Elysia stared at the old House and wondered how it had all begun. She was procrastinating, a bit nervous now that the House was in sight. She could hear the ruckus from here. The music, the shouts, the laughter. She'd never heard the House's origin story. To her, it felt like the House had always been here. That the stories were as old as Relaclave itself.

Before the Fall, the House had been hidden from sight. Thick foliage and tall, dark hedges protected it from prying eyes. Now, there was no ivy curtain and the hedges were long dead. Naked and laid bare for all to see, the House became emboldened. She was a strange pillar in their city, flaunting her secrets and what felt like magic, but couldn't be.

Elysia stopped her musing, her thoughts cut short by a new sound. A sweet piper played an entrancing tune. No words fell from his lips, but still, the song played. Bidding the people of Relaclave to come one, come all to the House where they would surely care for you.

Her feet were moving before she could even form a thought.

Prowling silently up the skinny cobblestone path, she followed the tune to the poisonous, envy-green front door. A sudden wind came, blowing her satin skirt out. Elysia hastily smoothed the fabric down before she unwillingly flashed any poor, unsuspecting bystanders. As she straightened, the door creaked and her night began.

Elysia's pulse hammered. This was *not* what she had been expecting.

The Doorman stood with her hand resting gently on the door handle, bleached white hair rolling in smooth waves down her back. Orbs of the darkest night stared widely at Elysia, set against a backdrop of shimmering gold-brown skin and rosy, cherubic cheeks. She was magnificent. A frothy, lush dream of a woman. Curves poured into a dapper cream silk suit like champagne, bubbling up and out of the vest beneath.

The door creaked open a little wider, and curiosity had Elysia straining to see who would appear next. Long feminine arms snaked out, wrapping lazily around the Doorman's waist. Fingers splayed across her soft stomach, inching up toward her breasts. The newcomer stepped into the light, draping herself over the Doorman. Nuzzling her face down into the crook of her neck, smearing lipstick as she went.

Elysia froze. *This wasn't possible.*

Only years of practice allowed her to keep her eyes from becoming saucers.

Because those arms. Those hands. *That hair.*

Her chest moved in small, rapid breaths. Her brain refused to comprehend the disaster in front of her.

She kept waiting for the sight to disappear like it was some hallucination of the House. It didn't.

That was her sister fondling a legend in the doorway.

With bloodshot, smoked-out eyes and silver hair, Beatriz Parker dragged her lips possessively up the Doorman's neck. Elysia forced her face to remain impassive, imperious even. *The gods must truly hate me.*

Beatriz looked out through the clouds of her eyes. "Show your token or get out." She stuck her face back into the crevice of the Doorman's neck, murmuring something that no doubt would have made Elysia blush to the higher realms. But then her head shot back up, her brows jamming together like they just might stick.

"Mother?" Disbelief broke through the drugs.

The Doorman let her head loll to the side, her large curved eyes unblinking and showing only the faintest sign of amusement. Her small hand brushed up against Beatriz's face. "The apple doesn't fall far from the tree, does it?"

Beatriz appeared to be broken, mouth agape and red eyes staring.

Elysia had been training her whole life for this moment. Chin level and voice curt, she stared at her sister like she was both unsurprised and unimpressed.

She took a step that had Beatriz straightening like a child. "You're slouching. Skip one more meeting and I'll have you escorted into the castle from whatever infested hole they find you in." Then she whipped a handkerchief out of her skirt pocket and began rubbing it vigorously against the smudge of wine-dark lipstick bruising the Doorman's neck. She tucked the handkerchief away and nodded. "There. You're welcome." *She's lucky I didn't lick it.*

The Doorman reared back, clearly unused to Georgia Parker's *polishing*. Elysia watched her hazy facade flicker, a vicious light stealing through her dark eyes. But then her face became a dream once again. Her hand dropped away from her neck and reached out expectantly. "Your token, Mrs. Parker?"

Elysia uncurled her fingers, revealing the burnished silver hair pin in the palm of her hand.

The Doorman's eyes narrowed briefly, but then she shrugged and stepped aside. "The House Gardenia welcomes you."

Elysia nodded, sweeping past the myth that was the Doorman and ignoring Beatriz as if she were nothing. Five steps in and she almost stumbled. The part of her that could feel the very pulse of a secret, yanked on her like there was a leash between her and the Doorman. An invisible tether drew her eyes and feet back to where she had just come from. She refused to turn her head. Gliding onward, she ignored the burn within her that demanded to be fed. Farther and farther she moved from the Doorman and her sister's heavily lidded stare. They were the last two people she should be near in this House.

But gods, she wanted to *know*. Her eyes darted back. *No, I can't, I can't.* The feeling was enthralling. The desire to know, to seek, to find.

The magic addled her thoughts, coaxing her to do what was natural. To find out how this soft, beguiling creature had become the Doorman. The Doorman who knew every token ever given. The Doorman who, it was said, could break men like twigs between her hands.

People whispered that she was beholden to another. That she was chained to some power beyond her, doing the bidding of a hidden master. Whoever the Doorman worked for—their power rippled through this House in spades. The threads that had called to Elysia since birth beckoned her closer, begging her to dive head-first into the dark pool of secrets surrounding the Doorman's dainty feet.

Elysia rolled her shoulders, breaking the spell. That wasn't what she came here for. The House and its mysteries needed to wait. *You need to focus.* This evening was going to be a far greater challenge than she had imagined. The wisp of a secret tickled her nose as a woman grazed past and she almost groaned.

This place was a death trap.

Eyes searching, she slipped into a dark jungle of fake trees and plants. Kavians loved using them as decoration. And it *was* stunning. The textured layers of leaves and branches created a mysterious thicket you could barely see through. The walls dripped a deep sanguine color, and warm mood lighting kept all the lies hidden.

It was stunning, but it set her teeth on edge. One room into the House and something about this place was already irking her. She thought she would love it here, but she was finding the illusion tasted sour in her mouth.

Running her fingers over a bunch of leaves, they came away with a sticky coating of dust and soot from poorly trimmed lamps. She could barely take a step without a fake leaf hitting her in the face. If the plants were *real*, then this room would be a masterpiece. A living piece of art that breathed and smelled so good that one's lungs grew bigger. Instead, its falsity felt like a warning. A rolling wave of dread and unease passed through her.

Secrets were true. *So why did everything in here feel like a lie?*

There was a muscular, dark-haired man who wore a suit that had been tailored to perfection. Small gold hoops lined one ear, marking him as staff. He leaned over a woman, whispering hateful things down into her mouth. Soon she dropped to her knees, apologizing over and over, for what Elysia didn't know. Her body went limp, sagging over his feet, gripping his trousers with desperate hands. Elysia shook her head at the sight. Humiliation was one drug she couldn't understand. *To each their own.*

She imagined that if she ever got a true invite to the House that there would be a room with a line of people who one by one poured out their confessions while she devoured what they gave. She wondered if there was a limit to what she could consume. Ugly, beautiful. She didn't care. She'd never been in a position to *indulge*. But here? The temptation grew stronger by the minute.

She exited the jungle and entered a sitting room where the gentlefolk of the House carried silver platters and fluted drinks. Sweet smells of honey and pastries chased away the forbidden air of the last room, enveloping her now in a sugared fog. Trays floated past with powders and vials and leaves meant for smoking. In the center of the room was a massive divan, ridiculous in its size. And sprawled out on the enormous bed-sized cushion was a cluster of women. Feeding each other, gazing deep into the other's eyes, giggling and touching. It was a candy heaven made flesh.

She felt herself drifting, her feet following the rhythm and pull she'd held closer than anything all these years. The sound of secrets never left her, and she doubted it ever would. The beat became a steady rousing thing that vibrated in her chest and brought a rush of color to her cheeks. Elysia was quickly realizing how easy it would be to simply wander room to room, acting as a voyeur upon other people's fantasies. Judging and enjoying. But between the dwindling effects of the pukeweed and the constant coursing murmur of secrets racing through the smoke-laden air, she found her stamina lacking. Her body wanted to bend. Her mind wanted to mellow. She wished to sink like a pebble to the bottom of the ocean and watch the secrets go past. There was a reason she'd never stepped through these doors before.

Following the siren call of just one secret was enough to dim her logic and send her tumbling through basement windows and dark lit alleys. A building built and thriving on the blood and bones of secrets? It was a slaughtering to her senses that she was in no way prepared to fend off.

She was close to whatever it was. So close.

She became a ghost sailing through the trees, up the heavy dark wood stairs, fingertips trailing the banister as she floated higher and higher.

The song did not have a crescendo. It became quiet and still. For the crescendo was the secret itself, and Elysia knew it lived down the hall and two doors to the right. The heart of the song beat inside that room. Waiting impatiently. Just for her.

She ignored the sound. *Don't worry, I'm coming for you.* And slipped into a bathroom down the hall, dropping her large purse to the floor. Her dress went up in the air, tossed over head. Oil poured out over her skin. A soft wash cloth was brought to her face, scrubbing away any last sign of Georgia Parker. Fresh faced, she switched her wig and clothes. Auburn hair, her mother's eyes, and a corseted curve-inducing dress she'd stolen from Remy. *As long as I don't look like me.*

Dressed as a stranger, she walked down the hall with a soft sway in her hips. She rested with her back against the wall, listening to the voices rumble and spill out into the hallway. She was unsurprised to detect the weaselly tones of Scarzan. He was her target after all, yet she still hesitated outside the door, apprehension sinking low into her stomach.

Her head fell back as she tried to muddle through logic, instinct, and the magic that ignored both. She'd made it this far, she reasoned. She'd gotten past the Doorman. Past her *sister*. Her own godsdamn sister hadn't even blinked at her appearance. This was no different from any other night she flitted from room to room, gathering secrets out of the dust in the air.

The brick in her stomach argued otherwise, but it was too late.

She was here. Scarzan was just steps away. And she had promised Beatriz.

Now or never. She reached for the door.

CHAPTER 12

THE DOOR SWUNG OPEN SMOOTHLY, releasing the sounds of scattering dice and slapping cards. Booming alcohol fueled voices shoved over the top of each other to be heard. She came in quietly, observant of the chaos billowing around her. There were men entwined in a corner, lost to the world around them. Players held in the grip of a games table, sweating with fear and money. And music drowning any inclination to escape before it was too late.

All the occupants were so entrenched in their games that nary a single eye turned in her direction. Her feet didn't make a sound on the thick carpet as she tiptoed past, girding herself for what was to come. Because he was here. And not even the magic in her chest could mute the growing feeling of foreboding zinging through her blood.

Scarzan sat at the center chair of the main table, his pointed face splotched and red with drink. Her nose wrinkled, watching his eyes twitch with each play of the game. His forehead looked moist, and even though she couldn't possibly smell him from here, she just knew the man smelled like stale sweat and onions trapped beneath his ugly suit. *Gross.* Between the drunk and high bodies and the size of the room, Elysia felt a wave of claustrophobia. Too many mindless people crammed into one space. It made her skin itch.

She was safe where she was—out of sight and with a good view. She couldn't *hear*, though. She edged closer, leaving the safety of the shadows where no one had noticed her.

Her earlier fear whispered that something was ever so very wrong, but Scarzan's secrets shushed the sound and filled her ears with promises of a payout worth her while.

She found herself folding into a chair two seats away from the rat. Her heart pounded. *What am I doing?* She forced herself to relax, crossing one long leg over the other. *Getting what I came here for, that's what.* There was no reason to panic. This was her job, for the undead gods' sake. Scarzan had just managed to crawl under her skin and make her doubt grow loud. But there was nothing to fear.

The dealer motioned for her to be brought a drink. "This round's full, miss. You'll have to wait."

Elysia nodded and curled her fingers around the damp glass, giving it a sniff. *Gin and juice.* She didn't want to play, anyway. The man to Scarzan's right turned to her with a laugh. "Are you sure you want to play at this table, miss? There's lots of other rooms in the House."

Elysia looked up with interest at the stranger next to her, smiling knowingly. "And why would I not? Do you think the stakes are too high for a girl like me?"

He let out a booming laugh that matched the slight crook in his nose and sat back in his chair. Crossing his arms over a broad chest, he leaned in close to her ear. "Our friend in the middle here is never happy with an ordinary game."

Elysia slid her drink around in a circle and considered his words. The dark honey colored liquid funneled into a mimicry of destruction. She dropped her voice. "You mean to say money is not the prize?"

The man slammed down his empty beer mug and laid three cards along with a tiny gem.

"No, love, not tonight."

She frowned. "Then what are we playing for?"

The secrets danced in a whirl around her head now, and she felt a single bead of sweat form on her brow. She hadn't trained enough for a place like this with secrets new and old forming and escaping with every breath and movement in the House.

By the gods, Beatriz was going to owe her.

Scarzan's ears turned up at their conversation. He appeared ready to bark until he registered what was resting two chairs away from him like a young, untouched daydream. Liquor-shot eyes groped downward, lingering where jewels glinted against skin.

He didn't even bother ripping his eyes away as he directed the dealer.

"New game. Deal the girl in. No one sits at this table without playing."

He looked her in the eyes with a certain smug satisfaction on his face. "The price is yourself unless there's someone else you'd care to bid. Winner chooses their prize from the losing participants."

Unsmiling, he held her stare several seconds longer than was comfortable. She would've expected the disgusting sludge of his insides to reflect in his eyes, but instead she found them to be flat and void beneath the red spider veins of alcohol. The man was an empty, hateful vortex, walking around, pulling in anyone and everyone he could into his depraved existence. Everyone knew too. And yet he remained a diplomat for his people. Practically untouchable.

But betting people? That was insanity. Kava had never allowed such practices. Servants were paid. Maybe not fairly, but they were paid and owned by no one. Yet here in this musty room they were betting people like they were gods and everyone else was an old watch to pawn for one more round.

All for a game that literally was nothing more than a means to pass the time.

Her fingers gripped the edge of her chair as she thought about bolting. Forget Beatriz. Forget whatever bullshit she thought she needed dirt on this man for—she hadn't agreed to sell herself off for a tip.

But the truth is right there... Can't you see it?

A heady rush of insatiable curiosity filled her. All she needed was for him to admit it.

She studied the players to her left. Three men. One woman. All willing to throw away someone else or themselves. When push came to shove, she was willing to bet they would sub someone in on their behalf if they lost. Her face remained serene, even as anger became a tense, unbearable force within her chest.

Her fingers trickled up her chin until she rested her face in her palm.

"Ever lost someone you wanted to keep?"

Scarzan's face flushed at her pointed question. She hadn't said, *did you gamble away your only daughter?* But she'd come as close as she could. Nerves jumped inside her as she waited for him to respond.

He started to sneer, but her neighbor with the booming voice cut in, elbowing her as he answered. "Thought I'd seen it all in the rooms at this House. But finding out about a politician swapping their kid's life out for their own? Seems the games in Bellia are even better than here. Wouldn't want to be that kid, though." He shook his head and made a tutting sound.

She blinked. He'd somehow lost his own life to the crime lords, but turned over his daughter instead. Her stomach felt sick, her mind's eye conjuring horrible images of a scared girl being thrown to the wolves.

The cool cut of Scarzan's voice raised the hairs on Elysia's arms, but she just smiled and played with her hair as he talked. "I've never once made a bet I wasn't prepared to lose. That was the best deal I ever made, getting rid of that impossible wildcat of a girl."

Hot rage as sharp as the dagger hidden beneath her clothes threatened to wipe the benign, vacant expression from her face.

The logic that had taken flight the moment she stepped through the House's front door screamed at her to make her exit. To blush and stammer, murmuring of her mistake. She'd gotten exactly what she'd come here for—she had everything she needed for both Beatriz *and* herself. The woman who had been collecting secrets for years knew this was the moment to exit.

It would have been perfect.

But the diviner within her begged her to stay, to let this man unwind more of his secrets at her table. The magic whispered to her that his secrets were worth the price. The music played on, wrapping around her, asking her not to go so soon.

If he had bet his daughter—had claimed this deed aloud to everyone without a shred of shame—then what else had a man like Scarzan done?

The question kept her planted in her seat.

The other folks at the half-moon game table waited to see what the girl would say to the monster in the suit. They couldn't decide if she was just plain stupid or if there was something more beyond her pretty face. She paid them no mind, barely sparing a glance their way. She was here for his secrets, not for their questions or stares.

That fading voice of reason reminded her she was rubbish at cards. It argued that this was a terrible plan. But she didn't really need to win. She just needed *one more* secret, and *then* she'd slip away before the time ran out. Just the one. Then she'd go.

She slung an arm back and tossed out a jovial grin. "Let's play."

The dealer hid a cringe, but nonetheless, he began shuffling the cards, resetting the trays of gems.

The game was rocks.

The story went that the game had first been made by a small boy out on the streets of Kava. A boy with quick hands and sharper eyes who could play cards like some sang to the moon. In the brilliance of his youth, he crafted a game like no other, and he called it rocks.

The game spread from the streets to kitchens. Past gated walls to underground tunnels where maids and guards alike played long after dark. And then one day the game found itself within the heart of the castle. The castle had swept up the game in its hand and thrown it back out in a tournament with a new name. They called it gems.

They were not dirty street children, but men with dignity and class. Therefore, the game would be gems. And yet, it was an open tournament, and one particular street boy with charm down to his toes swindled his way into their ranks.

He stole game after game until he took the whole damn thing. And when they swore in the young man with his ripped knees and broken-in cap as Kava's newest treasurer—well, he told them it had always been rocks and it would always be rocks.

Remy's daddy had changed since then. His cool dark skin gleamed under castle torchlights and he dressed finer than the king himself. He'd grown sharper and colder so that he did not wither in the heat of the castle's intrigues, but rumor had it that the King's treasurer still liked to find a game out on the streets now and then when the mood struck him right.

Elysia now found herself wishing she'd paid even a lick of attention to the man who'd invented rocks as he'd prattled on and on at Remy Wincraft's home about how to play Kava's favorite pastime. Because with a handful of cards and a full line of gems, she could only pray to those who did not listen for luck to be on her side.

The gentleman at the far end of the table kept his head ducked down and threw in a card without a gem. A safe opening to set the cards in motion. Elysia scanned her own hand, her heart dipping at what she saw. This was it, the truth was in, and the undead gods really, truly did hate her. She had never seen such a terrible hand.

The ox of a man next to her knocked her elbow. "Your turn, little lady."

Ew. She smiled and followed the first player's lead. Two cards. No win, no loss, no gems.

Elysia started observing the players rather than her pathetic cards. The furthest man remained hunched, hiding both his hand and his face. A woman with a pinched expression and brows permanently bunched had her knee bouncing beneath the table as if her body fought the urge to run away.

And then there was Scarzan.

His former smugness had been wiped clean, leaving his face unnervingly blank. The corner of his lips kicked up as he played a few cards, and he lifted his eyes to hers, daring her to notice the groundwork he was laying.

Elysia clamped down on the instinct to flinch or let any kind of fight rise up in her eyes, and instead lazily re-directed her attention to the cards he had played. *Why is he looking at me like that?*

Understanding settled like a weight around her neck. *Shit.*

Rocks was a complicated game. It wasn't solely your own cards that mattered, but how the cards all played together and against each other. Scarzan's cards took her lifeless throwaways and turned them into a play that scored him a gross amount of points. He was using her poor hand to taunt her.

The dread Elysia felt earlier returned as a terrible knowing. He was not playing simply to win the game, but rather to win her. Any magic induced delusion of gaining another secret from this man had gone silent. Her eyes shot between her cards to the other players, trying her damndest to dig herself out of this hole. But Scarzan pulled further and further away in the lead, leaving it impossible for someone else to win.

And so the rounds went, with Elysia making feeble attempts to play herself out and Scarzan boosting her cards to keep her alive. He was toying with her. He could just let her play out and still choose her as the prize as was the winner's right to choose from the lot, but the game had become a hunt, and like any prey she began to think that if she could not fight, then she should run.

Elysia slid her eyes to the door and wondered how much the House was *really* going to care if she dared to break their sacred rules and escape from Scarzan's clutches. It would be terrible to get away only to end up dead on the beach. Would there be men and women with hoops down their ears chasing her into the streets? She wished she had bothered to find out if the House's servants were the pretty type of decoration for wandering eyes or the kind that hid knives and tricks in their sleeves. *Both, of course,* she answered her own question with an internal sigh. *Gods, I'm an idiot.*

She had never dared explain what was really happening when she lost herself in the thrall to Gage—that it was magic and not some unquenchable thirst for the poison of this city. He'd told her over and over again that she needed a lifeline, an anchor if she couldn't keep her head while out on jobs. She always blamed it on the sweet surge of excitement and curiosity that made her head swirl and feet feel light. Pointed out that plenty of men lost their heads from something similar in fights and such.

But right about now, she was wishing she had taken his advice to heart.

She'd never thought it was that serious.

Except now it was, and with each hand played, she realized she would not be unearthing any more life-ruining secrets or happening upon the perfect blackmail before the game's end. A cloud of shame darkened within her chest. *How could I be this stupid?* Her magic had gotten the better of her, and it was no one's fault but her own for thinking herself invulnerable. The shame burned, turning her thoughts to the shoulds and woulds of it all. *I shouldn't have pissed Gage off. He would have helped.*

Sure, she'd barely smuggled herself out of stuffy apartments that she didn't quite remember slipping into and donned aprons to slide out of kitchen doors of homes she'd rather forget, but in truth there had always been a part of herself that loved it. A part that laughed with its head thrown back and hands stuck to her hips with the invincibility of someone who had never been caught. It was the part of her that did not have to be Elysia Parker, daughter of the Crown, but was instead allowed to be something so very, very different.

She hadn't blinked when Augustus Freer chuckled as he ordered the death of his first wife. Just like she hadn't blinked when her father let it happen because no one would have cared about a murder that was *stopped*. No, he needed something irrefutable. Like the bloody corpse of Freer's wife to hold over the man's head for the next twenty years.

She had not quaked when she hid a breath away in a wine cask from the bloodletters as they did their work.

She had not cried when her father repeatedly threatened to turn her into a bloodhound for the cursed folks of their land whenever she dared balk at his demands.

She had watched the life fade out of the men who had threatened her with an almost detached, clinical type of understanding. They had harmed women in unspeakable ways, they had wanted to harm her, and now the undead gods delivered them a mercy in killing them before they could further besmirch their souls.

It was important for her to remember that she was not a good person. Sometimes she almost forgot, but then there were nights like these to remind her of what she had known since she was child who could not stop her feet from finding others just like her. Those people were dead now. But she wasn't.

The Crown was a jagged thing, dripping in blood that was not its own, but that was how it survived—it took that blood and made itself stronger. This was its lesson to all its children.

Her magic had bested her. But she would not be anyone's prize this evening nor any other.

A man like Scarzan wouldn't take losing lightly. He would take it out on more than one woman in this House. And she knew that. Somewhere deep in her gut, she knew he would lash out, violating the women of this House for her escape. But it didn't change what she was going to do.

It couldn't.

She sat loosely in her chair, with an almost girlish naivete in the soft lines of her face and the wide set of her eyes. Yet if anyone bothered to pay even the smallest amount of attention, they would realize her languid posture, her countenance—none of it matched her wine-drenched hair or the daggers she couldn't quite kill from her eyes.

Behind her false serenity, Elysia realized she had never in all her schemes truly felt afraid until now. Not like this.

Her fear told her several things.

First was that it was pertinent for her to remember the violence beneath Scarzan's sallow skin.

Second was that the crescendo of this evening's song had not been the secret that so easily jumped from his arrogant lips. It was the now unescapable knowledge that she wanted to kill this man. Perhaps she simply had a sore spot for shitty fathers who peddled out their daughters for their own ends, but more than that, it was how when she looked into his eyes she saw everything that was wrong with her world. Beyond her disgust and vicious desires, she had the strange premonition that he was going to become a nuisance if he wasn't handled properly.

And third, it was really, *really* time for her to be going.

Elysia began to squirm in her chair, wiggling and clenching her thighs. She waved a server to her side with embarrassment flooding her cheeks and whispered, "Is there a bathroom on this floor?"

"Down the hall and to your right, miss."

Scarzan's eyes darted over as she stood to exit. He barked with the hardened assurance of someone who was rarely denied. "No one leaves the table until the game is done. No one." His eyes narrowed on her.

Elysia paused with her legs bouncing uncomfortably. "Sir, I really don't think this can wait..." She trailed off, as if flustered at his indecent behavior.

The man to her left seemed wholly unaffected by Scarzan's intensity. He waved a hand, brushing the diplomat's spittle and anger aside. "By the river, let the girl go to the bathroom. Do ya want her to piss all over the carpet? She won't be leaving the House unpaid—no one ever does."

The servers remained still, none wishing to defy Scarzan.

His fingers clenched. "Five minutes."

Elysia kept her shoulders from heaving in relief, nodding obediently as she scurried from the room. Five minutes. Five minutes to save her own neck and get as far from the House as possible. She willed her legs to behave normally until the door shushed over the carpet back to closed, and then she lunged like a madman down the hall, fingers scraping at the first door handle she came upon.

Shoving the door open, she stumbled into a sprawling leisure room and prayed her luck had returned. *Not that I ever had any.* She started with the window, straining and pulling to no avail. Of course, it was sealed. *Godsdammit.*

"No one in or out," she muttered to herself. She spun around.

She had maybe three minutes now.

The seconds dwindled.

Elysia took a long, ragged breath. She was better than this. She had trained for this. Not the magic. But for escape? Yes. There was not a building in Relaclave she could not hide in or escape from. An escape was nothing more than a secret.

She would get this room to tell her its secrets.

She closed her eyes and listened to the soft current of the old, smoky air.

There.

Like a catch in the fabric of the ether that made the room, she took hold of the thread and followed it in her mind's eye until she stubbed her toe. Her eyes opened. *What in the gods' names?*

She stood between two windows. The wall between them was plain and without any marks. The thread held taut, drawing her fingers to the window frame's edge.

Feet clattered down the hall.

Her fingers pressed to the wood.

A banging on the door began.

The wall popped with a hiss and slid back behind the other window, and in the space between stood the Doorman with a satisfied catlike grin and cunning eyes holding an oil lamp to break up the darkness.

Elysia startled and did the first thing that came to mind.

She swung. And gods, did she swing hard.

The woman's eyes widened right as Elysia's fist smashed her face.

The Doorman fell back like a statue and slid down the wall until she did not move.

Her heart thundered and bloodied crescents appeared on her palm where her nails had dug in. Elysia shook out her hand, cursing internally. *Fuck, that really hurt.* She stared down at the Doorman, taking in the woman's jet-black roots creeping into her bleached blonde hair, the dark lashes dusting her high cheeks.

She'd knocked out a myth, and she'd be damned if she didn't live to tell the tale.

Elysia stepped over the Doorman muttering an apology and yanked the hidden panel shut right as she heard the lock break and the door slam open. She shuddered, thinking of the rage Scarzan would emit when he realized she was gone.

Closing the hidden panel had effectively cut off the only source of light, leaving her in utter darkness. She couldn't tell her ass from her face in here. Elysia brushed her hands against the walls—to her right was the true outer wall of the House. Unsurprisingly, all the windows were sealed shut and painted so that no one could see in or out.

She began to jog, knowing she had no time. The passages were no doubt only known to the Doorman, and now, like so many other secrets, to Elysia. She picked up the pace as her anxiety ratcheted higher. *There has to be a way out.* No one designed a pleasure house without an escape hatch. She sprinted now between the walls like a rodent in a maze even though her puke-weed exhausted body begged her to stop.

The exit has to be somewhere.

From one thought to another, her foot caught and her shoulder banged against the wall as she crashed down to the floor.

A wet, garbled laugh sounded above her.

Shit. She tried to press back up, but the Doorman was already there, lighting the passage with the amber glow of her oil lamp. One hand pinched her bloodied nose while one thick shapely leg kicked out, her booted foot shoving Elysia back down to the dirty floor.

The Doorman peered at Elysia curiously like she was some newfound specimen that needed labeling. She nudged Elysia's face side to side with the toe of her boot until understanding filled her eyes and an impressed smile brought her face wide.

"You Parker girls sure do know how to make a woman work."

Elysia scrambled to stand and was promptly shoved back down. This time the spiked boot stayed over her throat.

"My people told me you were puking in an alley this evening."

She kept the pressure on Elysia's throat and smiled pleasantly.

"But here you are, causing almost as much trouble as your sister. Honestly, I'm not sure I can handle two of you. Imagine if you *actually* worked together." Her face blanched a little at the thought.

Elysia propped up on an elbow, pushing back against the boot.

"How did you know?"

She frowned. "That it was you? Haven't you heard any of my stories?" The Doorman seemed genuinely offended.

She chuckled, digging the tip of her boot into the soft flesh beneath Elysia's chin. "It was a bit of a surprise to see the terror that is your mother this evening, but it wasn't until just now that it all made sense. You, Elysia Parker, have most definitely never been given a token of entrance. As I said before, the pair of you would likely wreck this city, so I've withheld your token the last few years. Saved myself the headache."

She smacked her boot side to side on Elysia's face. "But here. You. Are! With that sweet doll face and a wig, wearing your best friend's clothes. As if I wouldn't know—insulting, really," she added.

Elysia grimaced. "You're the one who let me in."

The Doorman removed her foot and twirled, leaning back against the wall. She gave a complimentary tip of her chin as she spoke. "Well, to be fair, I didn't realize it was you then. Truly, your makeup—so good. I thought your sister was going to shit herself. But something seemed *off.* I couldn't imagine anyone hated themselves enough to steal from the Golden Seal. Or would go to the trouble of creating such a convincing disguise! But then when the prince trailed your ass like clouds to the sun into that godsforsaken room—*that* is when I knew."

Elysia held her blank expression even though she felt near vomiting for the second time this evening. *The prince?* She wanted to scream into the never-ending nightmare that was this night.

Instead, she groaned.

"Men," she said flatly. Specifically, *her* blasted man, ruining her plans. *And how had he even known she was here?*

The Doorman smirked and settled her hands on her hips, strumming her fingers against the silk of her pants. "Wouldn't know. I don't touch the creatures." She continued speaking, her tone brisk, "There are several reasons I am helping you today, Elysia Parker. The most pressing being that my girlfriend scares me almost as much as she delights me, and I happen to know she would be quite displeased if I killed her baby sister, even if you *did* violate the House."

Elysia choked on the word girlfriend. Beatriz was in a relationship? Did *Beatriz* know she was in a relationship?

The Doorman shrugged, considering Elysia from where she towered over her. "Beyond not wanting your sister or the prince to come for my neck, it does not escape me why you are here. You think you're helping your sister." Her brow furrowed as if Elysia was a riddle she hadn't quite solved.

"You *care* for her. How un-Parkerly of you." She smiled broadly, sounding like she was giving out a favor. "Nonetheless, actions have consequences. You're in my debt now, Elysia Parker, and I *will* come calling."

And with that, the Doorman's elbow drew back, her tiny fist cracking out like lightning as she clocked Elysia squarely, right between the eyes.

Elysia's head snapped back and the last thing she heard was the Doorman's laughing words, "Say hello to the prince for me, will you? Tell him we're even."

CHAPTER 13

Elysia smelled thunder and ozone. It reminded her of a storm blowing through the forest. She tucked her nose in a little closer to the delicious scent, feeling her bones relax into someone warm and strong.

And then a rough jostling that felt all too purposeful sent her teeth clacking, ruining the moment entirely. She strained to lift her head. It felt two sizes too large, and there was a vicious pounding between her eyes.

It all came back to her in a sudden, terrible flash.

Unholy gods. The Doorman.

Say hello to the prince for me.

She groaned. *Could this night have gone any worse?* Well, yes, yes it absolutely could have. *You could have been shelled out like a prize pony to that vile man.* But nowhere in the many possibilities she had imagined was there a scenario in which she had to explain to the *prince* what in the realms she was doing at House Gardenia. In a wig. Betting her own body.

Elysia tentatively opened one eye and found Topp staring down at her like he still couldn't believe the stupidity he had witnessed this evening. The sharp lines of his cheeks and jaw were in hyperfocus—his displeasure whittling his face into one she had never seen before. This man looked like he wanted to ream her out and shake her by the shoulders, or maybe tie her up and lock her in a room where she could never be such an idiot again. *Can't really blame him...* She pinched her eyes back shut, but Topp jostled her once more, forcing her eyes to fly open. She clutched his shoulders and glared up at him.

Ass.

His grip tightened. "Ah, ah, ah, little liar. Nowhere for you to run off and hide this time."

She was fairly certain she could break his hold and be gone before he realized what had happened, but she thought it best she kept her mouth shut. Nothing good seemed to come of her opening it. And running would only look even more suspicious. She had to salvage this. Fix the mess she had made. Her brain whirred, coming up with a dozen unbelievable stories explaining why she had been dressed as Georgia Parker and then a redhead in a pleasure house betting her body.

I. Am. So. Screwed.

Her body ached. She'd been drugged. *By herself.* Punched. And lost to her magic. If it wasn't for the fresh wave of anxiety forcing her hand, she could easily slip back under. She supposed it was a miracle that she hadn't left her body and traveled to that strange land or done anything else to get herself executed. Apparently, being unconscious was not the same as being asleep. A small mercy.

Topp came to a sudden halt, readjusted her weight, and pulled out a key from his pocket.

"Can you walk?" His voice was clipped.

She slid down his lean muscled body, her hands clumsily groping him as she went. *Whoops.* She giggled and had the faint realization that she was most definitely not quite herself yet. *Pull it together, Parker.* She brought her feet to the ground, stepping back and swaying slightly. Topp's arm shot out, holding her steady even as he fumbled with the key to unlock the door. Elysia slipped out of his grasp like an eel underwater. Leaning back against the rough, soot-covered plaster of the building, she tried to identify where he had taken her.

She touched the bridge of her nose absently as she looked around. "Ow." The word was almost said with surprise.

Topp shoved at the door and spoke to her like she was five. "Yes, Elysia, getting knocked out hurts."

She rolled her eyes. Like she didn't already know that. The buildings surrounding them were a bit more practical than she liked, and the smell of hard work and salt floated in the air. They were by the docks.

"Why're we by the—"

Topp grabbed her hand and hauled her inside, locking the door. She pulled her hand back roughly, scowling. "Was that necessary?"

He shot her a look over his shoulder that said yes, at this point, it absolutely was. Shaking his head, he walked farther into what was once a dockside warehouse.

He looked comfortable here. A little looser, the wild in him having room to stretch its limbs and play. She'd seen him like this in the forest, but never at the castle or any of the places they usually went.

The warehouse would probably always have the faintest odor of sea and the creatures that had come from it, but there were also the new smells that Topp must have started to layer into the foundation. Smoke from billowing fires and imported coffee dripping slowly, along with his ever present scent of crisp air.

There was hand-carved furniture made from woods she did not recognize and rugs and blankets with patterns she did not know. There were beautiful painted cups in shapes that did not belong to Kava that she longed to pick up and study.

But Elysia did not move. *This... All of these things. The smells. The creature comforts.* Her brain worked to catch up to her senses. *This was a home. A refuge. A sanctuary.* Much like her own flat was to her.

"How long have you stayed here?" she asked quietly.

Topp didn't answer, but continued poking at the fire until it roared to life before moving onto the sconces and lamps.

"You've had this place the whole time, haven't you? Since you came back here for good."

Topp kicked back on a long dark brown couch, hands tucked behind his head. "You know, I'm not sure I love the hair, Lys. And I especially didn't like that makeup."

He looked at her with mock horror on his face. His hand went to his chest as he spoke. "Do you know there was a moment where I had to question my entire existence? Because I couldn't understand *how* I could *ever* possibly be attracted to Georgia Parker. But Georgia Parker doesn't have an ass like that. Or legs." He shivered in exaggerated disgust before grinning and looking at her over the edge of the couch.

But his anger pitched higher beneath his ill-fitting joking mask. A sharp static sound bit her ear as she stared at him, her eyes tracing the shape of his lips that she needed to shut before he could peel her apart, truth by truth. He was just taking his time the way someone does when they have you pinned.

Couldn't have that.

She paced closer, irritation pushing her along. "How did you really know it was me, or that I was even there at all tonight?"

Amusement flitted across his face. Even in his anger, he could appreciate a good trick. But still, he shook his head and went for her heart. "You really do have a lot of questions for someone who has been lying to the Crown through her straight, pretty teeth all her life."

He was off the couch in a flash. "And I am fairly certain that *I'm* the one who gets to ask questions tonight."

His long strides cut her off, causing her to pivot away, but his fingers wrapped around her wrist, tumbling her back into his orbit. Green eyes dared her to contradict him. Begged her to lie to his face.

She folded her arms, unperturbed.

"And you're rather dense for someone who is in line for a crown."

Topp barked out a laugh, running his hand up her neck into her hair. He dropped his face close to hers and whispered. "Tempting. But I will not take your bait. Now tell me what in the name of the undead gods you were doing at House Gardenia. And don't fucking lie to me, Elysia."

Elysia felt everything come to a glaring, momentous pause. It was the frozen time between a breath and an exhale. Every choice, past and present, ran through her mind. Memories and emotion twisting and turning so fast she couldn't track them. And she *knew*, she knew this moment mattered.

This choice, these next few words—they mattered. She could stay, she could run. She could lie or tell the truth. There had been a time when being with Topp had been easy, natural even, but those days seemed further and further away with each sleepless night that passed.

She'd dreamt of being able to tell him the truth. How it would pour out like dark water from her mouth. Choking and gagging on all the decay she'd buried inside. But then the lies could finally trickle down and out of her for good. It would feel like turning your face to the sun, right before the ax fell, to stand there, honest and bare as she truly was—cursed, but free.

I miss him. The thought slipped in like a poison disguised as a tonic, almost fooling her with its aching echo in her throat and chest. She knew better than to give in to such sentiments, but it was still true. She missed when he was Topp and never the Crown Prince—at least to her.

Back when she had told him all the hidden things. All the hidden things that happened in a place like Relaclave. But perhaps not all the hidden things that happened to a woman like her.

He never asked her how she knew the trivial bits of gossip she whispered in his ear while laughing late at night. Nor did he ask about the more serious tips she fed her father so he could finalize a deal or blackmail someone out of their livelihood. And not once had he asked about the cuts, scrapes, and bruises on her muscled body.

But with his forehead pressed to hers now, all she could see were her own lies. All the things she never said. Because she couldn't. Her evasions and lies had multiplied with every conversation, with every day, until she was so far from him that their love had become a blurry, distant thing.

Topp tucked a hand against her face, brushing his thumb on her cheek. She stared at the faint freckles beneath his eyes, her insides squeezing so tight she could barely breathe. Spring eyes watched her wade through the depths, drawing a gentle apology of a smile to her face. *I'm so sorry, Topp, I am.* Guilt ravaged her. He deserved better. Someone who could speak without dead dirt falling from their lips.

And even though it broke her heart once more, she told a half-truth.

"Triz was in some kind of trouble. Asked for my help."

She felt herself float away. Away from his coffee-scented hideaway with its cozy fire crackling. Away from the hands that cradled her face like she was all that would ever matter. Just away. To where she barely heard her own words and the pain didn't own her name.

It was insane she had ever thought she could marry him. That she had believed it would bring her safety and security. After all, whether he was Topp, the boy she'd met in the woods, or the Crown Prince of Kava—neither version had ever given any indication he would protect someone with the undead gifts.

He wouldn't protect me. The thought was a knife through her misguided heart. The useless beating organ in her chest that wouldn't seem to turn off no matter how hard she tried to cut it out. But it was true. The prince had never uttered a single word leading anyone to believe he would protect the cursed. Topp Blatz may have preferred working outside of the Crown lines and dalliances in the woods over meetings and legislature, but when push came to shove, he followed his father's lead. Only a bleeding-hearted fool would stay with the man who was the face of the laws that wanted her dead.

Topp read the growing distance on her face and dragged her over to the couch. The movement snapped her out of her head and back to him. He sank back onto the broken leather cushions, pulling her down so her knees hugged his hips. Warm hands grabbed her shoulders, bringing goosebumps to her cool skin. She watched the electricity in his eyes dance, feeling his fingers dig in as he spoke.

His voice was low now. No longer angry or taunting. Low and soft with a touch of honest-to-the-gods fear. "You went up the stairs in the House like a wraith. It wouldn't have mattered if I called your name a thousand times. You never would have heard me."

Panic flared even brighter within her. *No, don't ask me this.*

His fingers pressed a little tighter, the next question dawning, but Elysia lunged, stealing his lips and breath before the words could form. Her fingers were in his hair, her breath inside his mouth. He tasted like the sun in a dark land.

She felt him freeze, caught off guard by her frenzied kisses. But whatever his next question was, she did not have an answer. She didn't want to answer any of his questions tonight, so she kissed him in a way that she hadn't allowed herself to in a long, long while. Not since the dreams had swept in and stolen her future away.

She kissed him as though he was not the one who would sign her death warrant, but as if he was still the one who brought light into her life. He groaned into her mouth, feeling every bit of her intention, the longing for both what once was and what she had hoped could be her life.

"Lysia, we—"

She ignored him and kept kissing him, hands reaching for his belt.

"Need to talk," he gasped, even as his hips sought hers. He finally wrested her back and eyed her like she was a dangerous creature of his woods rather than a woman with lips already plump from kissing. He held her there. Close, yet firmly away, and took a sharp breath, staring at the ceiling and muttering a plea to some god Elysia did not know.

He brought his eyes back down to find a rather sullen Elysia. He looked at her like her attempts at distraction were cute but ridiculous. "You took pukeweed rather than have a proper conversation with me and went and gambled your own damn body at House Gardenia not even three hours later. It's going to take a bit more than a kiss to break me tonight, Parker."

Elysia gasped, scrambling back and falling off the couch onto the floor in her haste.

The prince looked enormously pleased with himself.

"Not so dense after all, am I?" He leaned back against the couch, arms reaching out wide along the top.

She wanted to tear out her own hair. "How?" she demanded.

He dropped to his knees on the thin buckskin rug beside her. "You have your tricks, and I have mine. I must say, though, even I am surprised at just how much of a little liar you've become."

She bristled and he laughed, crawling over the top of her. "I didn't say I didn't like it."

Elysia fell back onto her elbows, scooting away and getting nowhere. Topp held himself just above her, shaking his head and eyeing her like he wished they could go back to doing what she had tried to start on the couch. Confusion climbed within her, but if he was going to look at her like that, then she wasn't above trying again. Her hands went to his waist, gripping his belt and tugging until he came closer. Pupils wide, his lips twisted up in a mirthless laugh, and then he was kissing her with enough heat to melt a glacier. His tongue swept out and tasted every corner of her mouth.

He stopped. Elysia panted, eyeing him suspiciously. He had already made it clear that distraction was not going to be an effective tactic, but her brain was foggy and useless from drugs and having her bell rung, leaving her with no clear ideas of how to escape. His fingers trailed up her bare thigh and she bit back a groan. Forget distraction, her heart and libido were traitors of the worst kind. She wanted to yank him back to her and pretend the whole night had never happened. That the last many months were a bad dream.

His hand tugged on her stupid wig, and he closed his eyes, breathing out over her. The scent of him flooded her, making her dizzy. This was insanity. She needed to leave, weave a tale to cover her ass, do something, anything.

He came closer, lips brushing against her skin. Her own hands clenched, digging into his back where she had slipped them beneath his shirt. And then he spoke in barely a whisper into her ear. "Should I recount your most recent deceptions? Pukeweed to escape my excellent company. Not telling me about men threatening your life. Gambling at the House with that disgusting bastard." He thought carefully and then smiled as he hovered over her. "And oh, that's right, I almost forgot about that little thing you've been doing while you sleep. Maybe that's where we should start."

Elysia went from outraged to silent terror and back in one breath.

There was no way to prove she could hear a secret. It wasn't an obvious sort of magic, or one that people reminisced about when they were sure no one was listening. But she had no idea what happened when she went to sleep at night and found herself falling somewhere else. Did the air shimmer and wave? Did a ghost of her float out over her body? It didn't really matter if these things happened, or nothing happened at all.

What mattered was if a Crown Prince decided she was guilty.

She was ready to argue until she was blue in the face how preposterous it was that a girl could be drawn to secrets. She had practiced the words so many times they were ready on the tip of her treasonous tongue. *Secrets? That was the most ridiculous undead gift one could ever surmise. It was offensive to even suggest that her endeavors to assist the Crown in trades and deals were not pure skill and talent.* The argument in her head went on until she'd so thoroughly confused the imaginary accuser that they were in an agreeable daze.

She had not prepared an argument for what happened while she slept. She didn't even *understand* what was happening while she slept.

The terror she felt now had been guiding her steps since she was a child, and the rage that ran beside her fear grew less and less contained with each passing year of hiding and narrowly escaping being found out. She could hear her father taunting her that it would be her own fault if she hung, and that he would make sure they did not say her name.

Because a Parker would never stoop so low as to be born tainted by the undead.

The undead have cursed you, he said, *and they will not save you from yourself.*

Her father's words held her in pause until the fear and anger began to slide down her nose in thick drops. She blinked rapidly, trying to force the tears back into her eyes where they belonged.

Embarrassment burned within her. There was nothing worse than crying when really you were angry and scared rather than sad. It seemed a malfunction of sorts.

But the undead gods must have remembered her for there was a harsh one, two, one, two thud on the door.

Both Elysia and Topp started at the sound.

His words were terse. As if he knew the moment was slipping through his fingers. "Just ignore it. No one's coming here."

She stared up at his familiar face, still looming over her as if it were perfectly normal to accuse someone of treason from this position with his knee shoved between her thighs. She wiped at her tears. "Just go check. It's not like I'm going anywhere."

He looked at her warily. She thought it might have been because of the tears, but she knew it was more likely that he was thinking of her propensity for disappearing. Topp slowly pressed up and away from her, and Elysia took a long involuntary breath once he finally took his eyes off her and turned to walk to the door. She watched him go—his back tense and steps quick. *I wonder how long he's known.* Her fingers ran over the soft buckskin beneath her. *But he hasn't turned me in.*

Contrary to her actions this evening, she wasn't a complete fool. The fact that he hadn't turned her in yet didn't mean anything, really. Other than he hadn't decided what he was going to do.

She rolled over off her back and got up, hurrying to follow him.

He opened the door and looked around. "See, no one there." Annoyance laced his tone.

Elysia stuck her head under his arm and looked as well, her eyes snagging on what he had missed.

A coin, half the size of her palm, propped against a small rock, already dirty and wet from the soot and rain.

She ducked under him and snatched it up before Topp could spot it or think about prying it away from her. On the front was a sword stuck in a pile of coins.

It seemed Gage was pissy and not above interrupting what he likely assumed was Elysia having sex with the prince. He was probably laughing wherever he was now. She'd completely forgotten she'd promised to go to his house this evening. Knowing she was out on a job for Beatriz, he'd gone looking for her like some worried, overbearing brother who sometimes killed people. A more nerve-racking thought struck her. She almost closed her eyes as it hit her—had word had already gotten to him about the House? *Shit, shit, shit.* She did *not* want to explain this evening to him.

Elysia shoved the coin into her pocket, dancing back and out of reach from Topp, into the street and heavy rain. The smell of fish and salt crashed down, mingling with the rain's fresh scent. Remy's dress stuck to her and she stood there for half a breath, staring at the man who held her heart and life in his hands.

She pressed her lips together with a shake of her head. "I'm sorry." The words were quiet, but she meant them. Gods, did she mean them.

He took a step closer to her, out into the splattering rain. Frustration marred his face, and the rain flattened his ever messy woodland hair.

"Why won't you trust me?"

She wanted to, but everything in her screamed against it.

Her whisper barely sounded over the rain. "I can't."

And then she ran.

Chapter 14

Topp Blatz pounded through the halls of the castle, his fingers clenching and unclenching. His guards fell back on days like today when they swore there was more than static charging off his fingertips.

Crown Prince of Kava, yet he had spent over half his life outside its borders. He could find no record of when the tradition had begun, but he was told that all the kingdom's princes and princesses were trained and schooled by traveling from land to land. Making connections. Learning other customs and cultures.

For a short while, it was a great adventure. He and his older sister, Isamaya, ran amok in all the beautiful corners of the world. They went through a string of nannies and tutors who all eventually threw up their hands, exhausted by the Blatz children. Even when she was old enough to return to Kava, she stayed with Topp, wishing to stick together even if it meant putting off her own adult life. But then on one fateful trip home, Isamaya, barely into her twenties, caught an illness, and the royal line was slashed to one. It happened so fast that he hadn't even been able to say goodbye. And then she was gone, leaving him alone and without his one constant in life.

Topp touched the thin gold band he sometimes wore on a

chain around his neck. He needed her today. Her laughter, her ability to remain a light even after their mother died. She was only five years old at the time and he hadn't even cut his first tooth.

Topp had no memories of their mother. Maybe that was why he had loved Isamaya so fiercely. She had been his closest friend and confidant, guiding and protecting him the best she could while their father was consumed with grief and trying to save their failing kingdom. Losing a wife and magic in the same year might have killed a lesser man, but Garrison Blatz had clawed his way through the black hole of his grief to do what needed to be done.

Topp had often wondered if it was as Isamaya took her last breath that whatever lived inside him had taken its first. That the undead gods had not wanted him to be so alone, and so they had both blessed and cursed him that day when he set a small storm free within his rooms and watched his pain ravage the place whole.

It was that same day after his sister's funeral that his father took him out into the city. He'd thought Topp ought to see the part of their work that he called the family business. Topp had gone along curiously enough, happy that for once they were escaping the castle walls and getting outside. As far as he was concerned, the Crown meant pushing paper and being dragged into meetings where you were forced to sit still and pretend to pay attention.

His father did not take him to any of the places he usually conducted business, though. Instead, they walked on foot all the way into the south side of the city. He'd never spent much time there as a kid. If he was in Relaclave, then he was at the castle or making a break for the forests that lined the landlocked portion of the city.

The buildings in the south side were cleaner, their lines sharper. Made of mainly new constructions from within the last twenty-odd years, the soot hadn't scarred their outsides as much yet. It was inevitable, though. There wasn't anyone or anything that could escape the dirty filter of their kingdom. The buildings had a certain efficiency in this part of the city. People needed somewhere to live that didn't steal their entire wages and the south side was happy to provide it. If the cost was beauty, then so be it.

The cobbled paths turned to smooth black as they entered Relaclave's younger half. Topp remembered listening to his father's feet strike down over and over, watching how assured and tall he stood, moving through his city like he was invincible. Or at least, that was how Topp saw him. An invincible beacon of truth. The hero who had saved their kingdom from decay. Garrison stopped in front of one of the short towers filled with countless little homes, all scrunched into one stilted rectangular box.

He'd questioned his father, filled with doubt. "*Here*?"

The king had placed a strong hand on Topp's back. "Today is about the safety and protection of not only the Crown, but the very soul of Kava." Garrison paused, ensuring that he had Topp's attention. His hand moved to Topp's shoulder as he looked him in the eye. "Magic is the antithesis to life, son. It tried to steal everything from us once."

His hand clamped down harder, and his face drew painfully tight just as it did when anyone talked about Topp's mother. "And I will not allow that to happen again. This kingdom will be made clean. This is the only way to keep everyone safe. You'll see." He looked mournful now.

He'd found there to be a strange religious undertone to his father's words that previously he had only heard in other lands. Kava was a land of no gods after all. No magic, no gods, no faith. He hadn't known what to make of it. Only that it made unease crawl inside his chest.

The barely hours-old secret inside him turned heavy as his father's words played over and over in his mind. And the youthful hope that he could tell him what had happened burnt to ash inside his mouth.

They walked past an old grandfather smoking in the hall of the apartment building. The man ignored the king, perhaps did not recognize him, but then he winked at Topp with a tiny bow of his head and took another drag. Topp could still remember the intense aroma of so many different families cooking dinner all at once and how his trepidation and curiosity had grown with every step. His father stopped and rapped on a door. There was a bit of shouting, the sounds of a mother herding children, and then a tentative crack of the door.

"Yes?"

The king caught the door, prying it open a little farther. "I'm looking for a lad called Pyre. I'm told he lives here." The king smiled pleasantly enough at the tired mother. She eyed him as any mother would, wondering if her boy was in trouble. Topp could tell she was trying to gauge her recognition of the man in front of her, but without any of the king's usual finery, his father easily passed for any other well-groomed man of Kava. Despite being in his sixties, Garrison still had a headful of Topp's same chestnut locks and his stone gray eyes sparkled kindly.

The woman called over her shoulder, "Jedd, there's a man here for you."

A teenager just old enough to be in that strange time between boy and man lumbered into the room. Topp imagined they couldn't have been more than a few years apart. The teenager towered over his mother and leaned into the doorframe. "What's this now?"

"I hear you can weld. Like the flame and iron run in your blood."

The boy shrugged, but the king persisted. "Come now, I can pay you well. Surely, a few extra coins can go a long way. The tip I received about your work comes from a reliable source, so I've no doubt you really are the best there is in the city."

Jedd sighed and ran a pale hand through flame red hair. "I'm booked for weeks. What kind of work are you needing?"

The king stepped back, giving an air of ease. "I'd really like to see you weld first. See the master in action."

The young man's body became rigid. "Nobody comes into the shop. Those are the rules."

The strong reaction confused Topp. Who cared if someone watched you weld for a few minutes? Getting a job with the Crown could set you up for life if you were any good. The smell of seafood stew drifted out the door, making Topp's stomach rumble.

But his father nodded slowly. "Yes, yes, I suppose I wouldn't let anyone in the shop either," he mused. He straightened, letting a bit more of his authority leak out. "Perhaps you will make an exception for your king."

All the color slid from the boy's cheeks and his fingers started to tremble. "K-king?"

"Come with me, boy. I have a job for you." The king turned heel and did not wait for the pale, trembling boy who was not quite a man to follow him because he knew he would. They always did.

The king brought the boy to his own shop within the castle grounds and set him to task with one word: "Weld." He waited with his hands loosely behind his back, patient as a hawk gliding over its prey.

Topp remembered how the boy's eyes flickered to his own as if begging him to help, but Topp hadn't understood until he started to weld. And then it was too late. It had been too late the entire time. Each of the boy's fingers alternated between catching fire and dashing out cold as he manipulated the iron with no fear of the flames that danced over skin and iron.

Topp thought of the furniture that had become kindling in his room. How his grief had taken physical form, escaping his body. He looked at the young man, anxious to know what would happen next. As if it was his own fate he was watching unfold. Cold, bone-deep despair filled him.

But he should have known.

As every child of Kava knows. The undead gods are friend to none.

The trajectory of Topp's life had changed somewhere between the time when he had risen and when he watched a young man weld for the last time. Garrison stared at the boy, his face devoid of any emotion or reaction. Topp had no idea who he was going to become. He'd never wanted to be a hero like his father. All he knew now was that whoever he'd been this morning was no longer an option. The carefree, reticent heir could no longer exist. Not after today.

It was an odd thing in Kava. That no one remembered the undead gods or their stories. People rarely spoke of the wondrous small and large magics that used to be so normal. Topp had only been a baby when magic had died, yet warnings of the dangers of magic were all that were left now. Mothers and aunties and grandmothers telling tales of those who had lost their lives for the mere suspicion that they'd been visited by an undead god. If a child asked a question about the Fall, or the gods, they would be hushed.

We don't talk about that. It was a long time ago. Things are different now.

Everyone had heard of someone who had suddenly disappeared. Maybe they'd painted a portrait that dazzled the eye in the most unnatural fashion, or someone swore they'd seen their neighbor dry their wet clothes with a single concentrated wave of their hand. It was hard to say just what marked you as someone who'd dabbled with the undead or been born with a curse upon your blood, but you could be certain that it would get your throat slit if you had.

The boy from the scrunched building with hair like fire did not walk out of the castle grounds that day. A common errand boy delivered a small bag of money to his mother with the simple note that Jedd would not be coming home. And that was the end of his story.

Today, Topp Blatz lived by one single rule. It wasn't that he could never let his secret be known—that was just a given. His rule was that he would put no one and nothing above himself.

This rule was forged as that fire-haired boy died. His father had met his eyes and given him a calm, resigned nod. As if this was unavoidable. As if he were leading a rabid animal out to be put down instead of a boy with fire and ice in his hands. Until that day, Topp had believed his father to be someone who would protect him. No matter the cost or cause. The boy's dying screams made it clear as the Kavian skies were not—no one would be saving him.

One day, he would have to choose between his life and his father's. And he was determined to choose himself. His mother, his sister—they were both dead. He refused to meet the same end.

Because whatever his father was protecting, it wasn't him and it wasn't the people of Kava.

His mission became to unravel Kava's greatest secret. Somewhere in their buried history was a story of Kava, the Crown, and the undead gods. A story of how and why magic had disappeared. Topp was convinced this was where Kava's redemption lay.

He shook out his hand, halting in front of the door to the meeting. There was not a single part of him that wanted to be here. All of this shit with Elysia had his anxiety cranked up with no outlet. Instead, it moved roughly inside him, pushing his magic to lash out. *Last night was a disaster.*

He schooled his face into indifference. Within these walls, there wasn't any room for his natural inclination toward dirty humor or honest, blunt communication. No, he had learned to lie and be as silver-tongued as the rest of them.

Well, he still fucked with people. It just wasn't out of the goodness of his heart.

And the only time he was honest was when he felt like being an asshole to the slugs surrounding his father. Outside of his obligations, he spent every possible free second under the open sky, wishing he could disappear. His ambition, sense of responsibility, and guilt held him here like an unwanted but necessary anchor.

He'd acted as the hands of his father too many times to count, wasted lives piling up behind his name. He kept a tally of them all. The tally kept his focus clear. It reminded him that he had one job and that was to find the antidote to whatever had swept through Kava, robbing every last citizen of their birthright. But he still hadn't found an answer—he was still clueless why magic had disappeared. He had a terrible feeling that if anything happened to his father, the truth and any hope of restoring Kava would die with him. So, he waited. And tried not to lose his mind in the process.

Time to go inside. Cool arrogance slid over his bones like a second skin. His feet did not pound, his fingers did not clench.

He opened the door.

The meeting was in full swing, probably half over as he strode to the empty high-backed chair beside his father. The din of the men's voices rose to the high beams of the room even as Topp relaxed into his chair. He shoved back loose tufts of hair, his thoughts straying to Elysia and who in the realms had summoned her at such an hour the night before. Of all the things he'd been worrying about, it had not been some other man swooping in like a vulture at a time like this. He didn't know it was a man. But he had a feeling. His fingers twitched against his leg.

"Topp?"

His father's warm voice drew him back into the present. The look on his face said he was well aware that Topp had not heard a single word of the meeting carrying on around him.

He straightened, leaning forward and spreading his knees wide. "Yes?"

Irritation shot through the king's generally even-keeled expression. "There appears to be a new wave of cursed souls cropping up. As we know, this happens from time to time, but they're banding together now, getting bolder." The king chuckled as if he felt bad for the poor folks. "I would like this handled efficiently—gather them all up, take care of it. No loose ends. Easier for everyone that way."

Topp steepled his fingers. It was just business, after all. "You want to set a trap for them."

The king appraised him. He was getting into his seventies now. Constantly pushing for Topp to actually be useful and engage in what he deemed the more important aspects of the Crown.

"I want you to take the lead. Find the rebels. Determine when they'll meet and get the job done." He pushed away from the table, effectively signaling the end of the meeting.

Men stood up, chairs scraping as they shoved off. Some glared, annoyed that Topp was stealing their thunder and getting to take point in spite of his often begrudging willingness to do his duties. Others patted him on the back, hoping he'd pick them to be on his team.

Topp ignored them all, stalking out of the room without another word. Unknown to his father, he'd already been trailing the rebels for months. Being ordered to find and execute them was going to fuck up everything. He raked a hand through his hair in frustration. This was the largest group of people with undead gifts he'd ever come across. Killing them would really get in the way of questioning them. *Obviously.*

His brain searched for loopholes. *Maybe I can make sure some of them get away.* His mind darted on to other solutions before the thought was even complete. That wasn't probable and he knew it. His father likely had the exact number and names of the people involved.

He'd felt certain that this group could at long last answer his questions. He'd picked up pieces of answers over the years, both in Kava and in his travels. Stories of a deal made long ago that once sealed had changed their kingdom forever.

He was convinced the answers were here in Relaclave. Possibly even within this rebel group. He just had to find them.

The now hunted Kavians usually met in small numbers. Kept their gatherings short and limited in size. They knew what would happen if they were found out, and until now, that had prompted them to exercise caution. Topp had spent so much useless time following their members. But then he'd heard them whisper about a distraction. That'd they'd finally be able to all meet. Excitement and danger hummed through their quiet words.

Further surveillance led him to discovering the meeting would be this week. The date had been tentatively set, but the signal that all was clear still had not been given. Members whispered over teas and gin to not hold their breath that all would go to plan. They were waiting for something, but he didn't know what.

Topp flipped the coin he'd stolen and rubbed his thumb over the insignia. The coin, he'd discovered, was given to potential members. Those who had not yet been initiated into the society's ranks.

The day he had swiped the coin off the counter and walked out of Elysia's flat, he'd been in a marvelous mood in spite of his girlfriend puking her guts out in order to avoid telling him the truth—that she was just as cursed as him. It pissed him off, but he had to respect the woman's game.

His little liar didn't have any practice telling the truth, and he would have been worried for her intelligence if she had simply folded after a few leading accusations from a prince.

They'd have their talk once she settled and realized the truth of him. She'd always been a jumpy thing, and he wasn't trying to rile her anxieties, but there was a part of him that wanted her to open her enormous brown eyes and really see him. Because if she did—then she would trust him, and she would tell him everything.

But he could hardly blame Elysia for what she'd done. If anything, he admired her for it. The tenacity, the drive to survive at all costs.

Even if she did not know it, he understood her more clearly than most others ever would. He knew why she'd withdrawn and held her secret tighter the second he'd started to look her way. Secrets were what had kept both of them alive all these years.

He'd wanted to come clean. Have them both lay it all on the table. Pool their resources and conquer Kava's riddle.

It was only within the last month that he'd been certain. He had stopped at her flat to surprise her and found her dead asleep in the middle of the day. Passed out over a pile of books. Dark hair splayed out in waves. Eyes wide open and blank. And a strange silver glimmer rising off her body like a rope that went into the ether.

The business that occurred at the House had been a *complete* surprise. She'd hidden that little tidbit well over the years. If he was a better man, he would have ripped her out of there the second she looked like she was in a trance. But he didn't. He might care for her, but the incessant desire to find out what happened to Kava—what his father had done—trumped everything. It had to and for that he couldn't be sorry.

He flipped the coin one more time and tucked it away. That being said, he wasn't a monster. Somewhere inside of him, a better man existed and growled at him to keep the coin, and to ensure that Elysia stayed far, far away from that meeting even if it meant locking her in her flat and barring the damn windows. But the creatures and trees whispered to him that there was another way, a more cunning way, and so he heeded their counsel like he always had and prayed it would not come back to haunt him.

Topp whistled the entire walk to Elysia's flat where he replaced the coin just as he'd found it. And when he locked the door, he tried not to notice that it was clear she had never come home.

CHAPTER 15

Elysia woke up in a surprisingly comfortable bed considering she was in the home of Kava's Shadow. She had always expected his house to look like a soldier's barracks. Bare. Functional. Boring. Nothing could be further from the truth. The man liked to live in comfort.

She was in the room she'd always taken on the rare occasion that she'd needed a place to lay her head. The bed duvet was a bright, cheerful blue and there were enough pillows to make you think a woman had been involved. There was a fresh herbal scent on all the bedding that felt both relaxing and clean.

It was the smell of breakfast frying that dragged her from the bed out into the warmly lit kitchen, though. Gage stood there barefoot and shirtless.

He turned around with an almost boyish grin slapped across his face. "Bathroom is just down the hall there, sweetheart. But you know that." He laughed, still grinning like an ass, and turned back to the food.

She touched her face in confusion when it dawned on her just why he was laughing so hard. Elysia darted to the bathroom and slammed the door shut with a bang. She could still hear him chuckling as he scraped the pan.

A long look in the mirror gave her quite the view. In spite of her best efforts to remove all the makeup that had transformed her into Georgia Parker at the House last evening—she'd clearly left some behind. Eyes like a raccoon. Contour smeared just enough to make her look like a haggard, broken-nosed swamp thing. And her wig... half secured, half flapping in the breeze like it was about to make its great escape.

Like any brother, blood or not, she was sure he would never let her live this down.

After a much more thorough scrubbing, she returned to the kitchen with a bare face and her dark hair swept up into a loose bun on the top of her head.

"Ah, there you are." Gage plunked down a plate of food in front of her and sat back, sipping a coffee.

Elysia ate a few bites before she gave in to the eyes that were staring pointedly in her direction.

"Do you have something to say, Gage?"

He smiled as sweetly as any lethal half-naked man could. "You seem to be doing a *superb* job lying low. Exceptional really." He took another drink of coffee. "Did I say exceptional? I meant to say the worst possible job I could have ever imagined."

She was tempted to kick him so hard that coffee would spill down his stupid shirtless self. *Overstuffed ass.* She tossed her head back, gearing up to give him an earful. There was something about Gage chastising her that always made her feel like a petulant thirteen-year-old girl instead of a woman in her twenties, and today was no different.

"Well then, *maybe* you should have helped me like I asked you to. Oh, I'm sorry—what was it you said? That I could handle Beatriz's bullshit on my own?" Her eyes narrowed at him.

Gage remained unbothered. "Dirty work. I believe I said dirty work."

Elysia stabbed at a bite of egg, rolling her eyes. She waved her fork menacingly as she spoke, bits of egg flying. "Topp knows everything. Which I'm sure you do as well even though you've been waiting for me to say it. He saw me at the House acting... strangely. Made a comment about my behavior while I'm sleeping, which no, I will not be explaining right now." She stabbed at the plate again. "I don't understand what he's playing at. He didn't even seem angry. Well, perhaps that I had lied, but now I don't know what his next move is." Anxiety scratched at her.

Gage sat with his fingers wrapped tensely around his cup. He didn't yell at her for the House, or for hiding the truth from him for so long, or even for not spelling it out now despite the fact that he had already made it clear he knew she was cursed. But he wasn't going to beat around the bush any longer, either.

"The king has been hunting and killing your kind since the Fall, but from my understanding, he hated magic long before that."

Elysia stilled and Gage's eyes softened just a fraction. "Did you really think that I didn't know what the trances and your skills meant, Elysia? I might not have all the details, but I am well aware of what the sum adds up to. And you obviously forget that I am not from here—my people never lost their magic. Every day that I am here is like being without a limb."

His deep tan skin creased. "I always knew, Elysia. Since the moment I met you."

She blinked, absorbing the blow he had just dealt her. She knew she should be angry, but all that rolled through her was a shock of hurt. "You should have told me..." She'd been so alone. Always having to hide. She hadn't realized he still believed magic to be *good*. No one in their right mind would move to Kava if they thought magic was natural or good.

She studied him now. Despite their sibling camaraderie, they usually stuck to conversations about training. Over the years, he'd learned more about her life, but kept his quiet. She'd assumed that was because of his work. Frankly, she hadn't really wanted to know more about what he did when she wasn't around. Whenever she felt the pull of his secrets, she ignored it the best she could, much like she often ignored the draw of finding out what Beatriz was up to. She had needed him to just be her friend. And on some level, it had felt wrong to pry into the business of one of the few people she actually cared about and respected.

It was bizarre for her to think about his life before Relaclave. Much like a child with their parents, sometimes she forgot he used to have a whole different life. One she clearly didn't know anything about. He'd been twenty years old when he'd plucked her out of that bloody food cart. Now somewhere in his mid thirties, she couldn't imagine why he had stayed in Kava all these years. All he'd ever been willing to tell her was that his family had sent him to work here, and that he didn't like to talk about them.

The lines near his eyes deepened. "You've been worrying this thread for too long. It was bound to break at some point."

He spread his hands out wide. "What will it be, then? A ticket to warmer shores? A land where your damn plants can actually grow? You can't stay here anymore. My family would welcome you."

She stayed quiet, and his voice became gruff. "It's only a matter of time before the prince shows his colors and you're dead or used for worse by the king."

When she still didn't answer, he looked at her seriously. "I will stuff you in a sack myself, Elysia, and watch you set sail as the steamship's luggage if that's what it takes."

Elysia sighed, the wheels of her mind racing, searching for answers she did not yet have.

She poked at her now cold food. "I need more time. There's a group," she explained. "Rollie is how I found them. A whole group of people that I think can help. They want some type of diversion as payment, but I can meet with them this week."

Gage's eyes were sad as he set down his coffee and leaned on his elbows over the high countertop closer to her. "You're not getting it, sweetheart. It doesn't matter what these people know—

they will not have a way to stop what runs in your blood. To stop you from escaping your body in your sleep. You did it last night, you know. Looked like a gleaming, silver tether coming out of your body. Eyes wide open. Maybe you've been doing it longer than you think."

Elysia's heart sank a little more because he was right, and it was no wonder Topp had known. She thought she remembered all of her nightly excursions. But this just proved that she didn't. She'd been desperate and irrationally banking on this unknown group of people who were ultimately just as screwed as her to help her solve what could not be solved.

What could they possibly offer her?

Answers about why and how would not stop her from spinning like a top after the secrets in her path.

Answers would not keep her sleeping soundly through the night.

Answers would not stop the prince from turning her in.

She'd been found out. The prince knew. Death or worse were her only options now. Her heart squeezed tight, refusing to accept this. She couldn't just leave. This was her *home.* Maybe this group Rollie had put her onto was nothing but smoke and mirrors, but then maybe they were more. The sweet song of magic that guided her hand told her what she needed was still here, and she clung to that inkling like it was truth.

She knew they wouldn't be able to kill the magic in her. But that didn't mean they didn't have anything to offer. The soft voice of reason inside her head pleaded with her to take Gage's offer and go.

"I'm going to meet with them. I have to." She lifted her chin, defiant even in the face of her own demise.

Gage looked her square in the eyes as he broke her heart. "Your prince helps him. He's hunted just as many of your kind as the king has. You have to live, Elysia. You don't understand how important it is that you live."

She could hear some meaning that she didn't understand behind his words, but she couldn't care about that right now. Not with the ghosts of Topp's hands pressed to her face even as her hope died.

Perhaps her father was right. She really was cursed, after all.

CHAPTER 16

Elysia couldn't decide if it was certain terror or elation she felt zipping through her like a spark as she traipsed through the castle. The hand of her beloved dangled a rope above her head, and yet she felt as though she might actually be closer to freedom than she'd ever been before. The prince could turn her in at any moment, but he hadn't, and if she knew Topp Blatz, that meant she wasn't the only one with schemes afoot.

But that wasn't why she was here. No, Topp, her handsome executioner, would have to wait. She was here to see the one man in her life who had always known her secrets. Her father.

She'd requested a meeting with the promise that she had a long-overdue payment. In a manner of speaking, she had been paying her father in secrets to keep her alive since she was a small child. She wasn't even five years old the day her father realized the truth about her. His demands and threats had started soon after.

On days like today, when payment was due, she wished she could go back and hush that small version of herself. *How different my life could have been.*

Elysia walked the familiar halls to her father's office, heels clacking in an oh-so-satisfying manner. Her hand brushed the cool stones, and the memory of that day replayed in spite of herself. She'd sat in the corner of the very office she now walked toward with a book, flipping pages and eavesdropping. Three, maybe four years old—her nanny had been sick that day. She'd been happy to be stuck in the corner with her book, listening to her father scoff and argue about the price of things. It was familiar, soothing.

Her father's guest had prattled on about the fine spiced meats he could ship to Kava. Delicacies and such. But there was a sound beneath his words that had caught her tiny ears. She had paused mid-page-flip to listen closer to what was being left unsaid.

She'd been able to do this for some time and hadn't thought much of it. She figured everyone could do it. Hear the story beneath the lies. It wasn't something she could turn on or off. It happened according to its own will, pulling her here and tugging her there. Sometimes it led her to overhear conversations. Other times, strange music enchanted her and sent her searching for its source. And then there were the times when she just simply knew something that she should not have known.

She'd made a mistake that day. Telling her father about the bad man and his spoiled meat.

From then on, her father's instructions were clear: she could only tell such things to him. He rarely let her out of his sight for years, taking her to meetings and on long travels. Even now, she wasn't sure if it had been out of fear of discovery or for the sheer usefulness of keeping her around. To everyone else, he appeared to be the world's most doting father.

As she'd gotten older and it was no longer so simple to keep her by his side, her father had changed the rules. If she was ever caught, he would deny to his last breath that he knew. That cursed as she was, it was her duty to protect the family, and protecting the family meant feeding her father secrets. Confirming his uncanny instincts for the market, and steering him away when she detected foul play. Spying on men he did not like and finding skeletons to cause their ruin.

She'd cut down more men from their seats of glory than she

could count at this point. Anyone important enough to be a nuisance to her father was bound to have a few dirty old secrets lying around.

But then she grew older. All of her peers began their adult lives, and she longed for the same. She grew restless with her father's demands. She did not want to act as a sieve for the gross sludge of politicians and merchants and financiers. Always sifting for the piece of shit that would make her father happy. They all had secrets. It was nasty, tiresome work, all to satiate her father's ambition and accrue the Crown more coin. The Crown had enough coin, and she'd had enough of her leash.

So, she had gotten a little sloppy. Didn't bother to share a few tips. Ignored a few summons. Her punishment had been thorough.

Her father had not cared for his silent prodigy's backlash, and he'd made sure she knew. All of her freedom had been ripped away for six whole months. She had been forced to follow him from sunup to sundown unless she was off slumming for dirt. His behavior gave her whiplash as he morphed from proud father to someone repulsed by the sight of her. That was a few years ago. She hadn't missed a payment since then until the dreams started and her life fell apart.

Then again, it seemed she couldn't help but step outside the narrow lines he had drawn for her. The recent incident with the bloodletters was the most glaring example, of course. The scars on her feet reminded her with each step just how far Jack Parker was willing to go to keep his daughter managed. But that was why she was here today. She knew she'd been pushing her luck and now wasn't the time to set him off. The last thing she needed was to lose his trust and be forced to live in the castle again, trailing behind his every step. She just needed to offer up a good enough tip to keep him satisfied and looking the other way.

The guard at the door nodded at her approach. "Miss Parker."

She smiled in response, wondering at his presence. *That's odd.* Her father didn't usually have guards stationed at his door.

He opened the door, letting her through to her father's office. The sweet smell of smoke cloaked her nose and a damp chill hung in the air. Her father, bear of a man that he was, rarely lit his fire even with all the rain and cold. Argued that he could not feel it touch his bones.

Jack Parker folded his hands atop the stack of papers he'd been evaluating and offered Elysia the full weight of his attention. His smile was so sincere it caught her heart. "If it isn't my favorite daughter here to offer her father an unexpected gift."

Like so many times before, Elysia wondered if she'd ever know how she really felt about this man or him about her. She'd never expected love and hate to be so confusing. But she found her lips playing into a small smile even as she stayed back by the door and leaned against the credenza.

"I am indeed." She pulled off one dark silk glove and then the other.

Her father stood from his desk, his head nearing the ceiling as he walked her way. "Save your gift. First, the king and I must borrow you." He brushed a hand over her mid back, steering her into the large meeting room connected to his office. "Gentle heart that you are, I know you hate to do this, but the king requested your help." He touched her face, looking remorseful. His tenderness only served to incite a full-bodied wave of anxiety. *No, not again.*

She looked into the room and felt the ground sway beneath her. *No, no, no.* Five chairs were lined up against the back wall. In each chair sat a young woman. All near her own age. All with dark brown wavy hair and big brown eyes. *They look just like me.* Her heart pounded in her throat. She could still smell her father's sweet smoke, except now it made her want to gag.

King Blatz stood against the gray stone wall to her right. He flipped a switch, further illuminating the cool, damp castle room. White sleeves rolled up and hair mussed, he looked far too much like his son. "Miss Parker, we were given word that a woman of a certain description has fallen to the curse. We gathered the most likely suspects within the city. Given your past history of identifying such culprits, your father recommended allowing you to weigh in. What can you share?"

Elysia, daughter of the Golden Seal, knew everyone. From distant Crown members to the best carpenter in the city, she knew their names, knew their vices. She stared at the women waiting for her to decide who would die. Claudia Brine trembled. Syren Herrin had anger screaming in her eyes. And Pen Weaver stared blankly right through them all. The last two women just looked at the floor, tears streaming, unwilling to see their death coming. Cold distance slid through Elysia's veins, their faces looking further and further away.

Her feet throbbed violently, keeping her from detaching entirely. Pain stabbed through the old cuts in a way it hadn't since the man next to her first delivered those scars. She kept her face pensive, considering as she swept it over the women in front of her. She slipped her shaking hands into the pockets of her skirts. *I can't let him see.*

She hardened herself, taking herself to the place where she felt nothing. Where no one could possibly touch her.

Her dark eyes met her father's. "Everyone knows that Syren Herrin's tinctures never fail." She lifted a shoulder, hating herself, but she couldn't stop. "I'd say that's a bit unnatural if you ask me. Never a single stillbirth. Never importing herbs like the other healers. You have to wonder what she's even giving them all." Bile crept up her throat, but she kept it down.

"You nosy fucking bitch. I *saved* you, fixed your godsdamn ugly feet." Syren lunged across the room, slashing at Elysia like her nails were knives. Elysia let her. Let her nails rake down her pretty face, marking her as the traitor she was to her kind.

Syren really did have magic. She was the best healer their city had until today. And now she was going to be dead.

Guards descended, pulling the thrashing woman off of Elysia.

Blood dripped into her mouth. She swallowed the salty rust down, not bothering to wipe her face. She sat there on the floor, watching the guards force Syren along. The king stopped in the doorway, barely pausing to look down at her. "Thank you, Miss Parker. Valuable as always."

She nodded silently. Soon, the whole room was all too quiet. Her father offered her a hand and anger that burned like ice filled her entire being. *He* had done this. Orchestrated all of this. Forced her to hand over another life.

And yet, like always, she accepted his hand, allowing him to guide her back into his office. They didn't make it two feet through the door before he was grabbing her chin. Smoke-scented breath clouded over her. "You do *not* disappear for weeks on end. Have you forgotten how this works?"

Every single muscle in her tensed. She stiffly shook her head no, his fingers still pulling at the skin of her face. His jaw flexed. "I thought we had worked through your little rebellions." He dropped her chin, practically flinging her away. She stumbled back, her face stinging with blood and now bruises.

He paced back to his office, cracking his neck and sitting down. "I hate that you make this so difficult, Elysia."

She nodded, tears welling in her eyes. How quickly her anger distorted into a shame she didn't understand.

"I'm sorry." The words were choked, her eyes gleaming.

He gave a heavy sigh, nodding his head and looking at her like he knew she couldn't help it. He grabbed his pipe, packing it slowly. "Let's put this behind us, then. Tell me about your little gift." Her father stretched out his legs, waiting.

Elysia slowly sat down in the chair across from him, accepting the silent handkerchief he handed her. She pressed it to her swelling face. "I happen to know you are not terribly fond of Diplomat Scarzan. An old deal gone wrong." Her voice shook and she hated it. She inspected her carefully filed nails instead of looking at his face. *Breathe. You can leave soon.*

It'd been more than a deal gone wrong. Jack Parker had introduced Scarzan to his favorite aged tobacco. A gentleman's secret, if you will. Scarzan promptly stole her father's favorite apothecary. The apothecary who made his favorite pipe tobacco, to be precise. There were some things a man just did not do, and beyond stealing someone's lover, Jack Parker considered this to be one of those things. He would likely go to his grave hating the man.

Her father's brow furrowed. "Go on."

She looked up, head tilting, and shrugged. "Rumor has it that Scarzan has been spending his time at the House. Seems he overindulged."

He began to brush her off. "Elysia, that is the point of the House. Now—"

Elysia cut in. "I wasn't finished, Father. His overindulgence killed a maiden of the House. Her neck was mottled like old fruit by the time he was done. The Doorman is owed payment, and it seems she is old-fashioned. Death for death is her wish."

All the warmth left Jack Parker's eyes as his true mind for machinations shone through. He finished packing his pipe with the tobacco that was not nearly as good as what he once loved and considered her words. "And how do you suggest one go about accusing a man such as Scarzan of this crime?"

It was Elysia's turn to smile as she slipped her gloves back on, readying to leave. "Don't you worry, Father. It will be taken care of at Mother's going away party for all the ambassadors. When this goes through, consider me paid in full for the next two months." A bold move considering she was still bleeding in his office. But he'd accepted similar deals before when she brought him something good enough.

Her father looked up in surprise. Always the surprise. He laughed like she was ridiculous. "Such a sense of humor on you. Don't know where you get it. You know the Raven Ball is coming up. As if I could set my best asset free at a time like this."

She nodded, biting her tongue and walking to the door. Her fingers gripped the door tightly, and she was glad for her gloves to hide the sight. "One month."

Exhaling a cloud of smoke, he looked at her from head to toe, with the softest shake of his head. "This was never a negotiation. Consider yourself permanently on call. I don't know what's happened to your commitment to this family. Do you want Beatriz to die? Do you want your mother to hang for your crimes? Figure out your priorities, Elysia. Next time, they won't just look like you." Disgust lined his face as he gestured for her to leave. He was back to his papers without another glance.

Elysia closed the door behind her. She had known going in that he would never give her the ball off, but even a few weeks would have sufficed. She just needed time to figure out her next move. Her head fell back, thudding against the door. Safe from his sight, her chest shook now, her body trying to make sense of what had just happened. *What a nightmare.*

She tore the handkerchief away from where it was drying to her face like glue. Her face burned as much with humiliation as it did with pain. Nothing about this afternoon had gone right. She'd walked in here so sure she could make a deal with him, and he'd been two steps ahead. Ready to smack her down where she belonged. She swallowed a tight lump in her throat. She would *not* cry. Not where anyone could see. Syren Herrin's face crashed through the walls of her mind, but Elysia expertly swatted it away. If there was a god of retribution after death, then he surely had her name. Because she was worse than filth and she'd never had any hope for anything like honor. Because Syren Herrin hadn't been lying. If it wasn't for her healing, Elysia's feet would probably still be as useless as the day Jack Parker had carved them up. And how had she repaid the woman? By handing her over to the king and his executioners.

The old thought crept in that maybe she really would be better off dead. It was a thought that liked to linger in the back of her mind. That at least then she wouldn't have to deal with the guilt or see another life snuffed out because of her insufferable curse. Elysia shook herself out of it. She didn't have time to fall into that hole. Her life may have been a series of choices she wished she could erase, but it was hers, and she wasn't going to give it up.

Fuck my father and fuck the king.

Chin held high, she dared anyone to say a word as she paraded through the castle with half her face scraped off. The rumor mill worked fast when someone like Syren Herrin was dragged through the castle screeching until her lungs gave out. Word of Syren losing her mind to the curse was already spreading like wildfire. She could hear them whispering as she walked by that poor, sweet Elysia Parker had been mauled, too. Elysia ignored the stares and comments, continuing on briskly. She knew better than anyone that there would be something new to blather about by tomorrow.

The air soon turned warm and lush with the smell of bread and meat roasting. *This is going to go well.* She let out a sigh. Lynd was not going to appreciate her bloodied face. If she could, she would avoid the woman until her face healed, but that wasn't really an option today.

She stepped into the kitchen, the tense lines of her body already loosening. There was something about the smells, the warmth—it felt safe. A feeling she didn't deserve but desperately needed after what had just happened. She watched Lynd cook with a tender feeling in her chest. She found Lynd's cooking to be in the same vein of how she felt coaxing life from seeds destined to die in Kava's feeble light. Both the most natural yet extraordinary of acts.

Lynd spotted her but stayed focused on her dish. She called her over without a second thought. "Taste this," she demanded.

Elysia put her lips to the wooden spoon and sipped at the hearty broth.

Lynd snatched the spoon back before Elysia could say anything. She looked aghast. "Your *face.* Did one of those street dogs attack you?" Her hand ghosted over Elysia's face, not touching, but clearly wanting to. Apparently, the gossip mongers hadn't made their way to the kitchens yet.

Elysia just smiled and shook her head. There really wasn't a good explanation, so she didn't bother. She just walked over to the cleanest spot she could find and pulled out two pieces of paper from her purse. She hastily wrote out her messages and stuffed the papers into their envelopes. Dropping a blob of wax onto a spoon, she watched it shine, turning liquid over the flames of the stove. Sealing her letter, she left the wax free of any crest.

"You come here just to write letters, then?" Lynd stirred her soup, throwing in dashes of herbs.

Normally, she would have barked at her and told her that her kitchen wasn't an office. Clearly, the scratches were earning her sympathy points. Elysia smiled as much as her face would allow. "Ah, Lynd, I could have done that anywhere."

Lynd continued stirring the broth, staring at it with dissatisfaction. "So, what is it you need, then?"

Her motives were hardly ever pure, but there would always be a part of her that simply wanted to hide in Lynd's kitchens as long as she could. It was tempting—the desire to hide here all day. Lynd was not wrong, though. She had come for business more than pleasure.

Elysia tucked her messages for Beatriz and Rollie back into her purse and stepped closer to Lynd, putting a hand on her shoulder. She curved in toward Lynd conspiratorially.

"Oh, just a little favor."

Chapter 17

It was early evening when Elysia left her flat with her mind a razor's edge and her face cleaned up the best she could manage. Beatriz had been warned to tie up her business with Scarzan immediately. Elysia wasn't sure she wanted to know what that was about at this point. She'd kept her word, though, and that was what mattered. Rollie was set to receive a message informing him to ready his people. The diversion they demanded would be upon them soon, and if all went to plan, her debt to the House would be paid as quickly as it had come upon her. Which was exactly why Elysia now darkened the doorway of the notorious House Gardenia.

Kava's meager sun had not yet set. Without the dark of night, the House's fading beauty seemed to warn you its sweets would turn to dust on your tongue and all treasures won inside its doors may disappear by morning. Elysia was not here for the decadence or the many sinful delights of the House, though.

She banged her fist on the House Gardenia door with a bold impatience, ready to be done with this entire mess. She was tired and run through. The mystery that her life had devolved into had lost its luster, and now she would fight to author its ending before some man in her life stole the pen.

She stood in the doorway with a dark cascade of hair and a twilight purple dress that floated out into the night. Soft pink dusted her cheeks and darkened lashes curled to the sky. She came to the Doorman this time as a flower who carried a blade. A sentiment someone like the Doorman ought to appreciate.

The door swung open and a young man with golden hair and trails of glitter spraying out from his eyes answered the door. "The House isn't open. Come back at dusk."

He made to slam the door shut, but Elysia shoved her foot in the way, smiling grimly. "Tell the Doorman that Elysia Parker has come with a proposition." Her fingers tapped the dagger sheathed along her tapered waistline. Curved with an intricate bronzed handle, she'd made sure to steal her favorite deathly toy back from Gage.

The worker squinted at her, astutely surmising that it was highly unlikely the stubborn woman with the knife would politely remove herself, and he, after all, was not the muscle of this place. He let out a curse under his breath. "Just wait a minute, will you?"

He started yelling over his shoulder, and Elysia could hear his fellow people of the House telling him to piss off before falling back into peals of laughter. She sighed, looking up to the sky. She didn't want to barge in and drag the Doorman out, but she would. Her mother would die if she could see this lack of manners on full display. The thought brought a reluctant smile to her face.

"Elysia Parker. Can't say I'm not curious."

The Doorman stood shamelessly in the doorway with a hand on her hip and a mauve dressing gown seducing her every curve. She turned on her heel. "Come. Get ready with me."

Elysia looked at the golden-haired man with *I told you so* written across her satisfied face and promptly trailed after the Doorman's dressing skirts. The House Gardenia was even more lively when its doors were closed than when guests tumbled through its halls. The men, women, and people of the House both scurried and lazed about all in different phases of preparation for their nightly performances.

Women in just their corsets basked over the edges of beautiful chairs, grinning like rogues, and men with shirts half open and top hats askew threw tiny arrows at targets, laughing as their drinks spilled. A pair of men sat still as statues, tracing each other's eyes with smokey liner and smudging it out to unholy perfection. Both the air and the chandeliers shook with music meant for dancing. And jubilant destruction took the form of tornadoes of children, all tearing through the House with little shrieks to announce their arrival.

Elysia did not realize she had stopped until the Doorman called out, beckoning her to come along up the stairs. There was something about this strange House with its makeup and illusions. Her first and only evening here had left a terrible taste in her mouth, but *this* was something altogether different. Before the lights went out and the evening show began, it appeared the House was a *home*. She followed the Doorman, her eyes still wandering back to the folks playing and teasing as they readied themselves. Her feet were slow as her fingers slid over the bannister. She didn't want to look away. Watching them brought an unexpected longing to life inside her.

She couldn't help but wonder if the House's real secret just might be love.

A different sort of love, but love nonetheless. The love found between people who did not have a home, but then found one in both this place and each other. The love that she imagined came from a space in which your soul felt its own freedom.

Her throat tightened. She thought she might like to know that one day. What it would be like to be both anchored and set free within love. Somehow, she doubted that was in the cards.

The Doorman looked back at her with questioning eyes, but Elysia said nothing. She just shook her head and followed her upstairs. Elysia found her words as she entered a lavish dressing room that swirled with soft tones of lavender and cream and gray. "The people of the House... They wish to be here, don't they?"

She spritzed on perfume from an ornate glass bottle and considered the question. Taking a deep inhale as the mist hit her neck and chest, the Doorman made a pleased sound in the back of her throat. A sugar-sweet scent with something sharp beneath its breath pillowed through the air. Elysia thought it matched her company well. Delectable but dangerous.

Racks and racks of silk and organza decorated the room. From suits to dresses and corsets, the Doorman knew how to draw the eye. She sat down on a cream footstool, turning to a vanity suited for a queen. The marbled vanity glittered beneath the soft glow of countless tea lights. Even when no one was watching, it was like she couldn't help but entice and beguile.

The Doorman pulled down a small pot of face cream from a towering stack of choices and looked up at Elysia through the mirror. "The House is not like other pleasure houses, Ms. Parker. The House is my home and I open it to those who would make it their own as well. Do you not care for the ones in your keep?"

Elysia remained silent. She had none in her keep, spare the ever-dashing Sir Larkspur and the tiny sprouts she tended, and she was afraid that even her cat was mad at her after so many days of simply piling food high and dashing back out the door. She would very likely be snubbed with a flick of his regal tail upon her return.

The Doorman watched these thoughts play across Elysia's face, and her shoulders dropped with a sigh. She scooped out some moisturizer and began rubbing it into her face with smooth circular motions.

"I forget. You're a Parker, and more than that, you're Crown. There is no one more important to protect than yourself." She scoffed, but was quick to keep talking with a wave of her manicured hand. "I'm not one to judge. I haven't lasted this long in my line of work without vigilance. But what is life without *someone* to trust and hold?"

She pursed her lips, looking at Elysia shrewdly. "It's a lonely life, putting your love into the wrong hands. But I suppose people underestimate the bonds forged in childhood. They're irrational and completely heart driven."

Elysia met her eyes in the mirror, but kept her mouth clamped shut. *She's not wrong.* All the Crown kids were grown up now. And yet, for better or for worse, they couldn't leave each other behind. Rollie bringing her into the fold even though it risked himself. Remy and Daphne subtly reminding her that deviance in behavior was how people found themselves ostracized or dead. And Topp hesitating to end her life and their love in spite of what it meant to be a Blatz.

All of their love was dishonest—at the end of the day, they would all choose their own necks. But if there was the choice to save each other *and* themselves, then they would every time. And in her world, that was about as close as it got to love.

The Doorman tipped her head knowingly, unaware of Elysia's musings. "It's a shame about Syren Herrin. She was a good but stupid woman, healing everyone left and right. But we're fools for those we love, and that's what I saw in my House the other night. You love your sister. And now your beau knows the truth of what you are." She paused, grabbing another jar. "Don't worry, unlike him, your secret is safe with me."

The Doorman stopped what she was doing and looked at Elysia with a stark sadness in her eyes. "From one woman to another—choose yourself, Elysia Parker, before time runs out. That man has a destiny to fulfill and love will not stop him."

Elysia blinked rapidly as if it could stave off the painful truth of the Doorman's words. Her voice came out thick. "I have always loved my sister. But this was my fault. Not hers."

She cleared her throat sharply. "But I did not come here to discuss the prince or his ambitions."

Heartbreak masquerading as regret twinged within her. Sometimes she wished she had never met Topp. She should have chosen a pretty but insipid man. Instead, she chose one with the security of a crown and clever, enthralling eyes. *Don't forget the part where he's why you die.* She was an idiot.

The Doorman nodded, accepting her words. "No, that is not why you came, is it? Tell me about your proposition, Ms. Parker."

Elysia dragged over a matching pillowed footstool and sat down, crossing her ankles out leisurely in front of her. "These people are your family." She sat with the thought for a moment. Everything in her plan depended on the Doorman agreeing to her designs. Looking back up, she found the Doorman studying her carefully, so she looked right back without any fear and spoke boldly.

"Scarzan killed one of your own. I would like to see him dead as well. If I'm going to be caught and executed, then I might as well take a bit of the trash out before I go." Her voice went tight, betraying the terror that raged inside her at the thought of being on the execution block.

The Doorman's eyes continued to slowly track over Elysia. She popped off the tops of several tubes of lipstick, humming as she swatched them on her hand. Setting the lipsticks down, she turned, giving Elysia her full attention. There was a generous portion of skepticism in her voice.

"I had not pegged you for one of the old ways. Tell me what draws your hand, Ms. Parker. Because I do doubt the death of a whore you did not know has begged your tears or blade."

She went back to her mirror, reaching for black ink and a brush. The Doorman's words were as harsh as the line she flicked out from the corner of her monolid eye, but Elysia had expected nothing less.

She switched to her other eye. "And how might one kill vermin like that, anyway? They always seem to escape through holes in the wall."

Elysia huffed a short laugh, not missing the Doorman's slight. "What draws my hand, indeed? The truth is, the world is crawling with men like Scarzan."

She looked down, her jaw flexing and emotion beginning to

leak into her voice. "One less is nothing in the grand scheme of things. But I am *tired* of fawning and hiding and running. If I was braver, then I would go after the lot of them—the king, my father. But I'm not. And there's still a foolish hope in me that I'll make it out of this somehow. And to be blunt, killing this one man will pay many debts for me."

Elysia implored the beautiful woman in front of her. "You watched him every night while he ransacked your House. You and your people know what and who he likes better than anyone else." A tiny dangerous grin crossed her face. "I would like to set a trap the night of my mother's farewell gathering."

The Doorman looked on knowingly. "And what do you need from me for this trap?"

A hint of vengeance glimmered in Elysia's eyes.

She snatched a scarlet red tube of lipstick off the vanity. "I'm so glad you asked. I will be in need of a woman who can walk and talk like sin whom Scarzan will not be able to refuse. Simple men deserve simple plans. One woman, one poison, one death."

The Doorman raised the brow she was currently filling in. "You expect me to call off your debt when you come here asking for my best trained courtesan to become an angel of death?"

Elysia smiled and dabbed at the shade she'd swiped on her lips. "Of course not. That would be absurd."

She looked up, waving the lipstick in the air as she spoke. "Everyone will get poisoned in different amounts. But only from the drinks, which come from sealed bottles. No poison in the food, keeping the kitchens free of blame. I'll also be bringing in some more muscled hands to do the serving. No servant will take the blame for my actions if I can help it. The woman I am requesting from you is simply a distraction to ensure he drinks his drink and stays long enough to die dramatically."

She clacked the lipstick back down on the vanity. "Everyone around him will begin to take ill. And with half the Crown falling down, shitting themselves and Scarzan dead on the floor—well, the guards will be in a tizzy. It will be perfect."

Something wild shone in her eyes as the plan played out in her mind, but then she coughed lightly and folded her hands primly, coming back to herself. "Well, what do you think?"

The Doorman's cool dark eyes were wide and her mouth was frozen in a half open pout. She blinked once, then twice, and turned back to the mirror, shaking her head and muttering. "The two of you are a menace. Crown-trained menaces."

"And?" Elysia prompted her, unperturbed by the Doorman's fairly accurate evaluation of the Parker sisters.

"And you'll have one highly motivated courtesan in your service. The drinks will go down, and then she will be gone, along with your debts."

Elysia's grin was just shy of unhinged. She just might be able to turn the tides of these games yet.

"I'll see myself out then."

She came to a stop in the doorway. "Oh, to be clear. You do know your girl will have to drink the poison like everyone else, right? Wouldn't want her to look suspicious." Elysia smiled innocently.

"Fucking Parkers." A spiked heel sailed in Elysia's direction, but she was already gone, laughing as she floated down the stairs.

Chapter 18

Elysia sighed for the tenth time in the last minute. Her patience was reaching its limits. With the party fast approaching, her nerves were stretched thin, ready to snap. A small dingy tunnel was the last place she wanted to be right now. Pacing back and forth like a trapped rat, she growled in frustration. *Where was he?*

Rollie had refused to meet anywhere else because he was the world's biggest pain in her ass. Well, there *was* always Topp and Beatriz to contend for that prized position. But today, Rollie had it in the bag.

Gods, it really does smell like shit down here.

Glancing at the walls in sudden concern, she promised herself it was just dirt. It had to be just dirt. She sighed again and even she found the sound annoying now. Rollie was late. It was highly inappropriate to be late when you were assisting in the plotting of someone's murder. *What was wrong with people?* She tapped her foot, wishing he would just show up already.

Footsteps sounded down the tunnel, and her pulse skittered. She strained to listen. *That sounds like two people.* And there was only supposed to be one. Her hand slid to her dagger, and just as she slipped it from its sheath, she heard the dry tones of Rollie's laughter.

The dagger went back in, and Elysia smiled stiffly at Rollie and his unexpected companion.

Rollie stopped a few feet away with an incredulous expression on his face, holding a lantern out so it shone directly into her eyes. "Were you going to stab us? Do you even know how to use that thing?"

"Would you like me to show you, Rollickus?" She smiled sweetly with her fingers still on the hilt.

Rollie balked. "No, I would not like you to *show me*." His voice dropped to a mutter. "Someone's gotten some new hobbies. I think I liked the flowers better."

Elysia gracefully ignored him. "And who is this?" Her voice was clipped but polite, her feelings about the unwanted guest all too clear.

A short, powerfully built woman stepped up beside Rollie, appearing completely at ease despite the hostility and smell of shit in the air. "You can call me Mari." Her voice tinkled like glass in the breeze.

Elysia gave her a short nod. "Rollie, why is the lovely Mari here?" Her impatience seeped into her words. What didn't people understand about assassination? This was not a group sporting event!

Laughter lined the woman's face. Even in the dark, Elysia could see she had beautiful tan-brown skin and full lips that easily smiled. Between her dulcet tones and laughing face, Elysia could tell she would be a hard person to dislike. *Too bad I'm not here to make friends.* She just needed a time and place and to be done with this disgusting tunnel.

"Rollie tells me you have everything ready?" Her voice was friendly, open.

Elysia eyed her speculatively. "Are you in charge, then?"

She shrugged, her face growing serious. "I am one of several who ensure our safety. Can you ensure our safety, Ms. Parker?

Some say it is unwise for us to make deals with someone like you."

Ah. So that's what this was then. The group was having second thoughts about letting her into their special, secret little meeting. Another test, as if setting up a massive diversion wasn't payment enough. She was willing to bet they hadn't expected her to come through. Thought she would run away from their exorbitant demands and they'd be rid of her. *You'll have to try harder than that.*

Elysia's teeth flashed in the light of Rollie's lantern. "Then perhaps I should call the whole thing off. Who says you all can help me, anyway?"

Mari straightened and leaned forward just a hair. "Oh, but I think we can help you, Elysia. Rollie tells me of your nightly travels, and there are those in our midst who may have knowledge on the matter. Not all the old books were burned, you know." Her friendly charm disappeared. "I just need to hear directly from your mouth that there won't be any *problems*. Given who you are and the company you keep."

Rollie shifted his feet nervously. "I told her you would never. Even if you do prance around with that insufferable prig of a man."

Only years of her mother's training kept her eyes from rolling into the back of her head. "I've told the prince nothing of these matters. I have no more wish to die than you."

Never mind that he already knows. She swallowed hard, trying to keep her thoughts from wandering to all those grating questions of just what Topp planned to do with her and when. *Maybe he'll blackmail me just like Father.* That would explain why she wasn't dead.

Or maybe she was his greatest hunt. The prey he had stalked the longest and enjoyed the most. A sick feeling settled deep in her gut. But she let none of this show, smiling cooly at Rollie's friend. "All you need to know is that the diversion is set. Treason bells will ring and every guard will be occupied."

Mari faltered for a moment at this news and then let out a low, soft whistle. "You don't do things by halves, do you?"

She crossed her arms and mulled it over before nodding to herself. Decision made, she pulled a small striated conch seashell out of her pocket. Mari slapped it into Elysia's palm and held her own hand over it, warm and strong. "The night of the meeting, this will tell you where to go. If it doesn't, then something has gone wrong. Be sure to bring the coin. You have no idea what you're in for, Crown girl." She grinned wickedly.

Elysia tucked the shell away safely and lifted her hood back over her head. "It's been a pleasure." *Meeting adjourned.* And with that she turned heel, plundering back down the tunnel until Rollie's voice rang out like a bell.

"Hey, Parker."

She paused, waiting.

"I hear the beast is hunting again. Be careful out in the woods."

Elysia looked back and feigned a sweeping bow as if there were a crown to take off her head just like when they were kids and thought it was the funniest thing in the world to make fun of the prince and his stupid outfits and crowns.

Beast or no beast, she would not cower at the feet of Topp Blatz.

CHAPTER 19

IT WAS the day of her first and what she hoped was her last assassination, and yet there she was in the market, ready to sell her wares as if it were any other day. She shivered both from the cold and anxious anticipation. *So many things could go wrong.* But assuming she wasn't caught and executed for treason or magic—something she was desperately trying not to think about—she'd have to pay rent just like every other month.

Because, unfortunately for her, it was highly unlikely that her landlord, Mr. Coppicus, would take kindly to her missing rent due to plans of assassinating a foreign ambassador. Mr. Coppicus cared about two things and two things only: the sound of coins in a bag and his terrible squawking birds. She often dreamed about letting Sir Larkspur loose in his flat to shut up those damn birds once and for all.

Elysia was set up in her usual spot, listening to Mrs. Branby shout about fish prices and cups of chowder while continuing to ruminate about poison and if she'd gotten the doses right. *What a strange day.* She looked up at the bleak, gray sky. The soot was worse today, falling down with the heavy mist and bleeding through her clothes until her skin would be stained. She rubbed at her arms, hating how the accumulating droplets created a cold, slick layer between her skin and the clothes that now stuck to her limbs. She jingled the coins in her pocket. At least she'd sold enough to cover rent.

The freezing mist whipped the small, pathetic tent she stood under. It was on its last leg, but buying a new one wasn't really a priority right now. Elysia watched the crowds of people milling about and clasped her chilled fingers together a little tighter. Only in Kava did the people not so much as blink when the sky rained and froze its way to the ground.

She'd sold enough to cover her bills, but one small frame remained. The violet bloom inside the diamond cut glass looked charming with the speckles of rain across the glass. Elysia considered whether it was worth staying for the possibility of one more sale. *I'm already freezing. Might as well carry on till close.*

A little extra money might be what she needed to buy a ticket out of this city if everything went to shit. *As if Father wouldn't find me.* She kicked at the sloppy ground with her boot and wondered what it would be like to leave Kava after all these years. She'd traveled with her father when she was young, but she'd never actually *seen* anything. He'd always kept her locked on the steamship or at the inn until she was needed at meetings. Had always argued it was for her own safety. All those kingdoms and cities and she'd barely seen a thing.

The thought of leaving had her eyes searching for the sea, but here in the center of Relaclave where old met the new, there was not a ship in sight. Only shops and stands, all centered around the enormous fountain in the middle of the square. Iron streetlamps lined the edges of the square, fighting to stay lit as the damp crept inside the glass. She knew the ships were there, though, past the square at the very edge of the north side. The docks and the sea waited for her there.

Lost in her thoughts, Elysia did not sense the sharp crackle in the air like that of a storm, or the earthen scent of woods creeping ever closer until there was a nose pressing against the skin of her neck and hands taking hold of her hips from behind. Hot breath stirred the damp strands of her hair, and Elysia's shoulders stiffened.

"Looks like there's something I need in the market today, after all." Topp's voice vibrated against her and she closed her eyes. She'd known she'd have to face him eventually, but she hadn't expected it to be like this. In the middle of the market, caught off guard and looking like a drowned rat. She'd wanted to be prepared. For it to be on *her* terms, not his.

Elysia barely dared move, for fear of her spiking heart giving her away. *Gods, he smells good.* Her body, traitor that it was, wanted to lean back into his touch like a damn cat arching its back.

She kept her voice cool, her words archly distant. "I would think that one such as yourself already has everything they could ever want."

He pressed his face closer, surrounding her with the warmth of his body. Tall and broad, his shoulders easily wrapped around hers. Voice rumbling into her ear and through her chest, he spoke. "Do I, Elysia?"

She fought not to squirm. Turning her face slightly, her cheek pressed against his.

"I don't know, you tell me, Prince." Her voice came out a little breathless, and she cringed. *Come on, Parker, have some gods-damned self-respect.*

"What good is being prince if I can't have the one thing I truly want? I think I'll have it no matter the price." His over-the-top words brought an unbidden smile to her lips.

But then she came back to herself, wiping her face clean. She needed to know what he was planning, not engage in whatever this nonsense was. Indignation shot through her, pushing away the previous moment's levity. He had some fucking nerve. Coming here, saying things like that, when he knew the truth about her. As if her impending death resting in his hands wasn't a serious, terrifying thing.

Elysia spun round ready to cut through his foolish words

before he was her undoing, but stopped short at the sight of his bright eyes latching onto hers, looking at her the same way he always had—intense and mischievous, as if this was all still going to be okay. Her heart stuttered. It wasn't fair of him to still look at her like that. It wasn't fair at all.

Water dappled his striking face, and she found her thumb brushing it away. A single drop right off the heart of his cheeks.

Topp watched her through wet, sticky lashes, unhurried and completely focused on her. Like he could stand there all day with her in the miserable, godsforsaken weather. She snatched her hand back, embarrassed at her own actions. *What am I doing?* Wiping her hand against her cloak as if her fingers had betrayed her, she scowled at him and moved away, claiming distance between them.

"I don't know what your aim is, but I would rather die than be your hound. Do you hear me?" Her words were a sharp hiss. She hadn't realized how true they were until she was spitting them at the prince. She was done collecting the cursed for the Crown. Her eyes grew fierce, her voice jabbing out like a sword. "I will *not* be why waves and waves of people die."

Topp became still, his eyes tracking over her as if she might spook. He spoke carefully, slowly, his hands going up placatingly. "I have no plans to harm you."

He took a step closer, but she backed away, bumping against the pole of her tent. His voice became soft. "You can trust me, Elysia, I promise."

Her body remained tense in spite of his words to reassure her. Gathering her arms tight to her body, she held herself together to his face. But inside, her fractured heart crumbled.

That was a lie.

Her magic thrashed, angry at the undercurrent of something false and oily beneath his last words. He might not have plans to harm her, but he'd confirmed what she already knew: Topp Blatz was not to be trusted.

He closed in on her, bringing them nose to nose and his mouth a breath from hers. The tent pole dug into her back, giving her nowhere to go. Hand slipping inside the pocket of her trousers, he dropped in a handful of coins, taking his time to squeeze her waist as he let go of her body. "I think I'll take it. I'd hate for anything to happen to a piece so rare as this."

She looked up at him in confusion. *What?*

He collected the last flower pressing from her collection and went about inspecting it. Like he hadn't just shredded the last straggling piece of hope within her.

Topp continued evaluating the flower pressing as if it were the most exquisite, intricate piece of art, when really it was the result of a night of too much wine and arguing with Beatriz. He looked up casually enough then, one hand shoved into a pocket, the other holding her art. There was nothing special about the movement or the look on his face. But she still watched the rivulets of rain roll down his face to his lips to the line of his throat. Frustration churned within her. It seemed no matter what he did, the mere sight of him would be enough to do her in, and yet, it wasn't romantic at all.

It was tragic.

Her body could not seem to comprehend that Topp was no longer to be trusted. That years of memories and touches did not outweigh what she knew now. He was a beautiful, honeyed trap set by the gods who hated her enough to curse her.

His lips quirked, mistaking her lingering stare for lust. His voice dropped into a lower, more intimate register. "Are you going to bolt away again? Like you always do when I get too close lately."

His words caressed her spine, causing an involuntary shudder. Green eyes looked down knowingly. "Wish you wouldn't. You know my door's always open, Parker." The look on his face turned sensual while hers went flat in annoyance and she shoved him, palms hitting his taut chest before she could think better of it.

"Hedonistic pig," she flung back, turning fast to leave. His money was as good as anyone else's, and she didn't need her ragged tent that bad, anyway. Topp laughed loudly, the sound suddenly terrible and infuriating to her ears. Jogging backward, he stayed beside her even as she marched away.

"I'll see you tonight then?"

She frowned, stopping in the middle of a swarm of people. "You never come to anything you're supposed to."

You have to be kidding me. Her internal alarms began to wail. Topp never attended her mother's societal functions. As a general rule, he couldn't be bothered unless his father forced him, or it was a proper ball with wine and gin that ended with people half naked in the bushes and frisking in dark corners like everyone couldn't see them.

Tonight was not anywhere on the scale of a Kavian ball. It was light food and drinks, maybe a few dances with boring conversations. A standard cocktail affair.

He shrugged, and a glint that she did not like appeared in his eyes. He backed away, out into the crowds. "My father has been more demanding as of late. I said I'd go, knew you'd be there, after all. There's not a reason you don't want me to go, is there, Parker?"

Elysia narrowed her eyes, knowing she couldn't say a damn thing without it sounding suspicious. She called out to his retreating frame. "I already invited the girls. I didn't expect you to come."

He didn't answer, weaving into the crowds, somehow never stumbling or losing sight of her until the throng of people swallowed him up.

Elysia threw her head back. She was already poisoning the king, why not the prince as well? *I'm so going to die.*

ELYSIA STOOD on a small wooden platform with a polite grimace plastered on her face. Attending her mother's events meant being scrutinized like a cow out for sale. Georgia Parker walked around her in a tight circle with the utmost seriousness. She fluffed a bit of Elysia's skirts and slowly brought her eyes to meet her daughter's. "You're wearing slippers with a cocktail dress?" The disdain was palpable.

Yes, Mother, because you can't run for your life in a pair of heels. But she couldn't say that. She also couldn't say that most heels were murder on her scars. So Elysia closed her eyes and asked the undead gods to give her strength. Not for the evening. Just to make it through the next minute with her mother without talking back. Grown or not, she would not put it past her mother to find some way to torture her if she so much as blinked wrong in her direction. Couldn't have her doll acting out. That would be just dreadful.

She was just about to fake an ankle injury when Daphne burst into the room with Remy a step behind.

"Ooh, Elysia," she cooed. "That dress is magnificent."

And it was. Delicate straps met a fitted bodice that acted as a corset, giving Elysia the illusion of a much more ample chest than was reality. All her training sessions with Gage had chipped away what had once been soft flesh, leaving behind only sleek muscle. But she didn't mind. She liked her toned arms and firm thighs she had earned from hours of weights and sparring. The tulle skirt fell in straight, opaque sheaths down to her ankles, giving glimpses of leg as she moved. And with her hair piled atop her head in a smooth bun, she could have easily passed for one of her favorite dancers. Lithe, deceptively strong, and ready to perform on the stage that was a Relaclave party. She'd chosen a stunning midnight blue that matched the sweeping waters of the Valvere Sea not only for the color but because it obscured the dagger strapped to her thigh.

Remy strolled up beside her, making a show of looking Elysia up and down before plucking a gin fizz off a serving tray.

"Sexy ballerina looking for her prince," she declared.

Elysia laughed. Biased but heartfelt, she grinned at Remy's comment. Spinning on her toes to face them, she kept her face aglow with excitement, pretending tonight was like any other where they would drink too much and cackle in the corner. She leaned forward, resting an arm around each woman's neck and hopping off the platform.

"If it isn't the most *brilliant* and *dashing* women in all of Kava here to be my dates." She gave them a quick squeeze before letting go.

Daphne took a bow, blonde hair falling over her shoulder. "At your service, madam." She straightened, a devious look coming into her pale, aqua eyes. "My vagina is going to turn to dust if I don't find some dick tonight. I need someone rich and ready to ravish me."

Remy choked, hacking on her gin fizz. She took another drink, soothing her cough. "Gods, Daph, I know it's been a while, but *wow*. I don't think I've ever heard you say vagina *or* dick before."

Daphne nodded seriously. "Dire times."

Elysia's mother sighed and dropped the edge of the tulle skirt she had been holding. Even she knew her complaints would not be heard over the noise of three alcohol-fueled women. Georgia glided on staggering heels to the door, calling over her shoulder, "Five minutes, ladies."

A resounding "yes, ma'am" chirped in her direction, causing Georgia to smile lightly as she exited. Elysia could practically hear the thoughts in her mother's head. How much it satisfied her to have all her chicks coiffed and in perfect formation. Her mother did love when the guests were as beautiful as her parties.

The door snicked shut and Remy and Daphne immediately closed in on Elysia, shoving more highball glasses around until there was not a single empty hand. Events like these were not meant to be done sober. They were only tolerable with a very specific amount of alcohol in your blood combined with the irreverent commentary of your best friends.

That being said, Elysia eyed the gin bottle in Daphne's right fist and cringed inside at the thought of all that liquor coming back up later. She pretended to sip her own glass while Daphne rattled off about the new tailor she'd found in the south end of the city. She was convinced this up-and-coming seamstress was being gouged by false taxes. And no one was more motivated than Daphne when there was a convenient injustice that suited her interests. Remy listened attentively though, her eyes completely zoned into Daphne's dramatic re-enactment, nodding and humming in all the right places. She promised to give the woman a consultation soon, leaving Daphne flushed and victorious. A true beacon for social justice and tailors everywhere.

Elysia stood there soaking in the familiar dynamics, her body relaxing in their presence. She really wished she hadn't invited them. It wasn't like she could spare them from the poison's path, but she was confident that all the guests would be well by morning—except for one.

The avoidant creature that lived beneath her skin beseeched her to crush the poison she carried between her breasts underfoot. To call the whole thing off and down gin fizzes until she was dizzy with false delight. She would laugh and tumble and dance in a whirl with Topp's arms around her, ending the night tangled in his bed as she had so many nights before.

The vial of *just in case* poison rolled against her skin as she moved. A cold, silent reminder of her task.

"Are you ready, Elysia?" Daphne and Remy, ever the gallant escorts, each held out an arm. Unaware of what was to come and half drunk, their smiles lit all the way to their eyes.

"Ready." Hooking her arms through theirs, they set off to meet the night.

The double doors swung wide, giving a sweeping view of the Golden Seal's latest feat. Dazzling light washed the dance floor. Labradorite swirls in the floor sparkled as those same chandelier lights hit them just right. And swashes of dark gauze fell from the sky. The fabric twisted and tied just so, to create miniature alcoves meant only for two. On any other night, Elysia would have floated between those gauzy nests, collecting secrets like helpless insects in a spider's web. But not tonight.

Her father's threats played in her mind as they took the final steps to the grand staircase where they would make their entrance. All those women who looked like her. Syren, dead and useless while she was still alive. Syren healed people. What did she do? *Exploit and kill.* She was no better than the man who raised her. Like most people, she had sworn to herself that she would never be like her parents. But it seemed no matter how hard she tried, she came up short in that regard. A numb, dead sort of feeling enveloped her heart, staving off the shame that stuck to her always. The staircase loomed, only steps away. There wasn't time for those types of thoughts right now.

But her brain persisted, shoving the image of Topp dripping wet in the market, his full lips spewing false promises of trust to the front of her mind. The image mocked her. *He knows and yet he still underestimates me.* Maybe he didn't understand the entirety of her magic—but she thought it bold to lie to her face when he had likely put together what she could do.

They stopped beside the carpeted stairs, and her stomach twisted into knots. She stared down at the mass of courtiers and politicians below. All resplendent in their silk and tails and top hats. None expecting to be poisoned. Innocent people about to be dragged into her mess.

The world wanted her to be gentle and quiet.

Pliable with her eyes wide shut.

Moldable to their every whim without thought or complaint.

And she had been. For so long.

Desperate to be the good girl who met their ever moving expectations. Desperate to wash the filth of her curse off her skin and be marked clean with a crown she didn't even want. She knew now that she was never going to fit inside their boxes.

But what they hadn't realized was that they created a court-trained nightmare instead of a pet. Docile and fragile to the eye with endless pits of rage below. Rage that could see no beginning or end. She was only just beginning to understand it herself. She had never wanted to be this person. But she would be. Because you don't get to choose the hand you're given, you only get to choose what you do with it. And she was done being a compliant, perfect doll.

Her feet ached in her slippers. Sliced in crisscrosses, and long curving scores, reminding her of what happened to women who stepped out of line. It didn't matter, though. She had always been outside the lines. Now she was just living like it.

Elysia stepped back, allowing Remy and Daphne to go before her. Each woman held the room captive with their own specific magnetism as they entered. Remy smoldering and sauntering down like a dark flame wrapped in umber silk. Her tight dark curls were free tonight, springing out to create a perfect halo around her head. Daphne glowing as if she were the first true day of winter, so bright that she just might blind you. And Elysia, feeling the heady weight of every eye in the room, lifted her chin as if she were already their queen. Topp, the one who could make it so, stared boldly back at her as if he could see right through her to her very core. Past the mask and into the depths of emotion eddying within.

She held his cutting gaze until one of Remy's ever present suitors paraded in front of them, blocking her view. The rest of the world seemed to rush back in around her, the music and sounds of the night boisterous in her ear. *Oh, Barry.* Elysia almost rolled her eyes. Poor man.

Barnett Vollen, Barry to his friends, was determined to impress the immoveable Remy. His father was responsible for building the majority of the south side of Relaclave, and he was set to inherit the budding construction empire. All those flats stacked on top of one another lined his pockets well. But Barry dreamed of more. Like having the lush vision before him throw in her considerable business savvy and political weight to his ambitions.

But unfortunately for him, magic would be reborn in Kava

before Remy Wincraft truly gave her heart away. Unlike the majority of women in Kava, Remelda Wincraft had plenty of her own money and had no need to marry, no matter how much her parents pushed for a match. She might play along with the man's affections—accepting gifts and extravagant dates—but it would take a force to knock Remy off her feet. And Barnett Vollen was barely a breeze.

Elysia used the distraction to scan the room, her nerves beginning to creep in to the beat of a slow march. Her eyes went to the towering pyramid of empty glasses, all waiting for gin or wine. All thinly coated with poison. Just a dash of liquid and the poison would activate. In less than sixty minutes, bodies would be writhing. The swarms of people would drop one by one like flies, contorting as the toxin overtook their systems.

She continued to scan the room, but still not did not see Scarzan damning any conversations with his presence. *Come out, come out.* Anxiety crashed within her now. She just wanted this over. He would be here, though. She knew he would.

Offering a coy wink to Remy, she clasped arms with Daphne. "Let's do a lap, shall we?"

She was fairly certain Remy was burning holes into the back of her head, now stuck with boring Barry, but her body needed the false security of movement. Arm in arm, they skirted the room, swishing past where their parents mingled near the king and the diplomats. Tipsy laughter filled the air and even the king looked to be having a good time. And yet, Scarzan was still nowhere to be seen.

The rat was hiding somewhere. She just had to find him.

Elysia swiveled, thinking to grab some of the delicious smoked meat she was smelling and scout out the buffet corner of the room. Might as well eat something before everything went sideways.

Daphne leaned in close as they walked, her words soft enough for only Elysia's ears. "Who in the realms is that woman?"

Elysia craned her neck, searching for the source of Daphne's awe. She barely kept the smirk off her face. It was not Kava's best courtesan drawing every stare in the room, but instead her sister's beloved bewitching them all in a curve-hugging crimson number. Hair freshly lightened, it rippled down her back. Dark lashes and a nude glossed mouth. Beatriz would have been drooling.

The Doorman rarely made appearances at court events, but when she did, rumors and whispers broke free like an avalanche in her wake. Her hips moved like water, as if she knew she could ensnare any soul she sought. But tonight, she had only one victim in mind.

The Doorman lifted two gin and tonics off a passing tray and made a sharp, determined line for one of the half-lit alcoves littered about, not so much as bothering to make eye contact with anyone as she passed. Elysia's chest heaved in relief. She must have spotted Scarzan for her to move like that.

She brought her lips back to Daphne's ear, her blonde hair tickling her nose. "That woman is the Doorman of House Gardenia."

Daphne blinked as though in a daze. She turned wide eyes to Elysia, her voice lifting with a note of befuddled surprise. "I am not sure if I want to *be* her or sleep with her. I think either option might be fine, actually."

Elysia snorted, steering them closer to where the Doorman had disappeared only seconds before. Her trust in the Doorman only stretched so far—she wanted to see his throat bob with each poisonous swallow of his drink, to hear the revolting gurgle as he swallowed, and be confident that the Doorman had blessed him with an extra dose. Her fingers twitched. She needed to see the signal. The coy wink that would tell her death was brewing in his entrails. *Then* she could make a swift exit. And be on her way to the rendezvous that actually mattered.

She paused a few steps away from where they hid, straining to hear their quiet voices, when a loud crack that sounded an awful lot like a hand meeting flesh echoed within the folds of the dark gauzy hollow. A breath later, the Doorman exited with blotches of pink high on her cheeks. Her face carved into a guise of serenity, yet her fingers trembled. Regardless of the face she wore, fury coated the air she left behind. And the signal was never given.

Elysia swore beneath her breath. Waiting, hoping the Doorman would turn any moment now and relieve her fears.

But the Doorman began to converse with other guests, never so much as blinking in Elysia's direction. What had gone wrong that a woman as well-trained as the Doorman had broken form? Surely, there was no way the man had not taken so much as a drink yet this evening—it was a party, after all. But she didn't need him sick. She needed him dead.

Elysia turned to Daphne with a wicked grin. "Would you like to meet her?"

"You *know* her?"

"You could say we have people in common," Elysia responded absently, her eyes still darting around the room as if Scarzan might fall dead of his own accord. She had perhaps thirty minutes now before guests began to crawl like maggots in the heat of summer. Her stomach twisted violently. She could practically feel an ulcer forming. Dead or not, she would have to bail at that point. But she had a debt to pay. And in spite of what the Doorman assumed, Elysia did feel horrible that some poor woman had borne the brunt of Scarzan's misdirected anger. Anger meant for her because she had slipped through his hands. She knew men like him. And she had known someone would feel his wrath. Her pulse settled as she remembered exactly why this man had to die.

Jack Parker's booming voice interrupted her thoughts, echoing over the music and all the others in the room. Her shoulders automatically rose at the sound. A protective, instinctive response. She stared at her father's broad back, hate coiling up like a serpent within her. Yes, she would do something worthwhile before this all fell apart.

Elysia guided Daphne to the Doorman, pushing through the growing crowd of gossip hungry onlookers surrounding her. The Doorman sent them all away with a flick of her wrist. No hello or niceties, she launched into conversation as if Elysia had been beside her the whole time. "Your mother's parties really are impressive considering everyone has their clothes on."

She turned her attention to Daphne, not waiting for a response, her eyes glittering. "And who is this you bring me?"

"Daphne Rieer," Elysia announced. "Meet the much esteemed Doorman of House Gardenia."

A charmed smile slipped onto Daphne's face. "I should have known the Doorman is a woman. Only a woman could run such a successful House of pleasure. And yes, the Golden Seal rarely disappoints."

A smile that Elysia could have sworn was real warmed the Doorman's sharp eyes. She wound an arm through Daphne's. "Help me to endure this evening of endless chatter, and perhaps a small token of my appreciation will land on your door."

Daphne let out a low laugh. "Oh, we'll need more drinks for that. Come on then. I'll show you how us Crown girls get by."

The Doorman called over her shoulder as Daphne whisked her away. "Elysia, there's a friend who would love to see you. He's waiting in the back."

A volcano of aggravation erupted within Elysia. The world's most simple, foolproof plan was coming down around her ears. All they had to do was get the swaggering, drunken baboon of a man to have a single drink, and yet here they were fumbling the entire plan.

She rolled her shoulders back. Never mind the plan. She would do it her damn self. Swinging around, she scored fresh drinks from a familiar face. Gage's man opened his fist. "Stones for your drinks, miss?" Soaked in an extra dose, it would have been the smart choice, but Elysia waved him off with a determined smile. Sometimes it was better to do things the old-fashioned way.

Drinks balanced in one hand, she ducked into the dimly lit alcove, and found Scarzan splayed back on an oversized pillow, puffing on a noxious cigar. He might have stolen her father's favorite apothecary, but he clearly did not have her father's taste. The fumes were downright disgusting. She sidled in closer, ignoring the smell. Nothing mattered but liquor sliding down that man's throat. Scarzan's dark eyes latched onto her, something smug and certain filling them.

She pretended to stumble, her free hand dosing out the spare poison before grasping at the tented fabric. The Doorman may have failed, but she would not. She gathered herself with a loose, drunken giggle. "Oh, I am so sorry. I do believe I've entered the wrong little tent."

She giggled again and turned to leave, wobbling on uneven feet.

Sweaty fingers gripped her bare upper arm, bringing her steps to a sudden jerking halt. "I was starting to think you'd forgotten about me and our date."

He shooed away the man and woman who he had been smoking with, still clinging to her arm to the point that it hurt. She took a small step closer, a confused smile lighting her face. "I am not sure I recall an invitation for such a pleasure, sir."

Elysia stared at the oily wrinkles lining his face and racked her brains. *A date?* She had no idea what this foul man could possibly be referring to right now. She offered her only thought. "Are you meaning when I told you I would be at this party?"

Scarzan continued puffing on the cigar. "No, no. We had a far more legitimate deal than a passing query." He blew a talentless cloud of smoke into her face, causing her to flinch back as far as his grip would allow, eyes watering.

For one single moment, her mind went completely still. Frozen as it tried to comprehend his meaning. *No.* Her own flesh and blood had not recognized her. Topp had only known because he had suspected her and followed her to the House. It simply was *not* possible that this despicable daughter-selling fiend could have had the perceptiveness to notice who had been sitting two chairs down from him at House Gardenia.

A broken laugh fell from her lips. It sounded like shattering glass. "I do think I would remember cutting a deal with a man like you. Would you like a drink, Diplomat Scarzan?"

He plucked a drink from the palm of her hand and held it from his fingertips. His mouth twisted in condescension. "That farce of a woman tried to come in here before as if I wouldn't have known that she must have helped you escape that night. I reminded her that not even the House can break its own rules without consequence."

A small oil lantern swung silently, casting both light and shadows upon them both. Scarzan took the barest sip of his drink before setting it down. Reaching into his jacket for another cigar, he patted around only to be disappointed. His other hand was still locked onto her upper arm as if she might bolt and not look back. He forgot his fruitless search, and a threat formed in his eyes. His voice dropped dangerously. "And I am more than happy to be the man who delivers the justice owed."

"You dare speak of consequences and *justice*." She bit out the sour words, the pit in her stomach already knowing where this was leading.

He nodded slowly, not hearing a word Elysia said as his gaze slid over her breasts. His damp hand stuck to her, tugging and pulling at her skin as it ran down her arm. Clamping down on her wrist, he yanked her closer. Flat eyes shackled her own, his face near enough that she could smell the rotting smoke of his breath. "That whore didn't have to die. But it was only fair, wasn't it? My prize running away into the night like that."

Disgust broke her indifferent facade into a tight sneer, but it was that damnable rage rampaging through her blood that was going to get her in trouble. It was no wonder the Doorman had not lasted more than a minute in his presence. Eyes burning, she forced her face and voice to return to even.

"And what is it you're hoping for now?" Unable to lock down her fury entirely, it came out half hissed, a venomous snake ready to strike. Clearing her throat, she fought for some semblance of poise. Chin lifted, she continued, "I would remind you that I am all but engaged to the prince, and my father already despises you." A slight edge of warning strengthened her words.

Wrenching her arm free, she gave him a close-lipped smile that her mother would have been proud of—a wordless *get fucked*. Anger poured out like a torrent of heat through her, but she knew better than to be rash. She'd grown up in this court, she could best this man without making a scene. As much as she wanted to whip out her dagger and stab him in the eye, she couldn't.

The party careened around them, frivolity and excess a blur outside of their gauzy tent. Music meant for dancing was a distant sound in her ear. She could barely hear it, though, barely see anything but him.

The clock was ticking and his drink remained full. *Drink it, you asshole, just drink it.* She swirled her own cocktail, gazing over the rim of her glass to find a grotesque, unashamed want on his face. Mission still unfinished, she carried on with the conversation. "Name your price because you know it's not going to be me."

Scarzan leaned back on the pillow, laughing at her fight. He shook his head and switched his drink to his other hand. "You know, you remind me of my daughter with a mouth like that. And look what happened to her."

He took another tiny, useless sip.

"I remember you always pouting around your father's legs all those years ago. And look at you now. *Ripe and ready.*" He grabbed the center of her corset, ripping her into his body. The force of it had her stumbling, hands grasping and reaching to no avail. Bent in half, her chest heaved. Soft wisps of hair tickled her cheek, broken free from her perfect ballerina bun.

His voice was hot and jarring against her ear. "I will *relish* telling your father just how I've ruined you and you will do nothing because *this* is what you deserve."

Her stomach rolled, a sick clammy feeling washing over her.

To her dismay, all her anger fled, leaving her bare and weak, his hand still shoved half inside her corset, up against her breasts. Her mind spun, wheeling through every possible move she could make. The smartest was to quiver and quake. Men like him lived for humiliation. It was intoxicating. A drug that would leave him open to mistakes.

Yes, he would like that. Seeing her crumpled and small.

She let her shoulders curl and eyes grow enormous with fear.

"You cannot sir, you would not..." Voice shaking, she cowered.

His eyes dilated, her fear an aphrodisiac. But then he went off script. Expecting her to go limp and compliant in his arms, his hands forced themselves beneath her skirts. One taking hold of her ass, the other plunging beneath thin lace, scraping against the softest skin. The feeling of his fingers, his *nails* pulled her from the glacial, immoveable depths of fear holding her body captive and plunged her back into the flames of wrath.

And with that, several things happened all at once.

The most important of which was Elysia Parker exploding through her porcelain mask. Shards and fragments of the doll she had been flew like shrapnel through the air. Composure broken, she found a vicious, vengeance-bent version of herself waiting to emerge. The Crown-welded collar and leash lay demolished, brittle pieces scattered on the floor.

Chains gone, something ancient came to life within her, lips snarling, teeth bared. She wished she had claws to rip through sinew and skin. Without claws or fangs, she was left with her hands. Hands that had struck Kava's Shadow a thousand times. Elysia drove her fist up and into Scarzan's gut, dark victory urging her on when his mouth gaped at the impact. Hands gripping his shoulders, her knee was a battering ram between his legs. He toppled sideways on the lounge pillow, denting it as he fell.

Mouth agape, still choking for air, his dark eyes were wild, but she didn't care. Her manicured fingers grabbed his jaw, nails digging in like half moon knives. She could barely feel his skin, or the throbbing frenzy of his pulse. Her eyes were on his mouth, jaw pried wide by her hands. She didn't care if he bit her fingers clean off.

She grabbed his drink and then hers, holding his head back as she poured them straight down his throat. Tears streamed down his face, gin spraying as he choked and spluttered. But she slammed his mouth shut, his teeth cracking loudly. Dropping the glass, she plugged his nose, refusing to let go even as he failed like a flaccid worm.

"Swallow it," she demanded. She sounded like a demon.

But he complied, and a hot rush flooded through her. She'd done it. He'd drunk the damn poison. He would be—

"The number of times I've imagined divesting every last drop of air from that man's body." Topp's voice was a strained rasp. But he only shook his head wistfully, like he wished it could have been him to poison the bastard. Deft hands closed the gauzy curtains, blocking any curious eyes.

"And here you are, my sweet little liar, fulfilling my every unspoken bedroom dream." He paused as if in question, his deep voice rumbling. "This *is* foreplay, isn't it?" A dark grin spilled in her direction.

Elysia's hands fell immediately to her sides. As if that would hide what she had done. Like he hadn't just seen her in a reverie of rage, assaulting a foreign diplomat. Trepidation prickled up her spine, and she eyed Topp warily.

She never knew what he was going to do. He was becoming more and more unpredictable. And it was a problem. Her heart rate calmed, though. Sounds of the party slowly returned, instead of the noiseless static that had overcome her.

She faced Topp, giving her back to Scarzan, who was still a coughing mess. There was no hiding what she'd done. He'd walked in on her forcing the undead gods knew what down a man of political power's throat. And that same man would be dead within minutes, the rest of the party taking ill soon after. It wouldn't take a genius to solve that mystery. She squeezed her hands into fists. *I need to get out of here.*

Sometimes the truth was more powerful than any lie.

"He attacked me. Tried to, tried to—" Her voice failed, arms automatically wrapping her body like a shield.

The irreverent flirtation cleared from Topp's face, his understanding quick even with her few words. He was familiar with Scarzan and his transgressions.

Hands flexing, his eyes grew electric amidst the soft dark of the gauzy tent. Suddenly he looked bigger than he was—but it wasn't the thick muscles under his dark olive shirt, or the width or height of him. It was the feeling of a storm crashing against your window at three in the morning, violent and ready to break through the glass. The feeling grew until it felt like rain and lightning might burst from above. "You *touched* her?"

The prince took a single step. A saunter almost. Confident and unrepentant of what he was about to do.

But Scarzan was already moving, having taken advantage of their brief distraction. Bloated hands wrapped around Elysia's throat, his thumbs crushing into her windpipe.

Poison-laced spittle sprayed onto Elysia's face with each of Scarzan's words. "You fucking cunt."

His fingers squeezed tighter, lifting Elysia clear off her feet. Panic surged like a tidal wave as she lost her breath. The woman he'd murdered at the House flashed through her mind. She'd been found bruised and mottled, her neck the broken stem of a bloodied rose.

Elysia's vision grew fuzzy, Scarzan's face going in and out. Her head snapped to and fro like a rag doll. But Gage's fierce bark shouted at her like a lifeline.

How do you break the hold? Elysia, show me you know how to break the hold!

Her eyes flung open, Gage's words ringing in her mind. Gritting down, she gathered the last of her energy and thrust both hands up. Scarzan swore roughly, his wrists breaking away from her neck.

And Topp was right there not even a second behind, plowing

into him, taking the canopy down as they hit the floor. Layers and layers of gauze fell around them. A shroud of death, fanning out around the two men like a dark corona.

No one noticed the nimbus of death, though. Not when Topp's hands were busy breaking the marble floor with the back of Scarzan's head. One large hand over the rat's face, he pounded it down.

Over and over and over.

The muscles in his back shortening, then lengthening as his shoulder came down hard and fast. It was rhythmic. Blood pooling and spraying out in flecks. Scarzan's eyes had long since gone blank, the light snuffed out within them. But Topp persisted. Like he couldn't stop.

Staring down, transfixed, Elysia knew she should be running, but her limbs were numb, her brain buzzing silently.

Around them, the party came to an abrupt halt. People scattered, avoiding the fallout while craning their necks.

The music cut with an ear-piercing shriek of a violin. Waiters toppled into guests, trays soaring into the air and drinks falling down like rain. Eyes wide, people couldn't look away from the heir to the Kavian throne—on his knees, bloodied and violent like an animal in the woods.

Court ladies screamed as if they hadn't seen hundreds of people swing, hundreds of necks severed in the main square. But somewhere across the room, far from being a lady of the court, the Doorman grinned.

He might not have ended up dead on the beach with the House's crest branded onto his skin, but his life debt leaked across the floor in a scarlet river and that was good enough. Elysia finally looked up from the massacre to see the Doorman holding up a glass in cheers, then disappearing out the door.

Seconds later, guards rushed to the scene. Shoving through the crowds, the king and her father fought their way to the front. She could hear them shouting for people to move.

Grabbing the back of Topp's shirt, the king heaved, tearing

his son off the diplomat and tossing him aside. The tangled canopy was left behind, a veil over Scarzan's body. Topp grunted, landing hard on his side. He shoved back up to his feet, anger still hardening his jaw.

Bits of gossamer fabric floated down in tiny shreds, several more of the gauzy tents destroyed in the chaos. Elysia watched it fall, sticking to people and the floor like confetti. *It looks like the soot.*

She jolted, feeling her father's large, warm hand settle on the back of her neck like a vise. Her eyes darted to Topp, a few feet away, shaking out his bloodied hands.

A dark storm of anger still vibrated out of him. And then there was Scarzan, motionless upon the beautiful marble and labradorite floors. Sprayed with blood, it wasn't his face that was the horror. It was the back of his skull. Caved in with bone and brain matter smashed onto the floor.

Her eyes went back to Topp. Everyone had masks. Roles they had to play. Characters to get them by. But *this*, this felt like his mask had cracked open tonight as well, revealing an ugly, but honest shade of him. He wasn't wearing a crown tonight. He rarely did. She wondered if it was because he knew it didn't fit. That *he* didn't fit.

Whatever his plans were, the man who had been her friend, her lover—that was who had just stepped up like a tempest made flesh.

The king's voice rang out with a quiet anger, silencing the whispers in the room. "Both of you, follow me." There was no question of who he was speaking to—everyone's face swiveled to her and Topp like they were on a stage. He strode for the door, muttering beneath his breath. "And someone, call the fucking medics."

Elysia swallowed. She didn't think the medics were going to be able to fix *that*. If he wasn't dead, then poison would finish the job. But she trailed after Topp, her father only a step from her heels. She could feel all the eyes in the room as they left—could feel the whirlwind of rumors being birthed, ready to race out into the night, far beyond these doors.

Let them whisper about a prince who would kill for his woman. It was a luscious tale even if it did end with brains on the floor. One that would have everyone forgetting the weight of a Bellian politician dead at the Golden Seal's farewell party. Hearing the clucking gasps as she exited, Elysia knew this was one story that would travel far and wide. Everyone loved a romance. Especially one with death and betrayal.

As the doors closed, she heard her mother's voice, light as air, drawing everyone's attention to a tower of imported effervescent wine. Maybe it was the lack of oxygen and then watching a man die, but Elysia laughed. One short, dark chuckle. Her mother was high if she thought a bit of sparkling wine could distract from a dead diplomat with his skull bashed in. Topp looked over his shoulder with a smirk, like he knew exactly what she was thinking.

The king flung open the door to a room that Elysia guessed belonged to a cartographer. Maps were strewn about, along with pencils and small sharp measuring tools. They all filed into the room, her father and the king taking up similar stances with their feet wide and arms crossed. She was used to her father intimidating her. But she would be safe for now.

It was their little secret that he loathed her more than he ever loved her. That he couldn't help himself from punishing her. With the king two feet away, he wouldn't lift a finger.

And Garrison had always been the picture of a patient father. Most kings would have forced Topp's hand by now. Late twenties, it was more than time for him to begin taking over the day-to-day duties of the Crown. But Garrison always seemed to trust that Topp would rise to the occasion, never doubting his capacity to one day rule in his stead.

But tonight they'd murdered a man. In front of the entire court. Maybe Topp had finally found his father's limit.

King Garrison stood tensely. His fingers pinching the bridge of his nose and eyes squeezed shut. The tone of his voice recommended that Topp consider his reply very, very carefully. "*Explain.*"

Topp met his father's eyes, green to gray, his expression slightly bored. As if he'd asked him about a game of rocks and not the brutal death he'd delivered five doors down.

His mouth went flat, expression shifting to one that said the answer should be obvious to anyone with a functioning brain. Shoving his hands into his pockets, he immediately took one out and ran it through wood-brown hair before finally answering.

"You know how Scarzan is. Always leaving a trail of mangled women in every city he visits." He pinned his father with a look, daring the king to contradict him.

In spite of the bold statement, his tone was dry and matter of fact. It was the voice of someone who'd experienced a lifetime of people always believing him—why wouldn't they now?

His father stared at him, impatient and wanting more of an explanation than that.

Topp leaned back against a map-covered desk, kicking his legs out and crossing one ankle over the other. He was the image of a prince, unbothered and completely unrepentant. He took his time to answer, his words slow and thoughtful.

"I went looking for Elysia, and when I found her, Scarzan had his hands wrapped around her throat." Topp looked at her briefly, his face giving away his uncertainty of whether he should say the rest of what had happened. His voice went gruff. "That wasn't all he tried to do."

He looked both of their fathers in the eyes, ensuring they felt the weight of his words. Gooseflesh covered Elysia's arms as the air in the room grew charged. Topp's hands gripped the desk, shoulders turning in as he spoke. There was a low, hard quality to his voice that gave no room for rebuttals.

"He would have killed her. You might not have given a shit about what he did at the House, but you're out of your fucking minds if you think I was going to stand there as he turned Elysia's neck black and blue. Fuck *diplomacy.* I am the *Crown* and you do not *touch* what is the Crown's. Or are we rolling over now and letting scum like that do what they want while in our kingdom?" His words ended in a near growl, his eyes searing into them.

Elysia stared, startled at the depth of emotion behind his speech. He was claiming her, protecting her—but why? What was the point? She was living on borrowed time. Time she was borrowing from him and her father, both.

It made her want to reach for his secrets, but she didn't dare. Her curse had already given her a gift in letting her know that he couldn't be trusted. Trying to read him any further was pointless.

Not that she could read him with any skill, anyway. Her magic was temperamental, untrained and acting according to its own will half the time. She was better than she used to be, but in a kingdom where magic was dead, her gift was erratic at best, showing up and giving out at the most inopportune times.

If she could go back in time, she should have tried to read him long ago, but she hadn't known then what was coming. She'd had no idea that she would stand here, shocked at his support and wondering about his motives and plans. It might make her naive, stupid even, but she had wanted their love to be real so badly she had left his secrets untouched. Sentimental and foolish, she had always left the business of anyone important to her alone the best she could.

She might go digging through everyone else's trash, but then there were the few people she illogically and deeply wanted to be able to trust. It had always felt like a line. Invisible, but solid. And crossing it would have meant admitting there wasn't a single person in her life who was safe.

Her father shook her, snapping her attention to him. His large palms swallowed her shoulders, grip tight and angry. His always loud voice felt like it was too much in this room, crashing over her, causing her to shrink and close her eyes.

Eyes closed, she didn't see it coming. His hand cracked against the side of her face like he could shatter it. Before she could absorb the blow, he was grabbing the back of her already sore neck. Yanking her head back, pulling strands of hair as he did. His voice was a barely contained bellow. "Look at me when I'm speaking to you."

Lashes wet with pain, her spine arched unnaturally, arms clamoring to take hold of something, anything, so she didn't collapse. She stared back at her father, embarrassment flooding her. He'd never done this in front of anyone before. She didn't want Topp to see her like this, to know this part of her—weak, useless, afraid. She could see him in the corner of her eye, moving and instantly being held back by his father.

Voice lowering, her father's tone was scathing. "Alone with Scarzan? Are you not any better than a stupid whore? Did I not raise you in every meeting and every court function I possibly could, so that you would know exactly who and what you would be dealing with?" Tears ran freely now, the room narrowing to only her and him. A dull, heavy throb pulsed in her ears.

Her father released her, throwing her down to the ground. Twisting, her knees and hips hit the cold floor hard, pain ricocheting through her bones. She pulled herself up, knees folded and hands pressed to the floor. Eyes glassy, she looked up at him, fighting for even a scrap of defiance, but much like her pride, it was nowhere to be found.

Jack gripped the door, and the wood groaned. "Do you really think anyone will still respect you now? I thought you were smarter than this." A muscle in his temple jumped. His disgust was palpable, but she didn't look away.

And then he was gone.

Elysia remained a statue on the floor. It shouldn't hurt. After all these years, she should be impervious to the pain. But his words found every weak spot and chink in her armor, seeping in through the spots made thin from years of abuse. The prince and the king were still there, but she wasn't listening.

He didn't even ask. The thought looped. He didn't ask what happened. He didn't ask if she was okay. Because it didn't matter —*she* didn't matter.

He hadn't balked at the bruises forming on her neck. He had given her new ones, a matching set. A nasty voice that sounded like the truth reminded her of what she had done. Going to the House. Getting lost in her curse and betting herself off. *This is my fault.* The tulle of her dress scratched at her skin. And she couldn't forget all the lives she'd taken. How high was that number now? *This really is what I deserve.*

Gentle fingers brushed over her hair, coming to rest silently against her head. The side of him pressed up against her, and her own hand wound around his ankle, latching onto him without thinking. His thumb stroked against her hair, but Topp's gaze was on his father.

The king looked tired. It was easy to forget he was getting older, but right now it showed. He looked like a man who knew his age and was suddenly afraid his heir wasn't up to the task. That his legacy would die when he did. His eyes flicked to Elysia, shaken and small on the floor, then to Topp beside her.

His eyes were distant in thought. "You're a grown man. If you say you were defending the girl, then that is the story we will tell. Scarzan's reputation precedes him. It was only a matter of time before something like this happened. The Bellians will only be angry that they didn't get to serve justice themselves."

And just like that, Topp's word was enough to fend off what could have been a political nightmare. Dimly, Elysia thought that must be nice, to have that kind of power.

Crisis averted, Garrison drew himself up to his full height, seeming to shake off the moment of bleak prescience. He walked to the door, pausing before he left. His hand made a soft slap against the stone wall and he looked at Topp, his eyes never straying back to Elysia. "Make sure the medics take a look at her neck."

He had one foot out the door when the screaming began.

CHAPTER 20

Screams, shouts, curses.

They all echoed with a vengeance out of the ballroom and into the halls. In the distance, the Relaclave city bell began ringing. Three heavy pulls on the rope, the hammer of the bell swinging in response. One long pause, then three more deafening peals laying waste to the security of the Crown.

Elysia scrambled to her feet, the tulle of her dress ripping in the process. She could feel the vibration of stampeding feet out in the hallway—likely the guards rushing to find the king. *Time for me to go.*

There was only one reason this specific bell pattern was ever engaged. It wasn't the mellow noontime chime that happened daily or the merry ring of celebration. It was sharp and deliberate, meant to catch every ear and turn every face to the castle.

Treason was afoot within the city. The Crown was under attack.

Within minutes, the entrances to the castle would be sealed, and no one would be exiting or entering.

Garrison pulled out a long, thin dagger from inside his black and red jacket. He looked down the hall into the eye of the hurricane, then back to Topp. "Do something with her. Her head's not on right and we don't need her getting trampled. Then find me."

The sound of groans and retching overtook the screams. Elysia grimaced, knowing the worst was yet to come. Mouth set in determination, the king walked out the door, when suddenly he clutched his own stomach, his back rounding as he let out a throaty grunt. A look of confusion marred his face. But there wasn't time for questions, not when the treason bells were ringing. Straightening, he barreled down the hall and out of sight.

That's my cue. But before she could cut away, Topp grabbed hold of her elbow, not bothering to look back as he broke into a run, pulling her along. Her feet complied given her choice was to either run or be dragged behind him. She stumbled, glancing over shoulder, cringing at the sound of bile splattering and pained cries echoing.

Topp's grip tightened, his voice hard. "*Move*, Elysia."

Guards pounded past, sweaty and red, forcing him to shove through like they were going upstream. Elysia yanked against Topp's hold, but his grip was a manacle. He shot her an annoyed look.

"Knock it off, will you?" His eyes were distracted, though, searching the surge of oncoming men.

One hand on her, his other snapped out, grasping a guard by the collar of his shirt. The man lurched back, his momentum cut short by Topp's hold. The prince dragged them both now, barking out an order to the man.

"You're with me, Lewis. Now keep up."

The guard changed course without a blink, taking up the rear and watching their backs.

A quick glance told her it was one of Topp's usual guards, one of the few he allowed near his rooms and even sometimes had a drink with in Relaclave. Frustration scrunched her face. The doors were being sealed, and it looked like she was about to be stuck with a babysitter. *Great.*

Elysia huffed, lungs burning and feeling cross from the unexpected exertion. She considered herself reasonably fit, but sprinting up several flights of stairs into the turret where Topp lived would knock the air out of anyone. Unless your name was Topp, of course. The man didn't appear winded in the slightest. *Ridiculous.*

Elysia leaned against the cool wall, panting. She hated these stairs. Stone and unforgiving, only a masochist would make you run up them. Topp ignored her heavy breathing, his eyes darting around like whoever had poisoned the court might appear out of thin air.

Shoving a key into the door for his rooms, he unlocked it. Arm suddenly wrapped around her waist, he herded her inside in front of him. Snarling one last order, he followed her in. "Lewis, man the door."

And with that, he slammed the door shut. Lights flicked on, a soft hum filled the room as they warmed.

His fingers, still covered in a dead man's blood, were on her neck in an instant, gentle and efficient as he examined her. He stepped back, seemingly satisfied.

"Stay. Here." He bit the words off, giving her a look before spinning around to leave.

Elysia stared at his back in bewilderment. The words were out before she could stop them.

"Excuse me?"

Topp stopped, his olive shirt rippling like water against his back as he breathed. Turning, his eyes latched onto hers, body taut like a bowstring. Her heart stilled. She had thought it a trick of the light earlier, but his green eyes were practically aglow in the evening light. She swallowed but did not move.

His voice was the sound of an animal pushed past their patience. "Tell me, was it for your father? Or just some hare-brained vigilante justice for the House's woman? *Why* did you go after him, Elysia?"

Two long strides and he was there, hands grasping her wrists firmly. His brows drew together, incredulousness lifting his voice.

"Do you have *any* idea how many women have met the undead gods because of that man? And you, you—"

He broke away from her, wrenching open the door like he couldn't stand the sight of her for one more second.

Lewis balked, his hand posed to rap on the rich walnut wood. "Sir, Benedict just reported that almost every person in attendance has taken ill. Even the king has fallen."

Another guard loomed over Lewis's shoulder, sweaty and out of breath.

Topp looked back at Elysia, his eyes narrowing in sudden suspicion. "You know, Lewis, I feel a touch of it myself. Benedict, you're with me. Lewis, you're staying here." Grabbing his favorite hatchets off the wall, he slung on a leather harness and stuck them in. Worn steel glinted against the green of his shirt, and Elysia swallowed. Forget looking royal, he looked like a warrior of the woods.

"No one comes in or out of this room until I return, and that includes Miss Parker." He glared at her knowingly before facing the guards again. "Benedict, go ahead. I'll be right behind you."

The guards complied, and Topp stalked out, whipping the door shut without looking back.

Elysia stood there alone, unease filling her chest. Guilt was such a sticky, inconvenient emotion. One she didn't have time for tonight. A twinge of pain ran up her back into her neck and she grimaced.

Her father's anger was a gross, misplaced thing. Logically, she knew that. Emotionally, that was a different story. But Topp—he was not so far off in his conclusions that she was playing some sort of lone, dangerous game. That she was in over her head and leaving a trail of destruction throughout Relaclave.

She should have pretended to be sick—but he'd dragged her up here so fast, and she'd been worrying about escaping instead of him. *Fuck.* That was a mistake. But it was too late to fix it now.

She pressed a firm hand to her sternum, but it did nothing to quell the uncomfortable feeling that she might be wrong about

Topp. He'd beaten a man to death. Stuck up for her to her father and the king. Put his hand on her head and gently stroked her hair.

Elysia bit her lip, not wanting to think about it anymore. Looking around Topp's chambers, she frowned, noting the utter state of disarray. He wasn't usually *this* messy. Blankets, clothes, food. It looked like a toddler had been set free without supervision.

She picked up a fuzzy coffee-colored blanket, tossing it onto a chair. Two things could be true at once, she reminded herself. His feelings for her *and* whatever his plans were that she knew nothing about. Even if he hadn't meant to, he'd told her himself that she couldn't trust him. The reality check that was her conversation with Gage reinforced this truth. Topp had helped find and brutally eliminate her kind. It was as simple as that.

Whatever his feelings for her may be, it did not and could not matter more than that truth.

Elysia picked up a marine blue shirt and held it to her nose, breathing him in. Still clutching the shirt, her eyes drifted to his bed in the next room over. Between his scent in her nose and the familiarity of these rooms, a warm nostalgia rocked through her.

A longing for the days when this had all been easy. Days spent in a happy haze. Days when she was able to forget about her father and the curse all because she'd be seeing *him* later that night. Blissful delusion.

They had known each other since childhood. Been together since she was twenty. What did it say that neither of them was willing to trust the other?

She dropped the shirt—she didn't want to know the answer to that question.

Besides, she needed to focus on her own plans, never mind his. She should be elated right now. Tonight had been a magnificent disaster. No one would point the finger at her about Scarzan, seeing as how the entire court watched the prince kill the man. Which meant no one would be the wiser that she had poisoned the entire guest list. Her debt was paid to the House, and with the entire castle distracted, she was free to pursue what really mattered: those idiots and their secret little rebel group.

Once more, her only true fear was the prince outing her. *And that's for me to worry about later.* She paused, a decision settling like a rock in her gut. She would talk to him. After tonight, she would talk to him. She didn't have to trust him to talk about what he already knew—and she deserved some answers. Like what he intended to do with her.

Tomorrow. Tomorrow, she would seek him out. Dangerous hope flickered in her, and tonight, she let it be. If he dashed it out tomorrow, then so be it. Tonight, she would hope.

That settled, Elysia slipped a hand beneath her skirts, popping open the small pouch attached to the holster for her knife. Conch shell from Mari in the palm of her hand, her brows rose in surprise. Empty before, it now housed a tiny slip of paper. She ran her thumb over the smooth shell in wonder.

It's magic. She never allowed herself to think much about magic. What Kava used to be like, what it could have been like. But here was someone's magic, right in the palm of her hand. Ever so carefully, she wiggled the paper free. Scribed in black ink was a simple message.

Below the docks where the sailors roam, but never does a fish swim.

Her hand flung down to her side, message in hand. They could not be serious. She'd poisoned the entire godsdamned court and *this* was their idea of giving directions? The paper crumpled in her hand. There was nothing but air and water beneath the docks! All this and they couldn't bother to give her a proper address.

Grumbling, she pulled out the coin Rollie had given her, hoping they were connected. Coin in hand, she began to pace, stress driving her to movement. Suddenly, a small ball of fur lunged, tiny bandit fingers swiping like an expert thief. Elysia shrieked, darting back from the creature. Breath coming quick and fast now, it took her a moment to realize what had happened. A *raccoon* had just stolen her ticket for entrance.

"You little asshole!"

She bounded after it, but the small raccoon scuttled away. Prize secured, it dove onto Topp's sheets, making small pleased noises as it rolled.

For the love of the undead gods. That's why it was such a mess in here. Elysia rubbed the edges of her eyes, smearing makeup she had forgotten about. The creature was holding the coin up to the light like it was gold. In anyone else's chambers, a raccoon mugging you would be unexpected. But not here. Not in Topp's rooms.

She had always found it charming. Coming into his chambers and finding a new creature to adore. The passion he lacked for politics could be found tenfold when it came to rehabilitating animals. Squirrels. Birds. A fox once—but he'd had to move the fox to its own special pen after it marked and tore up every square inch of his rooms. He hadn't minded, though. No, he had sympathized with the beast, always commiserating with it about what it was to be locked inside. Both a little wild, only one allowed to be.

But that raccoon had just stolen her coin.

She stalked softly toward the bed, trying to mimic whatever ease it was that Topp carried within him. The raccoon watched her with big black-rimmed eyes and a tilted head. It plopped back onto its haunches, and Elysia realized that it only had three limbs.

"You're very nimble and extra cunning, aren't you, little friend?" she murmured, creeping closer. A red collar with a wooden tag adorned its neck. Because, of course, he had given it a collar. *Such a weird man.* Grabbing a piece of fruit off a plate that had likely been Topp's breakfast, she broke it open and waved it enticingly.

"Come here," she breathed. "Nice and easy."

The raccoon squinted and appeared to be considering her

offer, but instead of dropping the coin from its one good hand, it merely stuck out a bottom foot as if she would place the fruit there. When she didn't, it bared its little fangs and hissed.

By the gods. She was going to kill Topp. Elysia shook her head.

"Greedy thing, aren't you?"

She dropped the fruit onto the bed where the creature gladly used its bottom foot to shove juicy chunks of fruit into its mouth. Fist in the air, the coin gleamed between its small black fingers.

New plan. She wasn't Topp, born to woo woodland creatures. And she didn't have time to be *nice*.

Ripping open his wardrobe, she snatched a rough-spun cloth bag from the bottom. It smelled like hay and animals. She did not have time for *any* of this. Glancing to the bed, she found the raccoon immersed in licking its dripping, sugared foot.

"Sorry, buddy." As fast as she could, Elysia snatched the raccoon up by the scruff of its neck. It dangled there in surprise, blinking at her. "You're just a big, thieving cat."

She shoved it into the bag.

The screech it emitted next was unlike anything she'd ever heard.

It was the sound of two starving cats tearing each other apart over garbage in a smelly alley. She dropped the bag with a curse. The raccoon promptly shut up and rolled out to a sitting position where it glared at her with baleful eyes.

She was about to give up and leave without the damn coin, when her eyes caught on what she realized was a long skinny leash resting on Topp's nightstand. Red and leather, it matched the collar.

Leash in hand, she raised her brows at the raccoon. Once more, she lunged, grabbing the collar even as the raccoon thrashed, throwing its small, fat body around. Tiny vicious claws swiped out, leaving thin red lines along her arms. Scratched and out of breath, Elysia stood up with a grin.

"Got you."

The racoon hissed, jumping into an offensive posture.

Elysia glared right back. "You're nothing more than an over-grown cat, and I've had to bathe and deal with cats aplenty."

The tag on its collar caught the light. Crudely carved, it spelled out a name. *Lina.*

"Well, Lina"—Elysia smiled dangerously at the squat ball of fur—"I do believe we have somewhere to be."

She had to laugh a little that Topp sincerely thought putting a single guard in front of his door would keep her from escaping.

"Stay in the room, Elysia," she mocked. Snorting, she kicked a half eaten apple out of her way. Like a door and a guard would stop her. As if she didn't know there were three separate exits from his room.

The main door. The window—which would be a death trap without the proper equipment for wall scaling. And the exit into the one place she had been traversing for years, the tunnels.

Elysia heaved, putting all her weight into moving the low slate table that sat in the middle of his living space. Books about animal welfare and a stack of paper with barely legible scrawls went flying. With a final grunt, the table was out of the way. Flopping the heavy brown and burgundy rug in half, she stared at the stone floor.

"There you are," she whispered. Dropping to her knees, she pried at the ancient stone. She hadn't used this exit in ages. It wasn't exactly subtle. But she'd discovered it one early morning, when Topp had left her warm and satisfied in his bed. Snooping was in her blood, and he should have known better than to leave her alone if he didn't want her going through his things. She wasn't sure he even knew this existed. *People really should pay more attention.*

The stone gave way, revealing old rusty hinges and a pitch-black hole. Everything in her wanted to slam the stone down, and try her luck with Lewis at the door. She *hated* this route. Several floors up in a turret, it wasn't easy getting down to the tunnels.

She stared down into the hole, scowling. A barely human

sized crawl space crunched between the floors of the castle. And she had to take a fucking raccoon with her.

Elysia stood back up and brushed herself off, her stomach dropping at the sight of the clock. Soot and storms, it was getting late. She hastily grabbed a plain black cloak from Topp's wardrobe, throwing it on over her ruined dress. The smell of rain and earth surrounded her, but she pretended not to notice.

"Alright, Lina, it's time for us to go." Elysia picked up the leash and tugged until the raccoon lazily hopped forward, still refusing to relinquish its new prize coin. Hopefully, it would give up and drop the coin before she had to drag it very far.

"Good, good," Elysia muttered to herself, coaxing the raccoon closer and closer to the gaping hole in the floor.

She tossed a piece of fruit down the hole, assuming bribery was the way to this creature's heart. Lina dove through the air like an arrow, nearly tearing off Elysia's arm out of its socket and pulling her down into the hole.

"Well, then," Elysia shook out her arm with a wince. Grabbing several handfuls of grapes and berries, she shoved them into the cloak's pockets. And with that, Elysia eased herself and a candle into the small tunnel.

Propped up on her elbows, she reached up out of the crawl space and pulled on the rug until it flopped over. Rug in place, she carefully took hold of the stone cover, easing it down until its weight and gravity were too much for her arms and the stone slammed down with a terrible, scraping sound. Her fingers barely dodged its fall.

Heart beating faster, Elysia double checked the leash and candle and then began scooting on her ass and elbows down the crawl space. "Come on then, Lina. We've got a meeting to crash."

The raccoon hopped along easily enough. Short in stature and with an animal's eyes, it was having a far grander time than her. Given that it wasn't straining at the leash, it seemed like Topp had likely been training the creature to walk like a pet beside him.

Looking at its furry rump bob up and down as it moved, she almost couldn't blame him for wanting to keep it.

Elysia scooted slowly, sending the heel of her foot out cautiously each time. At the right spot, the warped wooden boards would drop out completely. There was a rope to cling to—but she hadn't known that the first time and ended up with a broken wrist and bloodied face. *This* time, she would be using the rope.

Lina came to a sudden halt, squawking when Elysia's foot accidentally pushed up against her fur. Elysia peered into the dark.

"Well, aren't you clever," she murmured.

The raccoon preened a bit as if it could understand, and Elysia prepared to drop through the levels below. Once upon a time, the drop had started in the servants' closet in the upper floors of the turret and was used to send laundry down to the lower levels. Efficient and smart, it allowed the servants to avoid breaking their backs on the turret stairs while staying out of sight.

Now, several remodels later, someone had gotten creative. The rope wasn't on a pulley anymore, but instead tied to the thick beam above. She didn't know which crazy Blatz ancestor made the crawl space, or maybe it had been a servant who needed a route for thieving, but damn if she didn't love and hate them at the same time right now.

Elysia blew out the candle and inched closer to the edge. She paused, looking between the raccoon and the rope, unsure of how to proceed. She barely managed to drop the leash when Lina took a great jump and caught the rope, swinging back and forth in the air.

"Going somewhere? Maybe you could just toss me the coin then."

Lina bared her teeth in reply.

"Right." Elysia prayed the rope could hold her and jumped the short distance. Her hands slipped on the worn rope, flesh burning as she slid. *Shit.* Her knees snapped together, clamping the rope between them, bringing her to an abrupt and jarring stop. Forehead dipping against the rope, she paused, dangling in the dark. Stale air surrounded her, not even a whistle of fresh air creeping in from outside.

The rope swayed gently, and Elysia blew out a nervous breath. Scrunching her body like a worm, she made quick work of the obstacle, not wanting to be on the rope any longer than necessary.

Down, down, down, she went.

Until she came to the old servants' closet. Releasing the rope, she landed in a crouch. Fingers on the dirt covered floor, relief came with a long drawn out exhale. *So much better.* She stood, rolling out her shoulders, and snatching up Lina's leash. Out the servants' door and into the tunnels, it was only a short walk to the stairs that led to the castle grounds.

Elysia paused with her hands on the circular grate that would lead outside.

Tunnels.

Cold moisture dampened her hands as she gripped the iron grate. She looked out through the diagonal cross sections, letting the night air hit her face. What if there were tunnels or something like it beneath the docks? She had scavenged through countless homes, businesses, and buildings in the south side. And what did they all have in common? Hidden doors. Tunnels. Cellars with escape hatches.

Were tunnels beneath the sea so farfetched?

She didn't think so. Not when magic tugged on her bones in a land where it shouldn't exist.

The grate stuck, mud and moss sealing it to the ground, but she shoved, wiggling it side to side, loosening the debris until it gave way. Lugging herself out onto the cold, wet dirt, she lay there catching her breath, staring at the grim sky.

Gods, she regretted not being able to change into trousers or leather training pants. Bits of muck and gravel stuck to her bare skin, slimy and sharp they clung and dug, but it didn't matter. How she looked was irrelevant. She just had to make it to these people in one piece. Hope rose for the second time that evening, now a small flame in her chest. Not enough to warm her, but enough to make her carry on, foolish and headstrong until her brutal end.

Elysia, still holding the long line of Lina's leash, began pulling until she could grab the creature by the scruff out of the grate hole. "Sorry, friend."

She offered a grape as a peace offering. Snatching the grape with her foot, the racoon still clung to the coin like it was her life's treasure. The mist and wind whipped the loose strands of Elysia's hair. Standing there in the bitter dampness, her eyes caught on the torches held within iron sconces lining the walls of the castle grounds. Flames danced, refusing to cower even with the mist.

What am I doing? I can't bring a raccoon.

Mouth firming, she looked down at the fat, furry creature. "I can't take you." She pulled out a fistful of fruit and held it out, palm flat. Lina pounced and so did Elysia, ripping the coin out of her impressive grip. The raccoon screamed, but Elysia ignored it, untying the leash, so it wouldn't strangle itself.

Crouching, she looked at Lina seriously. "Topp will have my neck if anything happens to you, so just be good, will you? Weasel your way back into his rooms."

Coin finally in hand, Elysia looked up at the moon. A purple haze drifted past its pale yellow face.

Midnight moon, foggy and bright
Best to stay inside
Lest you meet your ruin tonight

The old children's rhyme played in her head. It was just a silly thing—something mothers said. A reminder that nothing good ever happened in the wee hours out on the cobbled Relaclave streets. But the words were pins and needles beneath her skin tonight.

Elysia broke the trance of the moon, setting off at a brisk pace.

She walked out of the castle grounds, pointing her feet in the direction of the sea. Nursery rhymes couldn't stop what was in motion this evening. She allowed herself one more glance at the moon's face, shrouded in warning.

She knew what she needed to do, but the coin burned against her palm, a reminder of how difficult these people had made this for her. They could have just helped her, but instead, they had made it practically impossible. Jump, they said. Giving her hoop after hoop.

Resentment, thick and oily, ran through her—fueling her every step. She was going to get into this meeting even if it killed her.

She had no idea just how likely that was.

Chapter 21

Topp Blatz still felt green at the ears, but thanked the undead gods that at least he was upright. The ballroom was a reeking, disgusting mess. It was as though everyone had completely lost control of their bowels in a matter of minutes. Vomit, feces, no one could move fast enough. They just hit the ground and wept from there.

He had a strong feeling that Elysia had once again misjudged the potency of whatever plant she'd been working with, much like she had with the pukeweed. The woman was brilliant. If she'd been a man, then she'd easily have been an intel officer within Kava's armies.

But she was *shit* at poisons. Absolute, complete shit.

It'd taken him a moment to work out just how she'd done it. But halfway down the stairs, the itch in his brain had relented. *The drinks.* There was nary a soul in the room who had not drunk something, even if it was just wine or tea. And he hadn't missed the servers either—her mother's usual staff weren't quite so *brawny*. His jaw ticked. Where she had met and hired men like *that* was a conversation for another day.

And then there was the obvious, that little moment in the privacy of the canopy, her prying Scarzan's jaw open until he was unhinged like a snake. Pouring liquid down his throat until he choked.

It'd been startling. And yet, the beast in him had pulled at his lips until there was a grin. He liked her like that. Dress ripped and a murderous expression on her face. It suited her. Besides, the man deserved it.

The scent of desperation had tainted the barely lit tent. He'd even heard a tooth crack when she'd slammed Scarzan's jaws shut. His delicate flower had been ready to wrap around that man like a vine, squeezing until his lungs gave out.

He'd known she was going to do *something* to cause a distraction. He hadn't expected her to kill a man. The ordeal with Scarzan had blinded him, left him off-kilter enough to believe that had been her whole plan.

Topp's stomach rolled and he swallowed against the poison's leftover nausea. He was just grateful he'd barely touched his drink. Otherwise, he'd still be on the floor with the rest of those poor folks.

He paused at the bottom of the stairs that led to his rooms. That had been an oversight—to think the chaos inside the canopy had been her true plan. No, in hindsight, it was obvious those particular actions had been the fruit of desperation and likely to pay off the House for her blunders. Her usual calculated self had disappeared in her panic and rage. Her real plans were always... *more.*

Because Elysia Parker never did things by halves.

He'd corrected her on the main export of another kingdom once, and she'd spent the next twenty-four hours putting together a lecture on why he was wrong. One hour into her lecture, he'd thrown her on the bed, not caring which of them was right if only she'd stop talking about lumber and maple syrup.

He knew that to some, her actions would be despicable. She had just killed a man, after all. Well, she'd started the job, and he'd finished it. There wasn't a shred of remorse in his heart.

Scarzan had assaulted her and now he wouldn't assault anyone else. Simple.

Topp wasn't sure he'd live long enough to have kids, but the idea of selling his own blood—heavy revulsion filled him at the thought. It was weak. And it was shameful.

Scarzan had sold his daughter not only in place of himself, as Elysia believed, but also to gain access to insider games and muscle. Topp hauled himself up another flight of stairs. Rumor had it that the deal with his daughter had backfired.

Either way, the man was a waste of perfectly good air.

The memory of his hands on Elysia's neck was a fire in Topp's blood. As if a small man like him could kill a woman like her. If she was nothing else, Elysia was scrappy. She would do anything, be anything to survive—to an extent that Topp was only now realizing.

The sight of Scarzan attacking her had been enough to blow his eyes out. Glowing and pupils dilated. And then he was moving. Destroying all evidence of her assassination.

In truth, it was hard to say what had really killed Scarzan first —the poison, or the death he had wished to bestow himself.

It was a rare moment that he was glad for his position. Most days the crown was unwanted, a nuisance really. But when he'd been thrown from Scarzan, hand bloody with bits of the man still stuck to his flesh—well, for once he'd been grateful. Grateful for the privilege and protection of his name and gender.

He'd pushed his father's limits since the day he was born. Woods instead of ballrooms. Animals instead of politics. Hatchets instead of swords. Quiet when he should speak. And loud when he was supposed to remain silent. It wasn't a small thing to cut down a foreign diplomat in the middle of a party honoring his departure. Yet, here he was, free and clear.

Twice, his crown had saved his ass tonight. Because no matter how infuriating or backward their fathers' interpretations of Scarzan's actions were, he had been able to quell that nonsense with the simplest of words. She was his. And they could not say a word against her if he spoke in her favor.

Too many women fell on the swords of men because their words were not held as true.

Two more flights of stairs. Soot, he needed some water. His mouth tasted awful.

Jack Parker, though. His lip curled as if he might snarl. The man could spin money and trades out of thin air, but Topp saw the way he watched Elysia. There was always an off-putting blend of loathful vigilance and something that wanted to be love—but was not—in the air when Jack Parker was near his daughter. It made Topp's skin crawl.

He didn't know what went on between the two of them. For years, he had thought they were thick as thieves. At some point, he'd noticed a shift. A bitter reluctance whenever her father demanded her assistance. That her mask was never more flawless than when she was by Jack Parker's side. He'd always assumed she'd come to him if it was something bad enough. But after tonight, he realized how much he must have missed over the years, caught up in his own problems and goals.

If Elysia's response was any indication, this evening was far from the first time Jack Parker had laid hands on his daughter. Their normal, sickeningly sweet public interactions had dissolved like sugar in water, leaving a sticky cloud of vitriol and violence.

Topp rounded the bend, coming up to the last flight of stairs. To be clear, he was furious with her. She was brilliant *and* terrifying. Her actions and deceit made him want to shake some cold, hard sense into her bones. A relentless pain in his ass, that's what she was—killing diplomats at parties and betting her own self away at pleasure houses.

Not to mention, it seemed like she was dead set on getting herself killed. Like she thought she was headed for the executioner's block anyway, so she might as well go out with a bang. Guilt landed heavy in his chest, stopping his steps. That was likely his fault. And he *was* going to talk to her.

Just as soon as she led him to the rebels.

Then they could clear the air. He'd tie her down if he had to, but he'd make it clear he had no intention of making her collateral damage. A dark voice in the back of his mind questioned this. If there was anything, *anyone* he wouldn't give up to achieve his ends. But he pushed it away.

He would never hurt her on purpose.

Topp climbed the last of the stairs. He'd begged off from his duties as quickly as possible. Told his father's men that he had a lead, ordered them to leave him to it. Had said it was urgent and would be out of reach by sunup, so he needed to hurry.

The best lies were the truth. He'd learned that from *her*.

Topp spotted Lewis still in front of his chambers, barely keeping his eyes open. He wouldn't be surprised if Elysia had just waltzed out the front door with security like that. But someone would have seen her, and the doors were sealed, gates drawn.

Anticipation brought a grin to his lips. He couldn't wait to see how she'd played this. Because there was no way in all the realms she was missing that meeting.

Topp stomped a little louder on the last stair and watched Lewis jolt to attention. The man blinked rapidly, clearing the fog from his eyes. "Any problems, Lewis?"

The guard paused as though he was unsure if he should speak, "Sir... Is there an animal in your chambers, by any chance? I know you, uh, have your hobbies."

Topp's eyes went wide, and he lunged for the door. "Shit," he mumbled. "I completely forgot about Lina."

He pushed the door open a crack, peering inside. Well, there wasn't a raccoon screeching bloody murder. That was a good sign. Relieved, he walked into his chambers and shut the door, leaving Lewis completely befuddled in the hallway.

Two whole steps into his rooms, he stopped, one half of his mouth hitching up. She was gone, as he'd expected, and now it was just a matter of tracking her. Excitement raced through him like liquid gold. He was finally going to get the drop on these rebels. He'd met with his father's men, and to his surprise, they only knew a few names for certain—there was still a chance he could make contact and save a few lives tonight.

He glanced around his rooms, and a frown tugged down his face. Tiny lakes of watery yellow-orange fluid were everywhere. Topp ran a hand through his hair, frustration and disappointment coming in a great swell. He'd thought Lina was doing better with her potty training. They'd been working on it nonstop for the last few weeks, and she'd barely had any accidents.

Grabbing a towel, he dropped down to wipe it up. He stopped, brow creasing. That sweet scent—it reminded him of summers spent in other lands. Lands that were warm and filled with the sun and magic. He took another delicate but wary sniff.

Mango. There was wet, sticky mango everywhere. A laugh rumbled in his chest. *Better than piss.*

"Lina, come here girl," he called, searching for the tiny bandit. She'd clearly gone on a mango binge when he hadn't been there to feed her dinner. Couldn't blame her. Poor girl.

Topp walked in circles, opening and closing closets and drawers when Lina did not tumble out of her usual nooks or crannies. His smile only widened when he saw the living room table shoved haphazardly to the side of the room.

He really was curious to see how Elysia had escaped. He'd half expected to find Lewis unconscious and sticking out from behind a tapestry. They were in a tower for the gods' sake, there really wasn't any other way out.

He walked closer, noticing not only the table, but how the rug was rumpled awkwardly. His booted foot kicked at the corner of the rug. Grabbing the edge, he hauled it back and let out a low laugh. "Tricky, woman."

Purposeful cracks in the stone floor stood out to his sharp eyes. He ran his fingers over the cool stone, feeling for a catch. Giving up, he grabbed an old sword he didn't care about and jammed it into the crack. Putting his weight onto the sword, he pried at the stone until it lifted and he was able to grab hold of the edge, opening it completely.

Staring down into the hole, Topp allowed his eyes to adjust. How in the name of the undead gods had she fit in there? He looked down at the size of his own body and groaned. This wasn't going to be pleasant at all.

Hunched and a little humbled, he stuffed his body into what appeared to be a crawl space. There was no light, no sounds—not even the softest flow of air. Anxiety clawed at his throat. Men like him did not belong in spaces like *this*. There was a reason he liked the forest and all her meadows. They were open, the call of freedom in every shriek and quiet hum of the wind.

But he had to follow her, had to find that group. With a single deep breath, he continued, even though every fiber of his body screamed at him to rip himself up and out of here. Arms and legs tight, he felt like a sausage in its casing, slowly wedging himself down the path, praying it would end.

And then all at once he was hot. Unbearably hot. There was no air, and it was too tight. He was going to get stuck and die here. His chest was moving faster now. The walls of the crawl space closed in, swallowing him whole.

Eyes shut, Topp counted at a measured pace until his heart was no longer about to burst through his chest and his breath not so fast.

When his eyes opened, the walls had stopped moving, and he realized his feet were about to plunge into nothing. Topp inched forward until he sat on the edge of the ledge, his feet dangling. The death drop before him didn't give him the warm fuzzies, but fuck, he'd take it over that crawl space any day.

No offense to Lewis, but he was really starting to wish she had just knocked the man out and used literally *any* other exit from the castle than this one.

"Not like sealed gates would have stopped you," he grumbled, staring at the fraying rope before him. His broad shoulders dropped with a sigh. This wasn't going to end well.

He looked up at the rope and the beam it was attached to, eyeing them both with skepticism. The rope was worn and frayed. And the beam looked more like a toothpick than a stability beam to a man of his size.

Can't wait to die. Topp took hold of the rope and began his descent. He slid a few feet down. "Okay, okay, so far, so good." The rope whined in response and the beam creaked, protesting his weight.

And then there was a loud pop. The sound of the rope snapping free, whistling as it hurtled through the air, free and untethered from its barings.

"*Fuck.*"

Topp plummeted. He was a boulder off a cliff with no idea what lay below.

Legs and arms reaching, he scraped against the sides of the chute, attempting to slow himself down. *There.* Pushing off the wall, he threw himself into the dark.

Topp hit the ground hard, skidding against packed dirt. Laying there, sore and dazed, he was infinitely grateful there was no one to see him sprawled face down like an incompetent moron. Up ahead, the faint gleam of light beckoned and he could smell fresh air drifting in. Lifting his face off the dirt, he spotted a squashed grape several steps ahead. He dropped back to the ground with a grin.

Right on track.

Topp broke out into the courtyard, mud seeping into the knees of his pants as he heaved himself out. He'd lived in Relaclave on and off since birth, and he was ashamed to say he'd never ventured into the tunnels. Right below his feet was an entire network of entrances and exits, but his eyes had always been out the window, looking into the distance.

Soot-stained mist and damp air kissed his face now as he glanced around the empty castle grounds. He'd spent many an afternoon training, right here in the rain and cold. Fingers practically frozen to his weapons. He could fight if he had to, just like any of the king's men. He was strong enough—fast and agile. But tracking and stealth were where he shone. All those hours of stalking through the forest, honing his eyes and mind.

Every bit of moss stamped down, broken twig askew, and scent on the wind called to him. Silent clues turning the path bright like a guiding star on a cloudless night.

Eyes to the damp ground, he strolled out of the castle grounds, certain of Elysia's steps. He followed her out into the fading light of Relaclave's streetlamps, feeling as though he might for the first time be able to do something good. A single strike in favor of his redemption. He knew it didn't hold a candle to his failures.

Never mind the many hunts against his own. That was a damage he could never undo. Beyond their deaths, in his heart of hearts, he knew he was a coward. A better man would have relieved his father of the throne, damning the consequences. But he hadn't. Endless lives lost as he bided his time, hoping to unravel Kava's secrets—no matter what everyone told themselves, magic didn't just disappear.

His time outside of Kava while growing up had changed him. Being with people and lands full of life and magic. There was no denying that Kava was sick, decaying before their eyes. It was like no one could remember the before, or maybe they just didn't want to—he couldn't blame them. What was the point?

But he would find an answer, and maybe these people were a start.

The black, iron streetlamps cast a warm, almost orange tinted, filter over the cobble streets and the people walking along them. A couple strode past, hand in hand, sweet grins upon their faces as they hurried home in the late hour. Soot from the sky, soot from the unkept lamps. The dark smoky glow of the streets could have been romantic. Between the mist dotting your skin and the shadowed light, he could see it.

But he wasn't hand in hand with his love. He was tracking her just the same as an animal in the woods or a man on the run.

The thought sent a shiver racing up his spine all the way to his head. He knew this feeling. The thrill of prey in his sights.

He was hopeful there would be no death or reports of treason to make in the morning like there usually was when he sank into this part of himself. If he was lucky, there would only be answers bringing him closer to his aims.

The breeze shifted, and he swore her scent was on the distant sea wind.

The volatile nature within him hummed a warning, but he was already moving and could no longer hear the sound.

Chapter 22

Elysia had almost reached the sea. Feet planted on cobblestones made dark with mist, her silhouette stood stark against the warm flame of the streetlamp beside her, sea wind blowing her hair back like thin tendrils of night. Fingers cold and curled beneath her cloak, she inhaled the damp salty air with its notes of dirt and fish.

She was putting off the inevitable.

There was only one way she was going to find Rollie's clandestine group of the cursed in time, but she was loath to do it. Her body stood stiff and rigid in its bid for self protection. Her magic was a liability and she knew it. She'd be lying if she said she never enjoyed the loss of control—the feeling of the magic taking over, heady and intoxicating. But tonight wasn't the night for that. She needed her wits about her if she was going to be successful. She was well aware her magic did not seem to have any regard for her wellbeing or her goals—only the secrets that it sought. And a secret like this, an entire group of illegal magic wielders meeting in the dead of night, was bound to pull her under.

There were some secrets that were simple. Short and sweet to the ear. Ringing out, then fading fast like the opening chord to your favorite song. So easy to catch and let go. Harmless, really.

And then there were secrets that were sticky like tree sap, refusing to leave your skin no matter how much you tried to wash them away.

It was too easy for her to become caught in the magic of all that wished to be known. Secrets, much like humans, simply wanted to be heard. For someone to listen, the presence of another soul to act as a light and shelter for their ragged edges.

But it was dangerous. There was always the risk of falling into a trance, the magic overruling her sense of self.

She was on the sand now, staring out at the sea. Slippers soaked through, she set off in the direction of the water beneath the docks, ignoring her painfully numb toes. Particles of sand stuck to the tops of her feet, kicking up and hitting her calves with each step.

Eyes glued to the dirty white foam of crashing waves, she gathered her resolve. If she fell into a trance, then every single thing she had done to gain entry to this society of magic wielders would be for naught. Her shoulders rose, tensing at the thought. She needed to be clear. Clear and ready to extract the information she needed from these people. *Easier said than done.*

A sharp wind stung her cheeks, and she clenched her fists. But she wouldn't learn anything at all if she never found them. Elysia looked up at the dark, nearly starless sky. For a moment, she felt loamy earth under her feet instead of sand and saw a haze of red cross over the moon. The flash of her recurring dream snapped her resistance, driving her out into the icy sea.

That haunting nightmare had started all of this. Icy water slapped against her ankles in harsh agreement. *If only my magic hadn't changed.* Elysia extinguished the thought before it could fully form. Because her magic had changed. And that wretched nightmare of a dream had led her to here, this moment, searching for a sliver of hope beneath the sea.

Grim determination settled her breath, bringing her focus inward. Unruly magic or not, she was going to find those people, and with them, answers. Her magic responded, eager to drown her in its rush. Heart rapid, she strained against the potent sensation, forcing herself to sift through the torrent of whispers and tugs this way and that.

Body swaying, her feet stumbled, water crashing over ankles and spraying against her. The sea's chill did nothing to deter her, though. Her mind's eye was locked onto the mass of dark, vibrating threads all converging in one death-riddled web. An undercurrent of fear coated the strands. Matte and dry, they looked as if they might crumble.

Distantly, she realized the life of their secrets looked to be at its end. Or maybe this was what happened when you lived each day in bone-deep fear of your own self. You dried up—frail and ready to shatter at any little thing.

Water punched into her gut, knocking her off her feet. The sound of rushing water filled her ears, and then it was pouring over her head into her mouth and lungs, bringing her down beneath its weight as if it were an anchor. Elysia's feet hit the seafloor, instinct powering her up and out of the water. Soaked, but no longer chained to her magic, she coughed, salt water burning her eyes and nose and throat.

Her frustration was instant. Forget treason or execution, she was going to die alone in the sea because she couldn't control her stupid fucking magic. She would haunt Rollie in this life and the next if she died out here trying to find his gods-awful friends.

Nails pressed into her skin, she plunged deeper into the water. The docks towered over her, and the water dipped and lapped against her waist now. She stared into the depths of soot-addled water, knowing her eyes couldn't help her here. The magic beckoned, though, enticing her farther and farther from the shores into the water's hold.

The fingertips of the wind were pure ice, dragging across her wet skin. Gooseflesh erupted with a shiver. Shoulders hunched, she looked back at the shoreline. For a moment, she swore she saw a shadow—someone standing at the water's edge, but then it was gone. A trick of the dark and her fear.

There was supposed to be a tunnel. Or a door. *Something* to take her where she needed to go. But all that awaited her out here was hypothermia. Slapping her hands down against the water's surface, she loosed a growl in the back of her throat. They were *here*. She knew it—her magic didn't lie. She had seen the mess of their secrets. She spun in a circle, ready to scream at the water and sky to tell her what to do.

Tell me what to do, and I'll do it, I'll do anything.

The thought she didn't allow herself to think was this: *Because I'm not ready to die.* Not here in the water. Not with a rope around her neck. And not with a blade against her skin.

The feeling of the wordless thought was enough, her magic taking it as an invitation and spinning the wheel of her fate soundly. *Tick, tick, tick.* The wheel spun, pointing to where it had always intended her to go.

And then her body lurched. The magic, no longer willing to be ignored, took hold of her with both hands, pulling her under with a scream. One hand flailed above the water, and then she was gone. Crashing hard to the bottom of the sea, mouth still agape, she choked. Water gurgled, a stream of tiny bubbles rising surfaceward.

And then her knees banged hard, a plume of blood drifting out and away into the dark. Eyes open, her hands tore frantically at the sea floor. It wasn't sand or rocks that had cracked against her knees. *Something* was there. Her nails struck gold beneath the sand, literal *gold*. Fresh energy fueled her now. Because attached to sea-worn wooden boards was a golden slot, gleaming as if it didn't know it was beneath the sea. The trapdoor looked ancient, seamlessly melded with the sand and mossy algae-covered rocks around it.

Lungs burning, Elysia fumbled for her coin. The clink was muted, barely making a sound against the muffling of the water. Sight unfocused and eyes stinging, she clung to consciousness. And then all at once, the trapdoor fell inward, revealing a dark descent of stairs beneath the sea floor.

Water did not flow or rush in as nature had designed. There was simply a gaping hole, ready to swallow her whole. Elysia dove headfirst onto cold concrete stairs, not caring how she banged her limbs. Spluttering, she raised her head, staring in wonder as the sea raged on, but never entered this secret space. The trapdoor lifted slowly, unhurried until it sealed, leaving her entirely in the dark.

She lay there, chest heaving, lungs and eyes still on fire. Her body continued to shiver uncontrollably, teeth clacking against each other. Fingers like lead, she fumbled to rip off her sodden cloak. It hit the ground with a heavy splat behind her, and she jolted forward, unsteady on her legs. Her hands clumsily steadied herself against the wall.

The stairs ended at a door. Circular with two black iron lines intersecting its center like a crossroads, there were small symbols all around the outer edge of the door. Scales and swords. Hands in strange postures. Skulls and chalices. Fingers still shaking, she reached out, the iron symbols textured against her skin. Water ran in a steady stream off her clothes and body, leaving a growing puddle beneath her feet.

I should go in. This is what I've been waiting for.

But a new fear held her in place. She'd never seen magic like that trapdoor. Magic that could rival the strength of something as untameable as the sea. She could hear voices through the door now, becoming more and more clear. Could *they* produce magic like *that*?

Her hand strayed to the door handle, ears honed in on the sounds she could make out. Laughter. Voices warm and unrestrained. She gripped the handle—she'd dreamed of this.

With a surge of anxious anticipation, she twisted the handle, letting the door swing open.

An entire roomful of eyes swiveled to her. Soaked to the bone and with a necklace of bruises from both Scarzan and her father, she met their eyes. Not a single one of them was so much as damp. Clearly, they'd had a method of arrival other than the thrashing sea dumping them on the trapdoor like a sack of wet trash.

Her mask slid into place with a swallow. She could handle this. She'd been in far tenser situations with far scarier people. By the gods, she'd killed a man tonight. Created a distraction worthy of the finest heist. And she'd unraveled the clue she imagined they had not believed she could solve.

Elysia lifted her chin and met their eyes only for Rollie to amble forward and break the silence along with her poise in one blow.

His face was horror-struck. "What *happened* to you? You look like you had the shit beat out of you. Bruises on your neck and scratches on your face." Honest and blunt as ever, Rollie's brow creased in genuine concern, his hands clasping and unclasping nervously.

Her cheeks heated, hand automatically reaching up to cover the bruises. But it was no use. She let her hand drop, foregoing her attempt and opting for her own shade of bluntness.

Face still warm, she looked at only Rollie, ignoring the rest of the stares. Her voice came out flat and harsh.

"It's been a long night, Rollickus. And I look like I had the shit kicked out of me because I did—and then I almost drowned trying to get in here." She fixed them all with a look that was somehow both her mother and her sister, and watched them quell and shrink under her glare.

Mari walked up with a wide grin, slapping Elysia on the back and ignoring her venom. "Knew you'd make it. Can't blame us for our tests—sacrifice, loyalty, magic. They're important here."

She turned to face the group of wary, but curious people in the room, delivering a stern expression. As if they were school children that simply needed a firm hand. "Everyone, this is Elysia. Let's remember not her place with the Crown, but what she did tonight, so that for once we could *all* meet. She passed our tests and made treason bells ring. Let her be welcome."

Some of the crowd relaxed at her words, but Elysia noticed

there were many who did not—pursed lips and scowls still staring back at her. A woman in heavy trousers and a thick sweater with the sleeves shoved up was one of them. Jet-black hair and pale skin, the woman spat when their eyes connected. Kicking back the wooden chair they all seemed to be sitting on, the woman stood, crossing her arms.

"I heard you're why Syren Herrin is dead." There was a vicious ache in her words. It was a sound torn between pain and vengeance, and the feeling of it was familiar as her own thumbprint to Elysia.

She met the woman's eyes, a certain coldness overtaking her. "Syren Herrin died because she healed without restraint or self-preservation. She was a dead woman long before I helped her along."

The dark-haired woman moved fast, her strides hard and purposeful, but a lanky young man with bright blue eyes flung out a hand, a gust of wind knocking her back.

"*Sit down, Jessa.*" Mari's light, breezy countenance shifted, and Elysia quickly surmised that all the muscle packed onto her short body wasn't just for show. Magic or mundane, the woman looked confident and ready to hold her own.

Eyes like slits, the dark-haired woman made her way back to her seat. She sat down with a huff, knees spreading wide as she leaned in. "Mark my words, we'll regret bringing a traitorous Crown bitch in our ranks."

Elysia ignored her now. She would carry her shame and regret over Syren Herrin until the day she died. But that wasn't anyone's business but her own. She hadn't come here to make friends, anyway. The twinge in her chest negated this, but she ignored it, plowing ahead. She needed information, plain and simple. Information to save her own neck and then she'd never darken their doorstep again.

The room, much like the door she had come through, was a large circle. The only way in or out was that very same door that led back to the stairs and the sea. Lanterns hung off the sides of the chairs, giving the room a quiet, cozy light. A myriad of faces sat in the old, worn-out wooden chairs. Pale like the moon, coppery and rich, to deep smooth brown—the crowd reflected that Relaclave had once been a place that people from all over the world made their home. Now, people avoided Kava, given the strange mundanity of their land.

The walls of the rebels' refuge were made of dark slate, white scribbles and notes etched onto them all. Elysia's eyes ran over the chaotic notes, wondering how long this place had existed. Volumes and volumes of books were neatly stacked atop each other and pushed up against the walls. She was willing to bet those books were amongst the titles that had been burned long ago.

Mari gestured to a chair and tossed Elysia a towel. "Sit. We're adjourning soon, given the hour, but I promised you information. And it sounds like you need all the help you can get."

Elysia squeezed out her hair with the towel, then patted it down the length of her. Dropping it to the ground, she stared at Mari impatiently, not bothering to sit. She gestured with her hand for the woman to go ahead.

Mari took a deep breath and began. Pride filled her words, and Elysia felt the room swell in response. "We are the ones the curse could not break. This land was once filled with every magic and gift you could imagine. Magic touched our food, our land—and every single heart and soul."

She paused, staring poignantly at Elysia, her mouth tightening. "And then it was stolen. The undead gods are alive and well. Even now, when we do not recognize them, they carry on both serving and preying on humanity. They may have lost their foothold in Kava, but trust me, they are not gone."

Elysia's heart thumped. "You're trying to tell me—"

"That our magic was stolen by a jealous god from a realm that does not know the sun but only death. Victoria"—Mari pointed to a slim brunette with round dark eyes—"has seen visions of a realm with a bloodied sky and river of charcoal waters."

Fear sluiced through Elysia, icy as the waters of the sea around them.

Mari closed the distance between them, clutching Elysia's wrists, fervent and impassioned. "Is this where you go? To where our magic has been stolen?"

Her throat closed and mouth remained half-open, but wordless. She finally choked out a response. "How is that supposed to help *me*?"

The mountain of her problems had just grown exponentially if this was true. The realm of a god who had *stolen their magic?* No, absolutely not, she wanted *nothing* to do with that. All she wanted was to be fixed. For all of this to be fixed. Her fingers clutched back at Mari as she stared incredulously.

Disappointment dropped Mari's full cheeks lower, but her voice was gentle. "We can hide you—but we need to know you're after the same thing as us. The restoration of our people."

Her voice broke off at the sound of an incessant thumping from above. Everyone in the room froze like rabbits in sight of a fox. It sounded as though someone was trying to break through the trapdoor.

Elysia's gaze went wild, darting around even though she knew there were no windows or exits, only the singular round door. *Could someone break through the trapdoor?* She had no idea how something mundane like man-made iron tools fared against a magically reinforced trapdoor, but it sounded like the wood was splintering the same as any other.

Elysia looked to Mari, but the woman with the long black hair had pushed to the front of the room, and this time no one held her back. They were all thinking the same thing.

That she'd betrayed them just as easily as she had Syren Herrin.

"What did you do, you Crown piece of shit?" Jessa's words were a growl, but she shoved past her, checking Elysia's shoulder as she went. The woman didn't waste another breath on the traitor amongst them. She stood tall and boomed her orders, preventing the panic that would turn into senseless chaos.

"*Quiet.*"

The room halted, terror filtering through the room like a paralytic. Jessa met their fear boldly.

"We prepared for this."

Heads around the room nodded grimly.

"Now *move.*"

She called out to a pair who were obviously siblings with the same sandy hair and clear blue eyes who were already taking hold of other rebels by the wrists. "Remember, take those who cannot fight first." Jessa spun, already addressing someone else. "Belinda, the masks!"

The siblings' faces pinched in concentration, and then they popped out of existence, taking their precious cargo along with them. Elysia stared openly, stunned at what she had just witnessed. The thumps continued above them, the beat out of time and frenzied now. As if they knew they were close to breaking through.

Elysia startled at Rollie's voice beside her. "Travelers. Not easy to take more than yourself. Well, not without real magic, anyway."

She nodded numbly, her eyes going to his in pleading. "Rollie, I swear I didn't."

He nodded, giving her a look that made her feel as pathetic and naive as a child. "I know. But I think we all know who is about to bust through that door."

Elysia opened her mouth to argue he was wrong—Topp was likely still puking with the rest of them at the castle, but the large beautiful woman named Belinda suddenly yelled for everyone to hold still. A breath later, there was a soft hooded mask disguising every face in the room.

Jessa pulled out two daggers from her belt, wielding them with practiced fingers. "Those who can fight stay to the front. If you're waiting to travel, get to the back and keep out of the way."

Rollie grabbed Elysia by the shoulder, starting to drag her back. "Come on. You heard her."

Elysia shook off his grip, slipping closer to the front. She gave him a worn smile. "I can fight. You can barely walk without rolling an ankle. Get out of here, okay?"

There was a loud shout and then a roaring. It was the sound of the endless sea, battering and mad. Angry that it still did not gain entrance to their sanctuary.

Elysia's hand went to her thigh and she swore under her breath. The dagger that had been strapped there was missing, likely lost to the tunnels or the sea. Tension wound her tighter as footsteps thundered down the concrete steps. In one quick motion, she ripped the tulle from her dress, leaving only a thin black slip and the corseted top, wet and molded to her body. Tossing the tulle aside, she prayed for the mask and adrenaline to cloud the incoming men's vision. There was a fair chance the men about to enter had seen her gliding about at the party earlier, but she doubted these sorts of men could tell a tulle dress from a silk one even on their best day.

Shaking her arms loose, Elysia slid into a fighting position, waiting for the wave of death to roll in, wiping away the singular safe haven the cursed had found within Relaclave. The clatter of pounding steps stopped, everything suddenly far too quiet. In the silence, all she could hear was the hard swallows of the man next to her, the nervous breath of someone across the room.

Stilling herself, she found a peace that did not make sense. Physically, she was under the sea, the king's men outside the door, ready to cut their lives short. But mentally she was on rooftops and damp forest floors and the sandy sparring ring all of Gage's men trained in. Years of his relentless corrections and guidance acted like a spark, sharpening her mind and readying her muscles. She was not a warrior, nor was she helpless.

There was the soft tink of metal against metal—the simple lock being picked, and then the strange round door swung open and the king's men surged in, a small wave of salt water coming in alongside them. Water sloshing, six of the Crown's men strode in, confident, wielding both weapons and wicked grins. The hunt had found their quarry. And what a hunt it had been to bring them beneath the sea.

Elysia clocked their faces, not guards then, but the men who lurked near Garrison, always ready to slip off and do his bidding. No questions asked, these men were happy for the excuse to break skin and bone.

And in the rear, with a face so cold her own breath stuttered at the sight, was the Crown Prince himself. Gone was the impish boy who had grown by her side. In his stead was a creature quiet and still as the forest yet angry as a storm. A man with cruel eyes and a predatory gait—her heart should have broken. But it didn't. There was only a second of sweeping grief, weighted and familiar. The kind that straightened her spine, refusing the emotions beneath. Because somewhere inside she had known—love was not to be trusted and people only let you down. Especially the ones who were supposed to love you most.

Her former lover, now a stranger, stood at the door, his hair and cloak dripping. Any warmth to his rumbling voice had been leached dry. "Remember your orders, captured, not killed."

And then he simply surveyed the room, staying out of the fray as if he were above the cursed blood that would drench these floors regardless of his orders. The men at his side were wild wolves, not trained dogs, and they would not deny themselves the hunt.

Anger warmed her muscles and loosened her limbs. His betrayal was a layered thing that she didn't have time to examine right now. All she could do was let it fuel her, let it be the kerosene that turned her to flame. He had ruined *everything*. She was a breath away from stepping into another life, one with people like her who could help—people who had a vision that didn't include heads rolling in the main square.

She had been *so close*.

A man launched himself at her, drugged cloth in one hand,

the other wrapped in a fist and flying for her face. A sharp crack echoed inside her skull, blood gushing. Elysia danced back, wiping the back of her hand against the torrent of bright red staining her skin and teeth.

Eyes flicking around the room, she understood the score. A little brutalizing followed by a quick drugging. That was their method. Out of the corner of her eye, she saw Jessa pick up a chair and slam it down over the head of a short, thick man with a head like a melon. His melon didn't crack, but he did crumple like a paper doll. Jessa threw down a lantern, lighting the man on fire for good measure.

Elysia blinked. That woman was on a whole different level.

Her pursuer attacked once more, but this time instead of darting back, she ducked under his incoming fist, gripped his neck and slammed her knee between his legs. Face purple, the man dropped, his hands cupping what was likely a disappointment, anyway. She was a practical woman who believed in doing what worked—and a sharp knee to the balls was effective one hundred percent of the time in her experience. On his knees and still clutching his jewels, her fist collided with his face, returning his favor and splintering delicate cartilage. Taking a cue from the demon by the door who had caused this all, she dropped to the floor and cracked the man's head against the concrete until his eyes rolled back and lids closed.

A strange sense of power ran through her, bright and invigorating. Inhaling, she stood, swiveling and scanning the room. The travelers had cleared the back of the room. All those who remained were either drugged and unconscious on the floor or still fighting. The young man with bright blue eyes who had stopped Jessa, shoved his arms forward, face furrowed in concentration, but nothing happened. Erratic and unreliable, his magic did not respond. Elysia's heart dropped, knowing it was too late. He was on the ground, writhing with a cloth over his face in moments.

Eyeing the exit, her mind flew even as her feet moved. The

travelers would not be coming back. They'd done their job—it was each man for themselves now. Which meant it was *that* door or death. Determination turned her body fluid, her focus narrowing to the single goal of escape. Masked and anonymous, she could make it out of this yet. There was only one body blocking the door, and she wasn't afraid of a backstabbing, spineless prince.

An enraged scream tore out, shredding her concentration and ripping her eyes to her left. Two men had Jessa pinned. The woman hadn't conceded to this fact and was screeching and fighting like a mountain cat. Nails, teeth, and limbs blurred, but they were boulders to her pebble. Whatever her magic was, it was either defunct or not useful.

Jessa flailed, spitting in their faces and biting at their drug-filled hands. Once again, Elysia realized it was only the prince who stood in her way. The prince who stood in the doorway, looking bored and distracted, like this was a picnic he hadn't wished to attend instead of a campaign of genocide.

I should run, I could make it. She knew better than to go back for the dying. But there were still rebels in the room, exhausted and deflated by the sight of Jessa being taken down. And deep down, she knew this was somehow her fault.

She hadn't even taken a step when Jessa's body went limp, her head lolling to the side and body sagging. Something in Elysia's stunted heart felt furious at the sight—the woman was a bitch that she'd only just met, but to see her out cold with a foot in the grave felt unnatural and wrong.

Her mind shifted gears, making a fast and reckless decision.

She barreled straight for the prince, gaining speed with each step. Blankly staring at his men hovering over Jessa, his head turned a second too late. Her body was already airborne, mouth torn open wide, crying out for everyone to run. Every last scrap of her rage broke free as she pummeled into the hard body of the man she had so deeply wanted to trust.

Surprise and fury had them soaring, landing in a heap before the stairs. The look of utter shock on his handsome face made her want to purr.

"*Prince*," she snarled mockingly before scrambling to her feet. She needed to lead everyone out. If they stayed in that room, they were dead. Two rebels had taken heed of her cry and were racing around her, up the stairs past the incoming water out into the sea. She shouted out again at the remaining rebels, but her words were cut short when wet fingers wrapped around her ankle, giving one sharp wrench. Arms grasping at thin air, she went down hard, ribs and chin cracking against the concrete stairs.

The impact deflated her lungs with a whoosh, and then the prince was straddling her. Knees shoved tight against her sides, his weight heavy on her middle. Pulse pounding, a crazed sort of flight or fight ran rampant in her.

"Hello, sweet liar," the prince murmured, his green eyes lighting in the dark.

Water continued to pour in, careening down the stairs, soaking her once more. Her nostrils flared beneath her mask, only her narrowed eyes peeking out. She had expected him to know it was her, he'd tracked her here after all. But that just meant he should've known better than to have such a sloppy hold.

Wrapping her arms around his center, she yanked him closer, hissing in his ear. "My love." Only to shove her hips up, twisting and toppling back over him. She grinned beneath her mask.

It'd been a beautiful reversal, really.

Fingers still covered in another man's blood, she crashed her fist into the prince's jaw. His lips curled up, unfazed by her violence, so she hit him again, right on his pretty mouth. Glancing over her shoulder, she saw the king's men dragging their victims to the door. *Time to go.* She let loose one more punch, cracking his skull against the stairs, but the prince just grinned, a dark laugh shaking his chest.

Blood speckled on his lips, he lifted his head. "Run, little liar, run."

His words slithered inside her chest, squeezing her fear-filled heart. Leaping away, she was at the top of the stairs when it started. The sea began to win the war against the stronghold's magic, pouring in heavy and fast, ready to drown and ruin. She looked at the wrecked trapdoor waiting for her to dive through and escape into the sea.

But Jessa's prone body flashed through her mind. She'd lost count by now, but there were still other rebels down there. Both conscious and unconscious, succumbing to their execution instead of fighting to get out. Whipping back around, she spied one of the king's vultures crouched next to the prince. She wasn't sure how many of the king's men were still fighting, but hopefully, at least a few of them were still out cold.

Feet nimble and sure this time, she raced down the stairs, grabbing a hatchet off of the prince's leather harness as she went. Taking the blunt end, she slammed it into the temple of the king's man, not bothering to stop as he pitched sideways down to the ground.

Standing in the doorway, she shouted. "Grab a body and get out, the water is coming."

She watched someone grab Jessa, then fixed her attention elsewhere. Taking hold of a short but muscular man under the armpits, she heaved, aiming for the stairs. Bump by bump, she dragged him, her lower back straining and water hitting her hard. Twice, she nearly lost her step on the drenched stairs, but she was almost there.

The prince was nowhere to be found. Maybe he'd gone after the escaped rebels, or maybe he just didn't give a shit whether anyone but himself lived or died. In the grand scheme of the Crown, it didn't matter whether the cursed traitors drowned or died in the square. And the king's men were replaceable. Broken, bloodthirsty men always were. Either way, it seemed the prince had fled, leaving Elysia to a watery grave.

She could hear people scrabbling below, but she'd done all she could. Their grace had run dry, and the Crown's unconscious men would wake with vengeance in their bones at any moment.

She dove into the sea, arms wrapped around the man's chest, kicking wildly. The trapdoor had been in waist deep water beneath the docks, but the sea was angry now—vicious and thrashing as she reclaimed her domain.

Adrenaline was all Elysia had left. She swam hard, feeling as though each kick required strength she did not have to give until finally, waves around her legs, she could walk. What had felt like a short distance when she first walked out beneath the docks now seemed to be an eternity. Her back and shoulders strained, lugging the waterlogged man in her arms even as the water rocked against her.

But then there was sand. So much glorious sand. A cry broke free from her lips as her now bare feet touched the slick, packed down shore. *I made it, I made it.* She did not stop. Heavy step after heavy step, she dragged the rebel until she finally reached the place where the tides did not touch. Dropping him, she collapsed onto her hands and knees, chest heaving and limbs shaking.

The gods gifted her one whole moment of sweet relief, and then there was a laugh that made her skin prickle. Head turning, a large boot connected with her face. Her teeth bit through tongue, blood filling her mouth as she flew backward, landing hard against the sand. Before she could so much as put her hands to the ground, another harsh blow broke against her ribs. Vomit rose in her throat and she retched, bile burning as it escaped.

Bare arms wrapped around her middle, and she tried to roll away. Short, wet gasps fell out of her mouth while blinding pain scored through her entire being, confusing her senses.

I can't breathe. The man was a looming shadow over the top of her now. His movements were slow and sure, the same as any animal when their prey rattles with death.

Tears blurred her vision. She had no idea which of the king's men he was—he could have been any of them. And it didn't really matter, did it?

His knees hit the sand with a soft thud. Leering, he stared down at her. "Does the magic make you stupid?" Drawing his elbow behind him, he rocked her face back with another punch, his fist practically the size of her face. Stars danced in her eyes briefly and then her vision was gone entirely in the one. He was talking, she was sure, but she couldn't think, couldn't hear.

"Should have run when you had the chance."

Her skin split beneath his knuckles once more, but then he was grabbing for her mask and the sheer panic of discovery blazed through her like lightning. It numbed every broken bone and soothed the raw nerves of pain branching through her body.

Elysia screamed her defiance out into the open shores, shocking him with her guttural, wordless cry. There was no special maneuver or class to what she did—her body just knew it needed to survive this man, this night. Bashing her already wrecked face against his, she raked her nails down his sea-dampened cheeks. The man fell away from her, clutching his face and cursing. Stealing the man's knife out of its holster, she plunged it straight into his throat. Hot blood spurted out the edges, his own personal fountain of death, hitting Elysia in the chest and face. Bloodied, she clambered to her feet wildly, tripping her way out of the sand and sprinting and panting toward the city.

Tears streamed down her face as she bit back sobs. Every breath burned like heated knives in her chest. Clutching her ribs, she forced her functioning eye to stay open and just kept putting one foot in front of the other. Nothing mattered as long as she kept moving. If she stopped, she would be dead.

Her broken breath and mind became one mantra. *I will not die. I will not die tonight.* Over and over, she sang this song through the old city and its wet, cobbled streets. It was all a blur as she pounded past. The creamy arched and sloping buildings all riddled with grime—the bright doors that refused to give up their color to the soot. She saw none of it. Her thoughts devolved to ill-formed, incoherent things. *Not die, not night.*

She ran until she could run no more, and when she stopped, she found herself staggering up to the door of the House Gardenia. One arm still wrapped around her aching ribs, the other rapped out two weak knocks, leaving behind dark smudges of blood on the green paint.

She just had to keep breathing. She did not even have to run any longer. Her single open eye closed, dimming the world to black. Plastering a hand against the doorframe, she gritted her teeth, fighting to stay conscious. But the black was more than just her closed eyes, it was all around her, pulling her far from the pain.

The door swept open, the Doorman laughing over her shoulder until she screamed, saying a name and something else over and over again. A tall, lithe body shoved the Doorman out of the way.

"Elysia, what—how?"

Long, thin fingers clutched at her arms. Distantly, she could hear her sister sputtering, and if her eyes had been open, she would have seen horror shaping her already angular face.

But Elysia had made it. Out of the water, through the city, and to this door. Her knees gave out and Beatriz stumbled, trying and failing to catch her sister. Intertwined, they sank down to the ground, Elysia's weight falling against her big sister's chest. And for once, Beatriz caught her, protecting her from breaking further.

She could feel Beatriz's fingers clutching against her hair, but she couldn't make out her frantic words. They floated away on the salted air like soot. She could feel her body shutting down, all the sounds indistinct and faded. The pain surrounded her now. Whatever had spurred her on from sand to cobbled streets to midcity had given out at the sight of a green door and silver hair.

A woman with black hair and sharp eyes flashed inside her head. She wondered if that terrible woman had survived. If any of them had made it out of the water, through the streets to their own green doors. Green doors, green eyes. Quietly, she thought of the man who had left her to die beneath the sea and if he had ever loved her at all.

Someone was carrying her now, each step jarring and horrible.

A sweet, weighted darkness crowded in, though, easing her from her wretched state. But for once, she did not fall through worlds or realms. Tonight, she stayed in her own dream world.

It was an old dream. One she'd had many times of a little girl in a red sash staring up at the gallows. Except this time it wasn't her sister or her mother staring down at her, it was a long line of rebels, just like her with dead, dead eyes ready to be pecked by crows.

CHAPTER 23

Topp Blatz stood dripping sand and sea water onto the lush, impractical white carpet. There was a ragged split he could feel in his chest. The longer he stared at her, the wider it grew until there was a cavern within his ribs. Heart in his throat, guilt ran like acid through every part of him.

Nose broken, one eye sealed shut, her face discolored and swollen, he could barely see the woman he had kissed and touched every inch of. With purple and red smudges from face to neck, he was afraid to see what was below the blanket pulled up to her collarbone.

She'd had the chance to leave, to escape—and she had gone back. He was so deeply, irrationally angry with her. If she would have just *left*, then she wouldn't be mangled and a breath away from dying. She had gone back in, and he had left. Guilt racked him. He had left because he knew what her going back in meant —she wasn't going to get away and he would have to watch the prelude to her death. Watch her be beaten, then corralled with the rest of them to be taken to his father.

And it was his fault. All of it.

He had known that his mission to uncover the truth of their kingdom's decay would require much of him, but he hadn't expected this. He had not prepared for the moment that he would walk away from his only friend in this wretched land, knowing it meant her death. That loving him had been her death.

He wasn't an idiot. He knew she had pursued him thinking he would be her refuge. His crown a shield and barrier from the noose that had stolen so many. Instead, he had become a reaper. Standing by idly, watching and waiting as she died, knowing he couldn't interfere.

The air danced in response to his thoughts. It shorted out with crackles that spelled out his anger, his hate. Crouching next to the bed, he breathed her in, letting her warm, dark floral scent wash away the pain and guilt eating him into oblivion. His strong, calloused fingers became feathers against her hair. Born and raised in the same fold, she should have known better than to get too close to him. There was no such thing as hiding in the shadows of the Crown. But then, maybe she had known better, considering she never willingly gave him her trust or her secrets.

He'd only wanted to observe, to listen in and find out what the rebels knew. He'd known he would have to give at least a few of them up. Hand their names over to his father as the price for what he learned. Nothing had gone as he'd expected.

He should have realized he was being followed. That his father's men would be watching, waiting for him to strike without them. That even the mention of a lead was going to send them all running after his heels. They thought him an arrogant man off to prove himself.

But he hadn't noticed. He'd been caught in the thrall of tracking Elysia across the city and to the sea. Blinded by the idea of finally gaining a solid lead, nothing could have stopped him. Her scent had filled him, becoming his sole and only focus until it was too late, and he was watching her descend into the sea with the king's men ready to rush the water once she disappeared.

It was a godsforsaken miracle that in the pitch-black of night, they could not see who had entered those deep waters. He closed his eyes, fingers still in her hair.

She would hate him now.

Her breath made a wheezing sound on an inhale and on her exhale, he let go of the woman he had loved. He would never admit it had been a mistake to leave her there. Because there wasn't an apology in all the worlds that could ever undo what he had done. Some choices were irredeemable, not even time able to soften the damage or pain. And he was a smart enough man to know this was one of them. But whatever happened next, he would not make the same mistake twice.

Love or hate. He would do what he had to, to keep them both alive.

ELYSIA WOKE to the smell of earth and storm lingering, but when she opened her eyes, it was the intense gray eyes of her sister staring into hers.

Beatriz deflated, dropping her head and mumbling, "They kept saying you would wake up, but gods, Elysia."

She reached out, grabbing Elysia's hand firmly, no hesitation in her grasp. "All I wanted was some intel on Scarzan. Not for you to kill the man, poison the entire court, and end up like this." A note of hysteria heightened and sped her usually low, ever unbothered speech.

Beatriz gathered herself, her face growing sharp as a broken bottle. She glared back at the Doorman, who had been hovering a few feet away. The owner of the House Gardenia's high, rounded cheeks deepened in color at her girlfriend's unspoken reprimand.

Elysia shifted, attempting to sit up, only for Beatriz to immediately fluff and plump pillows, shoving them behind her until she could sit properly. Elysia's lips twitched in a little grin. Her sister's sudden nurturing instincts were like watching a dog walk on its hind legs. She paid for her mirth though, the smallest movement of her mouth causing shooting pain throughout her face.

"Hand me the pain tonic, will you?" Beatriz called back, her eyes sharp with the vigilance of a seasoned war medic instead of the haze Relaclave's renowned party girl usually wore as a veil over her eyes.

The Doorman selected an opaque brown bottle from a rough-hewn pine nightstand, handing it off silently. Glancing around the room, Elysia felt it was safe to assume she had overtaken a male staff member's room. Natural pine furniture and a simple dark green blanket on the bed. One neat stack of books and two oil lamps providing a soothing glow. It was the sparsest room she'd seen within the House. Elysia accepted the small brown bottle from her sister, but only held it, rolling it between her hands. She needed her mind clear for at least a bit longer.

Closing her eyes, she made a decision. When she opened them again, her dark brown irises had gone distant and glassy. "Do you trust her?" Voice sore and covered in rust, she nodded at the Doorman.

Beatriz paused, taken aback, before answering quietly. "Yes. Entirely."

Elysia nodded. "Then you both might want to sit. I'll tell you everything. If you don't want to know, I understand, but you'll need to leave."

A smirk curled across the Doorman's face, lightening Elysia's heavy words. "Ms. Parker, I would think we're past that given we have a murder under our belts."

Elysia's face wrinkled even as she nodded in reluctant agreement. Beatriz sighed, staring up at the ceiling, muttering about not being able to get any peace.

She'd thought it would be cleansing to finally tell it all. That it would at the very least bring relief to fill in all the gaps of Beatriz's knowledge, considering she'd only known of the haunting dreams plaguing her sleep. Especially when there was so much more to tell. From the secrets that enchanted her to the blackmail of their father and the prince hunting her into the sea.

She didn't labor over his betrayal. Mainly because she couldn't even bring herself to speak his name. The very thought of him filled her with an anger that demolished all reason and set a painful fire to the love that had once consumed her heart and blinded her eyes.

Heart full of ashes, she didn't feel relieved at all after telling them everything. She felt as if a cold excavation had been done. Her ribs torn asunder, splayed and pinned out wide like moth wings, revealing all that was *her* for them to dissect and reject.

Beatriz, for once in her life, sat with no words breaking the thin line of her lips. She just sat, stunned, until a familiar indignation overtook her. She shook her head as if that could change what she just heard.

Her voice was a sharp whisper. "I am so *angry* that you did not tell me about Father."

Showing rare restraint, she blew air out through her nose like a fire breathing beast before continuing. "But I know... I know that I have given you no reason to trust me. All that you know of me is what I've shown you and the rest of the world. I would have gotten you out of there. I just—I thought you wanted that life. I thought you loved being a daddy's girl, always sitting in all those meetings and having the entire court fawn over you. I saw the way you looked at that crown, at Topp, like they were your salvation, but I didn't understand." Tears filled her hard, gray eyes.

Elysia stared at her hands, not wanting to see the soft lines of pity on her sister's face. "I thought I could make it work. That if I worked hard enough, pretended well enough—that I would be safe. That I could really be one of them."

She swallowed hard and looked up, eyes dull and bleak. "But I will never be one of them, and I was foolish to think I could be. There will never be a woman with undead gifts and a crown on her head. Not in this land." Her fingers tightened on the brown bottle. "It was a delusion. Necessary to survive, but a delusion, nonetheless."

A sudden knock on the door startled them all.

The sight of who stood in the door frame had apprehension

filling Elysia's voice as she struggled to sit up straighter against all the pillows. "What are you doing here?"

The woman entered cautiously, eyes roving from face to face. Elysia couldn't blame her—Beatriz and the Doorman had both shoved to their feet, practically blocking Elysia from sight as they stood like guards.

Elysia tugged on her sister's off-white button-down shirt that looked like it belonged to a man. "Stop it. Both of you. This is Mari. She's a part of the group I was telling you about. She's friends with Rollie."

Beatriz's unsettling stare did not falter. If anything, it grew even more unhinged, her eyes narrowing. "The people who expected you to poison the entire court, kill a diplomat, and almost drown solving their stupid fucking riddle?"

Elysia picked at the forest green blanket. "Technically, they just wanted a distraction... The killing was really for your girl-friend. Debts to be paid to the House and all..." Elysia trailed off, realizing she definitely was not helping matters.

The mythic Doorman of House Gardenia withered at how Beatriz tensed. She busied herself straightening the already perfectly organized tonics on the nightstand. Silver hair swinging, Beatriz turned her glare to Mari, uncaring if the woman deserved her wrath or not. "Well, what do you want?" The words were clipped and sharp enough to poke her eye out.

Ah, there was the Beatriz that Elysia knew and loved. So warm, so fuzzy.

Mari edged around the small bed, opting for the side that was free of Elysia's newfound bodyguards. Her usual bold and sunny countenance seemed faded. She clutched an old book in her hands. Black with gold embossments and gilded edges, it looked familiar as it glinted in the light. Setting the book down, one hand grabbed onto a bedpost, her brow creasing in thought.

"I heard you stayed. Fought the king's men and even the prince himself."

Beatriz grumbled about her sister having rocks for brains.

Elysia shrugged, twinging at the pain in her ribs. "We all know it was my fault they found us. The prince followed me."

Elysia shushed her sister's objections, but Mari continued staring at Elysia thoughtfully. She finally spoke. "I don't think I judged you wrong. You're ignorant and selfish, but not malicious."

Elysia swallowed, absorbing the woman's observations. Her tone was neutral, objective even, which only made it worse. She had been evaluated and this was the conclusion.

Mari's brow went up in surprise as she kept talking, her thumbs brushing against the uneven pages of the book. "Even Jessa had to admit afterward that it seemed unlikely you knew what was going to happen. She lived, by the way, thanks to you making sure everyone got onto the beach. She was able to escape when she woke up in the wagon they'd all been loaded in."

She looked down, away from Elysia's gaze. "There's quite a few people who didn't make it, though. Both ones who fought and ones who traveled. They had more men scattered around the shores waiting—imagine their surprise when we popped out of thin air right in front of them." She ran a hand over her hair, tiny baby hairs bouncing free from her thick braid. "Shit fucking luck."

Her warm brown eyes betrayed her sadness, and guilt rose in Elysia. No one would ever see those people again unless it was dead in the main square. But the king was efficient, smart. People disappearing without rhyme or reason was just as effective for putting the fear in the masses as a head lopped off on a Sunday afternoon. He knew when each method was needed and used them accordingly.

"But I didn't come here to talk to you about last night. I promised you information, and if you think it will help you stay out of the Crown's graveyard, then I'm happy to give it, even if you have no interest in our cause."

She slid the heavy book across the bed to Elysia and tapped it with her fingers. "Tell me what it's like where you go. When you travel in your sleep."

Elysia stared past their faces at the plain wall in front of her. Whoever lived here didn't even have a single painting or piece of art. She'd told Beatriz and Gage about how she left her body and found herself in another land, another place, but she hadn't divulged what happened once she was there. Right when she thought she'd told everything there was to tell, she found another piece of herself to lay bare.

It was all too easy to conjure up visions of the dream inside her head. After pushing away the images for months, they sprang up and unfolded like a story, waiting to be told. Body tired and aching, she told them her tale.

"I fall asleep the same as anyone and when I wake, it's in another land—another realm, perhaps." She paused, eyes lost in her memories. "Kava seems to degrade more and more with each passing year, but this is different. It's death and decay and yet there's life."

Beatriz coughed like an old man, hacking without shame or subtlety. Everyone stared, and the Doorman's brow pinched with concern, but she waved them off. "What do you mean?"

Elysia let out a soft breath in the back of her throat, wishing her ribs and face would stop throbbing so she could concentrate. She searched for the words to describe this other world she fell into while asleep. The first image that came to mind was her bare feet, planted deep in the loamy dirt, how it oozed and chilled her toes. How the overwhelming expanse of the charcoal atmosphere hung over her with foreboding.

"Death seems natural there, I suppose. The soil is dark and rich—fertile, beneath my feet. The sky is a swirl of black and turquoise with a blood red haze. The trees are like bones. White with needle thin fingers. I've never seen anything like them. And there's a river. I don't think it's one you would want to fall into." She blanched a little, thinking of the dark, oil-slick river. It was beautiful, but so were many deadly things.

Mari struggled to keep the fear and awe from her face. "What happens when you're there?"

Elysia chewed on her chapped lips that still tasted of blood and gently touched the cool poultice strapped over her swollen shut eye.

"There's this song. It's haunting, echoing out from nowhere and everywhere all at once. And I'm drawn to it, but the dream never lasts. The music feels like it's *for* me though, which I know doesn't make any sense at all." Her chest ached even at the thought of it.

She ran her hand over her face and regretted it at once, able to feel just how swollen and misshapen she'd become.

Mari paled now and her voice came out a bit choked. "Have you ever seen anyone while you're there?"

Elysia scratched at the dried blood on her hands. "I always have a strange feeling of someone watching. I even thought there was someone once, but no matter where I look, there's no one. Like I said, I'm never there very long."

Beatriz's face wrinkled in distaste. "Gods, Lys, of all the places —you managed to find somewhere even worse than Kava. Sounds creepy. Like dead people creepy." Her last words ended in a mutter.

Mari's face swung hard to Beatriz. "I think that's exactly where she is. Where death himself lives—they used to call it the realm of death and deals."

She picked at short, bitten nails and took a deep breath. "Elysia, magic didn't just suddenly disappear from Kava one day. It was stolen. By the man—the god who rules that land."

Elysia wanted to scoff and brush the rebel leader aside. They were a godless land. She hadn't grown up going to temples or making petitions with offerings or flames. Other lands still believed the undead gods were the source of magic, but who was to say? Growing up in Kava, the stories of the gods weren't even allowed to pass over your lips. The idea that this undead god of death had swooped in like a villain and stolen all their magic felt far-fetched and a little silly. Yet her skin prickled and she felt the weight of Mari's words. At the very least, Mari believed what she was saying.

Elysia chose her words carefully, keeping her skepticism from her voice. "Let's say that's all true. Why would a *god* need our magic? Isn't that where people who believe in the gods say the magic comes from? And *if* it is there, can it be taken back?"

Mari threw up her hands. "I don't know! All the stories paint the gods as extremely fickle. Maybe he was bored. Maybe someone pissed him off. Maybe he's just greedy." Mari closed her eyes, containing her burst of passion. "You don't know Victoria."

The small brunette from the night before flashed through Elysia's mind.

"But she's never wrong. Her visions are terrifyingly accurate, and I'm telling you she has seen the land you're describing over and over. If she says that's where our magic is, then I believe her."

Beatriz threw Mari an unimpressed look and turned back to her sister. "Sounds like a load of shit to me. Fuck Kava, fuck magic. Get out of here while you can."

Elysia rolled her eyes, but knew her sister was serious, and frankly, she had a point. Her mind conveniently glossed over the bit about there being a god powerful enough to steal an entire kingdom's magic. She knew the very thought ought to inspire fear and trepidation. But as seemed to be happening lately, her anger opened its eyes, ready to spit at the idea of someone being so arrogant as to doom an entire people all for a bit more magic. Their kingdom was rotting. Soot falling to the ground and turning people's blood black, and even though no one would say it, everyone knew it had started after the Fall. Finally, she had someone to blame, and it pleased no small part of her to think of stealing Kava's magic back.

She spoke darkly to none of them in particular. "It's hard to even imagine that Kava wasn't always like this..."

Kava, a dirty stain in their magical world, somehow still standing as the one mundane, godless kingdom in existence. She thought about all those trips with her father to other lands, and not for the first time, wondered if he had kept her locked away on ships and in carriages for fear of her seeing how beautiful the world could be with magic free.

Mari tapped the book again. "Read the stories. If you're going to be pulled into enemy land, then you should at least know who you're dealing with."

Elysia snorted. Where wasn't enemy land? She was a woman with undead gifts. She was an enemy of the Crown who had been stupid enough to lay with its prince. Maybe she should just take her chances in this new, unknown enemy land. How bad could this god be?

She finally looked clearly at the book, her heart picking up its pace. She grabbed Beatriz's arm. "Triz, that's the book. The book from the library!"

Beatriz's mouth formed a pinched, flat line of distaste. She snatched up the book, not bothering to ask for permission. Rifling through the pages, she closed the book with a clap. "Of course it is. Right, so magic lady, how do we stop it? Because whatever garbage you were just spewing about my sister trying to *save magic* isn't happening. This kingdom is a shithole and will die a shithole, no use getting taken down with it." She stared pointedly.

Elysia sighed, chastising her sister. "Her name is Mari, Beatriz."

"I don't *care*, Elysia."

The Doorman swooped in, her sultry tones diffusing the brewing sibling storm. "Mari, is there a way to stop what's happening to Elysia?"

There was a hint of pity in the soft press of Mari's lips. "I've never known there to be a plant or method for stopping magic. It's as much a part of you as the blood in your heart and veins."

Beatriz began to pepper Mari with questions about who else they could talk to and where they might go for help, but Elysia cut her off with an air of exasperation. "Triz, I don't want to stop it. I mean, I did. Before. But, now, I don't."

Her dark eyes grew resolute, her tone matter-of-fact. "The prince knows everything. He left me for dead last night."

Frustration had her shaking her head. "Nothing will change the fact that my days are numbered even if we did find some way to rip the magic out of me. If anything"—she turned to Mari—"I want to know if there's a way to control it. I want to be able to stay in that realm and explore. If our magic is there... Well, I'd rather go down trying to do something useful than trying to escape. Besides, it'd be a long shot getting out of here when every merchant ship and export is overseen by my father, traveling by horse would take forever, and the train construction keeps getting pushed back."

Beatriz, the older sister who had never protected or coddled until now, let out a deranged hiss. "Have you completely lost your senses?" She grabbed the newly acquired book and strode to the door, holding it open wide.

She stared at Mari. "Get. Out."

Looking back at Elysia, she snapped. "And you, take the damn pain tonic. If you're not out or loopy as a bat within the next five minutes, I'll pour it down your throat myself." She left in a whirl of feminine rage, her feet banging down the stairs.

Everyone left after that. The room grew warm and fuzzy in a pleasant sort of way. She'd taken the pain tonic, not minding the reprieve it offered from her thoughts and physical agony. The world softened, her discomfort and lingering anxiety flickering out until she was boneless. Sinking back into the pillows, she closed her eyes.

Beatriz might not be willing to help her, but there was someone who would. A loose smile graced her lips as she fell under the blanket of sleep. Yes, there was someone who would be more than willing to help her find a way into the realm of death and deals.

Chapter 24

She kept running even though her lungs burned and her ribs ached. Both eyes were open now, even if her face still was an ugly mass of bruises and scratches. A wiser person might have waited longer to train, but Elysia could not stop the feeling of foreboding. The feeling of her time trickling like sand through the hourglass, and because she could not stop it, she tried to outrun it. She bounded through the woods and reminded herself with each step that sometimes it wasn't enough to be clever. She needed to be stronger, faster.

She had no misgivings about her abilities. Her physical gifts were average, but sharpened to precision through years of training, and she had no intention of letting that change just because someone had managed to beat her halfway to death. If anything, what had happened with Scarzan and the king's men had only reinforced what she had always known to be true.

Men never expected women like her to be capable of much at all. Big brown eyes and a soft face. They saw what they wanted—a docile creature ready for their boots to stomp on. They didn't expect you to lunge and grab them by the jaw to force a noxious poison down their throat. They didn't expect you to get back up after taking rounds to the face and ribs.

Her anxiety countered this, arguing that stamina and physical prowess were still no match for a king or a god, but she ignored the thought. She couldn't control much right now, but she could control what she put her body through. Running and training until her body hit its limit, shaking and ready to keel over. The self-inflicted pain almost felt good.

If she focused on the whole of the situation she found herself in, then she would become a paralyzed, frozen mess. And what good would that be? None at all. Compartmentalization had a time and place, and it was now.

She made it back to Gage's house, a sweaty, mud-splattered mess. The gate shrieked when she pushed it open. She cringed, knowing he left it creaky on purpose. Not that he needed the extra security. He was no one to most people, and those who did know Kava's Shadow were not dumb enough to go looking for his home.

She walked through the arched, black front door to find the man in question in his study, muscular frame hunched over a ledger. Still dressed in a fitted shirt and black trousers from being out on a job, a spot of blood decorated his collar. Yet now he sat at his large desk with candles burning as he poured over a page of numbers, looking as frustrated as any other business owner balancing their books.

"Money problems?"

Gage looked up at her, rolling his eyes, and she raised a brow obnoxiously in response. The day Gage had money problems she'd eat her own foot.

He set his work down, leaning back in his black leather and wooden lounge chair. "Yes, there's a woman eating me out of my kitchen and distracting me to no end, when I should be out running jobs."

She smiled sweetly, ignoring the pillow soft jab, and plopped into one of the navy armchairs in front of his desk, making him groan aloud.

Benign disgust contorted his face as he looked on. "For the

gods' sake, Elysia, at least change your clothes before you sit on things. If you were one of my men, I'd skin you alive for tracking shit all over the floors and furniture."

Elysia shifted, kicking her muddied legs over the arm of the chair. "It's almost as if I should go back to my own apartment. It's been weeks—the prince has done nothing. He may have been happy to let me die, but he doesn't seem to want to do the job himself. The king's men clearly didn't identify me, *and* Sir Larkspur hates it here." She stared at him in exasperation.

Gage sighed, shoving away his work and sitting up to stare at her like she was a complete moron. "Right, right. Maybe invite the prince over for a little heart-to-heart while you're at it, just really clear the air about that little part where he *was going to let them kill you.*"

Elysia ignored the immediate ache behind her eyes at his words and how her body felt a wave of shock every time she allowed herself to remember the truth. But she didn't let it show, instead she smiled viciously at the man she saw as a brother, knowing it would drive him mad.

"Nothing a good chat can't solve."

Gage chucked a crumpled sheet of paper at her head. "For fuck's sake. You know I want you here, just take a damn bath, will you? You smell bad enough to scorch the hair out of my nose."

An actual laugh rolled out of her mouth. He wasn't wrong. The combination of sweat, mud, and the gods knew what from the Relaclave streets made a terrible combination.

She'd been staying here for weeks rather than the House Gardenia. She'd stayed there long enough to be able to walk without feeling like she was going to pass out, and then she'd disappeared.

There was only so much of the newly protective Beatriz she could handle. It was downright unsettling to witness. Besides, how was she supposed to carry out any of her plans with Beatriz trying to swaddle her like a babe in a crib?

As much as she jested about going back to her apartment, she knew it wasn't a viable option. The prince had proven himself to be not only untrustworthy but a wild card. It was best to stay out of sight and out of mind for the time being. And that left her here with her murderous and secret-laden mentor. It really was more pleasant hiding out at Gage's house, though. It was always warm and filled with an obscene amount of food. Excessively cozy for an assassin, really.

Elysia threw her feet down on the floor. Mud fell off in chunks and she winced. "I wanted to see if you were game to spar."

"No," he said flatly. "Considering I normally have to drag you out to train, I thought you would have burned yourself out by now. You can't keep training like this, Elysia. You're barely healed as it is."

Undeterred, she bargained. "I swear it looks worse than it is at this point. Just an hour?"

Gage remained unamused and unconvinced. "No. Now go bathe yourself before I decide that Larky boy would make a better dinner than a pet."

"That's disgusting."

"Tell him to stop pissing on my pillows, then."

Elysia stood begrudgingly, fighting back a laugh at the wet, muddy outline she'd left on the chair.

Both of Gage's hands landed on the expanse of his desk as he leaned forward. "*Bathe*, now."

She'd stepped onto the first stair when he called out, looking back up from his papers. "Dinner is in an hour. We need to talk."

<hr>

ELYSIA DIPPED down in the water to just below her chin, her eyes still peeking above the glimmering surface. The bathroom attached to her bedroom was stocked with every salt and oil and scrub one could imagine. Based on the selection lining the small shelf near the tub, it would be easy to assume that a pampered lady resided here instead of a man with more scars than she could count.

It wasn't vanity that prompted Gage to stock every bathroom with glass canisters of salts and oils, though. It was simple practicality. The salts soothing her strained and overworked muscles were just that—practical.

If Gage looked handsome, it was because it suited the job. If Gage looked rough enough to scare the piss out of you, then it was because it suited the job. Everything had a time and place in his world. Salts to soothe, oils and ointments to protect and repair. He always said his body was both his tool and his home, and he would treat it as such. That an assassin who did not take care of himself was an assassin who was dead.

She'd known him so long that she imagined she was a bit numb to the idea of him killing strangers. Even after all these years, there was still an endless stream of questions she wished she could ask him—like why he'd come to Kava or how his family's empire functioned. Whenever she approached such topics, he'd just give her an easy smile, evading her questions as skillfully as any courtier.

The truth was, the man could tell her he was a demon and she'd find a way to rationalize it. Because he was the man who had plucked her out of a blood-soaked festival and kept an eye on her ever since. He'd taught her to punch and throw a dagger, but also how to mend rips in her clothes and how to cook her own breakfast. He'd found her the proper herbs to soothe her cycles and also to keep children at bay. He'd introduced her to people who traded in weapons and poisons, but also to the old lady who sold sweets that rivaled anything Lynd could whip up in her kitchens.

He was a complicated creature, and that was something she could relate to. She had long ago accepted that most people were neither all good nor all bad. She herself kept changing by the day, and wherever she ended up would likely be as murky as the Valvere Sea.

Elysia scooped out a handful of the closest body scrub, sitting up to rub it down the lengths of her arms. The events from what was close to a month ago now still threatened to overtake her psyche in moments like these where she was still and there was no one and nothing to distract her. She'd killed two men in one night, and it hadn't been magic's fault.

She sighed, reaching around to her back, barely noticing the grit of the sugar scrub over her thoughts. Her death total climbed higher by the week it seemed, and yet where there should have been her usual self-loathing was only a strange emptiness, as if all of her emotions had slid just out of reach. Below the surface of the water, they darted away anytime she tried to look them in the eye.

Plunging back under, she rinsed off the scrub. The apathetic void she found herself in extended to her own life. The reckless-ness that drove her beneath the sea hadn't been beaten out of her, it had only been fortified.

Selfish and ignorant. That's what Mari had called her. Elysia dipped her head back, humming to herself. The words had landed. Because she knew they were true—her sights had always only been her own survival. Powerless and afraid, she'd never let herself dream of change. But the rebels had.

Nestling back into the tub, she inhaled the dark, woodsy scent she had dripped into the water. The scent of pine stung her heart, reminding her of *him* and making her wish she'd reached for any other bottle. Rippling her fingers through the water, she concluded there were no sane options any longer.

She was going to walk downstairs where Gage would once again peddle out his standing offer to smuggle her anywhere but here. Maybe it'd work, maybe it wouldn't. Her father's relation-ship with the men who worked the steamships was greased with years of money and the promise of continued work. The chances of convincing an entire crew not to turn her in were slim. Someone always wanted extra coin, and narcing on Elysia Parker would be a sure way to line your pockets.

Deep in her gut, she knew her story was here. The story was

not in one of the many lands that boasted of sun and flowers and warmth that healed your bones. Because beyond her apathy was a long wilted desire to live a story worth telling.

The story she needed, the story that was hers, was in the soot-riddled rain and once creamy but now ashen sweeping arches of her favorite buildings. The story was hidden somewhere behind the shining, colorful doors of her city and dead diplomats and princes who hunted magical beings beneath the sea.

Elysia stood, water dripping, allowing all the dead and dirt to fall away. Wrapping herself in a towel, her bare feet slapped against the floor. No matter how Beatriz or Gage cajoled or threatened, it was her choice to make, and she was staying. If she was grateful to her parents for anything, it was teaching her not to bend to the whims of others, no matter how loudly they shouted or quietly they begged. Parkers crafted their own aims in their own time for their own ends. And it was damn time she did so for herself.

It had been almost a month, and she had waited long enough. Gage and Beatriz would have to accept her decision whether they liked it or not.

Elysia slipped into a shimmering blue velvet dress that slid over her like a cascading river. Soft dark boots and a black as night cloak. She shoved a scrap of lace into her pocket with a few pins and walked slowly back down the stairs into the kitchen.

Gage looked up from the fish he was deboning, irritated. "Take that cloak off. We're eating."

She made no move to take off the cloak. Sneaking past him was an impossible task, which is why she hadn't bothered. Hands sliding into her pockets, she answered him. "I can eat when I come back."

He nodded tightly, his fingers gripping the counter behind him now. "So, you're coming back then?"

She spoke softly, cutting to the heart of the matter. "I will not run. I can't. I won't. The magic holds me here, and there are things I need to do. If you want me to leave, then I'll go—I know my presence threatens you too."

His face, his entire body, became stone. Turning back to the stove, he dropped the now boneless and chopped fish into a pot. "One second past midnight and the doors will be locked. I'll have my men throw you in a cell. Do you hear me?"

Kava's Shadow did not have any children of his own, but he did have one impossibly frustrating little sister. And it appeared he would do whatever he could in order to keep her safe.

Elysia blinked at his tone. She was fairly certain she'd just been given a curfew for the first time in her life as a grown woman. A smile cracked her face, and she forced herself to walk backward into the hall instead of burying him in a hug.

"Midnight," she answered, slipping out the door into the already darkening night.

CHAPTER 25

Elysia moved with purpose, wanting to be on these streets not a moment longer than necessary. If she could have tunneled her way across the city, then she would have, but unfortunately, that wasn't possible. The handkerchief of lace she'd shoved in her pocket was now draped across her face, hiding her identity. Tiny jeweled pins, snug and secure in her hair, held it in place. Better people think her in mourning than for someone to see her face and send word to the prince or her parents.

Her absence wouldn't be tolerated much longer by her parents—she'd sent a message informing her mother that she was traveling, but would be back in time for the Raven Ball. A risky move given her father's temperament, but better than disappearing without reason and having them send out a search party.

Her feet carried her like a whisper past folks stumbling out of taverns. Spirit Street was not somewhere she frequented if she could help it. Vile scents of piss and stale liquor with a hint of sea brine turned the air rancid. Beneath her veil, Elysia's face scrunched, unsure if it was worse to breathe through her nose or her mouth. Her foot stuck to the unpaved muddy street, releasing with a disgusting squelch. While most streets in the northside were paved with smooth, dark gravel, it seemed both the residents and the Crown knew better than to waste any money on the upkeep of this particular street.

The taverns and hideaways lining both edges of the street were not the softly lit, golden hued spaces that her sister frequented. Beatriz and her friends did their drugs off of marbled bars and watched rooms spin from rich, swanky couches. The dank taverns on this street met a different need. The crushing, relentless need of people who knew nothing would ever change, that tomorrow and the next day would be the same as yesterday, but a pint would always be just a few coins. People who toiled and toiled and toiled, yet still could barely afford the bloated prices for imported food. These were the same people who sailed the seas and traveled the continent to procure everything from spices and vegetables to the occasional fruit for those who could afford it, but then ended their days in a room they shared with five other men.

On Spirit Street, the men and women who would take your coin for pleasure were not trained and allowed choice like the gentle people of House Gardenia. At the House they could turn you away without a second thought or fear of consequence. The people you found on Spirit Street were desperate, and desperate people made terrible choices because they were the only choices left to make.

Elysia walked up to a mildew-ridden tavern with wooden boards warped from the moisture-heavy air. The window giving a glimpse inside had been broken, likely from a fist based on the size of it. She didn't find it promising that the owner hadn't bothered to replace the glass pane, as if they knew it wasn't worth the trouble. Stark white lettering spelled out her destination on a plank nailed high above the pea-green door. The Salty Rim.

She didn't bother to kick the mud from her boots before putting her shoulder into the door to open it. A brass bell clanged over head, heads turning with lingering stares. She knew why they were staring. The soft boots. The crushed velvet peeking out beneath her plain cloak. Even plain well-made items could scream money. Most importantly, this wasn't the kind of place that saw new faces often. They knew their own, and she wasn't one of them.

She'd expected as much, her eyes skipping over the patrons as she searched for the person who ran the bar most nights. Rumor had it the owner kept an old sea plank encrusted with rusty nails beneath the bar. The way people told it, no one started a fight twice in the Salty Rim. Elysia imagined it was rather hard to make the same mistake twice when you ended up with rusted nails planted in your skull.

The only law that seemed to be enforced in these parts was magic being forbidden like it was everywhere. Otherwise, the king's guards and soldiers tended to look the other way. If it didn't impact the Crown, then they weren't being paid to care.

Elysia found her target right where she expected her. Standing behind the bar, the woman's catlike laurel-green eyes looked like she already had her mind made up about Elysia, and the verdict was not in her favor. Bare arms crossed, she wore an oversized faded aqua-blue shirt with the sleeves torn off and the buttons split open just enough to reveal an ample chest. Mink-gray heavy trousers met old worn out thick-soled boots. Paired with the wild black waves coursing down her back, the effect was as intimidating as it was attractive.

From her face to her body language, Elysia gathered that Jessa Roberts did not have time for anyone's shit today. She especially did not have time for a two-timing Crown bitch's shit.

Elysia watched as Jessa stared at her, an undeniable hint of violence in her gaze. She continued polishing the glass in her hands until it shone brightly against the dingy light of the tavern. A warped reflection of herself and the shithole behind her danced on the glass's surface. Glancing away, her eyes fell onto the nail studded plank of lore an arm's length away from Jessa, and she started to wonder if this had been such a grand idea after all.

Against her better judgment, she tried to open the conversation.

"Jessa."

"Crown. Bitch."

Jessa kept polishing the already clean glass, her lips curled in disgust.

Elysia's mouth tightened, but she ignored the insult. Untying her cloak, she used it as a cushion for the splintered wooden stool. She sat down, folded her hands and tried again, cutting to the point. "Do you remember what Mari asked me that night? About what happens when I sleep?"

A flicker of confusion gave away the truth before Jessa's face smoothed.

Given the events that had occurred two seconds afterward that evening, she wasn't surprised Jessa couldn't recall what had been said. *Perfect.* That was exactly what she had hoped for.

Elysia smiled like she held a secret in her teeth. "Pour me a drink because I think you're going to want to help me."

Jessa scoffed. "Doubt it."

And yet curiosity must have trumped her disdain given she grabbed a bottle of gin and popped the cork. Pouring out two small shooters, she pushed one over to Elysia. "Surprised you're willing to show your face here—anywhere really after attacking the prince." Accusation hardened her eyes. "Or maybe you were in on it the whole time."

Elysia shook her head slowly, fingers toying with the edge of her glass. If Jessa really believed that, then she would have already chased her out of here or thrown a punch. "I don't think the prince would have left me there then, do you?"

The words twisted the irrepressible pain she had been trying so hard to keep away. "He followed me. Knows enough that he could have me killed. Maybe it's sentiment that keeps him from turning me in, but I doubt it. I wouldn't have come if I knew he was following me. I wanted information, not to get people killed."

She blinked, keeping the shine out of her eyes. This woman was a stranger who despised her, not a bosom buddy whose shoulder she could cry on.

Jessa's eyes tracked over the almost completely faded bruises on Elysia's skin. "Heard you got your ass handed to you on the beach." A dark smirk crossed her face.

Elysia's temper flared, her eyes narrowing. "I heard you'd be rotting under the sea if a Crown bitch hadn't come back to save you and your sorry ass. Your people need training. They stood around like helpless children waiting to drown."

Jessa grabbed her glass and held it up. "To not dying."

Elysia huffed a laugh, holding her own shooter out.

The gin was awful. But somewhere between their third and fourth drink, Elysia decided to go through with her plan. She winced as she took another sip of gin, glancing around to make sure no one was close enough to overhear.

"Your friend, Victoria, she has visions of another realm, right? That's where I go when I sleep. At least that's what Mari and I think. Mari also thinks the god who lives there stole Kava's magic."

She made a face implying she knew how crazy this sounded. "I figure I've got nothing to lose at this point. Might as well find out."

Jessa studied her, eyes slightly squinted. "You're just going to find this hypothetical god and ask him if he took our magic?"

"God of death," Elysia corrected and hiccuped.

Jessa's eyes went large and she shook her head. "You're a little crazy, aren't you?"

Elysia lifted a shoulder. "Maybe. What do you care if I get killed?"

Her answer was flat and fast. "I don't."

Elysia smiled. "Exactly. That's why I want *you* to help me figure out how to stay in that realm long enough to find this guy."

Jessa blew out a long breath, but didn't answer.

A bit drunk, blind desperation colored Elysia's words. "We could bring magic back—if he took it, then he can give it back. Kava would *change*."

Dropping her towel on the bar, Jessa scrubbed at her face. "Let's say you do find this god. The most likely scenario is you're dead before you can so much as bat your pretty brown eyes."

Elysia held up a finger in rebuttal. "Mari gave me a book, and I read the lore—he's known for cutting deals. And like I said, I don't have anything to lose. My life in Relaclave is over. I can go on pretending it's not, but it's only a matter of time before the prince or my father," she stumbled, wishing she hadn't said that, but continued. "Before someone turns me in. Escape is unlikely, and maybe enough people have died because of me and my magic."

Her eyes glassed over in spite of herself. "Maybe, maybe I'd like to do something good before I die."

Jessa looked at Elysia knowingly, her shoulders moving as she chuckled. "Mari got to you with her crusader bullshit, didn't she? She's got a gift for getting people to be better than they are." Her head moved side to side, then she shrugged. "Or maybe she's just good at making people feel guilty as shit. Either way, it works."

"I mean it, though. There is a list of names that grows longer with each month and year that I am connected to the Crown. I can only control my magic so much, and my father—" She tensed. "He demands names as payment. I don't know who she was to you, but there will always be another Syren. Please help me do this. At the very least, I can go there and find out if any of it is true. Isn't that worth it?" She held Jessa's gaze, hopeful but unexpectant.

Jessa stared at her for a whole minute, chewing on the inside of her cheek as she thought. "To be clear, I don't think this will work. From the little I know of the gods, you can't outsmart them, and what could you possibly have to offer them?"

Bitter honesty hardened the bartender's face, making her look older than her years. "I'll help you, but this is Kava—the gods only give curses here, and I don't see that changing just because you've grown a conscience."

The lanterns swung gently overhead, casting warm inconsistent light onto the bar, and Elysia smiled, holding out her glass with a shrug. "To tricking gods then. Because I'm done with being cursed."

Chapter 26

Elysia sneezed. The powdery scent of herbs and dried flowers from other lands kept tickling her nose. Crammed into the back of a traveling wagon, there wasn't a breath of space between her and Jessa.

"Why is it so hot in here?" Jessa grumbled, shoving up the sleeves of her thick, boxy sweater.

Elysia tried to give her space, but her shoulder hit a clump of plants, causing them to crumble onto the dusty wooden floor.

"Shit." She stepped backward now, only to knock into Jessa.

"Watch it." Her gruff voice held no real bite as she stabilized Elysia and kept her from taking down the entire caravan's worth of herbs.

"Why couldn't we have waited outside?" Another sneeze was building and her eyes were watering too.

Jessa bumped into her now as she tried to duck around a bundle of hanging flowers to stand closer to the door.

"By the fucking gods." She glared at the wagon and all its plants like she wished she could blow the damn place up. "Because these were the instructions."

Jessa bent awkwardly, avoiding damaging even more plants as

she combed her hair back into a high bun and secured it with pins she pulled out of her pocket. Mouth still full of hairpins, she recited the instructions. "Be inside the wagon by the desecrated temple of spring's fair maiden at dawn. Not outside, inside."

"Sounds like a trap," Elysia muttered. Patience worn thin, Jessa scowled at Elysia, her mouth shriveled and eyes a little wild. Elysia examined the dried flower in front of her. "Sorry, sorry."

Their friendship was not off to the most glowing start, she supposed. Mari had mentioned Jessa being in love with Syren Herrin, so Elysia assumed that reluctant assistance was about as good as she could expect. Especially when her almost betrothed had been the reason why so many more of Jessa's friends had met their deaths. There was a cloud of death clinging to her and she couldn't blame the woman for likely hating her guts.

Elysia gently brushed her fingers over a faded flower. Leaving her to die at the hands of his father's men counted as a breakup, didn't it? She hummed, picking up a new flower to inspect. Who had time to sort through those kinds of questions?

She paused, brow furrowing on a strange, unwelcome thought. She wasn't sure she had ever met a couple who loved and trusted each other in equal measure. If that sort of love existed, she'd never seen it. The gaping wound festering in her heart made her question if maybe, in a different life, that could have been something she wanted.

The wagon door banged open, coming close to crushing all the precious herbs and flowers on the wall behind it.

A wide, unsettling smile spread across the weathered face of the thin old woman who entered. Wrapped in a fiery red shawl, her bird legs stuck out beneath in soft cotton pants. Silently, she circled them, dipping in and around each woman, and examined them both to the point of discomfort.

Elysia and Jessa could barely keep up with this new dance, neither wishing to have the old woman's sharp nose in their face or to wreck her property as she looked on. Huffing, Elysia felt sweat blooming on her nape. Back where she started, the woman slammed the caravan door shut, clicking all the locks into place with bony fingers.

Anxiety brought Elysia's hands to rest over the top of her weapons. She'd worn warm, winter friendly trousers that she now regretted, with a belt made for securing the two daggers she had today. She remained unconvinced that Jessa needed weapons. From what Elysia had witnessed, she was more of a *use what you've got* type of fighter, carrying a confidence that even after years of training Elysia had never mastered.

The old woman clucked, tossing her red shawl over one shoulder and sashaying in close. "My, what an interesting pair we have here. Now, how did *this* come to be?" One hand shot out to grasp Jessa's cheek, the other to pinch Elysia's chin. Her eyes squinted as she gave a good sniff.

Elysia felt her body go ramrod straight. *Why do the elderly believe they're entitled to do whatever they want?* Falling back on her court training, she pointedly ignored the old woman's firm grasp and warm breath. Jessa did no such thing, her seemingly permanent glare melting into disgruntled disdain.

The tavern owner didn't mince words. "Sniff me one more time like some kind of dog, meela, and we're going to have a problem. Understand?"

Elysia blanched. Meela was the Bellian word for wise one—often used in place of the more formal title of priestess.

Her mind instantly brought her back to all those years ago. Escaping the castle, watching the Ryspurian priestesses with their faces painted like death. How they had danced and moved to death's silent song until the main square ran dark with their blood.

As an adult, she'd always wondered what had motivated them to embody such zeal—and if she was honest, such stupidity. Bellians were cut off from their magic just like anyone else who ventured into Kava. Those priestesses had been magicless and vulnerable, yet they chose to spit on the cornerstone of Kava's culture in the capital's main square.

The Kavian's were a godless, magicless people. And yet the priestesses had danced and sang in honor of an ancient holiday, stirring memories and longing in the hearts of the people willing to remember. As someone who had spent her entire life fixated on hiding in order to survive, she just couldn't understand what drove those women to such actions.

Whatever their reasons, the king's justice had been swift. Their deaths acted as a necessary reminder to his people that Kavians would not fall into such antiquated religion or be led onto false paths filled with unnatural magic. They would rely on themselves as was only right, undead gods be damned.

The meela paid no mind to Jessa's threats, instead smiling knowingly at Elysia.

"You," she barked.

Elysia's eyebrows went up. "Yes?"

The old woman grabbed a polished wooden cane from the corner of the wagon. "How long has it been, then?"

Perplexed, she looked from the woman to Jessa, who just threw up her hands like she couldn't be expected to understand the woman's nonsense.

"I beg your pardon, but I don't know what you mean." Uncomfortable, her court mask remained in place, stiffening her words.

The woman harrumphed and smacked her cane against a cupboard, causing both Elysia and Jessa to flinch. She grumbled unintelligibly before flinging her bony arms and hands wide, the red shawl slipping down her shoulder. "Don't be daft. That you've heard death's song, of course. What else would you be pestering me about? I might be forced to live like a mundane slug while in this godsforsaken land, but I can still recognize the magic I've studied my entire life when it barges into my wagon."

Elysia's thoughts and fears jumbled. Her voice was a scratchy thing, caught like a bird in her throat. "No, that can't be right." Her words became faster. "Are you sure? Because really, I'm just good at finding secrets. Practically a professional gossip. Not deathlike at all."

Jessa stared at Elysia like she'd lost her mind, crossing her arms in annoyance. "What are you talking about? Tell her about the dreams. I've got to get back to the bar, so—" She motioned for Elysia to get on with it.

The meela laughed knowingly. "You don't want to talk about death. No one ever wants to talk about death." She chanted the words rhythmically. Poking her cane in Elysia's direction, she continued. "Okay then, child, tell me what brings you to my store? Herbs for money? Love? Lust? I hear the prince knows how to delight, if you know what I mean." She cackled and made a thrusting motion with her hips.

Jessa cringed, and Elysia found herself looking anywhere but at the small, gyrating grandmother in front of her.

"Fine," she spit out, just wanting the woman to stop before she lost her breakfast. "I met priestesses from your land as a girl. They told me I'd been marked by death, and I never thought twice about it until now." The formal rigidity she'd slipped into in her discomfort had disappeared in the face of such strange, lewd behavior.

The meela gripped her cane. "Go on."

Elysia rubbed her dust-irritated eyes. "In my sleep, I travel to a land that I believe is where your god resides, and yes, there is a song. I need help with traveling there."

"Pfff, you're doing just fine if you're managing to dream travel at all while living in this festering excuse for a kingdom."

Elysia frowned. She looked at all the dried flowers and herbs, muted but still beautiful, wishing she was trying to go somewhere that could actually grow something for once. "Okay, I need help *staying* there. I want to stay and explore. I need to find your god and speak with him."

The meela made impatient noises. "So do it then. Stay, wander, talk to whomever you wish while you're there."

Jessa butted in. "She never makes it more than a few steps and she's waking up. Same thing happens every time."

Her eyes became unfocused as she considered the problem. "This soil curses you all. But yes, we can fix this. You'll be right as rain."

Elysia felt her shoulders relax. She tossed Jessa a grin—finally, *progress.*

The grandmother began to sing an unfamiliar song to herself. While Kava itself was godless, Elysia wasn't completely uncultured, and she thought it might have been a hymn. Both women watched as the meela set to work chaotically tearing, ripping, and crumbling plants into an oversized glass jar. Her short body moved to and fro within the small caravan, her cane tapping and smacking as she went. Jessa and Elysia once again became a mess of limbs and elbows, trying to dodge both the old woman, her cane, and the plants.

Jessa's shoulder rammed into one of the plant-covered walls, and she was rewarded with a hard swat to the rear from the meela's cane.

"Watch the merchandise, girl! Practically gold in this land." The meela tutted and raised her cane warningly before returning to her work.

Elysia bit back a laugh, her shoulders shaking at the sight of Jessa silently fuming, nostrils flaring. "You can't beat up a grand-mother, Jessa."

Jessa shot her a look that said otherwise.

Unlabeled liquids were grabbed from the small wooden cupboards. Measuring with the reckless precision of someone who has been practicing for damn near a century, the meela slopped what smelled like alcohol into the jar until it covered the plants. Elysia watched in fascination as the grandmother eyed the mix of herbs, flowers, and liquid. She grumbled to herself before tossing in a few more pinches of plant dust. As far as Elysia could tell, the concoction hadn't changed, but the woman seemed satisfied now. Screwing on a tight lid over the top of a black cloth, she shoved the jar at Elysia.

"You must wait at least a month. Take no more than a thimble at one time. Have this one"—she jerked her head at Jessa—"watch over you as you travel."

Elysia stared into the jar, the liquid already turning a murky purple-brown. She gave it a little shake, watching all the petals and leaves and twigs swirl before settling once more. She was going to be able to follow the song. That haunting, enchanting song she was half convinced was designed to lure her to her death.

"How long will a thimble give me?"

The meela shrugged, tapping a long fingernail on the jar's lid. "Eh, hard to say. Your magic is crippled, but not lacking."

"You have no idea how much time this will grant me?"

The woman hemmed. "Ah, well, you know how it is with these things."

Elysia's face flattened. "No, no, I don't."

"The tincture will simply smooth out all those pesky gnarled bits of your magic." Her face brightened. "Like ripping the brakes off a carriage."

With those words, a new fear took root within Elysia. "If the brakes are gone, then how do I come back? I *do* need to come back." She looked down at the jar in her hands. *This lady is going to get me killed.*

The meela's shrug was a little more infuriating this time. "Magic is like breathing, but how am I to say? This land has turned you all inside out." She gave them her back, apparently done with the conversation, and began cleaning up the remnants of herbs covering the floor.

Elysia caught Jessa's eye, who looked back at her with an equally frustrated expression. Like it wasn't dangerous enough to seek out a *god*. She could practically hear Rollie squawking away at her, telling her what a blazing idiot she was for this.

Tucking what sounded an awful lot like it might just be a

party drug gone wrong beneath her cloak, she turned back to the meela.

"Meela, how can I pay you for this?"

She pulled a handful of coins out of her pocket. It wasn't much, but it was what she had leftover from last month's rent.

The old woman fussed with Elysia's cloak and touched her cheek, suddenly sweet instead of a wizened terror. "There shall be no price. I do this as a gift to my god and the women who raised me."

CHAPTER 27

CURLED up like a cat on the cushioned bench beneath her bedroom window, Elysia stared pensively at the sealed jar of herbs. She gave the jar a little shake. After all these months, she couldn't imagine what it would be like to finally sink her feet into the river bank of her dreamland. To walk along its edge and follow death's song. Again, she wondered where the song would take her.

As usual, rain dripped down the window, smearing her vision of the outside world. Lost in her thoughts, she let her forehead press against the chilled glass, staring out into the gray nothing. Rousing herself, Elysia pulled the black and gold embossed book from Mari back onto her lap. She'd been trying for over an hour to immerse herself in its text, to no avail. Filled with stories and commentary on all the undead gods her people had once known, the book was dense enough that she found herself stalling.

She'd already read all the stories about the god of the dead, but now with her tincture brewing, anxiety drove her to believe there just might be a key she hadn't found yet within the text. Flipping to death's pages, she began to skim, hoping to glean something new and useful for making a deal with death himself.

Her fingers traced the charcoal sketch of a man standing with his arms behind his back in a scraggy field littered with skulls and bits of bone. She frowned at the image. *I really hope that's symbolic...* It was nothing like what she had seen in her dreams, but then again, she hadn't seen much at all. Maybe there really was an old decaying field of bones and dust.

Over the weeks, the potion had grown darker and murkier, still all purples and browns. During this time, she kept waiting for fear to seize her. Wherever this realm existed, it was death. The person in charge of such a place could not possibly be someone you'd want to run into on a dark night without your wits and a good knife in your hand. *Not just death, deals.* As if his ability to rule over death was too simple, too *boring*. He'd had to take up a second hobby: manipulating mortals into desperate deals. She supposed all gods accepted or declined petitions, some of them had simply become more active in the process.

The terror never came.

It made her wonder if some fundamental part of her had been broken by the vigilance required of her as a cursed individual being blackmailed by her own blood. Or maybe it was a latent effect of watching innumerous executions, knowing it could and should have been her. In spite of her dark thoughts, Elysia lounged on her bed comfortably, sifting through the pieces of herself as if they were cut from someone else.

She imagined that a normal person would feel a sense of revulsion at the idea of visiting the land of the dead while still very much alive. Maybe there was something irrevocably wrong with her. Either way, there wasn't much she could do about it.

A flurry of feet sounded on the stairs, causing her to turn her head. Gage was gone, and this wasn't a house that received visitors. Elysia rolled smoothly off the bed, landing in a crouch, dagger in hand, waiting for whoever was about to break through the door.

Chapter 28

The doorknob twisted, opening to reveal a smug but winded Beatriz panting in her doorway. Lips curled in victory, her sister nodded a breathless hello. One of Gage's men appeared behind her, grabbing at the back of her neck, but without missing a beat, Beatriz threw her elbow back into his windpipe, never losing her smirk. The man gurgled and dropped to his knees behind her. One solid donkey kick from Beatriz and he was toppling down the stairs.

Elysia groaned and shoved her dagger back into its sheath, tossing it onto her bed. "One of these days I'm going to stab first and ask questions later, and then you'll be sorry."

She ducked past Beatriz, gaping at the now unconscious man sprawled awkwardly halfway down the stairs.

"Gage is going to be so pissed," she muttered, slamming her bedroom door and leaving the man to his shame.

Beatriz just shrugged, her attention on Elysia's dagger that she'd immediately picked up and was now sliding in and out of the sheath. "Not my fault he's bad at his job."

Elysia snatched her dagger back. "That's not a toy, Beatriz." She shoved the weapon beneath the waist of her trousers.

"My, my, you have even more secrets down there than most women." Beatriz gave her a wink, lighting a fire in Elysia's blood.

Hands latching onto her hips, she interrogated her older sister. "How did you even find me here?"

Beatriz flopped back onto the bed, arms going behind her head like she owned the place. Ignoring her younger sister's question, her gaze slowly slid around the room, making obvious stops on incriminating items. The book on the undead gods. The discarded weapons casually strewn about. The juxtaposition of pretty dresses and leather leggings and training gear. Curiosity lit her gray eyes as they halted on the herbal tincture.

Elysia drew her attention back, snapping her fingers in front of Beatriz's face. "I asked you a question. Do you even know whose house you broke into?"

Beatriz's head rolled to the side, flashing Elysia with a grin.

Her eyebrows rose, giving Elysia a put-out look. "Of course, I know where I am. You said you trained with Kava's Shadow. What you didn't say was that you're close enough with the man to sleep in his beds and eat his food. But Lily is very rarely wrong about these things. She says everyone needs people, even Parkers, and he's yours."

She went pensive, interlacing her fingers and looking back up at the ceiling. A hint of guilt touched her words, but she didn't say anything else, just nodded like this Lily knew everything.

Elysia's brow creased. "Lily? Oh, the Doorman's name is Lily."

Beatriz grabbed a small practice sword and swung it dangerously in Elysia's direction, her shoulder dropping with the unexpected weight.

Elysia disarmed and admonished her sister in one smooth movement. "Stop *touching*. You're going to hurt yourself."

Unfazed, Beatriz plopped back onto the bed. "Don't ever call her Lily. Or tell anyone she's called Lily. She'd probably kill you." She smiled with extra teeth.

Elysia sat down next to her sister on the bed, throwing up her hands. "Fine, I won't call your girlfriend by her name. But I highly suggest that you're gone by the time Gage gets home, so if you would just tell me why it is you're here…"

Beatriz tilted her head, looking at Elysia like she was dense. The look was unfortunately a familiar one between them. Blinking, she sat up abruptly, her posture suddenly perfect and imposing.

"Mother is ready to send out the guards to bring you home. Your cute little note about traveling didn't land well with mommy and daddy dearest." Her gaze became shrewd, and her voice icy. "You made yourself indispensable and now you're paying for it. It's almost as if you should have left the fucking kingdom like everyone who cares about you advised in the first place."

A rumbling chuckle filled the room, causing both women to whip their heads in unison. "So, this is the famous Beatriz."

Gage took up the whole damn doorway, his hands grasping the top of the frame as he leaned in heavily. He lingered there with one brow raised as if he hadn't snuck up on both of them like a lethal animal trapped in a man's body.

Beatriz blatantly ran her eyes over Gage, not bothering to be polite. "Do you fuck people on the side then, or is that body just for killing?" She turned to address Elysia seriously. "Lily could use someone like him. She only has pretty boys. Needs someone more like that."

Mortified, Elysia choked and failed to respond.

Immune to her sister's discomfort, Beatriz continued giving her entirely unsolicited opinion, inspecting Gage like he was for sale. "You know, the whole *I could kill you as easily as I fuck you* thing really does it for some people."

"Beatriz! You can't just *say* things like that."

Frowning, her sister looked at her with pinched brows. "I just did."

Elysia grabbed a pillow, smacking her sister in the face hard enough to send her backward onto the bed. She held the pillow there and smiled. "Just because you can doesn't mean you should."

She released her hold on the pillow and Beatriz shot up, her silver hair a mess and eyes narrowed. Elysia's chest quivered with silent laughter.

"He's like family, Triz. Don't be so gross."

Gage froze for half a breath only to start laughing so hard that the entire door frame shook, his shirt straining as his arms and chest flexed.

Beatriz gestured again. "*See?* That right there. Money maker."

Elysia shut her eyes. "Please stop."

"Don't be such a prude, Lys. We all know what you and the prince get up to."

"I'm a grown woman, you can't make fun of me for having sex."

"I mean, I can when it was with Topp Blatz."

Gage cleared his throat, pausing their squabble. "Your sister is right, Elysia."

She floundered. "Excuse you! I don't comment on *your* sexual partners, and after being here for a month, I certainly could!"

Beatriz's eyes lit. "Oh, do tell. What's his type? I bet he likes the ones that'll burn your house down. I can sense these things." She glanced at Gage cursorily and nodded as if he had confirmed her suspicions.

Gage stared up at the ceiling, looking pained, and rubbed his face. "I meant about leaving Kava and your parents."

"Oh, that." Elysia looked down at her feet. "Right."

An emotion that Elysia couldn't place crossed his face. "The Raven Ball will be here before you know it, and you've been gone for almost two months, when you've never been given permission for more than a few days in the past. The prince has been lying for you, but it's not working anymore."

Frustration laced her words. "Why would he do that? I don't understand that man. Yes, he tried to talk to me about my magic, and I avoided his attempts to communicate because I was *terri-*

fied. But then he followed me! And got people killed, proving me right all along. I wish I could just have a conversation with him, which I know is insane, but I don't understand what he's doing."

"But you haven't spoken with him," Gage prompted her.

Her voice went hard. "No, I haven't. Before that night—I worked the market like usual. Topp showed up and he promised me I could trust him. My magic could feel it wasn't true. Even if he wanted it to be the truth, it wasn't. Between that and him leaving me to die while a bunch of innocent people got rounded up for slaughter, I don't think there's anything he could say to prove himself. Any conversation between us would just be sating my pointless curiosity."

Beatriz got to her feet, hands grabbing her sister by the face. "Who cares, Elysia, who fucking cares? Never mind that lying carcass of a man and his motivations—just leave. Leave and save your own damn life." She took a giant inhale, nowhere near done. "Forget about him. Forget about Mother and our blackmailing excuse of a father, and for the first time in your twenty-four years get your *own* damn life. A life that has absolutely nothing to do with secrets or politics or death. Go grow your flowers somewhere that actually has sun and soil that grows."

Her sister's face grew heated, but her eyes glimmered. A sudden coughing fit shook her frame, but she finished quietly once she was done. "Please Elysia, do not stay here. There is nothing but death. And whether it comes now or later, that is all there is for you in Relaclave."

Elysia held very still, her heart beating rapidly in her chest. A tight pain encompassed her throat as Beatriz's words sank in. She nodded, defeat filling her and pricking her eyes painfully. She stood and her fingers brushed over the tincture jar.

Voice breaking, she couldn't manage to look Beatriz in the eye. "You're right. There's very little I'm proud of and endless things I'm ashamed of—that's why I was trying to do something different."

Throat aching, her feet felt weighted to the floor. She glanced one last time at the tincture on her nightstand. *It was a stupid plan, anyway.* Kava was halfway in the grave and it wasn't like a *god* was going to suddenly care.

"If you think you can actually get me out of here without me being dragged back to the castle, then fine. Book the ticket. Set it up. I don't care." Gage reached out to touch her shoulder as she walked out, but she evaded his touch, aiming for the staircase.

Ripping the cloak off the still crumpled, failed, and unconscious guard, Elysia flew down the steps and disappeared out the front door. A maelstrom of emotions crashed inside her, turbulent and unrestrained now that she was free from the prying stares of Gage and Beatriz.

She was well aware that leaving like this wasn't mature for someone her age. But her thoughts beat against each other as if it were a battle to determine which would win, and if she stayed, it would only end in words better left unsaid.

The wind cut against her face as cold as her brittle insides. One strong gust and she would be dust. Huffing, she wrenched Gage's front gate open and strode through, pulling up her hood. Uncomfortable with the warring guilt and self-loathing raging inside her, she reached for anger. She wasn't sure her sister had intended to be manipulative. But it felt like she had preyed on Elysia's obvious shame, reminding her of just how spineless she really was.

Maybe they would both always be a little fucked up. Doing their best to be different from how they were raised and still likely failing in some very important ways.

The thought made her feel ill.

Beatriz's words rang like treason bells in her head. As if she didn't know how much her life had been dictated by the whims and desires of those in power around her. As if it didn't kill her every time she went against her own moral compass in order to appease the Crown. Elysia let out a dark laugh, throwing her head back to stare at the evening sky. Cold air stung her nose, cooling her temper as it blew by.

She felt like a coward. The second Beatriz cornered her—she had folded. She didn't even believe Gage *could* smuggle her out, but she still hadn't stood up for herself. Hands in her pockets, she kept her eyes up as if the answers were hidden amongst the faded stars. The moon stared back, wearing its usual gray veil, dulling the bit of light it might have offered.

Doubt raised its voice inside her. *Because maybe she's right. You let everyone push you around. You fuck everything up—there isn't a chance in the realms you wouldn't have failed. Who are you to do something like this?*

A soot heavy cloud moved fully in front of the moon, stealing the last shard of evening light. It should have been someone like Mari who could dream travel. Someone worthy and capable.

Elysia pointed her feet in the direction of further self-destruction. Face uncovered, she walked with fast heavy steps, not really giving a shit if she was spotted. She supposed that would put a nasty kink in everyone's plans to save her sorry ass.

The sour stench of Spirit Street hit her in the face like a brick. *By the gods.* Remind her to never venture over here in the summer if it smelled this bad during the cold season.

She found the Salty Rim as she'd last left it. Dirty, broken, but likely to outlast them all in its squalor and glory. Bursting in through the door, she felt eyes touch on her then bounce away in disinterest. Hair tossed into a windblown bun and dressed in a thick navy blue sweater with a pair of Gage's old trousers belted on tight, she melted into the crowd just fine tonight.

Jessa watched her approach warily beneath strong brows. "What's gotten into you?"

Throwing herself onto a stool, Elysia ignored her question. "Drink, please."

"There's blood all over your cloak."

Elysia looked down and grimaced. The undead gods knew what that man had been up to before returning to Gage's house. Not that it took a lot of imagination to guess with that amount of blood soaked into the wool.

Elysia wrenched it off, grumbling. "Who wears a light gray cloak to kill people?"

Jessa stared openly for half a breath before finally muttering that she didn't want to know. Reaching down, she grabbed a bottle of Kava's cheapest gin. Its real name was Sonder's Gin, but everyone just called it Sap because not only did it taste and smell like pine, the burn stuck to your throat long after your drink was gone. She poured two tumblers and held one out.

"You look like the trash I normally kick out of here."

"Your tavern looks like it's one bad day away from collapsing. Somehow I don't think my *bloody cloak* is going to be what ruins the ambiance."

Jessa's eyes narrowed, and she bent her fingers expectantly. "Payment. Now."

"Yeah, yeah." Elysia dug around in her pockets until she found a few loose coins. Slapping them down into Jessa's palm, she picked up her drink with her other hand and chugged. Eyes squinting and face twisted, she fought off the cough trying to escape from her mouth. "*Fuck*. How does that shit get worse every time I drink it?"

Jessa smirked, walking away to help a few patrons at the other side of the bar. While she was gone, Elysia grabbed Jessa's drink, throwing it back and choking a little as it went down. Eyes watering, she cursed.

Walking back over, Jessa spotted her empty glass and stared at Elysia incredulously. "Seriously? You're being more annoying than usual."

Elysia shrugged. "Yeah, well, bad news. The plan's off."

Jessa's eyebrows drew together in anger. "Do you have any idea how many favors I pulled to get us that meeting with the meela?"

Throat still burning, Elysia snorted and spun around on her stool to watch the locals. Faces smudged with dirt and soot, she knew they'd all spent the day working hard while frozen to the bone and breathing in Relaclave's noxious air. And yet they still managed to laugh and rib each other over glasses of alcohol that set fire to their bellies.

"I'm fucking talking to you, Parker."

Elysia turned back around slowly. Aggravating Jessa was as easy as pissing off her sister. She looked up dryly. "And?"

Jessa closed her eyes, mouth moving as she silently counted to ten.

"Does that actually work for you? The counting?"

"Listen here, you sniveling Crown brat, we had a deal and you're not backing out now just because you're scared. Grow up and keep your word."

"Can't. Decided I'm leaving." She waved a hand in a circle above her head and pulled a face. "Take a look around, Jessa. Do you really think this is worth dying for? I don't. So, I'm not going to, sorry."

Jessa's mouth was half open, ready to fire back when she paused, comprehension dawning. She grabbed the Sap and poured herself a fresh glass. Taking a sip, she wiped her mouth and stuck a finger in Elysia's face as she started back in. "Motherfucker. You almost had me. But, nope. Not buying it. Whatever this is, it's bullshit."

Godsdammit. She dug her heels in. "Doesn't matter what you think. Either way, it's off. I'm leaving."

Lips pressed tight, Jessa leaned over the bar, dark hair swinging. Her voice lowered, its natural rasp harsh as she shone a light on everything Elysia hadn't said.

"Let me guess, someone got in your face, pressed on all the right places and now you're just giving up. Gods, are you even capable of making a decision for yourself? Or have you been a puppet for so long that you don't even know how?" Her disgust was audible.

Elysia bathed in the shame Jessa willingly poured over her. It was almost heady to hear someone voice aloud the terrible things she knew about herself. Bittersweet confirmation rolled through her, ripping open every old scar and wound. *Worthless. Stupid. Spineless.*

Jessa's voice got louder, angry that she wasn't taking her bait. "So, what changed? Who's pulling your strings now, Elysia? Because I know this isn't what you want. Who is it this time, huh?"

Elysia's mouth was moving before she could stop herself. Her words were fast and voice louder than she would have liked. "It never would have worked! Some half-baked plan from a tavern owner and the Crown's favorite fool? As if we could steal Kava's magic back from a *god*."

She laughed wildly, shaking her head.

Jessa's smile ate up her whole face, her catlike eyes sharp as ever. "Why'd you come here then? Did you think I was going to pat your back and feel sorry for you? Tell you that it's okay? Poor, Crown bitch. Poor, poor baby."

She pointed at the door. "You want to leave? Then get out of my damn tavern and don't come back until your head is on straight. I am *not* the one to come to with your whining bullshit. People are dying, Elysia, and they will keep dying unless something is done. But go ahead, run off." A note of disappointment tempered her anger.

She grabbed a cloth and began to polish the bar roughly. "As if the prince or your father wouldn't find you wherever you went."

Nodding silently, Elysia inhaled the poison of Jessa's words, making sure to feel each and every bit of the pain. She stood, pushing away from the bar, and looked Jessa dead in the eyes.

"You're right. But I'm a spineless, selfish Crown bitch. What else did you expect?"

She snatched the bottle of Sap off the bar and threw down the rest of her change.

"For your trouble." Crown oil oozed from her words, and she grinned at the snarl on Jessa's face.

And then she swept out of the bar like a queen with her disgusting cloak and shitty bottle of gin in tow. Beatriz wasn't the only person in this family who could do a bender. She could still hear Jessa shouting obscenities as the door slammed shut behind her.

Weaving through the streets of Relaclave, she tugged the wool cloak tighter around her body. She wasn't sure if it was the cloak, the bottle that she swigged, or her general attitude that was keeping the people at bay, but no matter what street she took, everyone was giving her a wide berth. Aimless, she'd walked far enough that the desecrated temple of the god of death was in sight.

She stalked forward, stopping to stare up at the ruins. Giant hunks of stone littered the raised concrete platform. Covered in her home's trademark soot, only the barest hints of white peeked out through the grime. She remembered Rollie telling her the stones had once been a giant skull, large enough to house priest-esses and worshippers at once.

Polishing off the last of the gin, she lifted the bottle overhead and flung it at the stone ruins. The glass burst, the sound loud against the silence of the night. "FUCK YOU, YOU USELESS, THIEVING—"

"Excuse me."

There was a tug on her cloak. Elysia turned to find a small girl with dirt-brown eyes looking at her in displeasure.

"*What*?" She gestured at the temple, glaring down at the child. "Kind of busy here."

Gods, it felt good not to care. *Was this what it felt like to be Beatriz?* She'd really been missing out.

The girl rolled her eyes. "You were supposed to be at the Salty Rim. I've been trying to find your drunk ass for an hour."

She held out a letter pinched between two fingers, clearly not wanting to get any closer to Elysia than necessary. Elysia couldn't even pretend to be offended. She was drunk, covered in blood, and screaming like a raving lunatic at a bunch of rocks.

She grabbed the letter. "Thanks so much." She smiled with false sweetness.

The messenger just shook her small blonde head. "Whatever, lady."

Elysia watched the kid run off, waiting until she was alone to rip open the letter. Climbing up onto the platform, she found a chunk of skull to plant her ass on.

There was no message. Only an address and time in bold, unfamiliar script.

721 Hawking Street. Ten o'clock.

Elysia flipped the paper around, checking the back and front, wondering if the alcohol had congealed her brain, but sure enough there was no further message or name to be found. The address rang a bell in her mind, but with the alcohol slowing her recall, she couldn't place why it was familiar.

As she stared at the note, a sly whisper curled in the air. *Go*, it said. The voice sounded hazy, the pull of it warm and enticing.

Paper crumpled in Elysia's fist. She knew better than to listen to her magic. But you know, she'd never had a bender before. Rarely even got proper drunk. Not that she was drunk now. *Obviously not. I'm sober as a bird.* A burst of laughter fell out of her. She clapped a hand over her mouth, still giggling. She was always too busy being *responsible* and being bossed around by her father to let loose. She *deserved* this. Gin pulled apart the last strands of her logic until she walked right through the hole it left behind.

Elysia stood. Eyes roaming over the scattered remnants of the temple, her thoughts drifted to its deity. *He's probably old and gross and useless like every other ruler, anyway.* She made a face, talking to herself aloud. "The last thing I need is another decrepit pervert in my life."

Shoving her hands into her trouser pockets, she forgot about gods who no longer mattered and pointed her toes in the direction of 721 Hawking Street.

CHAPTER 29

A RUSH of anticipation mixed with alcohol and greedy magic pushed her along with a lightness to her steps. Cobblestones flew beneath her and creamy buildings blackened with dirt surrounded her while black iron lamp posts lit her path with their signature smokey glow. She ran her fingers over the building closest to her, liking how it darkened her fingertips. She loved the filthy beauty of the south side. At least it was honest.

The rational, life preserving part of her tried to argue that she should just go home. It was late. She was drunk. And this was a terrible idea. But any remaining logic had been soaked in Sap and was no match for the magic rearing up within her.

What had started as a whisper now sang into her ear. All she could hear was the song of the secret crumpled in her fist. It was strong enough now she didn't even need the address. Not with the weight of the secret yanking like a sharp metal hook inside her chest. This secret's song was not a pounding drum or storm crashing against her skin. No, it came in softly, teasing her and drawing her near with its familiar sound. Its clever, tantalizing melody ran up her skin like calloused fingers she couldn't forget.

Her skin dimpled at its touch as she wound through the streets like she wasn't a wanted woman. Between the alcohol and the secret pulling her close, she could have walked for miles and never felt the distance pass beneath her feet. The song came to a lull and Elysia came to, realizing she was in front of her favorite restaurant, the Boar's Bones. *No wonder the address was familiar.* She stepped back into the alley beside the restaurant, moving out of the dim streetlight and away from wandering eyes. Tossing the bloodied cloak next to a pile of rotted food, she shivered from head to toe. While her outfit may have helped her blend in at the Salty Rim, it wasn't going to do her any favors at the Boar's Bones.

Delicious aromas drifted out of the cracked kitchen windows, and Elysia inhaled, wishing she were here to eat like any other normal person. She peered at the restaurant's back door, wondering what secret pulled her here, of all places. As she bounced from foot to foot, the cold brought a small dash of clarity to her thoughts. An image inside her head of the warm bed waiting for her back at Gage's had her reconsidering her actions, but thinking of Gage only made her think about being shoved like cargo onto a boat she didn't want to be on.

One last night to do whatever she wanted in Relaclave.

She smiled. Chasing after secrets that didn't belong to her was both what had built her and what had ruined her. She couldn't think of a better way to spend her last night in the decaying city she loved.

She would be on a ship tomorrow no matter what happened tonight. She could do anything, and Gage would still shove her below the deck and tell the ship's men that she was just a fat goat in a sack. Maybe if she was lucky, he'd even pull out her personal favorite threat she had ever heard him utter. *"Keep your mouths shut or I'll stuff them with your dicks."* Dramatic but effective.

The secret taunted her again. Elysia leaned against the alley wall, her sweater catching on the rough plaster. The hook in her chest was back, persistent as it ripped against her ribs, demanding she give in and give chase. She looked at the door, her feet already moving and hand reaching.

Cool metal bit her skin as she pressed down on the door lever. Once inside, a swell of heat billowed out of the kitchen to envelop her. The cold still clung to her, a shiver racking her body after being outside for so long. Muted sounds of chatter and laughter layered over the clinking of forks and knives met her ear. Sounded like a typical evening at the Boar's Bones.

She suddenly had the fleeting fear that her parents could be sitting at one of those tables. The thought triggered a ridiculous and unstable hiccup of a laugh. Clamping her lips shut, she tried to see through the small circular window on the door leading to the dining room. Her mother would *die* if she could see her now.

Slipping down the servers' hall, she found the narrow entrance to the staff-only staircase to the upper level of the Boar's Bones. She paused momentarily, staring into the shadows with trepidation. Dark and narrow with shallow steps was a dangerous combination for an alcohol and magic addled woman. Swinging herself around the bend in the stairs, Elysia sprang along the steps like a drunk cat.

Pausing at the top, she breathed out a wordless thanks to whoever was listening. The balcony level was empty, tables cleared and candles blown out. Creeping into the shadows, she stayed low and out of sight. Thick, wooden balustrades blocked the people down below from seeing both her and most of the tables. Yet anyone eating on the upper level would still have been able to gaze down, people watching as they enjoyed their meal.

Crouching down, she scanned the room through a wide crack in the wood. For a moment her magic flared, pulling her attention in every direction. The dining staff eavesdropping. The couple pawing at each other in the coat closet. Two men growing louder as they argued about money.

But none of those were what stopped her heart.

An easy deep laugh trickled past her ears and with it Elysia's blood rushed up her face, making her cheeks and ears burn. Nostrils flaring, her eyes moved fast, searching for the guilty party. *That fucking asshole.*

And there he was.

Leaned back and relaxed.

Engrossed in some tantalizing conversation with a beautiful woman Elysia had never seen before at *her* favorite table. The warmth of the oil lamp chandelier created sensuous shadows that danced across their forms. Elysia barely paid the woman any mind, though. How could she while her heart caught and fractured on the light playing against his green eyes? How he suddenly leaned forward in one fast motion, fingers pressing into the woman's thigh as if she were the only thing *he* could see.

When she looked back at this moment, Elysia would say that she really hadn't meant to do it. She was sure some vengeful spirit had overtaken her body. Probably Beatriz's, if she was being honest. Seemed like something she might do. But it was her own hand that ripped the blade out and let it fly straight over the balcony's edge as if she truly were the sister of Kava's Shadow.

The blade shattered the thin glass that the prince's strong fingers were wrapped around and vibrated as it struck deep into the wooden table beneath. The woman screamed, her chair clattering to the ground as she threw herself back and away from the table. The rest of the restaurant seemed to inhale one last breath before their fear broke, and everyone was shouting and shoving to escape out the exits.

In the center of the chaos, the Crown Prince remained unmoving with smug satisfaction lifting the corners of his mouth. The cacophony slowed until the only sound was that of her blade now spinning between his fingers.

Elysia swallowed hard, ducking back beneath the privacy of the balustrades. Eyes glued to her dagger in his hand, she watched it glint as it spun around and round. *I shouldn't have done that. Why did I do that?*

Her forehead hit against the wooden board. She should've run for it while the rabble threw chairs and elbows in their stampede for the door. Not a single soul remained in the dining room now besides the prince himself.

He was alone.

Someone had just thrown a dagger at the Crown Prince of Kava, and there was not a single guard throwing the bastard beneath a table to protect him or charging up the stairs to where the dagger had clearly been thrown from.

Elysia closed her eyes, fighting back her panic and instant disappointment in herself. Her magic was a fiend with no regard for her well-being. And *she* was a drunk, jealous idiot who walked with open arms right into the prince's trap. He'd lured her the same as any of the creatures he trapped in the woods. And she'd fallen for it. She shook her head miserably, hating herself even more now that her foul behavior had led to this.

Amusement vibrated in the prince's broad chest, the sound carrying up over the balcony to her ears. "Real shame for you that I'll have to keep the dagger. Only seems fair, considering you tried to kill me."

Elysia snorted, shaking her head. As if she would ever try to kill him. *As if she would miss.* She'd aimed perfectly even if he didn't believe it. Reaching up, she slapped her hand onto the rough wood and pulled herself up. Dizzy from the too fast movement, she grabbed on with both hands, swaying a bit on her feet.

The prince's brow quirked as he took in her rumpled and unsteady appearance. "Bad night?" His eyes stuck on her much too large trousers. "Do I even want to know whose those are?"

She smiled sweetly. "Wouldn't you like to know?" Let him think she was fucking someone else. See how *he* liked it.

The prince's eyes narrowed. "Are you going to come down here, then? I'd say you at least owe me a conversation."

Her fingers gripped the wood tighter. "I owe *you* a conversation? *That's* rich."

His jaw tensed. Stepping closer to the balcony and into the light, he tried again. "Fine. We *both* owe each other a conversation." He paused, looking strained. "Please, Elysia, can you just not be difficult this once?"

Elysia threw her head back and laughed. Her body flowed

back then forward with the sound, draping itself over the balcony's edge. "Me? I'm the difficult one? Oh, you are funny, Prince."

She swung her legs over and let herself slide right off the balcony, landing softly on her feet with only the slightest wobble. Her head spun, but she closed her eyes until it passed. She would not be vomiting again.

The prince stood mere steps away, emotions flitting through his eyes.

Awe. Longing. Anger.

She stood, slinking over to a table and leaning against it. Suddenly hot, she shoved up the thick, heavy knit sleeves of her sweater. The room slanted, but she ignored it, keeping her eyes on the prince. Exhaustion kept bleeding in, making her feel fuzzy and heavy all at once. *If I'm not going to sleep, then I need another drink.*

Blowing past the prince, she sauntered to the empty bar, making sure to give his shoulder a solid knock as she swept past. He followed on her heels now, his hands shoved into his pockets.

She found a bottle of wine, tugging on the cork until it popped free. Elysia watched the prince's mouth twitch as the wine glugged softly, pouring out into a glass. Bringing the glass to her mouth, she finally snapped. "What? Having a laugh at how easily you played me this evening?"

A full grin broke across his face, one hand brushing against the stubble peppering his chin. Green eyes filled with mirth, he stole the wine out of her hands, taking a sip for himself. "I didn't think there was a chance in all the realms you'd fall for it."

Elysia looked at him darkly. "My fucking magic fell for it just fine."

Sarcasm entered his tone. "Right. The magic."

"Yes, the magic." Her expression dared him to contradict her.

"Definitely has nothing to do with the fact that you smell like you rolled around in a bottle of gin all night." His face went pensive. "I think the last time I saw you even close to this drunk was at your mother's birthday party last year. Remember that one, Lys?" His lips lifted with suggestion.

Any possible embarrassment had died several drinks ago. Instead of flushing like she normally would have at his insinuations, she looked him square in the eye with a smirk. "Must not have been memorable for me."

A gleam entered his eyes. "Whatever you need to tell yourself."

Keeping her in his sights, he stalked behind the bar, making her heart race.

Low and deep, his voice washed over her, tugging at her just the same as her curse. "*I* remember everything about that night."

Her hackles rose at the sight of his body blocking the exit. She cut him a brutal look.

"Just stop. Stop your playing. Stop your flirtations. Stop pretending." She pushed a final sort of severity into her voice. "Whatever we had died when you left me to do the same."

A flash of guilt had him pausing. "You know that isn't what I intended. Nothing went right that night. I never wanted anything to happen to you."

His hand moved as if it wanted to reach out to touch her, but she automatically stepped back, bumping against a stack of glassware.

Her voice became as cold as the winter sea. "Your *intentions* left me damn near dead and killed innocent people."

Face devoid of emotion, he answered. "I'm well aware."

Breath short and heavy in her chest, she pinched her eyes closed and shook her head as if that would do the trick. "Either kill me, or let me go and forget my name. I will haunt you past the grave if you turn me in to your father and his men. I swear to the undead gods, I'll find a way to do it. I will not be put on display in the square like—"

"Like all the ones you sent there yourself?" He gave a sad laugh when her eyes shot to his. "We're more alike than you want to admit."

"I was *exploited.*"

"You've had a choice for a long time now, Lys." His now harsh stare tore out the foundations of the stone walls she had built up around her choices. Walls that allowed her to carry on living in spite of the terrible decisions she'd been forced to make. Green eyes bore down on her. "You haven't been a child for years. No one can fault you for choosing your life over theirs, but you have the choice to do it differently now."

Hot tears threatened to break free. His words made her feel sick. Because he was right.

Warm palms cradled against her face. "I will do everything I can to keep you safe. Just tell me your plans—I know you've got something up your sleeve. Even if you hate me, I swear to you, I will not make the same mistake twice." His words brushed against her skin, soft and gentle.

A single, unbidden tear rolled out. Blinking back the emotion, Elysia pried his hands away. She shook her head, frustration stealing her eloquence.

"No."

She barged past him, trying to find the words. He didn't follow her this time. She stared at him once there was enough space between them that she felt safe again. Her eyes stayed on her feet.

"You don't get to judge me, *Prince.* You were my light. My single good thing in this life and you left me for dead." Jagged and sharp, she threw each word like a javelin. Her heart went numb as she brought her eyes to his. "Whatever you're trying to achieve, I don't care. If we're alike, then I feel sorry for you—because that means you gave yourself away long ago, and I'm not sure there's redemption for people like us." Bleak and terrible, she meant every blackened word.

The wide angles of his face gave away nothing, and she hated it. She wanted her words to pierce his heart and shatter the courtly mask he now wore to hide himself from her. Arms crossed, he didn't shirk away from her condemning words or gaze, though.

"I will lose myself a thousand times over to save this land," he answered slowly.

A bitter laugh fell out of her. "Oh, you're a hero now? Is that it?" She gave a little clap, the sound echoing in the empty room. "People fall like bloodied leaves while you just taint that precious soul. It'd be poetic if it wasn't such utter shit."

The corner of the prince's eye twitched and a flash of satisfaction flitted across Elysia's face. His fingers clenched once, then twice. Offering him a dark smile, she leaned back against the table behind her. "If you were so interested in saving this kingdom, then you wouldn't have led your dogs to the one group of people who might have done something."

The prince looked away, then back at her, his green eyes flashing with specks of light. "I know you've been working with the rebel women who survived, and I want to *help*."

She grabbed a steak knife, weaving it between her fingers before snatching it by the handle. "And why would the Crown Prince care? A broken kingdom is easy to control, and you've never seemed to care before."

"Did you ever stop and think that maybe I told you as little as you've told me?"

The knife clattered to the table, and a pang ricocheted in her chest. It was hypocritical of her to be hurt by his lack of disclosure. But the heart minds its own logic and his words stuck into her like the sharp end of betrayal.

She cleared her throat. "And it appears I was right to withhold. Why are you folding now? I have nothing to give you."

The prince took three long strides, stopping once he was close enough to stare down into her face. "I want to know what you know. About magic disappearing. I want to know what your plan is, and I want to help."

"You're too late."

The prince kicked at the chair closest to him, sending it flying. He loomed over her now, frustration sharpening his face. "That's bullshit. I know damn well when you're up to something, Elysia."

She leaned into him, her words rolling past his ear. "There's no plan. I'm leaving tomorrow. Sailing far, far away from here." She let her back arch as she reached her arms wide. Body snapping forward, she tapped him on the nose. "And you!"

His face tightened and he shook his head, his voice coming out rough. "No, you're not going anywhere. This is our home, and the Elysia I know, the woman who is clever and infuriating and as reckless as she is dangerous, would not be bullied out of it. I don't care who's been whispering in your ear to leave. They're wrong and they don't know shit about what's going on."

Fresh tears returned to her eyes, but she warbled out a final answer. "There is nothing more to know. If I stay, I die sanctioned by the Crown you wear on your head. Whether it's tomorrow or a year from now. I guess I'm not as sanctimonious as you because I'm not ready to die."

His fingers slid against the nape of her neck, up into her hair, forcing her eyes to him. His words were hard. "No, I am standing here offering you my help, and you are not *listening*. I realize I fucked up and it will never be forgiven. I can live with that. Hate me, despise me—that's fine. But right now, our goals are the same. You want a Kava in which you can be free, and so do I. The woman I knew was fearless in spite of having every reason to be afraid. She walked through the castle with magic in her fingertips and waved to the king who would have her dead. She fucked the prince and made him love her so that she could wield his crown. And now you run? You run when you can finally do something that matters?"

She stopped. In spite of not knowing her plans, he knew exactly what to say. Green eyes beat down on her like a summer storm as he waited for a response that wasn't coming. He released her neck and she stumbled.

"Perhaps you are tormented by secrets because you refuse to hear the truth." He walked away, crunching over the broken glass. "Good luck running, Parker. Somehow, I doubt you'll get far."

CHAPTER 30

SHE STOOD outside the house for ten whole minutes before giving up on the notion of going inside. She was somewhere between drunk and hungover and had no desire to explain the sheer stupidity that had been her behavior. Instead, she clambered up the side of the house just like old times and flung herself onto the roof. She lay there on her back, staring up at the foggy night sky, wishing she could see a single star.

Just a single light of guidance would be good enough.

But not here, not in Kava. It was the darkness that would guide you here. She let the soft gray and black smudged sky loosen the knots in her body, her mind. The alcohol dulled the edges that the sky could not find as everything grew distant and her worries faded out. Body heavy, her eyes closed, and the darkness seeped from the sky into her consciousness, pulling her down, down, down.

It happened just like it did every night.

In her liquor-laced sleep, Elysia fell through time and space until her toes, now bare, touched down on cold, damp soil. Awake within this other world, she gingerly pressed her toes and fingers into the earth and looked around. She hadn't expected to come here tonight. Then again, she'd been so drunk that she hadn't really worried about it at all.

She stood and dusted the dirt from what appeared to be a nightgown. Cream silk flowed over her body, the antithesis to the blackened river off to her right. It rushed past, dark and foreboding, much like the rest of the landscape she found herself in.

A single note of music rippled out. The song was starting, just like it did every night. The realm around her began its lament, and Elysia listened, enraptured as always. But this time as she felt the world shift, readying to send her home, she dropped back to her knees, and grabbed hold of the barren tree beside her.

She gritted her teeth and growled at the dirt, the river, and the sky. "I am not *leaving* until I get some answers." Her finger nails raked into the bonewood, cracking with the effort of hanging on while the realms tried to spit her back out to her home.

She wasn't sure how long she'd hung on when a voice as dark and musical as the song playing around them kissed her ears.

"You're here."

His voice reached down into every crevice of her being, filling her with its soothing sound. A poem written just for her, she inhaled the sound. Her neck twinged as she contorted, twisting to find the owner of the voice. She stilled. There amongst the grove of bonewood trees just beyond the river was a man staring at her like this was Kava and she was the sun. In a blink, the man was crouching before her, not touching or speaking, just staring.

She wasn't sure he even realized he had begun to speak aloud, his voice a dusky murmur. "It shouldn't be possible." His fingers slid through her hair, letting it slip and pool through his fingers.

Head foggy and body burning, she knew she couldn't last much longer. Her tongue flopped uselessly, struggling to form the words. "You're him? The god—the deal broker..."

His hand fell. "You're—you're here for a deal?" His eyes closed, brow furrowing. Flat resignation extinguished the sun from his eyes. "Of course."

She gave a weak shrug and nodded, no longer capable of speech. She could feel the fabric of her being tearing, ripping as it sought its way home. Something warm dripped down her face, and she watched him shudder.

With a surprisingly gentle hand, his thumb wiped away the blood, red and stark against his skin. He stared down at that drop of blood before silently sucking his finger clean. He stood tall, his face creased with emotion she couldn't understand.

"Well then, I'll be here, Elysia Parker. Ready and waiting to spin the deal of your dreams." He gave a slight bow at the waist. And then in one violent motion, he ripped her hands free of the trunk.

With a cry, her body jerked. The last thing she saw was the god of the dead staring at where her body had just been. Hands clasped behind his back, lean and tall as the bone tree beside him. There was a pained expression upon his face. Devastated—the god of the dead looked devastated, and much to her dismay, he wore it beautifully. The strong lines of his face sharpened, the familiar resignation setting into dignified worn grooves. All of it telling her he was no stranger to the darker emotions that plagued humans and gods alike. He wore his pain aloud and for some reason, she found him all the handsomer for it. The thought troubled her, a silent warning sounding beneath her curiosity.

But then she disappeared, the image of him burnt into her memory like a brand.

Elysia flinched awake.

A tiny black padded paw repeatedly smacked her in the face. Large brown-black eyes stared intensely into hers as the paw came down on her cheek rhythmically. *One, two. One, two.* She lurched up, and the raccoon scrambled back from her, nails clicking on the tile, chittering and hissing at her as it waved its arm. Darting forward again, Lina grabbed a handful of sweater and tugged, grunting as if she could possibly move Elysia away from the roof's edge.

"Okay, okay, I'm moving." Elysia groaned and began to climb back down, pausing halfway to see if the raccoon was following. Sure enough, her rotund behind appeared over the ledge, dark feet dangling before getting a grip.

"You know, Topp is probably looking for you."

The raccoon grabbed a fistful of her hair and yanked.

Pain shot through Elysia's scalp, causing her to yelp. She glared at the creature. "Gods, you're a fucking demon."

Lina gave a terrifying grin full of little teeth and relaxed her grip.

"If I find out you're spying for the prince, then your next life will be as a hand muff. Got it?"

Elysia dragged herself up the front walk and stood staring at the black door of Gage's house trying to prepare herself. Her mouth tasted awful. Her head was thick and pounding. And she had a feeling this was going to go terribly. But before she could even reach for the knob, the door flung open.

Gage stood there, frazzled with chaos in his eyes. "Your funeral, kid."

Her brow creased in confusion.

But then the hurricane that was Beatriz pounded up behind him. She shoved him aside as if it were normal for her to throw around professional assassins twice her size. Gage grunted as he toppled into the coat rack, but Beatriz's eyes were drilling into her sister. Her normally sleek silver hair was fuzzy, and her silk button-down wrinkled. Beatriz Parker looked like a mess.

Elysia smiled and the fury her sister hadn't been hiding in the slightest erupted.

"You are still every bit the pain in my ass that you have been since the day you were born!"

Elysia tried to respond, but Beatriz reached out and slapped a hand over her mouth. "Do *not*." She stepped over the threshold, getting close to Elysia then quickly stepping back as her nose scrunched. "Don't you dare try to lie to me about what you did last night. And gods above and below, you smell like a fucking distillery."

Red crept up Elysia's neck. Her words were garbled behind her sister's hand. "Which part?"

Her fingers pinched into Elysia's skin. "What do you mean, which part? Are you telling me there's a part beyond where you showed up at that disgusting hole-in-the-wall trying to provoke a brawl? Are you *trying* to get executed?"

A disgruntled noise sounded off from somewhere farther in the house. Beatriz rolled her eyes, calling back with only a smidge less bite in her voice. "It *is* disgusting. Use a mop or something." She shook her head. "Fucking peasants."

Elysia licked her sister's hand like a dog and grinned when Beatriz ripped her hand away, as expected. She craned her neck around her sister. "Jessa's in there?"

Beatriz looked down at her suspiciously. "Yes, because she's a better human than you."

She went to push past her sister, but Beatriz shot her arm out, blocking the doorway. Her voice came out low and then a little nervous. "You're not telling me something. And for the love of all the undead gods. Please tell me you didn't have anything to do with the random knife attack on the godsforsaken prince last night."

A grin bubbled up and crept across Elysia's face. She spoke delicately. "First of all, it wasn't an attack. That's very dramatic. It was a well-placed knife that shattered a glass he was holding." She paused. "And second, you know, Triz, I think you're finally starting to understand how I felt about you all these years!"

And with that she stuck out a leg, causing Beatriz to stumble, and ducked under her arm into the house, strolling into the kitchen as if she didn't smell like a drunk, dead cat with a raccoon trailing two steps behind her.

Gage's voice followed her. "Did you really shatter the glass he was holding?"

"He was touching another woman, and I didn't like it. My knife must have slipped."

A choked laugh escaped him. "Is it bad that I'm proud?"

She smiled, biting back her own laugh.

Elysia grabbed the kettle, gathering what she needed to brew a little something to stave off the worst of her aches. She didn't bother looking at Jessa. Her insides twisted uncomfortably. She'd been such an ass last night. An unbearable, childish ass.

Fingers deep in an herb jar, she spoke, "Surprised to see you here. I was awful last night."

The admission cost her, shame making her wish she could forgo the conversation altogether.

Jessa just leaned back against the kitchen table and crossed her arms. "Yeah. You were. But I know bullshit when I see it." She paused, sounding uncomfortable. "Look, I'm not the most well-adjusted person myself, so I'm willing to overlook an outburst or two. But more importantly, I don't care what these assholes say. Fuck your sister and that overmuscled mother hen. You're not getting on that ship."

Beatriz walked into the room, eyes flashing. "I told you we shouldn't have let this street rat in here."

"Shouldn't have let either of you in here," Gage muttered.

Jessa rolled her eyes and spoke tauntingly. "Elysia, your little dog won't stop barking."

Elysia rubbed her temples, looking at her sister's bony hand make a fist as if she'd actually do anything with it. "Degenerates, both of you."

"I realize we have more important matters to discuss, but can someone please tell me why there is a raccoon in my home?" Gage stared in consternation at Lina.

Plopped on her haunches, her grubby little paw was rhythmically snatching forest berries out of a bowl on the counter. Cheeks full and face stained red with juice, she looked rabid.

Everyone stopped squabbling, falling silent as they watched the raccoon. Elysia opened and closed her mouth. Shifting on her feet, she answered weakly. "This is Lina."

More silence.

She waved a hand. "You know how the prince is—always rehabbing animals. Lina was in his room the night everything went to shit." The raccoon spit out a berry, leaving a glop on the counter.

Elysia grimaced. "Why she's here now... I don't know."

Gage answered slowly. "None of that makes any sense."

Elysia interrupted before he could continue. "Anyway, I have news."

She ignored the glare she could feel scalding the side of her face, shushing Beatriz before she could start spitting nails again. "Just let me tell you!"

Using a towel to hold on to the kettle, she poured hot water over the herbs in a green clay mug.

"I had the dream." She frowned. "Or traveled. Whatever we're calling it—last night. But this time I managed to stay a little longer. And I met him." She grinned viciously.

Jessa balked. Her raspy voice dropped to a stunned whisper. "You met a god?"

Elysia shrugged, setting the kettle aside. "He didn't seem especially god-like, but he's the one we're looking for, alright."

"And?"

She paused, her mind's eye flashing back to how shocked he seemed to be to see her. Almost as if he thought *she* was an illusion or dream. Not to mention the bitter ire he couldn't seem to swallow when he realized she wanted a deal. Her mouth pursed. What else would she be there for? A tea party? Gods and kings were the same as far as she was concerned, and it was only too typical that he would act all high and mighty about her wishing to procure a deal even though *he* was the one who had stolen Kava's magic.

"He didn't like it when I asked if he was the deal broker. Ripped me out of there right fast."

Gage sent a parental sort of look her way. "Remember how I taught you not to chase marks you weren't sure you could take?"

Elysia huffed. "I'm not trying to *kill* him. I just want to get our magic back."

He drummed his fingers and shook his head. "No, you're just trying to swindle him. You have no plan. Next to zero knowledge on this *god*. You'll be throwing yourself into another realm to your death."

"We could still stuff her onto the boat like we talked about."

"Could you just *try* to be a supportive sister for once?"

Jessa ignored them much like she ignored the drunk idiots at her bar, musing to herself. "You're a Crown kid."

"I mean, I suppose that's better than when you call me a Crown bitch."

Jessa looked at her in exasperation. "No, what I mean is—you're trained in this stuff. The diplomacy, the politics. People say that you work with your father on trades. Why couldn't you go meet with him as *that*, Elysia?"

Elysia and Beatriz both gaped while Gage frowned as if he was hoping no one would bring this up.

The sisters considered one another excitedly and spoke like lightning.

Elysia grabbed her sister's wrists, eyes going wide. "This could work."

"You could go as an emissary."

"We have enough of that brew for me to go as many times as I need."

"I could help you craft the deal."

"You would do that?"

Beatriz wrapped her fingers around Elysia's wrists as well. "There's a lot you don't know about me."

Intrigue played into Elysia's voice. "Really? Are you a Parker after all?"

Beatriz answered quietly. "Maybe I always have been."

Elysia appraised her and nodded before turning back to Jessa and Gage, who both looked winded by their conversation.

"It's settled. I'll take the tincture and attempt to strike a deal." Her words were matter-of-fact. "*Everyone*, gods included, has a price."

CHAPTER 31

BEATRIZ HAD BEEN RIGHT. The excitement of meeting an undead god could not deter Elysia from the practicality of her situation. She was a daughter of the Crown and she had not shown her face around court in far too long. Long enough that whispers were no longer whispers, but brazen lies curling off jealous tongues.

She's a Parker. Probably cheated on the crown prince and ran for her life.

I heard she fell into drugs just like her sister. Won't be seeing her again.

That's what happens when you piss off Georgia Parker. You disappear.

Her personal favorite was a particularly luscious tale of her finding true and scandalous love with one of her father's steamship captains and steaming away to pirate the seas. She *was* rather good with a sword even if she did prefer the agility of a dagger.

She lifted the precious cargo she was carrying higher as she carefully clipped up the front steps of the castle to the curved double doors. Behind her, on the iron gates that stood between the castle's courtyard and the rest of the city, were heads. Rotting heads shoved on pointed iron fencing. In spite of the bloat and rot and bird-picked bones, she knew exactly who was on display.

All the rebels who didn't get away that night under the sea.

The prince's offer to *help* felt hollow and thin inside her chest as the scent of human decay lingered in her nose. He thought her difficult. She was beginning to think him particularly dense.

Her slowly shifting perspective on the prince eased some of her heartache and muted the questions that hounded her in the quiet hours. Questions like, was there ever even anything real between them? She wasn't sure it mattered at this point, but the question remained, aggravating her late at night.

As for right now, she needed to soothe her parents' anger before they did something stupid and ruined her plans altogether. In other words, she had to proceed as if everything were normal.

Elysia smiled easily at a guard and laughed to herself. *Normal.* As if anything about her life was normal. Shocked faces corrected themselves into hurried nods of greeting with every step she took. She shook her head, loose waves brushing her face. As if any Parker would ever disappear that easily.

The moment her mother's office door was in sight, it began a slow glide open. Elysia stifled the grin trying to form on her face. Someone must have run awfully fast to make sure Georgia Parker knew her wayward daughter had returned to the castle halls. As expected, of course. She imagined they'd received a fat tip for the matter. Good for them.

Her mother appeared in the doorway with lies like honey for all the burning ears. "My sweet girl, I've missed you so. Come in, come in."

It was no wonder Beatriz had received countless lashes for rolling her eyes when her mother spouted off bullshit like that all the time in front of people.

Elysia dutifully followed her mother in and took control before her mother could flatten her like a bug beneath her beautiful shoes.

"Before you say anything, look at what I've brought." She

held out the luxurious garment bag like the obvious peace offering that it was. She smiled wickedly and looked up at her mother. "Go on. Look."

Georgia rested a hand on her hip, the lines of her face deepening in displeasure. "I really ought to send you to your father. The absolute amount of trouble and embarrassment you've caused us. Did you know your father has been secretly sending his personal guards on searches for you? He didn't believe for one moment your message or the prince's excuses about your *extended* travels."

Her heart thudded anxiously, but the heat that flushed her face was not fear—it was that cursed anger she couldn't seem to rid herself of anymore. She smiled politely over the roiling sensation. *Send her to Father?* Like she was an errant child in need of reprimanding instead of a grown adult. Gods forbid she threaten their name.

Her scarred feet twinged though. She was convinced the pain was psychological half the time at this point—no less real, but triggered by even the thought of being forced to endure her father's punishments. Face fixed, she ignored her mother's comment.

"It's for the Raven Ball. I thought I might want something... unique this year."

Curiosity winning out, her mother finally surreptitiously stole a peek at the garment bag only for her brows to raise in surprise. A small sound of wonder escaped her as her hands glided over the raised signature sewn onto the dark red garment bag. Still staring at the signature, her voice dropped to an almost reverent whisper.

"How in the realms did you acquire a *Pleur* creation? Is it vintage?"

Elysia replied airily with a wave of her fingers. "Called in a favor, gave a favor. You know how it goes."

Kava's most reclusive and renowned designer had not made a gown in years. Elysia did not blame the poor soul. His magic was in every stitch of every creation he'd ever made, but by the gods did he make beautiful gowns. He'd had no choice but to pretend his magic was gone after the Fall. No more magic, no more gowns.

She'd heard he wanted proper papers that would allow him to start over in one of the lands where magic still ran free, and she'd been more than happy to assist. For a charge, naturally. One divine gown to be worn at the Raven Ball, to be exact.

Georgia deftly worked the ties, gently opening the protective bag. She stared silently for a full minute before turning to Elysia with her eyes wide. "The cost?"

Elysia sat primly on the edge of the nearest armchair. "I haven't the faintest. Sent the bill right to the prince."

Her mother gave her an approving smirk and reached to touch the fabric, but Elysia shot forward, pulling the dress away to safety. "Ah, ah, ah. No touching until the ball. This beauty will be locked away like the fine piece of art that it is until then."

Georgia looked at her from the corner of her eye and moved to take a seat. She crossed her legs and folded her hands.

"Should I be expecting you to disappear again before then? You created quite the headache for your father and me."

Elysia tied the garment bag up tight, picking it up like it was made of gold. "Highly unlikely, but now you have a brilliant story to tell everyone about where I was, and that's what matters, isn't it? That you have a story to tell? Have a lovely afternoon, Mother." Her smile was sharp as glass.

She left her mother standing in a shroud of regret that she had raised two daughters every bit as conniving and dangerous as herself.

ELYSIA STOOD BAREFOOT AND UNDRESSED, staring at the garment bag. Her mother may have been put out by her disappearance, but she knew that the story of Elysia Parker securing a Pleur gown would be halfway across the court by now. Some nonsense story about her parents not wanting to ruin the surprise, but wishing to alleviate concern about their darling daughter.

Sir Larkspur swatted at the ties hanging down from the dark red garment bag. They'd moved back into her flat now that she was certain the prince wasn't about to immediately turn her in for treason. Gage hadn't loved it, but she needed space and the freedom to do what was needed without anyone squawking at her about safety.

Elysia looked between the cat and the dangling ties for all of a second before swiftly removing the garment bag. Anyone with a cat knew how *that* was going to end. Her armoire wasn't quite tall enough for the floor length gown, but it was better than the dress becoming kitty ribbons. A solid knock struck her door just as she closed the armoire.

"Jessa, right on time," she muttered, picking her way through the clothes and shoes strewn about her floor to the front door.

She unlatched the numerous locks trailing down the door and gave a shout for Jessa to come in. Padding back into the living room, she yelled over her shoulder. "This tincture better work like a charm because it smells *disgusting*. I don't know how that old meela thinks I'm supposed to choke it down."

Larkspur darted through her legs, almost tripping her as he shot by with a jovial mewl. Elysia grabbed hold of the closest chair, struggling to right herself. "Larky boy, what are you trying to do?"

As she got her feet back beneath her, a low chuckle hit her ears.

That motherf—

The prince grinned like a fox and plucked Sir Larkspur up into a cuddle where the traitor purred lazily, rubbing his dark little face against the prince's grown out stubble. "At least someone misses me."

Elysia reached for her dagger only to swipe against bare skin.

The prince struggled to contain his laughter, chest shaking

with the effort. "Missing something, Parker?" His eyes trailed pointedly over her body.

Embarrassment scorched up her chest and neck.

She was still walking around in her undergarments.

Unclothed. Unarmed.

And she'd quite literally unlocked her front door and let him in her home.

A boyish grin took over his face as he watched her struggle to regain any semblance of dignity.

Bastard.

She lifted her chin and strode away silently, her feet pounding loudly against the floor as if her ass was not firmly on display. Which it was. Snatching a dressing gown from her bedroom, she tied it on with haste. Dagger in hand, she stalked back out to the living room only to find him perched on the arm of a chair without a trace of apology on his face. The traitor Sir Larkspur was now draped peacefully over the prince's shoulders, sound asleep, looking like a damn fur stole.

Unsheathing the dagger, she smiled pleasantly enough for someone who was pointing the sharp end of a weapon at someone. "Get out. We've already had this conversation, and it ends with me telling you to *get out*."

The prince sighed loudly and ignored her. Walking into the kitchen, he leaned against a counter. One ankle crossed over the other and her cat draped over his shoulders. The sight made her want to scream.

"As good as you are with that knife, we all know you're not going to stab me."

She raised a silent brow in reply.

"Elysia." His voice caressed her name dangerously.

"Fine." She bit out the word and then flung the dagger the moment his body relaxed. It struck and vibrated in the space between his splayed fingers on the counter's edge.

The prince didn't so much as flinch. He pulled the dagger out cleanly, thoughtfully, and held it back out to her as if she hadn't just almost relieved him of his fingers for the second time in so many days.

"I can't believe I never even considered knife play." He leaned forward tauntingly. "All you had to do was ask."

"Oh my gods, you're impossible," she muttered, reaching to rip the dagger out of his hand, but he grabbed her wrist and, with one sharp tug, pulled her into his body.

"Have I turned you in?"

"No." Her face was muffled against his chest. Idiot smelled good. Like the forest and fresh rain. It was terrible.

"And how long have I known?"

She tried to squirm, and his arms turned to bands of steel.

"Ugh. Yes, we get it. You're so amazing for not having your girlfriend turned in for execution. Well done, you're practically a saint."

She stomped her bare foot down on his booted one knowing it was going to hurt her scarred soles but not caring. He swore and she twisted. She shot out of his grasp only for his long leg to wrap around hers. Her knee buckled, both of them crashing down to the floor. Scrambling on all fours, she tried to crawl away, but was yanked back and flipped over.

Thick thighs settled on either side of her, reminding her of that night beneath the sea, and all her air whooshed out.

"Gods below, you weigh a ton. *Move*," she choked out, slapping at his sides.

"As if I'm going to fall for that."

She huffed and pinched him sharply in the soft flesh of his waist.

"Hey!" His hands shot out to pin down her wrists before her nails could be directed at his face. "Such a pest sometimes."

Glowering, she considered if she could jacknife her leg up and rail him in the back of the head. She might pull a hamstring in the process, but some things were worth it. Like clocking him in the skull so she could get away from his overbearing ass.

He frowned down at her. "Are you going to listen now?"

She didn't answer, busy wiggling her hips down to give herself a little more flexibility.

He sat down harder, trying to quell her movements. "I'll take that as a yes, then. Tell me about this tincture. What are you trying to do with that rebel girl? Why were they so interested in you even though you're connected to the Crown?"

Elysia batted her eyes. "Oh yes, now that you've broken into my home and pinned me like some common thief I'll surely tell you everything! Come closer, I'll whisper all my secrets in your ear."

The prince's shoulders dropped in annoyance. He leaned in, ass lifting off her waist as his face became exasperated. "Why do you have to be like this? You're acting more and more like your sister lately."

Elysia preyed on his error, using her core to lift her own hips as well. Her leg flew up, foot slamming into his neck and head. The prince toppled, his hands grabbing at where she'd struck him as he swore, while Elysia rolled out from beneath him.

Back on her feet, her breaths came fast. "You say that like it's such a bad thing." She grabbed a glass, filling it with water and gulping it down. "You keep coming to me, begging to be let in on what we're doing. Telling *me* that I refuse to hear the truth, but you don't even have the balls to admit what this is really about."

The prince clambered to his feet, his steps heavy and hand still clutching the base of his skull. "And what truth is that?"

She set the glass down, meeting his bright gaze. Lifting one hand, she gestured at his chest. "That festering ball of pain living inside you."

The prince's face became stone. But he didn't say a word.

She spoke softly. "I can feel it, you know. Hear it too, sometimes. It sounds like it will bleed you dry."

His eyes shot to hers, wild and electric at what she knew. Fingers flexing by his side, he gritted out his reply. "You don't know what you're talking about."

Her own anger melted into a deep sadness. She shook her

head, feeling the fight drain out of her. She spoke quietly again. "You stand in front of me tangled in years of secrets, lies, and omission, and you want me to trust you? I know secrets better than anyone, and you? You're made of them."

She studied him. The man who was once familiar was now strange.

"I won't make you say it aloud. But we both know what's at the heart of it."

His mouth was a thin line, body tense at what she was implying, but he didn't stop her, so she kept talking. Made sure her voice was gentle and true.

"Death, grief, rage. That's what lives inside your chest." She paused. "Losing your sister changed you, didn't it? More than you ever let on."

The prince took a half step back as if the weight of her words had knocked the rugged arrogance clean out of him. His mouth hung open as if to reply, but a furious pounding against the door tore the moment away.

Elysia stared at him tiredly. "If you have any self-preservation, then I would recommend the window as a means of exit."

He glanced over to her in question, but didn't move, seemingly unable to process their interaction.

She shrugged and walked over to the door. "Don't say I didn't warn you."

The door kicked open before Elysia could reach it, and in strode the eldest Parker. Each and every confident step exuded a very specific type of elder sister bossiness. For some reason that Elysia couldn't quite put her finger on, the sight didn't bother her as it once had. It might have even made her smile just a little.

Beatriz stopped cold when she saw the prince. She looked like she'd stepped in shit and could smell it under her sharp, thin nose. "I don't recall anyone inviting a fucking Blatz to this party."

Her eyes went to Elysia. "He looks like you kicked his puppy. Tell me you kicked his puppy."

The prince seemed to shake himself free of his constraints, a mocking smile returning to his face. Rolling his broad shoulders, he cracked his neck.

"Business take a turn lately, Beatriz? You seem more agitated than usual. Or is that just the drugs just wearing off?"

She shot him a dangerous look. "The House is as it always is."

Elysia watched their standoff and felt her usual irritation with her sister spring right back.

"What business, Beatriz?" Her voice sounded a little too shrill, and she knew she shouldn't have asked. She'd very purposely never pried or sought after her sister's secrets. If her father ever came asking, she didn't want to know the truth of it.

Jessa swung the door shut, strolling over to lounge beside Elysia. She silently eyed the prince, her shrewd cat eyes going up, then back down. It was an obvious evaluation. Something the Crown Prince was not often subjected to—at least not by tavern owners who kept nail-studded planks behind their bar. Jessa frowned like there was something she didn't understand, as if perhaps she found him lacking. But her face smoothed and she turned away, leaving the prince looking disgruntled.

Beatriz looked on laughingly. In a voice more prim than Elysia had ever heard her speak, she asked, "Yes, Jessa? Your verdict?"

"It's just..." She looked at Elysia, speaking slowly as if she were working out her thoughts. "We might have our issues, but you're smart, educated, one of the few women who works for the Crown, and you're even pretty when you're not getting people killed." Her eyes cut back to the prince, confusion rippling her forehead. "You know what, I date women. I'm sure you're just fine."

She patted the prince on his generous bicep. Stunned into silence, he blinked—his head swiveling between all three women.

Beatriz snickered, then became falsely serious. "While I have enjoyed my time with the men of this fine land, and they may even draw my eye... Thank the gods for the House." She gave a wicked grin.

Elysia rolled her eyes. "Yes, yes, I'm an uncouth, unfortunate soul who has been twice cursed. Once with undead gifts and twice with falling for this creature, but he was just leaving." She leveled the prince with a withering glare.

The corner of his mouth hitched up a notch. "Knew you still loved me."

Elysia felt the honest happiness beneath his words like a sharp kick to the ribs. Did she?

She rubbed at her arms, trying to push away the uncomfortable sensation. "Can you please leave already?"

He relaxed back into one of her prized stolen arm chairs. "I think not. You all look far too irritated by my presence, which means you are obviously up to no good and I'd be stupid to leave."

Hands smacking against muscular thighs, he leaned forward as he continued. "So, what are we doing this evening, ladies? Elysia did mention something about a disgusting tincture. Or are we plotting to take down the Crown? Is that it? I may have a few pointers." His last words ended in a whisper.

"Maybe just its heir," Triz muttered.

The prince flashed a grin and waited.

Elysia finally snapped, her fingers now clenched into fists. "You can't stay!"

She internally groaned the moment the words left her mouth. The light in his eyes had just shot sky high at her reactive response. Good luck to any of them getting him out now. Would have to throw him out the window by his damn ears.

He settled deeper into the cushy chair, brushing his fingers over the worn leather. "I cannot fathom what has you riled into such a tizzy, but I can't wait to find out."

Beatriz sighed and cursed at no one in particular before flopping dramatically across the couch. She rolled over and threw an arm behind her head. "Princeling, what's your thought on the ole magic situation here in Kava? Why it's gone, if it should be recovered. You know, all that." She gestured broadly.

Elysia's eyes were stealthy on his reaction, but the inscrutable face of a prince stared back at Beatriz. His eyes narrowed just slightly. "Interesting questions, Beatriz, but curiosity breeds trouble in a place like Kava, doesn't it?"

A disparaging snort came from Beatriz. "Completely shit answer. Fucking politicians, all the same." She rolled over and slapped her legs in a mimic of the prince before springing up and eyeing Jessa with a determined lift of her brow. "Shall we, darling?"

Jessa smirked, taking a step closer. "Oh, I think we shall."

An animal cry tore from Beatriz's throat as both women rushed the Prince and ripped him up by his arms. He flung forward unsteadily on his feet, and was promptly driven farther along by the dual force that was Beatriz and Jessa.

"The door, Elysia, the door!"

Two steps ahead of them, Elysia, was already there swinging the door wide with an ear to ear grin. She wriggled her fingers in a wave as the prince was unceremoniously dumped outside her door as if he weighed no more than a small child. "Bye-bye then!"

She slammed the door shut on his once more stunned face and locked every single one of her ridiculous locks from Gage.

"Good riddance," she grumbled. "Thought he'd be here all night."

Jessa and Beatriz were already rummaging through her kitchen as if they hadn't just tossed the crown prince out on his ass.

Jessa stuck her head out from a cupboard. "Do you really not have any gin?"

Beatriz grabbed two mugs and made a face. "She normally steals her booze from the castle. You'd think she was poor."

Jessa paused her rummaging, looking impressed. "I wouldn't mind a glass of stolen Crown liquor."

Elysia ignored them both and climbed onto the counter, pulling an old decanter down from the top of the cabinetry. She handed it off to Jessa who pulled out the stopper. "You both have terrible manners. You know that, right?"

"They say when you can go right into the kitchen and make yourself at home—those are your real friends." Beatriz nodded sagely as she bestowed this tidbit.

Elysia just raised a single eyebrow, her expression flat. Beatriz ruffled her hair as she walked past and Elysia almost fell off the counter trying to slap her hands away.

Unperturbed, Jessa poured out two mugs, cheersing with Beatriz before taking a sip. "So, where're we doin' this? Your bedroom?"

Elysia watched the two women swagger through her home with mugs of gin sloshing in their hands and cheeks turning rosier by the second. These were the geniuses that were supposed to watch her physical form while she took herbs powerful enough to launch her through the realms. *What could possibly go wrong?*

She walked into her bedroom to find Beatriz had traded her mug full of gin for the tincture. She held the large jar up to her face so that her nose smushed against the glass while the dust of herbs and plants swirled inside.

"Anything interesting in there?"

"Just grateful that I'm not the one drinking this sludge."

Elysia played with the ties on her robe. "Yeah, yeah. I don't think it really matters because I always end up in the same damn nightgown, but I think I'd rather get dressed, just in case. I've had enough people see me half naked for one day."

Jessa's head swung her way. "Who saw you naked?"

"I will never understand the grip that man has on you." Beatriz set the jar back down and shook her head.

Pulling her favorite dark blue knit sweater over head and fluffing out her hair, Elysia responded. "It wasn't like that. And from what I recall, there was a time when you and the prince were friends."

"Youth is a mystery, Elysia. It's best we leave its transgressions unexamined."

Elysia sat down on the bed, rubbing her hands together nervously, and watched Triz pour out a thimbleful of the tincture with the confidence of a woman who had poured out one too many shots in her day. She stared down at the small gulp of tincture, her nose wrinkled in distaste. Dark, murky liquid stared back at her, promising to taste foul if the smell was any indication.

"Right, okay." Elysia took the thimble and gave it another cursory sniff. It smelled like a dead animal.

The girls held out their respective mugs, and Beatriz grinned darkly. "Bottoms up, sister dear."

All three downed their glasses, but only Elysia began to fall.

Through time, space, she didn't know.

She could hear the river's song, and she followed it closely until she fell harshly on the cold, damp ground.

CHAPTER 32

Elysia sat for a breath, feeling the dirt between her fingers, the damp against her legs. The sky and lands were awash with shades of the ever darkening twilight, but in the distance, she could still see where the day bled into night. Rusty cardinal ink blotches dispersing into the dark. The blood sky made the hairs on her arms stand upright. She had grown used to only gray, and the bloodied copper above made her nervous.

For the first time, the song which haunted her dreams did not play out into the night, nor did she wear the ethereal slip of a dress she had expected to find herself clothed in. More importantly, she did not feel as though she was about to be ripped back to her true body, which rested in Relaclave. Bare feet planted in the damp river bank soil, she realized she felt solid and anchored to this place.

Fear shivered up her skin, making her pull at the sleeves of her sweater. She couldn't think of things such as being stuck here. It would do her no good. She was here now, and that was what she had wanted.

Elysia stood and began walking alongside the iridescent oil slick river. It appeared endless. Winding through the twilight into the burnt red over the horizon. Her bare feet became chilled, numbing with each step along the shore. In the distance, the bonewood trees stood sharp against the barren landscape, their fingers whittled to severe points.

Silent nothingness wrapped around her, making her spirit uneasy. She'd grown up in the capital of her kingdom. Someone was always shouting. Builders were always banging. Feet and wooden wheels cracking against cobblestones. Silence was a made-up construct in the heart of Relaclave. But here, it felt as though it might smother her.

Cloaked in eerie quiet, she wondered if she had imagined the man in her dream. Because how could anything or anyone possibly live here? And yet, the ruddy sky and rushing purple-blue water gave her hope that somewhere past her line of sight there was not only life, but the answers which she sought from this realm.

Soot fell like a soft blanket of death upon Kava, stealing the color and warmth a little more with each passing day. The decay was as gentle as a lullaby, coaxing her people easily to their doom. The process so gradual that no one even bothered to protest. She hadn't realized just how bleak it really was until she stood here, in death's home with its strange silence and jagged trees, and yet there was still color blooming across the sky.

Elysia walked for what felt like ages with no idea if she was growing closer to where she needed to be. She hadn't the faintest idea where to find the god of death, only that he did indeed live here. Tired and frustrated, she stopped walking and blew out a long breath.

I could be going in the entirely wrong direction, and I would have no idea.

Crouching low beside the river, she reached out to let its dark waters brush her hand. It moved swiftly beneath her skin. Hand hovering, but not touching, she watched, mesmerized by its colors.

The silence broke with the sudden terrible sound of snarls loud enough to jolt her back from the water. Falling onto her ass, she scrambled to stand, immediately snapping to attention. She scanned the seemingly endless expanse all around her, searching for the source of the sound. Heart racing and body now poised to run, she saw nothing. This fact did nothing to ease her anxiety. She was the only person for miles—if an animal was snarling and barking, then it had likely fixed its sights on her, and being unable to see her oncoming attacker was not a good sign.

All at once, three small dogs with barks twice the size of their bodies were diving and snapping around her legs. Elysia froze. There had been *nothing,* and now there were three dogs pawing at her ankles. Clearly, this realm did not work as hers did. Then again, she'd never lived with magic and knew nothing of its rules.

Heart slowly calming, she kneeled now that she knew death was not imminent. Tiny with apple shaped heads and big brown eyes, the dogs greeted her warmly. She smiled, running her hands over their small frames. One was fluffy with shades of black and copper. The other two sported matching tan coats of gleaming cropped fur.

"Where did you come from?" she murmured.

The dark fluffy one instantly sprang into her arms, clambering up to nuzzle into her neck. Holding the creature securely, she stood, brushing her fingers over its soft body. The other two acted like little demons, nipping at her pants, growling and tugging.

In spite of what looked like extremely sharp small teeth, the small dogs didn't hurt her as they nipped and headbutted against her legs. She'd spent time with enough of the prince's creatures to understand when she was being herded.

"Alright, alright then. I'm right behind you."

Pleased with her answer, they turned tail, immediately trotting off to the undead gods only knew where.

Walking leisurely behind her new escorts, she peered down at the one who'd been smart enough to mooch a ride. A burgundy velvet collar circled its small neck, but she couldn't see a name sewn into the fabric or anything else that would give her any information. She brushed a thumb over the smooth velvet.

Still rubbing her thumb over the velvet collar, her fingers curled into the animal's fur. It slept on peacefully, a soft buzz blowing out of its dark lined lips with each breath. A thin layer of wariness soaked through to her bones as she walked. The heavy beat of her heart played in her ears and each exhale sounded trapped in her chest.

Over her shoulder, the river disappeared while a forest of barren trees loomed ahead. Toes numb and aching, she entered the woods. The silence grew even thicker alongside it the darkness of night. The Lovestone Woods in Relaclave were a sanctuary, but there was no peace to be found here tonight.

Feet sinking into the dirt, she paused at the mouth of the forest and let her eyes roam. After a moment, she realized that no matter how long she stood there, her eyes were not going to adjust. Not when the reddish-black sky swallowed the light whole. Her guides let out a huff as she resumed walking. Unafraid, the two dogs moved swiftly into the dark.

The naked trees and their branches scraped up like spindly fingers, curving and pointing with gothic judgment. It felt as though the forest mocked her. As if it knew she was unprepared for what was to come. The quiet patter of her canine guides kept her placing one foot in front of the other despite her instincts. She couldn't help but wonder if their ease was misplaced. The forest was silent. But that didn't mean there wasn't danger.

It was the silence before the sky fell and beneath these naked trees, there would be nothing to break its fall. Her steps hurried as her mind twisted, thoughts turning as gnarly as the forest around her. She wanted out of here, wanted to find the god of this realm and be done with this.

The pup in her arms squirmed, begging to be let down. Once on the forest floor, the three dogs sat down, no longer interested in racing ahead. She tried to walk past them, but one of the short-haired dogs grumbled and circled around her until she was back where she started. Hands in her pockets, she studied her surroundings.

What had been one simple worn path now split into four. All dark and unlit. All likely terrible options.

"A crossroads," she murmured to no one.

One path behind her. One path before her. One path to her right. And one path to her left.

A woman slunk out from behind the pin-thin trees, moving like the night itself. She had wood-brown hair cropped to her chin and smart gray eyes that tracked Elysia's movements. A few freckles stood out faintly on her fair skin. Wrapped in a light pink ankle-length dress with chunky boots, she seemed both out of place and completely at home in the forest.

Her entrance had been as silent as the woods around them and there was an air to her that reminded Elysia of the women in her city who tended the dead. An ease that only came from looking death in the eye over and over again until the false enmity faded into something gentler. Elysia couldn't say she understood, but between the hangings and the death moths she had developed something of a fascination with death. One of many secrets she never told. Good girls and daughters of the Crown didn't wonder about such things.

The woman's voice was soft, caught somewhere between youth and the adult body she bore. "Elysia Parker. The fates do have their jokes, don't they?" She stared unflinchingly, taking in the measure of her, before gesturing almost demurely around them as if this were a throne room instead of the most unnatural forest Elysia had ever had the misfortune to enter. "You've come upon a crossroads."

Elysia met her gaze, thinking that she seemed familiar. "You know my name, but I don't know yours."

The woman's face didn't so much as twitch, but a pleased mischief entered her stone-colored eyes.

"Don't you?" Her lips almost smiled. "You can call me Maya."

She sat on a fallen log with perfect posture. Her palms turned up, gesturing to the paths surrounding them. "This is only your beginning, Elysia Parker, and your indecision will ruin you before you even embark on your true quest. So, I have come to grant you a boon."

Apprehension skittered through Elysia. "And what is the price of your gift?"

Maya's mouth curled up, pleased at her question. "Our goals align for the time being. No cost."

Before Elysia could respond, the woman, who appeared perhaps a decade older than her, stood and her tone turned brisk. "The choosing of the path—fate's first query into whether *you* are worthy." Hands inside the pockets of her dress, Maya surveyed the four paths.

Elysia eyed the woman as if she were possibly mentally unstable. "I think there's been a mistake. I need to speak with the god of the dead. If you could point me in the right direction that would be much appreciated. No need for... *this*."

"And you will. But first, your decision." Seeing Elysia's expression, Maya continued, sounding exasperated. "Look, you came here and clung to a tree like a barnacle. It caused a stir. And now you drugged yourself to get back here and speak with him *again*. For better or for worse, you've got the fates' attention after those little stunts."

A flash of frustration coursed through Elysia. She forced her voice to remain even. "Those were not *stunts*. I simply have something to discuss with the god of the dead. *Fate* has nothing to do with any of this. Besides, where I'm from, the gods and fates do not hear nor care." Bitterness darkened her voice.

Maya smiled at Elysia's rancor, but a strange pity softened her eyes. "Hardly the truth, but I believed that once, too. Either way" —she gestured around them—"you still have a path to choose."

Elysia threw her hands up. "Fine. You want me to pick a path?" She started to fling out an arm, but Maya caught it in midair.

She lowered Elysia's arm slowly, anger swirling in her eyes.

"You would do well to respect what you do not know. And if you cannot respect it, then at the very least have curiosity."

Embarrassed, Elysia intuitively knew she had almost just made a possibly mortal mistake. She stopped, closed her eyes and breathed. Nerves needled under her skin now. She had no idea how to find the god of this realm, or which way to go. It wasn't like she'd been dropped off with a map and a bundle of snacks for the road.

"I am sorry." She spoke stiffly, the words unfamiliar and unused on her tongue.

Maya relaxed, stepping back in wordless acceptance of the apology. "You will find your magic is accessible here. I imagine it may *illuminate* your path."

Elysia's eyes shot to her new guide's in surprise. People from Kava were magicless no matter which land they slipped into— sure, someone like her would retain the crumbs they had started with, but it wouldn't bloom into anything more just because they crossed a border. A painful feeling of vulnerability overcame her. She had no idea how to use her magic properly. If anything, her magic used her.

Nervous, she scanned the four paths surrounding her. Even as she strained to look beyond what was visible to her physical eye, she saw nothing but dark empty paths cutting deeper into the woods. Eyes closed, she listened, hoping to hear what was hidden out of sight, but not from someone like her.

At first all she could feel was tension, all she could hear was doubt. Muscles knotted and feet aching. Thoughts as twisted as the trees around her, telling her she never should have left Rela-clave. But then the silence that had smothered her sunk into the spaces between her thoughts, quieting and soothing until she could finally hear.

Inside her mind's eye, it was the breaking of dawn. The sun she barely knew, cresting the land—its light just enough to see within the shadows. Through the light and beneath the shadows, she found the truth. Sepia-toned images flashed through her mind, faster than she could track. Music overlaid the images, adding texture and depth to what she saw.

A small hum that turned to a soft sigh escaped her mouth even as her body staggered, unused to the toll of magic. But the magic slid through her, potent and heavy like hot fire in her veins, burning away any illusion or dogma that magic was something to fear or squash.

She had not realized just how dead and broken magic really was within Kava. Because here? It was ease. It felt like freedom— like *her*. She wanted to roll in the feeling, bask inside it until she never forgot what it was to be *her* again. She wanted to laugh like the undone child she had never been and bottle this moment for when she inevitably did as all humans do, and forgot this feeling.

It was unfathomable how the people of Kava had survived for so long without magic. The fact that her people had lumbered on only spoke of their resilience, and it made her wish that every last person in her land could feel what she was feeling.

A branch crackled somewhere in the woods, and Elysia's eyes startled open.

Maya watched expectantly, tapping a long thin stick in each of the four directions. "Ready to make your choice? Whatever your decision, after today, you cannot say you didn't know."

Elysia took a breath, the nerves flitting back from where they had hid. She heard what Maya wasn't saying. That after today, she could blame no one but herself for what was to come. She had looked with her magic wide open and chosen her path. And more than that, she could feel the weight of every past decision settling around her shoulders. It was neither heavy nor cumbersome. It was simply the truth. There were always going to be unmovable variables. Her parents, her home. But there were endless tiny decisions that no one could claim but her. This moment was about admitting her role in the mess that was her life. Picking up the reins and loving herself enough to acknowledge the power in her yes and in her no, in what she did or did not do.

Turning around silently, she peered into the darkness of the path behind her. She spoke quietly, almost reverently, in the wake of meeting her magic. "The path behind me is diseased, but enticing in its familiarity. I saw a tangle of roses. Soft, beautiful, thorny roses with petals of blood and velvet. It felt familiar. Like falling into your bed at the end of a long night. But the thorns and stems were snarled so tight—I am not sure it may even be entered." Her brow creased as she stared into the nothingness, her arms wrapped around her middle.

Maya held still, her face serious and eyes distant in contemplation. Elysia continued describing the paths that lay open to her.

Her voice took on an almost eerie quality now. "The three that remain are different yet the same. They run through the woods on different trails, but all remain the same. One with brambles, rivers, and vines. Another with creatures, teeth, and claws. The third with gambles, vice, and lies."

Maya nodded, still deep in thought as she considered these new paths. She pointed her stick behind them. "You can go home. It would be as if you never came here."

Swinging her stick, she tapped it down to the right, to the left, and then finally straight ahead. "Three paths that are so very different yet bring you to the same place. What you lose and gain along the way will not be the same. Who you *become* will not be the same. What will your choice be, Elysia Parker?"

Her eyes darted between the paths. She was not the slow and patient sort. Nor was she a warrior at heart—not the kind that lived to battle tooth and nail to feel victory spray upon their skin. There was no point in lying about who she was in a wood so dark with no one here to see.

She spoke her judgment steadily. "What's another gamble?"

The world responded to her words and the will beneath them.

The crossroads vanished. All paths but one disappeared, trees suddenly surrounding them.

"And will you take the path alone? I am more than happy to escort you to whom you seek." Maya's voice came from behind her, the much taller woman looking down over Elysia's shoulder.

A bright green thread whispered to Elysia, and it sounded like suspicion. She watched the thread evaporate. It might have sounded like suspicion, but it *felt* like meddling. It made her think of the interference between siblings—how she would happily muck up Beatriz's plans if only to watch her squirm. Sidestepping the question, she asked one of her own.

"Why doesn't the undead god of this land know I'm here?"

Maya leaned back against a tree now with her arms folded, the small amused lift of her lips the only acknowledgment of Elysia's insinuations. "Oh, he does. He's just a little occupied."

Elysia persisted, narrowing her gaze. "Last time I managed to hold my form here, he appeared rather immediately. Although, I did seem to upset him." She frowned.

He's a god. Why would he care about a measly human in his realm?

Maya scratched her nose before her hands went back to the pockets of her dress. "Yes, I imagine he might have been a bit sensitive about that. If he has any common sense, he'll have gotten over it. But we don't get humans here often. Well, *live* ones anyway. Lots of dead ones." She grinned to herself, but then continued, her gray eyes growing serious. "While I have certain hopes for you, this decision was sacred. You grew up in a world where your choices were stripped from birth. I thought it was important to allow you the gift of clarity and choice before your journey begins without a god swaying your decision."

Her expression warmed, a sharp sort of mischief entering her eyes as she pushed off the tree. "And I wanted to meet you for myself."

Elysia bit her lip, thinking through Maya's words. The idea of a perfect stranger holding space for her to meditate on her path—all so she could feel a sliver of trust and confidence in herself in the time to come was strange and unsettling. Instead of feeling grateful, she felt wary. When in doubt, she reached for the diplomacy that was second nature.

"Then I thank you for your hospitality and kindness. And I would appreciate your guidance in finding your god."

A low whining growl came from near her feet, and Elysia smiled. She reached down to give the pup some pets. "Yes, you can come too."

Maya stretched, her arms reaching up and back. "Time for us to go, then. It's getting late, and I imagine his deadliness will be feeling a bit frustrated by now." Her shoulders shook with a silent laugh, but she didn't explain, just set off at a steady pace down Elysia's chosen path.

The dogs galloped off with loud barks, darting around Maya's heels as they plunged ahead. Something about the sight gave Elysia pause. The tall bone-white trees, Maya's self-assured form, and the little dogs. It had all been such a strange day already, from her conversation with the prince to drinking tinctures and magical tests in a dark wood.

And now she was to meet a god. If her path was to be filled with gambles and risks, she imagined this was only the first of such strange days.

CHAPTER 33

ELYSIA AND MAYA emerged from the woods into the night only to come upon the mouth of a great body of silver water, mirror-like in its sheen with an old stone bridge for safe travel. They stopped at the bridge's highest point, and Elysia found herself staring down into a cityscape covered in mist. Gulls cried and Elysia could hear the wordless chaos of a marketplace. There was even the familiar scent of salt and fish in the air. She frowned and spun around to look at Maya, her body tensing in confusion.

"Why does it look like Relaclave?"

Maya's brows rose as she looked at Elysia consideringly. "We are passing over the waters of the unlived life. We house so much more than the dead here."

Elysia examined the people below her a little closer and felt her stomach drop at what she saw on the shining surface of the water.

Her sister. Hand in hand with the Doorman, looking lighter than she'd ever seen her. Pulling her girlfriend through the crowds. Movement to their right caught Elysia's eye and a soft cry fell from her lips. Daphne examined a bolt of fabric that she showed to a sandy-haired man who had the look of someone who works with his hands. Her smile was enormous, his gaze on her soft and crinkled. Standing in front of rows and rows of attentive women who sat behind desks was Remy. The women waited, writing utensils in hand, poised and ready to begin. Muddy with axes strapped to his chest was the prince. Strolling through the forest, his shoulders were relaxed and a bottle of wine hung from his fingertips. Lina hopped along beside him and the grin on his face belonged to the boy she once knew.

Her eyes began to sting. "Unlived lives? They aren't dead?" Fear constricted her insides. They couldn't possibly all be dead, and yet their ghosts swirled on around her.

"People are always dying, Elysia." At Elysia's panicked expression, she took pity. "Life is constant death and rebirth. Some consider it practice for the real thing, you know. But everyone, no matter how well they live, has lives unlived. And *here* is where it all goes."

She looked at Elysia intently. "Even the dead can get stuck here. It's best not to dwell on what never was." With that Maya walked on, never looking down into the waters once, her eyes set only on the path before her.

The waters swirled, then settled into a silver mirror once more. A red mist rolled in, heavy and thick, hurrying the women to the opposite shore. Past the waters, they walked for what felt like hours. The night stretched on and Elysia's strength grew thin. She was tired, hungry, and worried about how long she had been here in this realm.

The topography finally shifted, kindling hope within her chest. Long grasses and hills replaced the bonewood trees and barren landscapes. Even in the dark, she could see foreign blooms hiding amongst all the green. The dirt path they walked on now looked well traveled and when they made it to the top of a hill, she could see a large estate nestled in the valley .

Smoke curled up and away from numerous chimneys and a few windows still glowed with golden light in spite of the hour.

All three dogs charged down the hill, running faster than it seemed their legs should be able to carry them.

Elysia looked at Maya as reality sank in—a *god* lived inside the home below.

"Any pointers for meeting him?"

Her guide shook her head. "I don't meddle with his deals. I value my neck too much."

She nodded, trying to mute the building anxiety of what was to come, when a question occurred to her. "Will I be able to use my magic on him? Would that be rude?"

Maya responded under her breath as the estate grew closer. "Please, for the love of the dead, try."

Elysia frowned. She couldn't tell if her words had been sarcastic or some sort of black-humored plea.

They were almost to the front door now. Gorgeous rusty brown bricks surrounded a green door that was so dark it was almost black. In the center of the door was a skull knocker with dice threaded onto the loop in its mouth. Through that door was the undead god who could solve their problems. Thief and deviant, she would steal Kava's magic back from him.

Whatever the cost, she was determined to make him yield.

Flickering sconces of flame lit either side of the door. Her eyes remained glued to the flames as her stomach flipped like a trapeze artist. One hand fluttered to her throat, rubbing at her skin. Was she supposed to address a god as you did a king? Did he have a name? What was the protocol, the expectations for a situation like this? Her nerves climbed higher, a flush starting to rise from her chest. She hated being ill prepared, and she was now realizing she didn't even know how to properly greet the person she was aiming to do business with today.

Gage had been right. She was in over her head and likely about to drown.

But resolve filled her despite the anxiety thrumming through her limbs.

She reminded herself who she was—the daughter of the

Crown, the sister of an assassin, and a woman with nothing to lose. She could see through lies and feel the truth. Steal secrets and hide in plain sight. And most importantly, there was no length too far when one was already good as dead.

The door unlocked with a pop and Elysia mentally shook herself free of the doubts threatening to hold her in place. Stepping inside, she cautiously looked around. She wasn't sure what she had been expecting. Black and red, perhaps? Dark and creepy with dust coating the furniture?

The dogs ran ahead, leaving the foyer behind, but Elysia moved slowly, studying her opponent's home. Rich wooden paneling and stone floors. Thick rugs to still the cold trying to rise up from the ground. Candles that danced with too-tall flames and dripped wax down the iron candelabras. A blue-flamed fire that pushed delicious heat out in waves. Lingering in the air was the smell of bergamot and orange, hinting that someone in the house loved a strong cup of black tea.

She was loath to admit it, but his home was *relaxing*. More than relaxing, it almost felt romantic. As if you would find its owner stretched out on a leather couch with a drink and book in hand and the fire blazing behind them. Tiny dogs and a home that made her want to curl up and nap? She was half convinced they must be in the wrong place.

Eyes roving as if she were going to find a dead body or someone being tortured, she walked farther into the house behind Maya. "He really lives here?"

A man with dark brown skin and black hair worked into smooth, tight waves strode into the room with an apple in hand, lost in his own thoughts. He mumbled a hello to Maya, and then froze with his teeth stuck into the apple. His eyes and brain finally shook hands, alerting him to the fact that there was a stranger in the house.

"Isthather?" The words were garbled and spit around his apple.

Maya made a face of disgust, but her tone was amused. "Yes,

and this will be how she recalls meeting you always. With an apple stuck in your mouth like a piglet and spittle running down your chin."

The man crunched through his apple and glared at her as he chewed. "Don't piss on me just because he's going to hang you from the ceiling for what you did."

Elysia's eyes grew large. "He would hang you for helping me?" Her question was cautious. What was she getting herself into, and why was every ruler the same? Dead or alive, god or mortal, they just killed anyone who upset them.

Both Maya and the newcomer turned and looked at her carefully, noting her distress. The man tilted his head, his thick brows going together. "Not literally, obviously. Do you really think he would do that?"

Maya slapped a hand over his mouth. "You need to stop talking." Taking the apple, she shoved it back into his mouth. "Much better. Come on, Elysia, you're running out of time. Say goodbye to the piglet."

Grabbing her wrist, Maya dragged her into a hallway, walking until Elysia no longer knew all the turns they had made. Even as they hurried, Elysia's eyes drank in the endless paintings and small sculptures decorating the halls.

Speaking over her shoulder, Maya gave Elysia a devious look. "Should be right where I left him."

Throwing open a pair of double doors, they entered a large, beautiful but minimal room. Stale air and a general sense of disuse had her looking around curiously. Elaborate oil lamp chandeliers with black iron flowers and vines hung from the ceilings. On the floors were pewter candelabras almost as tall as herself with half-burned black candles flickering steadily as wax puddled onto the stone floors. Splitting the room in two, a long burgundy rug directed you to the room's purpose—the plain black dais at the very back.

Elysia had been around enough riches and power to know that the people who demanded gilded chairs and piles of glimmering stones were not the ones to fear most. It was the ones who were silent, unimposing, and felt no need to boast who made her shiver. Because behind their quiet was a certain confidence—a certain security in the depth of their power and reach.

She shivered now. Because upon the dais was a black throne. Simple in construction, the only adornment blackened skulls staring out from the posts of the throne. The chair bore no cushion as if its owner knew a throne wasn't meant to be a comfortable thing.

And on the throne sat the man she had met at the river, looking absolutely unbearably pissed.

"Maya." Not even his velvet voice could hide the irritation shooting through her name.

Maya's face remained guileless. "Yes, my most feared deadliness? Wouldn't you like to come and greet our guest?"

Even the dead themselves likely felt his displeasure. It crept out like shadows from behind the throne, the air growing cooler as it neared.

Maya picked at her nails, sliding her eyes over to Elysia. "He hates when I call him that." She glanced back at him and shrugged. "I'd say I'm sorry, but you have your goals and I have mine."

The god before them appeared vexed, his long face that might as well have been hewn from stone by an artist's hands stared at the ceiling. His lips moved as he spoke silently to himself.

Elysia looked at Maya. "What is he saying?"

"I think he's chanting that he can't kill the dead. *Can't kill the dead. Can't kill the dead.*" She nodded even as her eyes remained trained on the god upon the throne, who was now releasing a slow controlled breath. "He's been working on his communication skills. One of the dead here used to be an advisor for some mortal king. Suggested that he use a mantra whenever he feels like losing his shit. Spends half his day reminding himself he can't kill us now."

Glaring down at her, the god of the dead responded with tight politeness. "Maya, I am going to need you to undo your magic. *Please*." The added please sounded as though it cost him, the word barely fitting through his lips.

Maya's eyes lit with a very satisfied sort of pleasure. "I knew you overexerted yourself the other day. You're really stuck, huh?" She turned to Elysia thoughtfully. "Maybe you should present your deal now before he figures out how to move."

"He can't move?"

She answered matter-of-factly. "Not from the waist down. I left him with full control of his upper body."

"You stuck a god to a chair."

She lifted a shoulder. "And from now on, he won't let his power get so low. If anything, I deserve a thank you."

The man stuck to the throne interrupted them. "Maya, if you don't release me from this throne, then I'll be forced to assume you aren't a fit guide for anyone. Roles can be revoked, do you understand?"

She narrowed her eyes. "You don't have that kind of sway."

"Don't I?" He stared at her, unblinking and looking a little bit murderous before finally speaking again. "Release me."

Maya must have believed his threat because she threw her hands up in defeat. "Sorry, new girl." With a snap of her fingers, he jolted forward, falling onto one knee as if he had been straining to break free.

But Elysia hardly noticed Maya now. Breath caught in her throat, her eyes were held captive by the man crouched at the foot of his own throne. Dark hair falling out of place, royal blue eyes flickered behind the disobedient strands. Long, elegant fingers steepled against the floor, his back rippling as he rose back to his full height.

He towered over them now. His body neither thin nor thick, it reminded her of the men in Relaclave who could cut through the sea as if it were nothing for their bodies to move through such tumultuous waters with ease. Entranced, she watched his fingers redo the button on his jacket, tugging his cuffs back into place.

With a roll of his shoulders, the man moved his neck from side to side. Smoke dissipated in his wake as if his power, while apparently diminished, could not be contained within his body. Elysia swallowed at the sight of him. He was a dark, beautiful god. And she was deeply in over her head.

He was looking at her now. She forced her face to remain even, her eyes on him, but inside her head, she rallied once more for what was to come. She was Elysia fucking Parker, forced into the world's most boring business meetings since she could walk, and she could cut a deal with anyone. Even the god who reigned over death itself.

He took another moment to compose himself before wordlessly gesturing at Maya to leave.

Maya dipped her chin, her back bending in the smallest of bows before walking leisurely to the double doors. Light spilled in as she held one of the doors wide and all three dogs bound into the room, charging for the god near the throne. The long-haired tri-colored pup reversed course, pawing at Elysia's legs.

Elysia silently picked the dog up, stroking its small body while watching an undead god act like any other mortal with their pets. The tan short-haired dogs let out pathetic whines until he reached into his pocket, scattering treats for them to hunt.

Fiery blue eyes turned back to her. "She likes you."

There was a quiet humor to his words.

Elysia continued running her hand over the creature. "You're a dog person—a small dog person at that. How unexpected."

He nodded, slipping his hands into his pockets and walking down the stairs. "I wouldn't underestimate them." There was a wryness to his tone that had her glancing down at the animal in her arms, but it merely licked her nose and stared back at her with sweet brown-black eyes.

He kept talking, understanding what she left unsaid. "You expected me to be *different*."

Before she had a chance to respond, he scooped up the two other dogs and strode over to a small rectangular table hidden in the corner of the room. The heavy black iron table matched his throne and contrasted the warmth she had noticed throughout the rest of the house. Two chairs placed on opposite ends awaited them.

Down to business then. Apprehension climbed higher with each step she took, her bare feet still cold on the stone floor. The god of the undead waited for her, his eyes glittering as if he could see how her pulse raced beneath her skin. As if he could taste the regret that had already begun to sour in her mouth.

Sitting down, he smoothed one hand over his dark hair, fixing the loose strands with a practiced motion. Face clear, she observed him. The fastidiousness, the sharp clarity to his blue eyes. The meticulousness that he couldn't hide even if he wished he could. There was an arrogance to him, but in this instance she feared it was warranted. Intelligence shone in his face, and there was a shrewdness to it that made her heart stutter.

Elysia joined him, still studying the hard lines of his face. She sat with one leg tucked up under her before quickly planting both feet on the ground.

His face twitched in amusement at her nervous movements.

Her words came out in a blur, her hands clenching beneath the table. "I'm sorry she restrained you. I didn't know. What I mean is—"

He spread his own hands across the iron table, interrupting her apology. "Maya's actions are not yours to apologize for, Ms. Parker. Now I understand you've traveled a long way and want to make a deal."

Mouth tensing, Elysia leaned back in her chair, crossing one leg over the other. *If that's how he wants to be.* "You seemed quite affronted by my desire for a deal the last time we met."

Her eyes drifted to a crystal chalice at the end of the table. Dark iridescent liquid rippled of its own accord, light glinting off its surface, but the god of the undead snapped her attention back to him with a lift of his shoulder.

He unbuttoned his jacket, allowing one arm to reach back and drape around his chair. "Your request was unexpected. And I'd rather talk in front of a fire with a glass of wine, but we haven't got the time, have we? Besides, you seem quite insistent on business."

His response surprised her. "Why else would I be here?"

A short, curt laugh escaped his mouth. "Why else, indeed." He studied her now, not bothering to hide it. Eyes roamed over her face, from her hair to the tips of her fingers. Elysia fought the desire to squirm.

"I should have known you'd be beautiful. Eyes like a doe to cover all the unholy thoughts inside your head. Because you're not an innocent, are you? You couldn't possibly be." His firm mouth almost smiled as he looked down at his hands before looking back at her, waiting for her to answer.

The tone in which he delivered these words implied a double meaning. She gathered that he somehow knew much about her life in Relaclave, but also that he wanted to unsettle her. See just how easily she reacted.

Elysia colored, anger simmering beneath her surface. He thought he could toy with her. Make her slip up just because he had a pretty face and a voice that ran like fingers up and down her spine.

Steel entered her eyes, hardening her against the deceptive allure of the undead god before her. She redirected their attention as if this were any other meeting where the participants couldn't quite stay on task. "I believe this could be mutually beneficial. A deal for both of us."

A small knowing smirk sharpened the angles of his face. "Ms. Parker, I'm not the one who should be worried. The deals I cut are rarely to my disadvantage." His face shifted, all mirth disappearing in an instant as his voice lowered. "I'll give you a secret since I hear you love them so much. There was only *once*. One single time that I fouled a deal."

Elysia found herself leaning in closer. "What happened?" She clocked every tiny twitch of irritation on his face, how his shoulders tightened and cheeks drew gaunt. Whatever his mistake had been, it haunted him even now.

"I was new to my throne and trust me, I have learned my lesson every day since then. I hope you're prepared for what you're asking to do because once a deal is struck, there's nothing that can change it. Understood?"

His response left endless questions bubbling up inside her, but she quelled them with a firm hand. She knew better than to let her curiosity take the lead. Instead, she met his frigid condescension with an unyielding spine. She lifted her dark eyes slowly to his, her voice taking on a sultry quality that startled even her. "Then I suppose you have nothing to worry about. Since you always come out on top."

A soft laugh huffed out of him. "Don't start games you can't finish." Amusement shone in his eyes now, as if he was calling her bluff.

"With all due respect, I've played scarier games. Are you willing to hear me out?"

He frowned at that, pinning her with a stare. "You've thought this through? There's no shame in changing your mind. You haven't even tried to read me with your magic yet."

Elysia stiffened. "I'm not so presumptuous as to think I can freely use my curse on a god."

The allure of reading this man's secrets felt criminal, it was so tempting. She looked at him plainly now. The serious crease to his brow. His eyes shifted between a fissuring coolness and passionate embers of heat. There were some things even she knew not to touch.

"I'm here for a deal. I don't need your secrets to do it." Her voice came out terse, and she sat up a little taller. She wasn't going to let some handsome stranger get under her skin.

And yet her eyes went back to his face, seemingly of their own magnetic accord. It was no wonder the god before her had no difficulty swindling those who came to him for deals. She could just imagine the women panting after him while he barely even noticed. He appeared to be the kind of man so entrenched in his own endeavors and passions that for him to look up at all would be a miracle. *But if he did...* She couldn't help but wonder how his intense severity translated to *other* activities. To have that type of focus, attention to every last detail... Her thoughts trailed off, and her cheeks went pink as the sound of his voice drew her back in.

The undead god of the dead looked at her warm cheeks, his mouth lifting slightly in response. "Perhaps I'm feeling amicable. Look, listen. Do your worst. Learn my secrets while I'm giving you the chance." He leaned across the table, not looking apprehensive in the slightest.

She blinked, thrown by his fervent words. Cautiously, she allowed the volume of the whispers surrounding him to increase. Within a moment, the whispers became screams, and then it was her own voice joining them as her hands covered her ears, body doubling over until her head was between her knees. As if her physical hands could stop a sound that wasn't even there. Abruptly, her magic cut off, the sound dying. Chest heaving, she stayed curled over until her head quieted.

Tears leaked out of her eyes, leaving wet tracks down her face. The god of the dead looked pained, his fingers clenched and jaw hard. His mouth opened, but she closed her eyes, diving back into her magic's grasp. This time she focused specifically on what *she* needed to close this deal with *him*. Instead of an onslaught, tiny threads and wisps came to her.

Eyes open, she found a hint of nerves in his expression before he dashed it away. Her voice was a rasp. "The weight of all their pain will kill you."

He gave her a tight pinch of a smile. "Temporary fix for a temporary problem. What did you discover in your second attempt?"

Elysia considered her response, making him wait. Hoping it

made him sweat. "I learned there is something you deeply, desperately want, and you hate that it is so."

She could have heard a pin drop.

The intensity in his blue eyes blazed like the sapphire fires of his realm. He turned his face as if struggling with himself before he came back to her, and when he did, his voice was cutting and harsh. "You did not go deep enough nor are you understanding correctly. Given the chance, you looked away. Remember, you had both opportunity and choice, Ms. Parker. Let us move on to the deal, then."

Heart beating faster, she shook her head, feeling as though she had made a fatal error. "I... I can look again. My magic is new."

Composure restored, the god across from her gave a clipped shake of his head. "No, we need to move on. What are your opening terms?"

Rattled, she steepled her fingers and appraised him. "I have reason to believe you played a role in my kingdom, Kava, losing access to its natural relationship with magic."

His jaw ticked. "And?"

"And I would like this remedied."

His chest strained beneath the black shirt and jacket he wore. Each breath seemed to be a strain until he finally spoke. "That's what you want? No matter the cost?"

"Can you do it?"

He stared at her and she worried at the scrutiny in his gaze, the tension lining his shoulders.

In an abrupt movement, he crossed his arms, his stare still heavy. "You're asking me to break someone else's deal."

She frowned. "It was a *deal* to end Kava's magic?"

"Dealer-client privilege." He shrugged, appearing indifferent to the shock ringing through her.

Anger reared its head in response to his evasion. His blatant disregard for the ramifications of what he had done set off the fury that slumbered within her. *How could one person be so thoughtless and careless?* She took in his face, devoid of empathy or compassion. *And such an asshole.*

Elysia fought to keep her own face neutral, but based on the way his eyebrow was rising, she wasn't winning that battle. Leashing her anger, she responded with a shrewdness that would make her father proud.

"You made a deal to cut off Kava's magic *forever*?" She smiled knowingly.

The undead god pursed his lips, running one hand through his midnight hair. "No, and as much as I enjoy your aptitude for the finer aspects of a magically binding deal—it's not that simple. I can't just give Kava its magic back."

She looked back at him, challenge lighting her eyes and a taunt lifting her voice. "Too difficult? Impotence problems?"

That same amusement as before shone back at her. He considered her a moment longer before his face grew serious as he came to a decision. "Something like that. Deals are tricky things. *Magic* is a tricky thing. There are three deals in conflict at the moment. One that came into effect when I became god of this realm, the one you would like to be broken, and the one you would like to forge."

He tapped his fingers on the table, and a slow smile crept across his face. "Would you like to know one more secret?" His laugh rolled out low and deep, knowing that he had just hooked her completely. Anyone whose magic revolved around secrets was likely to have a weakness for personal truths.

Elysia's mouth pressed tight and she narrowed her eyes. "Don't think I don't see what you're doing."

"Ah, but it's working, isn't it? Your magic just stretched like a cat, you can barely contain it. I can feel it winding in and out around me. Not that I mind, of course. Your magic has *such* an interesting sensation."

She rolled her eyes, ignoring his blatant attempts to provoke her, so he persisted. "It's only fair. I know your tragic little story.

Girl grows up in magicless land, is exploited for the very gift they revile, and still tries to save her people. Well, this is mine."

He clicked his fingers, transporting them from the table to the dais. Except now there were two skull-adorned thrones and they sat facing each other on them. Startled, Elysia grabbed hold of the arms of the throne. Traveling like that might be commonplace for him, but it was foreign and deeply uncomfortable for her. Hands gripped the arms of her throne, and his knee brushed against hers as he brought his face close to hers.

"You were correct when you asked if I was impotent."

Elysia blinked in surprise. "You've displayed magic several times in the short time I've been here."

The god of the undead's face twisted, tension cording through his neck. "I am impotent for a god."

Elysia found herself caught in his story, curiosity flickering to life and a question tumbling out of her mouth in spite of herself. "Really?"

Instead of answering, he snapped his fingers, bringing them back to the table with the chalice now in between them. As much as he tried to lounge back in the chair, she could see the frustration peeking through his body. The subtle roll of his shoulders, how his nose flared for the briefest of seconds.

He finally answered. "I was a reluctant god. Combine that with the reckless anger of youth and the fates and their penchant for a good story, and here we are."

"The deal that went wrong."

He looked up at her, one corner of his mouth lifting as he echoed her. "The deal that went wrong." His smile became grim. "But also tradition. Tradition and a deal gone so very wrong. The perfect storm."

Elysia considered all he had told her carefully.

"If you were to regain your powers, then you could grant me my deal?"

The god before her paused, uncertainty bringing distance into his gaze. The uncertainty disappeared. "What I need is my talisman."

"A talisman that holds your power." Her words were flat. He had to be fucking kidding her.

He nodded. "Yes, something like that. There is a talisman that belongs with me. Every god of the dead has to find their talisman in order to come into the full power of their position. It's a terrible tradition and there's nothing I can do about it."

Elysia knew her face was rude. That she should be hiding her obvious irritated disbelief.

"And how exactly am I supposed to find this talisman? Is it in your realm, mine? Is it big, small, metaphorical? What exactly are we talking about here?" Her anger spurted out in fits. This task would be impossible.

Her anger was nothing to him. He flicked it away and held her gaze as steady as the bone trees of his land. His jaw tensed, but he brought a gentle hand to the curve of her face. Smooth, warm fingers rested against her skin. "If you accept my offer, then I will provide you with every last resource within my grasp. I will be at your complete disposal. The power I do have will be yours to direct so long as it brings us closer to the talisman. Our situations are much the same—your kingdom, my realm—both magically impoverished, decaying before our eyes."

The depths of his blue eyes held her silent as he made his case. "I can do *nothing* without the talisman, so either we have a deal, or we both carry on knowing our homes are slowly dying an unnatural death that could have been stopped."

Elysia bit down, her teeth grinding as she chewed on his proposal.

"What happens once you have the talisman?"

He gave her a funny smile. "The talisman will do its job and we will pursue the restoration of our homes."

"You still won't be... how you should be, though? Because of the deal gone wrong."

He emitted a long sigh, chin tilting up to the ceiling. "Correct."

Elysia gathered her frustration, releasing it back at him as logic. "What you're offering me is an impossible quest for an undefined talisman. A talisman that won't fully resolve your impotency, or guarantee we can restore our homes, which effectively makes this the worst proposition I've ever heard." She threw him the most flat, unimpressed look she could muster.

"Would you prefer I lie to you? Tell you that I'll be able to restore your land from rot to vitality in the blink of an eye? Trick you into taking my deal only to leave you feeling betrayed?"

"No—"

"I am not going to begin this relationship with lies. I have told you all I can within the constraints set by the fates. Is there more I wish I could tell you? Yes, of course, but for now the talisman is where we must start. Whether you come to hate me or trust me by the end of this, please know this was my only choice. You will understand once you find the talisman." The god of the undead leveled her with a stare that saw right through to her quaking heart.

"And this all goes back to the deal that went wrong. The reckless deal *you* made that is now slowly killing my kingdom and your realm." She held his stare, her mouth drawn tight. She knew it was unkind, but she needed to hear him acknowledge *why* they were all in this mess. A mess that he was now expecting her to clean up.

His eyes darkened. "Yes, Ms. Parker, because of my error. Trust me when I say that I have spent every day regretting that deal for a myriad of reasons, but one above all the others."

"And what would that be?"

Blue eyes blazed into hers. "A conversation for another day. Do we have a deal?"

Elysia closed her eyes, disappointment crashing over her. The sorrow burrowing through her was not just for herself, but for all the Kavians who would not be getting their magic back.

Not tonight. Possibly not ever.

She knew an unachievable deal when she heard one, and she was wise enough to know when to walk away. She exhaled a small, bitter sound. "It sounds like we're both just going to have to live with our regrets then. Then again, I'll probably be seeing you soon enough unless I leave Kava." Elysia looked around as if the dead were suddenly going to appear and she could ask them what it was like to die.

"You shouldn't speak of such things."

Elysia's eyes flicked to his, noting how terse he sounded—as if it angered him to hear her speak so flippantly about her own death. "I didn't think someone like yourself would be so precious about death. Happens to the best of us after all, doesn't it?"

There wasn't a shred of humor to be found on his face. "While the timing of mortals' deaths is out of my control, I am deeply aware of the undue trauma of an early death upon a soul."

Elysia softened at his response and found herself wishing she could keep talking to the pale, blue-eyed god in front of her. He appeared harsh, maybe a little compulsive or even obsessive, but there was a depth to him she found alluring. She got the feeling he was someone who would be happy to muse and ponder the mysteries long into the night so long as his day's work was done.

"Since we're being honest, I think I might like you. I feel like you're someone I could talk to, and that's a rare thing for someone like me. But my answer remains the same—no deal." She studied him openly now, feeling oddly at ease with her disclosure.

The god of the dead wore a practiced impassive face. "I will give you two weeks to change your mind. Return when you are ready and give your final answer. Simply call my name three times."

"That won't be necessary." Her words were matter-of-fact. His offer was nothing more than a wild goose chase without even the lure of a golden prize.

She stood to leave, but paused, giving him one last chance to give her a better deal. "There is an entire kingdom decaying and its people alongside it. People who are sick and people who are being hunted for being unlucky enough to be cursed with some broken remnant of magic. And your best offer is a quest for a talisman?" She stared at him beseechingly.

The fires in his eyes cooled and his shoulders drew back. "My name is Aidan. Until your return." He touched his fingers to his lips, and then cupped the back of her neck, pressing his fingers firmly behind her ear.

There was a small twinge of heat upon her skin, and then she was gone. Ripped from the land of the dead with nothing to show for her efforts.

She had failed. Kava would remain exactly as it was—hopeless.

Chapter 34

Elysia's eyes flew open, and a cold sweat coated her body. Her fingers grasped the bedding reflexively. Checking and testing. Making sure this was real.

She'd made it back. And she was in her room. She patted a hand down her body. In one piece at that.

Beatriz sat slumped and sound asleep in a chair with her feet propped up. Drool trickled down the corner of her mouth, and one hand was half shoved into the waistline of her pants. Jessa lay stretched out on the floor with an arm folded behind her head.

Footsteps sounded outside the door. Elysia was standing with her knife drawn before the door so much as cracked.

The Doorman entered with an amused smile. "Charming, aren't you?"

Elysia's shoulders slid back down, and she tucked the dagger away. "Is it odd that I'm almost glad to see you?"

The Doorman wrapped her fingers around a mug and nudged Jessa with the toe of her pointed leather boot, but Jessa's mouth just opened wider on a soft snore. "Between these two, you would have been dead had anyone else snuck in here." The Doorman glanced up. "Also, did you know there's a man sitting on your roof? Looks an awful lot like a certain prince, but what do I know about these things..."

Elysia groaned and grabbed a pillow off her bed, launching it at her sister's face where it hit its target with a satisfying smack.

Beatriz startled awake with a garbled sound and promptly snatched a brass candlestick holder from Elysia's nightstand, brandishing it violently through the air.

The Doorman stared at this as if it were the most adorable sight. "You're getting much faster, my love. Well done."

Elysia looked between the two of them incredulously. *Seriously?* "She was asleep with drool running down her face. As you *just said*, I'm fairly certain she would've been dead if anyone had broken in here. That *I* would have been dead."

The Doorman frowned. "Positive reinforcement is a much better tool than verbal flagellation, Elysia. Sometimes I think you two were raised by demons the way you respond."

Elysia rubbed her eyes, mumbling to herself, "The Doorman. The Doorman is telling me my damages. Perfect."

The bedroom window popped open, and the prince stuck his head in from where he had been apparently sitting on the ledge and surveilling the situation.

"They really are snarly little beasts sometimes. I've tried training her, but..." The prince shrugged as if it were too great a burden for even him to bear.

Elysia grabbed the nearest tome from her desk and chucked it with all the force she could gather straight at his chest. The book hit his chest with a thump, both his arms reflexively flapping and letting go of the building.

Elysia watched him fall straight back and down out the window. Good riddance. A muffled groan echoed up to the flat. She turned and faced the room again. "He thinks *now* is the time to find his sense of humor again? Ugh."

Jessa sat up with a yawn. "What the fuck was that noise?"

"Elysia's bound and determined to assassinate the prince. I

tried so hard to stop her…" The Doorman fanned her fingers and examined her nails.

Still off kilter from her travels, Elysia's temper cracked. "I swear to the undead fucking gods if you all don't get your shit together—do you think this is a carnival? A time for laughs and half-assed measures? I go to the realm of the dead and you're taking a *nap?* Are you kidding me right now?"

Elysia marched over to the window, slamming it shut and locking it this time. "You couldn't even manage to lock a window, Beatriz? Honestly, it's like you wanted something to go wrong."

Jessa cleared her throat and cut in before the Parkers could scratch and hiss away the time. "If we could redirect our attention to Elysia visiting a death god?"

All the girls fell quiet, and Elysia deflated, the familiar restriction of shame and fear tightening within her. She'd failed them. She'd failed all of them. Her beloved home with its beautiful, stubbornly colorful doors and all its people. Not that they'd ever know. But she had.

"Do you think we could make some tea?" Disappointment softened all of their faces, and Elysia swallowed against the sinking pit in her stomach.

Jessa hesitated as she walked past before finally wordlessly clapping a hand on Elysia's shoulder in silent solidarity. Elysia looked down at the floor, feeling her face tense against tears that suddenly wanted to flow. This wasn't how it was supposed to happen. It had been a long shot and yet she clearly had been banking on it more than she realized to feel this bleak and miserable now.

A few minutes later, they were all curled up like cats amongst the couch, pillows, and blankets of Elysia's living room. Scents of chamomile and lavender curled into the air. She was glad she'd remembered to snag some tea off of Lynd because tonight called for a little warmth and was well worth the indulgence.

Beatriz plunked down her mug, seemingly tired of waiting. She'd been making faces for the past five minutes while she sipped her tea and apparently had hit her limit of pretending to like the taste of dead plants.

"So, death god, undead god of the dead. What're we workin' with? Negotiations? A deal? Hit me." She rubbed her hands together.

Elysia took in the razor glint of excitement and something akin to lust shining in her sister's eyes with some perplexity. "You get off on this shit, don't you?"

The Doorman grinned with pride and ran perfectly manicured fingers down Beatriz's silky locks. "Obviously. You're not the only talented Parker, Elysia."

Triz shushed her girlfriend by pressing an indelicate hand over her painted mouth and didn't seem to mind when sharp teeth caught her fingers. "So?"

Elysia set her mug on the floor and avoided eye contact as she answered. "There's no deal. No negotiations. The bastard wants me to find a *talisman* to unlock his bound powers. Long story short, he fucked up a deal and now Kava and his realm are screwed. He's useless." She bit off the words and folded her arms.

Triz waggled her brows. "What kind of talisman?"

"For the undead gods' sake, Beatriz, I am not hunting for an object that could be *anywhere*. I'm not a treasure hunter! It's a terrible deal. Actually, it's worse than a terrible deal. It's a trap. I refuse to be the one who pays the price for this god's stupidity. He got us all into this mess and he can figure out a solution himself."

The Doorman toyed with a strand of Triz's hair. "Then what do you propose? Since he's *so* useless."

Elysia sat up and shot the Doorman a look. "I propose that we do what we should have done in the first place—we get the dirt we need to make a better deal. I don't buy that this is the best he can do. If anyone can find a chokehold on someone, it's me, and I swear I will find the secret that will bend this god's will. He gave me two weeks to return."

The Doorman shivered and fanned herself. "Good *night*, you could have just told us he's hot as the death realm itself and that your panties are in a twist. No wonder you negotiated so terribly." She patted Elysia's knee. "It's okay, darling, we can train that out of you. You've spent far too much time with only one man, but the House always provides what you need." She dropped a coy, understanding sort of look in Elysia's direction.

Beatriz made barfing noises, while Elysia glared silently at them all.

Jessa's eyes went wide at Elysia's reaction, her eyebrows practically to her hairline. "Oh my gods, you really did have it out for the god of the dead. Soot and storms, Elysia, first a prince who could turn you in and have you hung at any last breath, and now the god of the dead? You need serious help." She hooted mercilessly, and Elysia turned a vibrant shade of red.

"I do not," she muttered. "And his name is Aidan."

All three women blinked.

"He has a name?" Beatriz looked repulsed by this.

"He has three pint-size dogs and a beautiful home."

They all sat back and pondered this for a moment until Beatriz finally got down to it. "Alright. So, he's sexy. He's got three tiny-ass dogs. And we need a secret to force his hand. Anything else I'm missing?"

Elysia nodded at her sister's summary. "We each belong to an important sector. Beatriz, you've got the undead market. I don't know what your business is, but I'm not stupid—you're moving something. Jessa, you run a bar that caters to people who travel the seas and keep our city running. People treat them as if they're invisible—which means secrets are spilled around them constantly, so get nosy, ask questions. And Doorman, well, you have the House."

Beatriz's mouth flapped open wordlessly as she sputtered at being found out, but her girlfriend just patted her hand and shushed her.

Jessa frowned. "What about you? You're the one who can sniff out a secret like a dog's behind."

Elysia grimaced. "Thank you for that, Jessa. What a painting of my skills. I will assist all of you, but... I will also visit the librarians and the office in charge of the census. Find out if any of the death priestesses survived the aftermath of the Fall. Oh, and I want to see if that old meela is still around."

Jessa leaned back on one elbow. "I thought it was common knowledge that all the priests and priestesses were killed by the king's edict after the Fall, and I hate to break it to you, but the meela is long gone. She never stays more than the days it takes her to get to Bellia."

Elysia shook her head. "There were some priestesses so powerful that they were afraid to kill them. The thought being it's best not to murder those with a supposed direct line to the gods even if magic is gone."

Everyone fell silent at that. Lost in thoughts of abandoned temples, rituals, and magic long buried. The people they knew and didn't know who had lost their lives over the years for so much as a spark of magic surviving.

"It's not likely we'll find anything. There's every chance we'll be right back where we started and I'll regret not getting on a ship out of here, but what we're doing matters. If there's a chance that someone else can grow up differently... then it's worth it," Elysia said quietly.

The words were as much for herself as they were for others. Even though the women in her living room knew that none of them called her on it. Instead, they raised their long-cold teas in the air.

Beatriz shoved her mug against the others. "To the women whose names are never known who fix the mistakes of men that we all may have better lives."

Chapter 35

Topp Blatz had found himself in some strange and unfortunate places in his life. Much like today, it was usually completely and entirely his own fault. He was made for direct confrontation, not hiding in cabinets half his size. Yet here he was, feigning he had any skill at this sort of thing.

The blinding pain in his knee felt like it might be an indicator that he definitely did *not* possess any skill for subterfuge. To be fair, it had only been a few days since catapulting out of Elysia's window, and his body still hadn't entirely forgiven him for that little stunt. Shifting his already contorted frame, he tried to pretend the ache in his knee was not trying to murder him. One false move and he would be found out, so he bit down on the pain, refusing to so much as breathe wrong.

He'd been waiting in his father's office when he heard not only the king coming but also Terrin. He would say that Terrin reminded him of a weasel, but he'd rehabilitated a weasel once, and that would be rude to vermin everywhere. Terrin was King Blatz's favorite sort of advisor. He had no wife or husband or lover of any sort, no kids—he had nothing.

Nothing but ambition and his king.

And by the gods, did Topp hate the miserable man. Anyone

with their nose that far up his father's ass ought to be made a snack for a pig. Or just needed a good punch to face. Either would be fine, so long as he didn't have to listen to Terrin snivel anymore.

Topp tried to adjust his shoulder against the confines of the cabinet only to find his arm now dead and numb to the point that he couldn't even tell if it had moved at all. He gave an inaudible sigh. Throwing yourself into a cabinet in order to eavesdrop on someone was downright uncomfortable. He much preferred intimidating people into confessing what he needed to know.

Except his father was the one person his tricks would never work on. Never had, never would. That was the problem with family. Anyone who's seen you butt-ass naked, waving your cloth diaper in the air as you run through the castle halls, is never going to see you quite the same as anyone else, even when you are a grown man.

His arm throbbed painfully as it decided to come back to life. He didn't know how Elysia did this sort of thing all the time. She *was* rather bendy. The thought almost helped him forget the shooting pain spreading from his knee to his thigh. Almost.

Hearing his own name tossed out amongst the rubbish they'd been blathering on about, he tilted his head to peer out the small crack between the door and the framing.

Money. Killing off that irritating group of vigilante magic users.

"Was surprised Topp led that charge, Your Grace."

His father edged his response with the appropriate amount of derision. "You question my son's loyalty, even now?"

Topp focused on keeping his breathing both silent and steady —hearing them speak of the dead rebels triggered him to retreat into himself, but that wasn't an option at the moment. He needed to listen even if he'd rather disappear than hear about his failures. Years of hiding and studying other culture's magic as he traveled —and what had he accomplished? Nothing.

All he had to his name was a long list of people who never made it home.

The pressure on the corners of his mind increased, demanding he block it all out like he normally did. How else was he supposed to survive? No one could be responsible for such atrocities and actually function like a normal human. He'd recognized the shift in himself over the last decade. He used to laugh and joke more readily than most. Now he found himself ready to swing a fist at the slightest provocation. Hiding it was a full-time job—not to mention the fact that he was just as guilty as any of them.

It was his own fault that Elysia didn't trust him. The thought of allowing someone in far enough to see how fucked up he really was inside—it was unbearable. And beyond that, he was obsessed. Obsessed with righting these wrongs. With finally figuring out how and why magic had left Kava.

"Do you really think he will be able to continue your good work? He acts as though it's beneath him rather than the most important work he will ever complete."

Topp peered through the crack in between the cabinet doors.

The king popped the crystal stopper out of his favorite decanter. While everyone else in Kava drank cheap gin, he kept a steady supply of imported whiskey for himself. He held the intricate bottle for a moment before pouring out two tumblers and handing one off to his advisor.

His father's eyes sat heavy on his advisor, clearly not appreciating the open critique of his heir. "Topp may push to see how far he can wander, but at the end of the day, beyond whatever fanciful notions he may hold, he knows exactly what I am willing to do to maintain what we have created in Kava."

The king took a small, burning sip of whiskey and stared straight through to where Topp hid behind thin wooden doors. "Rooting out magic, killing it at the source. I have foot soldiers for such brutality. I don't need my heir out there, hands bloody. I need him right here." The king made a fist, squeezing his hand tight. "My son knows what his end will be if he can't fulfill what is demanded of a Blatz."

The king set his whiskey down, now staring blatantly at the cabinet. Terrin glanced over his shoulder nervously before his eyes darted back to his king.

"No one knows this story, Terrin, but I think it's time I tell someone."

The king took a seat behind his desk while Terrin stood there sweating, looking torn between the intelligent response of anxiety and the fact that the king sharing his secrets was all the man had ever dreamed of for years.

"I made a promise after my wife died—that no one would ever die from the inhuman curse of magic ever again." The king's voice shifted from the benevolent caring ruler to one of iron and blood. "I did what was necessary to free our people from the affliction of magic and false gods, and it is my most sacred duty to maintain this freedom."

Taking a small drink, he continued. "My father was a hard man, an angry man. He had an affinity for air magic, and he liked to use that magic against my mother. Inevitably, there came a day where he went too far." The king's jaw worked and he crossed his arms. "Without my mother around, I became his target. As you can imagine, I am intimately familiar with the dangers of magic, but it wasn't until it killed my wife that I did something about it."

Terrin stuttered. "I thought, I thought that was a riding accident, Your Grace."

The king nodded, looking out the window into the gray before switching on the lights behind him. Warm-toned bulbs fixed to the wall behind his desk like modern sconces came to life, reviving the office from Relaclave's natural gloom.

"We'd argued that day. She thought I was losing perspective regarding magic. Went for a ride to clear her head, and some fool's fire magic spooked the horse."

Inside the cabinet, Topp froze, hanging onto every word. He knew he'd been caught, but there was nothing he could do except listen. His father was finally revealing what he had been afraid of all along. The monster was not outside of him. It had raised him and ran through his blood.

His eyes latched onto Terrin. The advisor was going to wish he had never entered this room. If there was one thing dating Elysia Parker had taught Topp, it was that all secrets came at a price—some much steeper than others.

The story wasn't finished though.

"My daughter knew how her mother died, and yet even after all I did to secure a safe, magicless future for our people, she carried on flaunting her curse like she was above the law of this land. She could have ruined everything. I had to stop her—for the good of the Crown. Topp has never caused such problems. He burns with questions, but he's obedient. He knows his place is supporting the Crown." The king's gaze drilled into the cabinet. "Or maybe he just knows that if he wants the Parker girl to stay alive, then he'll do as he's damn well told. Besides, there's nothing he could do to bring magic back, anyway. I saw to that."

Topp's chest heaved. His father was right—he had burned. Burned for years as he questioned the deaths of his mother, his sister, and how magic left this land. Burned as he questioned if it was he who was insane or everyone else who saw a saint and hero when they looked at his father. Burned as he tried again and again to find answers to questions that no one but his own flesh and blood could resolve.

He wanted to bellow so loudly it would shake the castle's very foundation. Wanted to free the magic that pushed against his skin, hot and electric.

The air within the cabinet began to tremble and even shimmer as light danced along its current. He tried to disconnect from it all. The pain, the anger. The part of him that screamed for vengeance against his own blood. But it was no use. His magic knew two very simple things. His father had killed his sister. And Kava's king needed to die.

The cabinet exploded as Topp's magic surged out, searching

for its target. Bits and shards of wood flew everywhere with dust falling in a cloud. But Topp was right behind his magic. Launching himself across the room without a thought other than the target that filled his sight.

And then everything stopped.

It was as if his magic had been ripped from the room. Like his power had been cut off at the knees. All the oxygen had disappeared, and he had no fire to burn.

He fell helpless to the floor, his body making the softest of thuds against his father's richly woven rug.

Sweat ran along Topp's brow, his body contorting into an unnatural shape. Head lolling, he stared brazenly into his father's eyes and found them cold. His words were choked. "What... What are you doing?"

His father's fist was closed and his voice strangely even. "I am doing exactly as I said. I am keeping you. Right. Here."

He squeezed his fist and Topp felt the last of his magic deflate as if it never existed. Even though he'd only lived with its remnants, his body felt stripped to its bones and powerless. All his muscles flexed and tensed, fighting against this invasion. Whatever his father was doing was unnatural, and his body was unlikely to remain conscious much longer if he didn't stop. Heartbeat erratic and vision faltering, his breath turned shallow.

He laughed openly, coming out from behind his desk. "Did you really think I didn't know? That I'd spend my whole life hunting your kind and wouldn't see it in my own son? You've hidden it well enough all these years and that's what you will continue to do."

He crouched down on the rug, knees coming close to Topp's face. "I've no desire to sire a new heir. Your mother was it for me, and her son will take my throne."

Topp's nostrils flared. Words wouldn't come, but he knew his father could see exactly what he thought of this.

The king smiled. He stood, looking down at his son. "You'll come around. Even if not for yourself, then for Elysia's sake. All it takes is one accusation, one whisper of magic, and a person's life is mine to turn to dust. You wouldn't want that, now would you? You may have grown harder over these last years, but somehow I doubt you have the balls to let her die."

Even if Topp had the voice to speak, he wouldn't have been able to—his father, executioner of the masses, didn't think he was capable of allowing someone he loved to die. But he *had* become someone who did such things. And he had no idea where that left him.

"You will continue as before, but with shall we say, renewed fervor? And you will ensure Elysia is at the Raven Ball. Both of your behavior has been unfortunate as of late, but I'm sure you'll see to it that she gets in line." He paused. "Or don't. But you know what happens then, don't you?"

His father turned to Terrin. He spoke regretfully. "I *am* sorry about this."

He closed his opposite fist now, his power striking out and stealing the only magic this man had: his life. A gray pallor overcame the king's loyal advisor. Knees giving out, he toppled down, his face an inch from Topp's own, his glassy eyes no longer seeing anything at all.

The king walked casually from the room, whiskey glass dangling between his fingers. "Clean up the mess, will you?"

His father's magic released him, and Topp fell onto his back, chest quaking and magic darting feverishly back through him like all the candles in a room coming alight.

Physically he would be fine, his body would slowly return to its natural stasis. But what his father revealed had caused a permanent fracture that would likely never heal. It was one thing to question and long for answers. It was another to have your roots ripped out from beneath you, leaving you with only ashes and death to sustain you. No matter his suspicions, it turned out the final moment of truth was still painful.

The image of his sister filled his mind. Gray eyes that matched his father's, a thick smattering of freckles softening her delicate face. He so rarely allowed himself to think of her—she may have motivated his search, but think of her, he did not. Because to see her face was excruciating. He'd even had all of her paintings removed from the castle. But right now, she was all he could see. Her wood-brown hair and gray eyes stared into his soul, and he knew what she would have wanted.

Revenge.

It had always been about answers. Where did the magic go? How did his family *actually* die? What would it take to restore his home?

Tomorrow he might care about Kava again. But tonight, he was a brother and a son, and he wanted nothing more than to make the man he called father feel his pain.

The inner turmoil he'd long felt about his father had been put to rest today. In its place was the newly ignited need to shear the life of Garrison Blatz from fate's tapestry.

He had no idea what his father had done to secure a future in which magic didn't exist in Kava. All he needed to know was that his sister was gone, and it was because of him. Topp sat up, rubbing his hands roughly against his face.

He knew what fear and hate could do, and he saw it in his father now. Somehow, his father's past had driven him mad. Because it was madness to wipe a land of its natural magic. It was madness to cut down your own daughter. And it was madness to wield the magic of the gods while cursing their name.

Over the years, he'd seen behind his father's mask often enough to wonder if Garrison Blatz was really a hero after all. But he'd still felt guilt over his questions about his sister's death. Because what kind of father could possibly kill his own daughter? His suspicions left him feeling like a terrible, ungrateful son. On the days his father looked at him with happiness and pride in his eyes, the guilt was almost incapacitating. He would look around his kingdom—at all the people who parroted Garrison's words and cheered for the man who saved them from the destruction of the Fall, and convince himself once more that he must be the one who was wrong.

Garrison Blatz was a good man who spoke the truth. Magic was a curse, and the undead gods did not hear nor care.

But if magic was a curse, then Topp Blatz was the ultimate sin. He couldn't have stopped the magic in himself if he'd wanted to—throughout his life he'd lurched between feeling dirty and ashamed back to angry and searching over and over and over.

In his guilt, he'd stop all his efforts for a few weeks, but then the anger and questions would return, and his big sister would whisper in his ear, show up on the pages of a book, or in the love of the animals he cared for, and then he'd be back in the thick of it, trying to find answers.

And now, at long last, he knew the truth.

His father may wear many faces: benevolent king, loving father, wise counselor, but beneath them there was only one truth, one face, and it was one of decay. Only a soul who had already lost itself could kill their own daughter. Could rip the very essence out of an entire people and send countless faces to the gallows.

Topp stood, feeling calm in his resolution. He took hold of the dead weight that was his father's advisor. Throwing the man over his shoulder, he exited his father's office.

There would be no pleasing his father. There would be no falling in line. Revenge was the only sustenance for his spirit now.

He would solve the riddle of Kava's decay, and he would rid his kingdom of the plague that was his father.

Topp set off at a brisk pace through the castle halls with his father's fresh kill swinging behind him like yesterday's rabbit. He hummed an old song that his sister had always sung.

Death be a fog, but death also be a newfound sight, and Topp felt like he had never seen more clearly in his life.

Chapter 36

Elysia reached over the bar, rummaging around for the gin. Her belly went heavy on the bar and her legs kicked up dangerously as she tried to grasp the bottle she spied beneath the rail. *Just a little farther.* She strained, fingers swiping.

"What in the realms are you doing, Parker?" Jessa's voice startled her and Elysia twisted precariously to look up at her.

"Getting the booze, obviously."

"Aren't you supposed to be in a library skulking after priestesses, or dazzling gross old men at the House into telling you their secrets? You may need a few more lessons on that." She stared pointedly at Elysia's indecent position.

Elysia scowled and, with a move that Gage would have applauded, sent her legs over the bar, landing lightly on her feet.

"I am the most charming, thank you." She yanked the gin bottle out of its home and poured herself a smidge.

She took in Jessa's scrunched face and set her glass down heavily, leaning against the bar. "It's been seven fucking days, Jess. Seven days and I've got nothing. But since you asked..." She hoisted herself back over the bar and onto a seat.

"Already wishing I hadn't."

Elysia ignored her. "I learned there are several high-level

romantic affairs commencing at the Raven Ball. The usual, you know? Rooms reserved with false names. People trying to hide their little once a year sexcapades. But then there are the people who use their true names—they're going for the spite approach. A really clear *fuck you* to their partner. Normally, I'd have one of Gage's men squeeze the former for coin, or better yet, a more useful piece of information in exchange for my silence, but not this year."

She took a gulp of the throat-burning gin. Coughing, she kept talking. "Oh, there's a financier on my father's team who is *absolutely* lining his own pockets, and by the gods, he is an idiot about it. Haven't decided what I'm going to do about that. Part of me is like, good for you, because who doesn't hate my father? But this guy seems like a real shit, so I kind of want to fuck with him, but now doesn't seem like the best time, does it?"

Jessa raised a brow, looking a little winded, but nonetheless she poured out a tiny bit more, gesturing for Elysia to continue. It seemed like her stamina to tolerate the Parkers was growing. The thought made Elysia's lips twitch in a smile. She held up her drink in thanks before continuing.

"But most importantly, I learned there are absolutely zero death priestesses left in Kava, and you know what's funny? I was there the day the last of them died! Trounced my little boots through their blood. Guess they joined the death temples of other kingdoms after the Fall rather than be pushed into a life they hadn't chosen. They should've known better than to roll back through Relaclave with that nonsense. They were gutted like pigs."

"Soot and storms, Elysia," Jessa muttered. "That's a little bleak even for me."

Elysia shrugged. "There's a death every other day in this city. Let's not act like the sun is shining on any part of this land. I heard the weirdest rumor, though. I heard it several times, actually. Reliable sources too." Her voice trailed off, a note of confusion coming through.

Jessa made an exasperated sound. "And?"

"They kept saying that the prince was spotted parading through the castle with a dead man slapping at his back. One of the king's advisors, flopping like a limp fish. Said people were terrified because the air was doing strange things around him."

Jessa's dark eyes dragged over Elysia like she was dense. "You already know what I think."

Elysia made a face.

"Oh come on, Parker. It's obvious. The man is just as cursed as you. He might be an ambitious, heartless son of a bitch, but I think it's clear that he couldn't give two shits about you having magic."

She stared at her glass. "He went after all your friends, Jessa. Maybe he didn't intend for so many to die, but there's no way he came after me without knowing very well that he'd have to turn some of them in."

Jessa folded her arms. "Sounds familiar, doesn't it?"

Elysia's head shot up, her eyes narrowing, but Jessa kept talking. "He is the reason my friends were murdered—he's why *I* almost died, why *you* almost died. I have no love for the man, and I would be perfectly fine if I found out tomorrow that he was dead, but let's just face the facts. It would make a lot of sense if the prince was as cursed as the rest of us."

Elysia chewed on this, hating how it felt weighted and true. Her nose wrinkled. "I will be so fucking pissed if he's cursed."

Jessa's brows drew closer in question.

"Everything could have been different! If he had just told me before that night. It wasn't until that night on the beach when everything changed. We could have had each other—I wouldn't have had to escape his rooms like some common court whore for months because I was terrified he'd find out! And you know what? Fuck him if he is cursed because he let me live in that terror."

Jessa started shaking her head subtly, eyes going wide as they looked past Elysia.

"What?" Elysia slammed her glass down, fully worked up now. "Do we need to repeat *again* that the asshole left me for dead? And how he had your friends killed?"

"Elysia," Jessa hissed.

"Don't *Elysia*, me! I am so godsdamn sick of all of this. Topp Blatz can fuck *all* the way off. If he wanted to be useful, then he'd stop trying to kill us and start trying to get rid of his heinous father and his laws. Like oh, you're sooo manly with those *double* axes you carry." She suddenly pressed up, leaning over the bar. "Well, why don't you fucking do something with them, then, Blatz? Like godsdammit. Be useful already."

Jessa's lips were stuck together now, a heavy breath coming out of her nose. Her words came out through clenched teeth. "For the love of all of Relaclave, please shut up."

Elysia frowned, a slight twinge of unease tempering her for half a breath. She sat back down, still frowning, but unable to squash the urge to finish her speech. Another prickle ran up her spine, one she knew better than to ignore, but unfortunately, she was a Parker, and her mouth kept moving in spite of her body's warnings.

"I'm just saying—we'd all be better off if the king was dead. Would it fix magic? No. But at least we wouldn't be getting executed anymore. It's a more solid plan than trying to make a deal with death."

Jessa closed her eyes now.

A familiar vibration hummed in the air, causing Elysia to straighten. *Shit, shit, shit.* And then an even more familiar voice was in her ear, his lips tickling her skin as he murmured. "Such filth coming out of your mouth. I think the least you can do is buy me a drink if you're going to talk like that."

All the tiny hairs on her ear and neck stood up.

Son of a bitch.

He spoke again before she could move. "And what do you mean, *make a deal with death?*"

She spun on her stool and stared up into the ever-vibrant green eyes of the crown prince.

"This bar doesn't serve people like you." She spat the words and probably a little gin right at his broad, handsome face. He was so close she could see the faint dusting of faded winter freckles along his nose and under his eyes. She used to kiss them in the summer, when they popped against his skin. Even the slightest hint of light brought them back. She had always wondered if he'd be covered had he lived anywhere else.

The prince toyed with the edges of her cloak, his hands moving to grasp the outside of her shoulders. He looked torn between his intrigue regarding her ill-timed statement and saying whatever it was he had come here to say. He settled on the humor that sat awkwardly upon him, like a sweater he'd outgrown, but couldn't quite part with.

"I'd chastise you for your loud proclamations of treason, but we all know it wouldn't do any good, and I don't have much time. I came to warn you."

Elysia eyed him more carefully now. Beneath the freckles were the bruised smudges of a man who hadn't slept well for a very long time. The corner of one eye jumped and his shoulders were strained. She frowned.

"Warn me of what? Tell me." Anxiety closed her lungs, her thoughts going to all the worst places. Her hands wrapped around his wrists, heart pounding unevenly.

The prince gave her a crooked sort of smile, one he used to make all the time, but never did anymore. Her fingers dug into his skin. He was trying to soften whatever it was he was about to say, but he was only making it worse.

"Just say it. Is there a warrant for me? Is Beatriz okay?"

His brow smoothed. "No, no." His eyes went out of focus for a moment before they latched onto her once more. When he spoke, his voice chilled Elysia to her core.

"You're right. The king does need to die. I'm afraid that's going to prove difficult, though. I came here to warn you that he knows—what I am, what you are, and he can rip the magic right out of your body. I watched him kill Terrin using the same power."

Elysia stared at him. The entire bar disappeared. She didn't hear the glasses clinking, or stools creaking while people shouted, only her blood rushing in her ears.

One last time, it was just her and him. Eye to eye, soul to soul—she leaned in, letting him be the rock her wave broke against. She held onto the feeling for one breath, two breaths, and then she exhaled out and the room slid back in with reality.

"You should have told me—about you." Her words were barely a whisper.

The prince looked down at the mud tracked floor, tension lining his mouth. "But I didn't. And neither did you." He squeezed her shoulders. "He'll kill you, Lys. In a heartbeat, if you do anything brash. I know I said we should work together, but I think you should leave."

Elysia took a step back, shaking her head. "I don't believe you."

The prince heaved a short, frustrated breath. "He said he would kill you the second you step out of line. He thinks he can manipulate me through you."

A small, sad smile moved Elysia's lips. Her words were soft. "But *we* both know that isn't true. You almost let me die once, and you would do it again no matter what you say if it meant saving Kava."

The prince started to open his mouth, but Elysia spoke over him. "There's something you're not telling me. You've gone senti-mental for the moment, but I know you, it won't last. It never does. So tell me, what did you find out?"

He glared fiercely at her. "Don't use your magic on me."

Elysia laughed, feeling more and more drained the longer this conversation continued. "I just know you. No magic necessary."

He scraped at his face, his stubble making a scratchy sound

against his palm. He refused to meet her eyes when he finally answered. His whole body tensed.

"He killed her. My sister. I know you didn't know her. She was always gone or being hidden away. Guess I know why now, but—I think he had something to do with the Fall. He made all these comments about my grandfather and how my mother died." The prince regained his focus, and his face hardened. "I won't be responsible for him killing you, Elysia, and I don't know if I'm going to like who I am at the end of this, so I am begging you to leave. Because you're right. My grief will blacken, and there is no telling what I will or won't do to stop him."

A flash of guilt entered his eyes, and she knew what he wasn't saying. Whatever promises he had made that he would never hurt her were now void. He had one mission and she would only get in his way.

His large hands swallowed her face. "Just tell me what you know, and I will get you out of here. You want Beatriz or your friend to go with you? Fine. Just tell me what you've learned and I'll handle the rest. You can pick the kingdom. I have friends everywhere, there's nowhere you can't go."

A slow, all-encompassing sort of anger began to warm her cold heart. "You'll ship me off so you don't have to worry about my blood being on your hands, is that it?" She kicked her stool to the side and leaned against the bar. "How sweet. How *romantic.*"

Each word that fell from her snarled lips was a poison dagger. "What happened to *we could be a team, Elysia? We could work together?* This is exactly why I didn't tell you anything. You used to be so *different*. Was I so busy hiding myself that I couldn't see you? You're just another domineering asshole who thinks he knows best, and I've had about enough of that for one lifetime." Elysia stared at him, both furious and bewildered.

Her jaw set firmly. "Get fucked, Blatz, because I'm not going anywhere."

Jessa moved from behind the bar, coming beside Elysia. One armed wrapped around Elysia's shoulders, and the other gripped her trusty nail studded plank. "I think it's time for you to go, Prince."

Hands clenched, the crown prince bit back the anger holding his body prisoner. He turned to leave, but not without one more parting shot.

His full lips twisted with disgust. Spreading his arms out wide, he sounded as if he thought he were magnanimous. "Pathetic. You were willing to do *anything* to hide behind *my* crown. I understood that you just wanted safety. I wasn't going to stand in your way. But this is unacceptable. This is childish and petty. You're risking our kingdom's future because I hurt your feelings?"

He encroached on her space, his vitriol increasing by the second.

"Get over it and grow up. You don't matter. I don't matter." He straightened. "Nothing matters except fixing this."

The Crown Prince of Kava left without another word. The bar door slammed shut, rattling all the foundational beams and swinging lanterns like it always did, but Elysia was in a daze. She slowly slid her gaze over to Jessa, her voice barely her own.

"Is he right? Should I just tell him what we know?"

Jessa looked at her like she was insane before quieting her face into a more even-keeled expression. She steered Elysia back onto her barstool and took a seat beside her. She shook her head before resting her chin in her hand.

"That piece of shit was just playing you, Elysia. Ten steps down the road he's going to regret those words, but he'll never have the emotional maturity to admit it."

Elysia stared at her, unsure of what to think. "You were right about him being cursed."

"Should have put money on it." Jessa groused as she stood to go back behind the bar.

Back where she was comfortable, Jessa set down her plank and kept talking. "Telling him won't do any good—he's completely run by his emotions right now. He'd probably do something stupid, and it's not like he can get to the realm of the dead to make a deal, anyway."

"People do somehow—sounds like it could have been his father."

Jessa crossed arms, considering this. "Suppose you're right, but I don't think Daddy is going to hand that secret over to him anytime soon."

"True." Elysia pushed her glass away from her, not wanting to drink anymore. She looked at the woman who had, against all odds, become something of a friend. "I hate that this is what's become of us. He's going to get himself killed."

Jessa poured out a drink for a burly dock worker before answering. "You've gotta let it go. He's a grown man, and we have our own mess to manage. You need to stay off the king's shit list—especially if what the prince said is true. The king is even more dangerous than we already knew."

Elysia nodded wordlessly. Jessa was right. She knew Jessa was right. Standing, she rapped lightly on the bar to snag her attention.

"I'm going to step outside."

Outside, she watched the people of Spirit Street, not really seeing them, but just needing to let the biting wind sting her face. The sharp cold matched the pain cutting through her chest, and she found she didn't mind it at all.

She should be at the House. Listening in and drawing out words from painted lips. But she'd walked out of Jessa's bar with her insides torn up and trying not to cry. Try as she might, she couldn't shake the image of the prince from her mind.

Looming over her, condescension and contempt ruining his beautiful face.

She had read stories of forest gods that lived for chaos and tricks while researching the god of the dead. Sometimes they were depicted with two faces. One light and one shadowed. She wondered if she was seeing his shadowed face now. Because she had fallen in love with a man so filled with kindness and curiosity it drove him to care for broken animals. A man built like a warrior but who preferred the contemplation it took to sit in silence with trees, who had a laugh so booming you could hear it from one end of the forest to the other. The person who stood in front of her today was still him, but a version she no longer recognized. As if the old him could only peek through the new him in moments and glances before it was overpowered.

The wind flung dirt and soot until Elysia was wiping her face. She wished she would have noticed he was fading. Or that he would have told her about his sister. He never did speak about her, always kept his grief and his love tight to his chest.

She swallowed hard, not allowing her tears to form. What she really wished was that either of them could have just been honest sooner. They were so similar—cursed to hide while bowing and pretending. Stuck navigating families held together with threats and false affection, both terrified of trusting anyone besides themselves. And look where that had gotten them.

It could have been so different. But a second thought, a whisper-quiet thought, questioned this. Because maybe, no matter what she had done, he would have left her behind. Maybe the only person who really mattered to him died a long time ago, and he had simply become the world's best pretender, fooling even himself into believing his lies.

It was too late for honesty to fix this. It had been too late since he left her to die on a beach.

But he was right about one thing. Kava deserved better.

She pulled her cloak tighter around her neck and let her feet guide her home to the castle walls, knowing what she had to do.

Chapter 37

Elysia found herself beneath the castle, deep in its safety. She used to use this path all the time to escape into the forests with no one the wiser. The stale, musty scent of dirt and rat shit was as terrible as it was familiar, but her mind was far from the vile stench of the tunnels.

Life so often stole people away before she ever had a chance to say goodbye. Whether they died or walked out of her life of their own volition, it was rare to end things with everything she wanted to say clear from her chest. Instead, she carried the unspoken words like iron weights inside her heart, knowing they would never grow wings to leave her mouth and kiss the other's ears.

Whoever Topp Blatz was to her now—he had once been everything, and if she was going to do what she needed to do, then she was going out on her terms. She had her plans and he had his, both unwilling to bend ambition for love. All she wanted was one good final memory to take with her.

A memory that was hers alone, untainted by lies and chaos. That way, she could pull it out of her pocket and remember the good instead of how it all went wrong.

She exited the tunnels outside the castle walls, feeling the tug of her magic, but not needing it to guide her. Swaths of pines and ash and oaks rustled in the wind, the few lingering winter leaves and needles bending in a familiar wave. A damp chill enveloped her as she entered beneath the trees' open arms, bringing goosebumps to her skin. Inhaling deeply, Elysia felt her spirit relax in the forest's shade. The moist earthen smell of soil and dying leaves was the next best thing to the scent of flowers. Invigorated, she followed the familiar footpath into the forest's dark.

The sudden crescendo of her magic didn't startle her, not when she'd come here knowing where he would likely be. Staring up into the trees, she tilted her face, knowing he was somewhere in the branches' shadows.

"I'm calling a truce."

She received no response.

Elysia untied her cloak, letting it drop to the forest floor. Hands on her hips, she kept staring into the black. "I want one last night. And then you'll get your wish, and I'll be gone."

Eyes adjusted, she realized he was sitting on the lowest branch of the ash tree, considering her offer. The prince pushed off of the tree, landing in front of her. Elysia swayed, leaning into his ever present smell of rain and ozone. Her hands drifted to his chest, and he stared down at her with a wary face.

"Since when does Elysia Parker ever call a truce? The woman I know isn't satisfied unless she's steamrolled her opponents into submission."

"It's a one-night-only offer. Consider yourself blessed."

His lips lifted in spite of himself, and one hand slid to her waist. Mouth brushing her cheek, his face dipped down closer to hers. "I was an asshole."

She gave him a small, close-lipped smile. "You were."

Just like that, with a few soft words and a lingering touch, the past few months were tossed from mind and memory while their bodies remembered what had once been so easy.

She pressed her face against his, the scent of his skin cascading through her in a swirl of warmth. A sigh fell out of her parted lips as her shoulders relaxed and the tension eased. A steady chorus of want and need began to hum through her. "You really, really were, but I don't want to talk about that right now."

He leaned back, a slight crease forming in between his eyes. "Why do I trust you even less now that you say you're here for a truce?"

She pulled her sweater over head, her skin bare and dimpling in the night. "Because you're an asshole, not stupid."

His fingers tightened on her waistline, his green eyes bright and pupils wide. "You're sure about this?" His much longer legs were already walking her back toward a tree. Rough bark scraped against her smooth back and she laughed, jumping to wrap her legs around him like she had a million times before.

Large palms caught her ass, holding her there easily.

She licked her lips, tracing his face with her eyes. "This isn't our first time, Topp. Whatever heart I had to break, it's already been done. I want this—I want you. I want one last memory that isn't us flinging knives at each other because everything has gone to shit."

Understanding clouded with his own pain was there and then gone in his eyes. He held still, so still as he weighed out her words and what she was asking for tonight under the dim moon.

Elysia stared back at him, the tree digging into her skin and cold turning her blue. She barely noticed the cold, though. Not when the anticipation and vulnerability of her request left her feeling far more bare than any lack of clothing. She waited for him to move, to say something, anything.

Then his mouth descended in a blink, covering and claiming hers like it truly was the last time. One slow, deep kiss left her head spinning and blood rushing, and then it was a frenzy. Mouths moving frantically, tasting each other over and over beneath the trees that had always kept their secrets.

Topp unlatched her legs, planting them back down to the ground as his mouth moved down her neck to her collarbones, kissing a trail that left her eyes closed and hands fisted in his shirt as she drank in the sensations. Moving lower, he captured one rosy nipple in his mouth, tongue gently bringing it to a peak and her pulse even higher. His thumb rolled over her opposite breast as his explorations continued downward, causing an impatient sound to vibrate in her throat.

Lips smiling against her stomach, Topp found the button to her trousers and worked them down until he was kissing her from the ankle back up. Elysia grasped the bottom of his shirt, tugging it up and over so she could run her hands up and down his back. Once upon a time, Topp had been muscled but lean. Now in his late twenties, he was thick and muscled with a chest like a bear. Hands full of him, she squeezed his upper arms, enjoying the feel of him. The cool wind slipped past, turning her nipples even harder, and she fought the urge to writhe against him. *Gods, I've missed this.*

Her thoughts shorted out altogether as his mouth finally reached where she had wanted it all along. Head cracking back against the tree, she barely felt the hurt as his mouth worked with the steady skill of a partner who knows you all too well. Over and over he laved, devouring her whole.

Fingers fisted in his hair, she squirmed, but his hands held her still, not yet done enjoying the taste of her. With one final kiss, he looked up at her as she panted down at him. His lips glinted with her upon them, and he held her gaze as he slid his fingers into her and curled.

Her knees damn near buckled, and a pleased rumble of a laugh moved through his chest. Deft strong fingers reached for the perfect spot again and again as she rocked into the palm of his hand. Vision hazy, she looked down at the man she had loved, and the sight of him crouched beneath her, working her perfectly, sent a thrill of power through her. She bucked against him, urging him on, and Topp complied, increasing his ministrations to the rhythm she demanded.

Heat spread through her like the flames of a furnace as she reached higher and higher. Breaths short and fast, her body folded into him as a brilliant feeling flooded her entire being like a cosmic shot of light, racing to every last corner of her. And then it wrecked her, plowing through the flimsy walls she held and bringing an unwanted wave of emotion to her eyes. She stayed where she was as he held her there, planting small kisses along her hip as she rode the final waves.

Topp stood, the question back in his eyes, if they should continue as he saw the wet emotion in hers, but Elysia didn't want to talk or acknowledge what she felt—there was no point, so instead she reached for him, ridding the prince of his trousers. Elysia pushed his chest, bringing him down to the ground where she sat astride him, taunting him as she slid over the length of him.

Hands digging into her ass, the man's eyes squinted shut.

"You're fucking killing me."

She grinned, tossing her dark hair over shoulder, naked and triumphant like a dark goddess of the woods. Ducking down, she nipped kisses and small bites along his neck.

"Good."

And then she allowed him to slide into her, a groan escaping her lips as the hot length of him filled her.

Two breaths to adjust, and then she was riding him, one hand on his face, demanding he look at her as she brought him home. She slowed her pace, rocking her hips until she could see the strain upon his face, and then she slammed down and watched him break. Back arching, he made a muffled sound as he collapsed back down to the dirt. He lay there sweaty and spent, and Elysia allowed herself one last look at his face. Cheeks warmed, hair messed, and chest still moving fast.

A hollow pain crept into her heart. She'd gotten what she wanted, and she wouldn't ruin it with words. Standing, she grabbed his undergarments, using them to fix herself, and then she was pulling her own clothes back on.

The prince propped himself up on one elbow. "Running out already?"

She looked back over her shoulder, moving her hair to one side. "Truce is over. I'll see you at the ball and then I'm gone."

Elysia could see him swallow back whatever emotion or words he truly felt as she'd known he would do.

"Right." And then his head tilted, eyes suddenly focusing on her intently.

She stepped into her trousers. "What?"

The crown prince stood next to her, unbothered by his own nakedness, pulling down the collar of the thin sweater she had just donned. Elysia twisted her neck, trying to see what he was looking at and failed.

"What is it?" she asked again.

His thumb brushed over a spot below her ear. He repeated her earlier words slowly as a dangerous look entered his eyes. "You didn't *try* to make a deal with death. You *did* make a deal with death. Elysia, what have you done?"

Her shoulders drew back, body stiffening. The memory of the god of the dead pressing his fingers to his lips before touching her skin played back in her mind, clear as day. Her hand shot to her neck, covering where she presumed the mark was and stepped back from the prince.

"I haven't done anything. There's no deal." She took another step back. "You do what you need to do, and I'll do what I need to do."

She felt like she was cornered by a wolf. Except she hadn't trained her whole life just to feel like prey. No, she didn't care for the feeling of her hackles rising defensively at all.

Shooting him a look of warning, she kept backing up, not liking how his body seemed poised to attack. Hand drifting to her pocket, her eyes remained on the threat.

"Tell me how you found him. Tell me what you know, Elysia."

Maybe if he'd asked calmly or given any indication that he could handle the information like a reasonable person, she would have told him, but he didn't look like a calm or reasonable person.

He looked like a forest gale ready to rain down havoc until she broke.

She looked him dead in the eye, mouth drawn tight. "No."

The single syllable of her response had barely left her lips when he threw himself at her, plowing into her middle and holding her down to the ground. Eyes flashing, he swore at her as one hand came down hard beside her head.

"This isn't a fucking game, Elysia, tell me what you know."

But she'd been ready, had known he would explode with temper instead of noticing how her hand had found the small dagger in her pocket. She pricked the tip of the dagger against the thumping artery in his neck.

"Get off me, or bleed out beneath the trees, Blatz." Her voice was as cold as the steel she pressed to his neck. The prince flinched, conscious awareness once again entering his eyes.

Slowly, stiffly, he clambered off of her.

Elysia stood up, dusting herself off. She shook her head at him in disappointment. "All I wanted was one night, one memory." A bone-deep ache filled her, but she kept the dagger lifted as she started walking backwards. A certain sadness flitted through her voice. "I don't know how anyone else reaches him, so don't bother. Trust me that I'm going to do all I can."

When she reached the edge of the woods, she lowered her dagger and whispered to the trees. "Truce over."

Inside her, a little girl in a charcoal dress with a red ribbon sash watched one dream die as another was born. She would never wear the Kavian crown or stand beside the one who did, but maybe she could be someone who helped save her home from the ruin of rot that swept it now.

The dark-haired little girl looked out at her, dropping her red ribbon to the forest floor from her hand. In its place, a bronze-handled dagger shone bright and true, a flower appearing behind her ear where a skull and dice now lived.

Chapter 38

Elysia stood in her living room with her feet leaden and heart in tangles. The wicked delight that normally enthralled and disgusted her in equal measure at the thought of loosening her grip on her magic until she nearly lost her head was nowhere to be found this year. She hated working for her father, but she had deep down loved the chance to break free of the constraints that normally chained her. The Raven Ball was a time for debauchery. No one ever batted an eye at strange behavior, it was practically expected, which meant it was the one night she had felt free.

This year the enchanting veneer of freedom was cracked and worn with the dinge of Kava's plight and her own slick fear.

She knew she needed to hurry. Yet she stood silent in her flat, her body weighted and unwilling to move. A sense of foreboding came over her like a dark cloud, but she shooed it away. It was only natural that she felt dread. This could very well be the last time she saw her friends and family. No matter how horrible things had been, leaving her family behind without a word of explanation still felt like a betrayal.

She thought back to last year's ball and wondered at how different her life had become in such a short time. She no longer sought the perfect secret to please her father, or believed she might one day earn his love. She no longer yearned to crack open the ribs of her mother, so she could peer into her chest and see the shallow depths of her cold, unfeeling love.

The sense of possibility—a frivolous lie that felt like hope and wide-open paths—had left her for good. She had watched all of her possibilities shrivel up and turn to dust.

No longer was she burdened with false dreams of safety and love. The life she had imagined with a crown and her family finally embracing her had dried up and blown away. She now knew that these were merely delusions that had carried her for years. They were a child's dream, and sometimes those were the hardest to kill.

Now that little girl stood calm and ready, her dark eyes serious and a dagger in her hand. She was the girl who had been found in a pool of blood inside a vendor's cart. Trained and loved as if she were his own by Kava's Shadow. She was the girl who had disappeared into nothing while her father carved her feet. She was the girl who threw herself at a man who did not love her to secure a better future. But now, she took all of it, and walked toward a future that was her own.

She told no one about her plan. She'd listened to all the whispers and hidden in the darkness of the House for two weeks, and while she didn't learn anything to strike a better deal with death, she had learned something very, very interesting.

Tonight would be a night for the books—the most memorable Raven Ball that Kava had ever seen. She only hoped she lived long enough to see her mother's face when it happened.

Elysia pulled out the garment bag from her armoire and grabbed her cloak, readying herself for the walk to the castle. Once at the ball, she would be demurely alert. She would swish and glide amongst the guests as expected. She would pretend to be a beautiful woman wearing a beautiful gown who hoped for nothing more than a man to bend his knee.

Her nerves jumped at the thought of the prince. All she could do was pray to the undead gods that the man didn't do something insane like try to kidnap her now that he knew she could reach the realm of the dead. If he did, she would be ready.

Bending low to scratch beneath Larkspur's chin, she murmured softly to him. "If anything happens, Jessa has a key. She's far more responsible than Beatriz and will take good care of you."

She stared into his purple eyes for another moment, her heart breaking. Throat thick, she ran her hand over his sleek black fur one more time before standing and walking out the door before she could change her mind.

ELYSIA HAD ONLY JUST ARRIVED at her room within the castle when there was a shout outside the door.

"Let us in, Elysia!" There was a shuffling and clicking of high heels followed by more muttering. "Fucking freezing in these halls. You'd think they could afford a fire or two."

Smiling, Elysia opened the door and found the friendly faces of Daphne and Remy popping into the doorframe like meerkats. Unlike her, the two women did not smile.

"Oh my undead gods." Daphne looked traumatized. She looked at Remy for support, now gesturing frantically at Elysia while making aghast faces of disbelief.

Remy strolled in, sliding off her gloves and calling back over her shoulder. "Procrastinate much? We barely have twenty minutes and you're a mess."

Elysia followed her in. "You should have seen me before the bath. And I might have sent my mother's servants away. I couldn't deal with their fussing."

Remy looked down at the pile of muddy clothes on the floor. "You went to the forest, didn't you?"

"Felt necessary." She hadn't planned on it. But the forest wasn't only his, it was hers too. She'd needed a longer walk than just from her flat to the castle, and had found herself ankle deep in muck, soot, and mud before long.

Remy wrapped a strand of Elysia's wet hair around her finger. "You're nervous."

Daphne bustled in, shutting the door and flying around the room to gather supplies. "Of course she's nervous. Only the entire city knows the prince is supposed to propose this evening."

She held up two different pairs of heels, her face deep in thought. "What color is your dress? The rumor mill kept saying you got your dirty claws on a Pleur."

That made Elysia grin. She walked over to the garment bag and made quick work of the ties. She stood next to the dress, face alight with anticipation. "Well, what do you think?"

Remy looked thoughtful. Daphne had a hand on her throat and looked dismayed.

"It's *black*."

"I know, I love it."

"I just—I just, isn't it a little dark?" The words came out in a rush and Daphne hurried on, "I mean I know it's the Raven Ball, but you're getting engaged, for the gods' sake. Engagements are happy, Elysia, and happy is not black." She sniffed and prodded at the gown as if it might magically reveal itself to be the pink of a blushing bride.

Remy continued to study it for a moment with one hand drifting to her hips. "Art tends to have a message, doesn't it?"

Elysia held the fabric of the dress between her fingers, her voice equally musing. "Yes, yes it does."

Soon the gin was flowing and the girls were cackling. If she allowed herself to, then Elysia could have easily forgotten what was coming, but the events that were to come were a steady, ever-increasing drum beat in her mind. Every sip and laugh felt surreal, as if it were someone else being buffed and coiffed into someone who might wear a crown.

She kept waiting for someone to grab her and tell her not to do it, for someone to beg her one last time to leave. But she'd expertly avoided Jessa, Beatriz, and Gage this last week. No one had been able to catch her in spite of them stalking her front door and badgering the residents of the House.

She tapped a no longer muddied nail upon a deep wine-red lip stain, the shade so dark it might as well have been blackened and dried blood. "It's perfect."

Face painted and body gleaming, she stood in front of the Pleur. "It's time."

THE SOUND of string instruments carried up the stairs to where Elysia stood, waiting to descend onto the dance floor filled with all of Kava's finest. Her silver satin slippers tip-tapped while the guests in front of her were announced one by one. Finally, she glided up beside the man who was booming out their names as if anyone truly cared who was about to walk down the Crown-red-carpeted stairs.

But yet, as she stepped into the light, she felt a pause sweep through the crowds below. The air stilled and breaths were held. The elder gentleman calling the names gestured for her to begin, and as she did, he cried her name.

"Lady Elysia Parker, daughter of the Crown."

Her gown might as well have been the most eloquent *fuck you* she had ever offered. What her mother had not seen with the dress limp in its garment bag was that the fabric was alive. The threads became vines and leaves that cascaded up her throat. The blackened greenery acted as nature's hands as it strangled and wrapped around her neck. The same decaying vines and leaves caressed her shoulders, running down her arms to end with a leaf like a teardrop upon her hands. Dark tulle roses fell down her body to the floor, leaving a trail behind her that marked her steps.

No mundane hands could have ever cut such cloth. It was obvious there was magic infused into every stitch and bit of its production.

King Garrison's gaze met Elysia's like a blast of the coldest night, and she smiled warm enough to dazzle the entire city in this room.

A hand touched her elbow as she at last reached the bottom of the stairs, and she knew whose eyes she'd find behind it.

"I hope you know what you're doing." His words were low, reverberating amongst the nerves that fluttered in her gut.

She turned on an inhale, eyes wide with innocence. "As you mentioned, Prince, I believe in—how did you put it?" Her head tilted and voice gained an edge. "Steamrolling my opponents."

Elysia slipped into a curtsy, aware of the many eyes she doubted would leave their sides tonight. As she lifted back up, one brow went up as well, and she held out a hand.

"Will we be pretending one last time? Or are you going to do something stupid and rash?"

Annoyance slipped through his fixed face. "I don't think I'm the one who needs a reminder not to do something stupid."

"Then dance with me."

His large calloused palm swallowed hers, and then they were sailing chest to chest across the black-and-white patterned floor. While the prince may have preferred the rhythms of the streams and trees, he was more than capable of leading her through every dip, whirl, and leap.

Breathless and cheeks growing pink, she laughed and laughed as they moved. At the sound of her true laugh, Topp Blatz couldn't help but smile, eyes crinkled and freckles barely there, and it was a beautiful, heartbreaking thing to behold. She looked up at him with glassy eyes and a full heart. *This* was the memory she would hold on to, the feel of him warm against her and looking at her like she was someone to be loved or even adored.

Her mother had reached deep into the essence of every Raven Ball of the glorious past and pulled out radiant shades of charcoal that she cast out like a glamour across the ballroom. Smoky grays and plumes of night tricked the eye into believing they walked through a beautiful rolling fog. Dim candlelight flickered, creating the faintest warmth to soften the dark.

She had recreated the soot that fell upon every inch of their home and made it look like something beautiful instead of dead. Casting her gaze around, Elysia wondered at the effect her mother had managed to create.

It was a night for secrets, for trysts, and the strange magic that happens when one believes no one is looking.

The song slowed, and she brushed the back of her fingers against the stubble on the prince's face. Voice near breaking, she spoke. "I may have wanted to hide behind your crown—but I was always glad it was *yours*, and not someone else's. I never pretended. I may have omitted, but I never pretended about my heart."

They came to a halt, dresses and dark polished shoes still dancing around them. His gaze turned penetrating as he caught her fingers and pressed them to his mouth.

"Tell me your plan, Elysia."

She nudged him into motion once more, part of her loath to let the moment end. But she didn't answer him. The music carried them a little longer until the prince couldn't stand it anymore.

His exhale was ragged, but he kept his face clean of the desperation she knew he must be feeling.

"Please, tell me. I swear I won't interfere. I just want to know how to reach the god of the dead—I *need* to know. You have to understand that." His grip on her hand and waist tightened uncomfortably.

She opened her mouth to respond, when Rollie stepped out from behind a fast moving couple and shoved himself in between the prince and Elysia, causing Topp to stumble down to one knee on the hard tile floor.

Rollie, true to himself, did not cast a spare blink in the prince's direction. His pale hands grasped Elysia's forearms indelicately. "You need to leave."

Her heart clapped into motion at his words. Adrenaline made her focus crystal clear, though, and a certain calm spread through her chest. *It was time.*

But aloud, she feigned confusion. "What are you talking about?"

He shook his head, his eyes darting around nervously. "No time. Let's go, we can take the tunnels."

Elysia nodded, taking hold of Rollie's hand and allowing him to drag her across the floor and out of the ballroom's thrall. They moved with as much haste as one dared without drawing eyes.

"Rollie, no matter what happens, thank you. You're a good person and a good friend."

His pale fingers tightened on her wrist, still pulling her along. Eyes still forward, he threw tense words over his shoulder. "Just keep moving, Parker."

Elysia could only imagine the expression on Rollie's face based on how the throngs of people were parting for them now. She smiled easily, laughing and offering gentle pardons as he tore ahead. Soon they were in the halls, heading for the stairs. Velvet curtains blocked off the staircase to the tunnels, and Elysia finally yanked back, causing Rollie to stop and stare at her as if she were mad.

"Rollie, you need to go."

Frustrated, he gripped the velvet and turned to her, gesturing at the stairs. "That's what I'm *trying* to do. He's coming for you, Elysia. I don't know what changed, but your time is up. Jessa sent Gage to the tunnels to help you escape."

Elysia swore and moved him away from the stairs. She was hissing now, not caring if people noticed. "Why did you all have to meddle? Gage is probably down there planning ten different ways to infiltrate this ball and murder everyone. Never mind, just *go*. You need to get far away from me, Rollickus. There's no reason for you to go down, too."

His face creased, hesitation sticking his feet to the floor. "You're up to something, right? You're not just giving up?"

Her voice softened. "Run. I mean it."

Rollie vanished without another word, effortlessly melting back into the crowds and aiming for the castle's main entrance. The man had been the castle's underground ghost for years. If anyone could slip away, it was Rollickus Timmons.

Salvation had never been in the cards for a girl marked by death, though.

This is really going to hurt.

And with that thought in mind she plunged behind the curtain.

Guards were waiting as she'd expected. His face was a familiar flash and then a boot punched into her stomach. Doubled over, she peddled back only to be grabbed and thrown. Caught by the back of her dress, another guard slammed her face into the stone wall. The telltale crunch of her nose echoed inside her skull. Hot blood gushed down her face as tears formed in her eyes. But no matter how it hurt, she didn't fight back. She let them take their licks and bided her time. Blood continued to gush until she imagined there was no difference between her painted lips and the skin around it.

The guard holding her released her, and this time she stumbled into a chest she knew all too well. Strands of hair tore free of her scalp as the king wrenched her way from his tunic-covered chest. He leered down at her bloodied and wrecked face, saying not a word. Eye to eye, they stared at each other until the sight of his complete lack of remorse ignited her disgust. Lips lifting into a snarl, she refused to play the gentle doll.

He gripped her hair tighter, drops of blood trickled out, soaking into her dark hair. Neck taut, her head was pulled so far back her spine arched.

Garrison made a disappointed sound at the broken, cursed

creature in his fist. "Just couldn't stick to the shadows, could you, girl? Coming here with that dress. Should've killed you when it was easy, but I do admit I had plans for you. Your father's ambitions were always so small—I would've used your curse properly." He sighed and shoved her away into one of his guard's arms.

Elysia didn't say a word, but she didn't flinch from his gaze either. His story was a farce. Even if she had waltzed into the Raven Ball wearing a perfectly mundane dress sewn in the red and black of Kava, she would have ended up exactly here tonight. The king of Kava had walked into this ball with plans to make an example out of the crown prince's beloved.

He should have known better than to deceive a woman cursed to bend to the whims of whispers.

Mouth full of copper, she swallowed blood, waiting for him to get on with the show. She was dizzy, likely had internal bruising, and wanted to cry from the pain, but none of that mattered. Gage had once told her that there would come a moment she had to choose between her life and her morals. He had been right. That moment had come and gone. She no longer cared who saw her as good or bad, or avoiding the punishment that always seemed to be looming over her head.

Now she aimed for retribution. She bore a lifetime of scars. Physical ones on her body and endless upon her psyche.

She was cursed. The moth women had anointed her marked by death. Asked her if she had heard their god's call. And now, behind her ear was a tiny skull and pair of dice resting patiently, waiting for her to admit death was her future whether she liked it or not.

The king looked weary but determined. "If Topp didn't understand me before, then he will now."

She smiled up at him so pleasantly with her bloodied teeth gleaming. The king flinched and her grin grew wider. "Are we just going to chat all evening, then?"

Garrison let out a scoff and started dragging her back

through the halls and into the ballroom. "People behave so strangely right before they die. Thought you'd fight like a wild animal."

The people of Kava parted, their faces blanching and gaping at the sight before them. Their hero, their king—dragging the prince's sweetheart by her hair while her red blood dripped down onto the tiled floor.

Winded and gasping for air, Elysia bent awkwardly beside the king as the band came to a terrible halt. Instruments clattered to the ground and chairs screeched as musicians flung themselves away. The king held her on the stage. He wanted everyone to see, to hear, to *feel* what was to come.

"Garrison."

The king looked down at her, perplexed that she was speaking. Elysia smirked and stared him dead in the eyes as she raised her voice loud enough for all the room to hear. "How'd you kill her?"

The king blinked, but she kept going.

"Tell the people how you killed your daughter for being born with magic. *Did she fight like a wild animal?*"

The king's arm swung so fast she didn't even see it coming. His palm broke against her cheekbone, her eye instantly swelling from the impact.

She kept going. "Or maybe we should talk about why magic disappeared because no one knows how that happened, right?"

Her mocking skepticism rang out loud and clear. The silent room suddenly filled with the sounds of quiet gasps and people stirring anxiously.

The king's hand slid from her hair to her throat, squeezing to cut off her words. His face was splotched with wine stains, eyes bulging as he growled, "You will shut your mouth, you insufferable abomination."

"Or what, you'll kill me like your daughter?"

With a crazed sound, the king threw her down against the stage. The crowds murmured, crying out in dismay. The woman they believed would wear their crown was being forced to her knees in front of them all.

Two guards held her and heavy steps sounded behind her. She could feel the presence of the king. Heard the soft whine of his sword pulled from its scabbard.

Her time in this world was short.

Yet her eyes ran over the crowd.

She found her parents front and center. Frozen and unmoving. Her father's face was blank, waiting for his king to tell him what to wear. Her mother was flushed with panic, whether for herself or her child, Elysia didn't know. She didn't move though —or scream or rage the way a mother does when their child is in danger. Silent and still, her mother told her truth.

Remy's firm grip kept the blindsided Daphne in hand. Her gaze remained steady on Elysia, the heartbreak in her eyes clear from across the room.

Clawing her way to the front like a feral beast was her sister. Screaming and bloodying anyone who didn't step aside.

Suddenly, the air became a cracking whip, a static buzz rushing through the room as the electric lights cut in and out. Topp stalked closer and closer to the stage, violence in his eyes and the hair on Elysia's arms stood on end.

The king started his speech, relaying how she'd fooled them all. She was a poisonous snake, a fruit meant to condemn, but he would save them from her bite and poison on her lips. He wrapped her long hair around his fist once more and raised his sword.

The crown prince was almost to the stage.

Guards were attempting to slow his path, but he shook them off like flies, the remnants of his magic shocking in and out.

You have one chance. And you better make it count.

She reached beneath her skirts, twisted, and plunged. The bronze handle of her blade protruded grossly from the king's stomach, but even as he folded, he still clutched her hair and swung his sword. Wrenching herself back, she ducked his sword as the guards scrambled to regain purchase, grabbing at her dress and yanking until she was beneath them all again.

The king was a furious, bleeding mess, but she was yelling out into the ballroom, unafraid of the man behind her.

"Your magic *cannot die!* For every life we have lost, there is another still hiding because of this man. How many Kavians must lose their lives before you see his lies for what they are? Find each other, support each other. Do not let him ruin you!"

There was a whistle in the air.

She wished she could have looked the king in the eyes as she did it.

But her eyes were on her sister, screaming and thrashing against the arms of five guards because they couldn't hold her. Elysia smiled, she wished she had told her she loved her.

And she finally whispered his name: *Aidan, Aidan, Aidan.*

Cool steel touched her neck, cutting into skin.

But she was gone, with Topp's roar echoing all around her as she went, a delirious and bloody smile still slapped across her face.

She had heard death's call, and now, he would answer hers.

Acknowledgments

Much like you, dear reader, I am just another person who has been shaped and held by countless stories that now live inside my bones and heart. It's only right that my first thank you goes out to story itself. I believe stories are living, breathing things—they want to be told and heard by the people who need them. I'm honored to tell Elysia's story, and I hope you found something for yourself in these pages.

Thank you to my sweet little family. Alec, thank you for never once doubting my ability to do this. Thank you for believing in me when I said I didn't want to practice therapy anymore and that I was going to write books about magic and love. More importantly, thank you for being you. You might not be a romance book character, but I think you're better. You are solid and tenacious, and you have a voice that would make theatre kids cry with envy. I am the luckiest to laugh with you every day. You are my anchor, and yes, I would like a snack. Devi, my sweet, three-legged floof of love, you are the light of my life. My little soul dog. Like I tell you every day, long may you reign with your iron front paw. I hope you live forever. Dobkins, you are quite simply the world's best cat.

Thank you to my parents for allowing me to hide in my room and read ninety-nine percent of my childhood. To be honest, I wish I still could most of the time. I love you both. I'm also going to pretend you haven't read any of this book. Maybe you would accept a redacted version? No, too late? And thank you to my brother for being one of my very first readers. I'm so glad we can still share our love of stories between us. And thanks for finally convincing me to read Rothfuss all those years ago. It cracked me open, and I knew I had to write, even if it took me my whole life to publish a book.

Megan and Yoshi, my dream team, cheerleading squad. Your kindness, love, and generosity are unmatched. Thank you for letting me awkwardly talk about my book when I would have rather crawled under a table. You're both the best, and I can't wait to come see what you've built together. And Megan, thank you for being a friend who flies across the world even when your own is on fire to watch the cinematic masterpiece that is Twilight on my couch. You're more beautiful than Cinderella, and you smell like pine needles.

Chelsea and Kathy, my rogue goddesses and midnight sirens, I love you both. Thanks for being my weird, wonderful friends. I'd like to insert a meme Chelsea sent me about siamese cats and soul friends, but that sounds hard. And please, please, don't make a cutout. Love you both!

To my amazing editors & cover artist:

Elora—thank you for telling me to drop the reader into my story. It took over a year, two separate unrelated first drafts, and a lightbulb, but I finally understood, and it changed this book immensely. You are a gift, and I'm so grateful to have met you in the strange, wild lands of the internet.

Emily, thank you, thank you, thank you. You are incredible at what you do. Thank you so much for your attention to detail and thoroughness.

Brittany, thank you for being my final pair of eyes!

Story Wrappers aka K.D.—thank you for giving me the most beautiful cover! She's a stunner and I'm smiling just thinking about it.

To my street team: Thank you all a million. It blows my mind that you were all so generous with your time and help. Thank you for helping Undead Gods get its start. You're truly the best.

And finally, thank *you* for taking a chance on an unknown,

indie author. Your support means the world to me—every single page you read, every comment, and every review. Thank you so much. And on that note... If you loved Undead Gods, then please consider leaving a review. Reviews and recommendations are what make the book world go round, and I would appreciate it so very much.

All the love,
Caitlyn

ABOUT THE AUTHOR

Caitlyn grew up on faeries, folk-lore, and late-night reads. Her dream is to write fantasy stories that will keep you turning the page long after everyone else is asleep. She lives with her partner, tripawed floof of a dog, and the world's friendliest tuxedo cat. If you can't find her, then she's probably escaped to the forest, but will provide updates from @caitlynbattellebooks on social media and through her newsletter. Subscribe below to never miss out!

Trigger Warnings

Gore.
Torture.
Death and violence.
Physical and emotional abuse.
Sexual assault and predatory language.
Brief mention of passive suicidal ideation.
Familial neglect and abuse dynamics.
Drugs and alcohol.
Explicit language.
Sexual content.
Physical illness.